/

THE KEEPER OF LOS

Veronica L

Production by eBookPro Publishing
www.ebook-pro.com

THE KEEPER OF LOST DAUGHTERS
Veronica Leigh

Copyright © 2025 Veronica Leigh

All rights reserved; no parts of this book may be reproduced or transmitted in any form or by any means, electronic or mechanical, including photocopying, recording, taping, or by any information retrieval system, without the permission, in writing, of the author.

Contact: veronicaleighbooks@gmail.com

ISBN 9798288170607

The Keeper of Lost Daughters

A WWII Historical Fiction Novel

VERONICA LEIGH

ReadMore Press

DISCOVERING THE NEXT BESTSELLER

Sign up for Readmore Press' monthly newsletter and get a FREE audiobook!

For instant access, scan the QR code

Where you will be able to register and receive your sign-up gift, a free audiobook of

Beneath the Winds of War
by Pola Wawer,

which you can listen to right away

Our newsletter will let you know about new releases of our World War II historical fiction books, as well as discount deals and exclusive freebies for subscribed members.

Prologue

Friday, 22 February 1946
Krakow, Poland

Lidia leaned over the kitchen sink, the muscles between her shoulder blades knotting as she scrubbed a spoon until it gleamed in the dimly lit room. Wisps of her golden hair sprang free from its clasp at the nape of her neck and the steam from the scalding water made her skin slick. Her day at the factory had been an arduous one, followed by a long walk home that made her calves ache. An hour was spent preparing dinner. She was exhausted and she ought to be in a bad mood. Instead, she was amused.

Her daughters', Sophie and Eva, lively chatter from the table brought a smile to her face. They were sketching everything from Father Cieslik to a neighborhood cat, using the nub of a pencil on a scrap of paper. Life was a constant struggle but they were worth it.

An impatient knock interrupted their solitude. Lidia dried her hands on her apron, passed through the sitting room and answered the door. A man in a worn three-piece suit was on the doorstep, his palms braced against the handle of a cane, his left ankle curved awkwardly. Only slightly taller than she was and spare, his graying hair was uncommonly long, brushing against the upturned collar of his coat. Twin lines made parentheses beginning at his nose and ended at his chin, barricading his thin lips. He wasn't old, per se; she estimated that he was in his early forties. But by his haunted brown depths, he had lived a thousand years.

"Yes? May I help you?" She asked, when he didn't immediately state his business.

"Is this the Sobieski residence?" He inquired. She had to strain her ears to make out his low tone above the wind gusting through the naked tree limbs. "My name is Adam Altman. I'm Suzanne's father."

"Suzanne? Suzanne who?" Lidia frowned, completely bewildered.

Then she remembered.

Five years ago, she found Sophie abandoned in a basket on the doorstep of the cottage she shared with her husband, Tadeusz. There had been a letter from the birth mother hidden beneath the basket's lining. Bits of it came flooding back, but the exact wording had been lost. She did recall that Sophie had originally been named Suzanne Altman. However, for the last five years she was Sophie Sobieska, and she was Lidia's daughter, heart and soul.

"There is no Suzanne here." Lidia ground the words out, her conscience scolding her for speaking such a terrible falsehood.

The man's piercing gaze met Lidia's and her heart pained her, as if he plunged a knife into it.

He raised his chin a notch, peering over her head. "I can see my daughter. Suzanne is right there, at the table." A mournful gasp escaped from between his lips. "She has my wife's eyes."

Lidia cast a backwards glance over her shoulder. Sophie was thankfully oblivious to the monumental change that had suddenly taken place in her life. She was still leaning on the table ledge, focused on drawing her picture. However, Eva ceased sketching and turning towards them, she eavesdropped on their conversation.

"No, sir, you're mistaken. That is my daughter, Sophie." Lidia replied, facing the man once more.

The gentleman may have fathered the girl – if he was indeed Adam Altman – but that hardly gave him the right to disrupt their lives after a five-year absence. One portion of the letter Lidia did remember was that the birth mother surrendered all rights to Sophie. Mrs. Altman never said a word about reclaiming the girl.

I'm her mother. She had been the one to change every diaper, wipe away every tear, offer every cuddle.

Besides, this man had yet to prove he was in fact Sophie's father. Peculiar things had happened since the end of the war. Survivors from the camps returned to reclaim their children and their property. However, there were those who still wanted to harm Jews. For all she knew, this man was a troublemaker looking to upset their happy little home.

"Don't lie to me!" He raised his voice.

Lidia placed a hand on his chest and guided him back a few steps. "Sophie is my daughter." She insisted.

"Did you give birth to her?" He slammed the point of his cane on the snow-covered sidewalk. "No, you found Suzanne in a basket on the doorstep of your old cottage in the Debniki District."

No one could have known that...unless he is who he says he is. She swallowed. Well, on the off chance he was Sophie's father, it didn't mean he was a good man and she was not about to hand the child off to him.

"Stop it!" Lidia racked her brain for a solution. Something, anything to prevent this man from taking the one thing she couldn't bear to lose. "I will send for the police if you don't leave!"

"Very well, Mrs. Sobieska." Rage seethed off his taut frame and from his expression, she knew he wouldn't give up without a fight. "But I will return, with a lawyer-"

She went back inside and slammed the door before he could finish his threat.

Lidia collapsed into the chair by the fireplace, pressing her face into her coarse hands, she wept. *This can't be happening!*

Chair legs scraped against the floor. Seconds later, she felt a tug on her sleeve. "Mama," Sophie's innocent voice broke into her thoughts. "Who was that man?"

She sat up in her seat and sniffed, she found both girls at her side.

"Mrs. Sobieska, was that Sophie's-" Ewa didn't say it out loud, but she mouthed the word *father*.

"No one important." Lidia said to Sophie. But to Ewa, she gave a discreet nod. She wiped the remaining tears from cheeks and forced a half-hearted smile. "Why don't you show me your pictures?" she suggested.

Sophie fetched the drawings from the table, hopped onto Lidia's lap and showed off her creations. The child didn't give a second thought to the angry man who showed up unannounced. Out of sight, out of mind. *Thank God for that.* Young as the girl was, she shouldn't have to think about him at all.

Ewa perched on the arm of the chair, appearing downcast. A rare mood for such a lively girl. But she sensed the gravity of the situation.

Lidia kissed Sophie's cheek and tried to focus on the girl's drawings, in an attempt to distract herself. However, she could not seem to put that man out of her thoughts. She would see him...Adam Altman again.

Her gaze briefly flickered to the calendar on the wall and noticed the date. *February 22nd*. She let her head rest on the back of the chair, closed her eyes, and asked for strength from Above.

How could it have slipped my mind? Of all days for Adam Altman to show up in their lives! It was the fifth anniversary of when Sophie was left on their doorstep and the second anniversary of Tadeusz's death.

February 22nd haunted her, continually leaving its mark on her life.

Lidia's Story

Chapter One

**Saturday, 22 February, 1941
Krakow, Poland**

Lidia peered out the window facing the street, feeling a sharp pang of guilt settle in her belly, on observing her husband's grimace as he trudged down the road. In the colder months, the wild wind off the Tatra Mountains cracked his cheeks enough to make them bleed, but for her sake, Tadeusz plied his razor daily and kept his face smooth. He never wore a beard, conscious of her dislike of wiry hairs that would irritate her when they kissed. To heal and protect his skin, he massaged petroleum jelly into his forehead and cheeks.

She shivered at the sight, let the curtain fall back, and resumed her morning chores. Her husband would be gone for hours, traveling on foot in the woods bordering the city. Tadeusz was hesitant to leave her behind, but she insisted she would be safe while he checked the animal traps he had set out to catch meat for their dinner table. The meager rations afforded to them by their German occupiers wasn't enough to fill their empty stomachs. Her husband resorted to hunting. Well, his version of it. Since the beginning of the war, Poles were not permitted to carry rifles, or any other kind of weapon. Tadeusz was a good provider and unwilling to allow them to starve. He ingeniously laid out traps throughout the woods and kept track of them using a map he drew by hand. Setting out traps was in all likelihood illegal too, but it was a risk they were willing to take to ensure their survival.

Lidia's mind was on the laundry and scrubbing a stubborn spot from one of her husband's shirts when she heard a knock at the door. *Tadeusz shouldn't be back so soon.* Her heart fluttered as she went to the door, wary of who might be visiting this early in the morning. For all she knew it was a German soldier. She'd like to believe that the Nazis would leave her and Tadeusz alone, since they were ordinary Christians. But considering what they were doing to the Jews, they couldn't be trusted. Her husband was convinced once the Nazis finished with the Jews, they would start in on the rest of the Polish population. In the Germans' eyes, the Poles were only a level or two above the Jews.

She prayed for protection and opened the door. At first glance, no one was there. *A foolish prank.* Some silly youth with too much time on his hands was looking to stir up trouble. She was about to go back inside when a mewling whimper, begging for its mother's attention, drew her attention downwards. A large picnic basket lay on the doorstep.

Lidia crouched down next to it and raising the lid, a tiny human face was revealed. She gasped and covered her mouth. The baby's wide eyes focused on her and it let out a belting wail that echoed off the mounds of snow and barricades of houses. She carefully eased the baby out of the basket and cradled it in her arms. The child's delicate features and feminine golden curls hinted that it was a little girl.

"Who would abandon such a beautiful baby?" She asked aloud.

Instantly, she knew the answer. *The baby is Jewish.* A Christian mother would have taken the child to a church or a Christian orphanage. A Jewish mother wouldn't dare take their child to a Jewish orphanage, not with the Germans in power. The Nazis had emptied some of the Jewish orphanages, taking the children to only God knows where.

A penetrating wet chill cut her to the bone, reminding her how cold it was outside and how it wouldn't take long for the baby to be frostbitten. Or for the neighbors to notice, as they were beginning to leave for work. Grabbing the picnic basket, she tossed it inside, and drawing the child closer, she nudged the door closed with her foot. She sat on the divan, wrapped the little girl in another blanket, and let the baby suckle on a knuckle to sooth her. Despite the freezing temperatures, the girl couldn't have been in the basket for more than a couple of minutes, as she still bore the warmth from being cuddled to her mother's breast.

Lidia figured the mother had to have watched her take the baby in, just as the Biblical Miriam watched Pharaoh's daughter lift the Baby Moses out of the bulrushes. And like Pharaoh's daughter, Lidia knew precisely what she planned to do about this baby.

Tadeusz didn't return until after noon, with a sack of carcasses slung over his sturdy shoulder. "What is this?" He asked, the second he noticed the bundle in her arms. He dropped the sack on the floor.

"It's one of the Jewish babies. She was left on our doorstep." She replied.

"Jesus, Mary, and Joseph!" Tadeusz sat next to her; his mouth slackened. "We – we have to bring it back to the Kazimierz District and return it to its people." He said. "That's where most of the Jews live. Her people will see that she is sent back to her family, or one of them will look after it."

After bonding with this child for several hours, there was no way she would let this child go. Never having been blessed with children of her own, she didn't know the joy of motherhood. She had settled for mothering stray cats and cats were a poor substitution for a child.

The baby's hand squirmed out from the blanket and it seized Lidia's index finger, seizing her heart as well. The Lord was offering them a chance, their only chance to have a baby. She wouldn't reject His blessings.

Lidia shook her head. "If we do that, she will die. You've said it yourself; the Nazis want to kill the Jews. If we send her back, they will murder her too." Tadeusz held up a hand in protest, but she grabbed his broad chin and forced him to meet her gaze. "Can you not see this is a miracle?" Not even their priest possessed the fervor that she did in that moment. "Look at her, she is special. We have to save her and make her our daughter."

Tadeusz gaped at her as though she lost her mind. For a second, she feared he might refuse. He never seemed prejudiced about the Jewish people, whenever he spoke of them, it was with sympathy. But it was one thing to have sympathy for the Jewish people and another to be willing to risk your life for one.

He ran his thumb along the curve of the baby's cheek, and stroked her hair. His fingers dwarfed the little girl's head. "Well, if we're to raise her, she must have a good Christian name and baptismal records." He concluded, his eyes glistening. He, too, was falling in love.

"Sophie Maria?" Lidia suggested. "Sophie for short."

"Sophie it is, then." Tadeusz nodded, cracking a smile.

Lidia sent a prayer of thanksgiving heavenwards. After eleven years of marriage, without any hope of having a baby, at long last she had a daughter of her own.

Tadeusz drug out the metal tub for her and Lidia prepared a warm bath in the kitchen for the baby, to warm Sophie and rid her of any filth. The water revived the pinkness to the baby's delicate skin and she was soon cooing with gratitude. When bath time was over, she wrapped the child up in a fresh, clean blanket and spent the rest of the day hovering around the child.

From her estimation, Sophie was too young to be weaned from her mother. She was tinier than she ought to have been, but what else could be expected if the mother had to live off Jewish rations? The German occupiers allotted the Jewish people less rations and calories than the Poles, which contributed to malnutrition. *In time, in my care, Sophie will fill out beautifully, with rosy cheeks and dimples in her elbows and knees.* In her mind, a plump child was a healthy child.

On a quick examination of the basket, Lidia discovered a slip of paper under the lining at the bottom. She didn't have to read it to know it was from Sophie's mother. Tucking it into her apron pocket, she decided to read it later.

Following dinner and dishes, she usually spent the evening losing herself in a good book. Books were her own form of entertainment since the Germans forced the Polish population to turn over their radios. However, instead of curling up with a good book, Lidia drew her chair near the fireplace and cuddled with Sophie. The little girl captured her attention better than any novel.

Sophie was beautiful. She possessed a harvest of golden girls, large blue eyes, and a fair complexion. A heart-shaped birthmark was nestled on the left side of her neck, which seemed like a sign that she was a girl after Lidia's own heart. No one would question her when she introduced Sophie as her daughter.

Lidia remembered the letter she had found, and withdrew it from her apron pocket. The script was full of flourishes, having been composed by an educated hand. Her throat constricted to the point it was difficult to swallow, but she made herself read it.

Dear Madam,
My little girl is named Suzanne Altman; she was born Saturday, 12 October, 1940 and she is Jewish. My name is Mina and my husband's name is Adam. We lived in the Kazimierz District but we will soon be relocated. The Germans are moving all of the Jews to a ghetto in the southern part of the city. I'm an artist and my husband is a tailor. Our families have lived in Poland for generations and we were happy until the war began.
While I can't be certain of what the Nazis have in store for us, I fear my husband and I will die. Please don't ask me to watch my daughter suffer the same fate. I beg you, spare her life. I don't know if you recall, but I once approached you and you gave me some bread. I have since watched you and found out where you live. I thought anyone who would risk their life to give food to a stranger, must have a loving and courageous heart.
As long as Suzanne is safe and happy, even if Adam and I do not survive, we shall live on through our daughter. Love our child as your own and when she is old enough, tell her the truth and assure her we loved her more than life itself.
Thank you.
Mina Altman

Lidia sighed. A month ago, a woman wearing the Star of David, sought her out. There was something in the woman's demeanor, her vulnerability, her pathetic appearance, that emboldened Lidia to hand over the loaf of bread she bought from the baker. The woman thanked her and left, and Lidia never saw her again. But evidently Mrs. Altman kept an eye on her.

Suzanne. Sophie's real name was Suzanne Altman. The name wasn't Christian enough for the child to use and still pass a Christian. No, from this point on, the little girl would be Sophie.

Tears rolled down Lidia's cheeks. She had Sophie for only a day and couldn't imagine parting with her. *Poor Mrs. Altman.* She made the ultimate sacrifice, one that most mothers would dread making. But in giving up Sophie, she gave the child the gift of life for a second time.

"Someday, Sophie, you'll understand." She planted a kiss on the baby's pert nose.

Tadeusz chose that moment to amble into the house, bearing large chunks of firewood in his arms. He stacked them next to the fireplace, feeding one log into the blaze. He hung his coat on the peg and sank down into his chair near Lidia's, he stretched his limbs and moaned.

"What is that, darling?" He asked.

"A note from Sophie's mother, Mina Altman. It was in the basket." Lidia explained, flashing the piece of paper in his direction. "Mrs. Altman asks us to love her daughter and when she is old enough, we must tell her the truth."

"We can't do that." Tadeusz shook his head. "For Sophie's safety, she can never know she is Jewish. That piece of paper threatens her life and our and were it to fall in the wrong hands, Sophie would be killed."

She bit her lip. Tadeusz was right. Whoever was caught helping a Jew – even giving them a loaf of bread – was shot.

Notices hung around the city, warning what would happen if the Nazis were disobeyed. She lost count how many times he had seen entire families – children included – marched off, knowing they would never be seen or heard from again. Sophie was worth this risk, but they had to be careful, for her sake as well as theirs.

He softened his tone, as though to make what he said next easier for her to hear. "If we are to save Sophie, to raise her, we must stay true to our story forever. That she is our daughter and a Christian, because there is no guarantee that this war will end. Harsh as it may seem, we must destroy the note."

"Tadek, that feels wrong." Lidia protested. Every part of her conscience rebelled against his plan. She could understand destroying the note, it was dangerous to have in their possession. But certainly, one day, when it was safe, they could tell Sophie something about her parents. "To deny Sophie her heritage, that would be a sin."

"Better to deny her heritage than deny her a chance of life." Tadeusz eased forward in his seat and held out his hands. "May I?"

Lidia begrudgingly passed the baby to him, fearing her little body would be crushed in his muscular arms. He had been patient about waiting his turn, but now it was his chance to bond with his daughter.

Tadeusz cradled Sophie as he would a piece of china. The child snuggled peacefully in his cumbersome arms.

She sat back in her chair, marveling at the sight. Tadeusz was a bear of a man. He could be fearsome to those who crossed him, but to those he loved, he was as soft as a stuffed bear. His gentleness radiated through his warm amber eyes and his round face often displayed a placid expression. As a laborer, he was all muscle. He did carpentry work along with offering his expertise as a handyman to various businesses and churches and families. The pads of his palms were rough, the skin eroded by dirt and years of work.

"Perhaps in time, Sophie will have a brother or a sister." Tadeusz whispered.

Lidia shot him an icy glare. Her husband could be oblivious at times, but this was uncharacteristically tactless of him. It was no secret: she couldn't have children because the Lord closed her womb. No amount of weeping, prayers, or fasting made a difference. Unlike the Biblical Hannah, God did not change her circumstances.

Tadeusz understood, or at least she thought he had. He never faulted her for being unable to do the one thing a woman was expected to do. *You and me – that is enough, darling. That is more than enough.* He had sworn to her time and time again when melancholy overtook her and not a morsel of food could pass her lips.

"You know that isn't possible." She responded shortly.

Tadeusz's usually dusky face paled. "I only meant; we could adopt more. Many children need a good home. Especially now with the war going on." He jutted his chin towards the letter. "Please, destroy it."

Lidia nodded, but she still hated to steal the truth from Sophie. The little girl had already lost her parents, to lose the last connection to them and to her heritage would be too much. Yet her husband had a point. Better for Sophie to live as a Christian than for her to be murdered.

A dark little voice murmured in her ear: *Sophie would be ours forever.* Whatever the outcome of the war, no one – no distant relative – could swoop in and reclaim the girl. The evidence of her origins would be lost. Sophie would be raised in the church and she would become a good Catholic, never facing the temptation of embracing the religion of her birth.

Lidia wadded the note up and pitched it into the fire, committing it to the flames. The inferno spat back a hot breath into her face. She watched as it disintegrated into a pile of crispy ashes.

She laid her smaller hand on top of Tadeusz's large one. "I would love to have more children with you, Tadek. Nothing would make me happier." She kissed him and then kissed the baby.

But for now, Sophie was all that she wanted in the world.

Chapter Two

Monday, 3 March 1941

All of Krakow was humming with news of the Nazis' preparations for a Jewish ghetto in Podgorze District. The Christian inhabitants of Podgorze were relocated and large cement walls were erected to close off the area. An edict was issued commanding all Jews to move into the ghetto by the 3rd of March. With the exception of Sophie, neither Lidia or Tadeusz had much to do with the Jewish people. This new law didn't directly affect them one way or another. Yet on the morning of the 3rd, they bundled up and ventured out to watch the procession.

Tadeusz and Lidia pushed Sophie in her pram, joining the other spectators who gathered on the sidewalk, maintaining a safe distance from the souls paraded past. She didn't know what she had envisioned when she heard the Jews were moving into the ghetto, but she assumed moving trucks and cars would be involved.

Not this. Lidia exhaled and curls of white froth froze in the air. *Anything but this.*

Hundreds, perhaps thousands, of Jews marched down the street, with suitcases, rucksacks, bundles, pulling wagons, carrying chairs – toting all the worldly goods they could. Men, women and children, young and old, rich and poor – all on the same unfortunate journey.

Lidia thanked the Lord that Sophie was safe in her pram, cozy beneath quilts, cuddling a cloth doll. If Mrs. Altman hadn't left the baby on their doorstep, the little girl would be amongst them, heading towards certain death. No one in the crowd of onlookers gave the little girl a second glance, let alone suspected that she might be Jewish. She was perhaps the only Jew in Krakow spared of the ghetto.

She began to unconsciously scan the procession, searching for a young couple. Two distraught individuals who resembled Sophie. But no one seemed to stand out to her.

"Which ones do you suppose they are?" The words tumbled out of her mouth before she could stop them.

"Who?" Tadeusz's thick brow was furrowed. He noticed her gaze subtly flick back from the exodus of Jewish people to Sophie and back again. Her husband lowered his mouth to her ear. "Oh, Lidia, for Sophie's sake you must put them out of your mind. We are her parents now."

Lidia nodded. Tadeusz was right, this was not temporary. They were Sophie's parents in every way that counted. However, she couldn't deny the connection that she felt to the Altman's. *Is this how all mothers feel when they take in an orphan?* Well, their situation was different. Sophie's parents were going to die, if they hadn't already.

A few standing beside them, started to shout insults at the Jews. Others picked up rocks and clods of mud to throw at them.

Lidia clamped her hand over her mouth to stifle a whimper. These were the same folks they went to church with. "This is terrible."

One boy ran over and skidded to a stop, a few paces from where she and Tadeusz stood. He jammed his hand into his pocket, he pulled out a handful of stones. The boy squinted and aimed at the heads of the poor people. Each one that he hit, he pumped his fist into the air.

"Goodbye, Jews! Goodbye, Jews! Goodbye, Jews!" He shrieked in the ugliest voice imaginable, his spittle spraying.

The boy struck another, this time a woman, sending her to her knees on the cobblestones.

"How dare you!" Tadeusz whirled around, grabbed the boy by his collar, and gave him a harsh shake. "Stop that!"

"They killed Jesus." The boy smacked at her husband's arm, but was no match for the one who held him in place. "Let me go!"

"No one killed Jesus, He gave his life for all." Tadeusz's little sermon fell on deaf ears. No one ever needed a logical reason to hate because hatred was never logical. "If you don't leave, I'll whip you myself!"

"Fine, I'll stop." The boy vowed, but the second he was released, he ran off screaming and shaking his fist once more at the Jews.

Tadeusz threw his hands up in defeat. "I can't watch this any longer, I have to go to work." He left a kiss on Lidia's upturned cheek, then he brushed his fingertips to his lips and placed them on Sophie's forehead, tracing an invisible cross. "See you later." He wove his way through the jeering crowd, shaking his head.

Lidia nudged the pram along, regretting that she had shown up to watch another's misery. It had been in bad taste, to not only go but to take Sophie, to possibly catch a glimpse of the little girl's parents. She was no better than the ones who jeered at the Jews. To repent for her actions, she intended to light a candle for the Altman's the next time she was at church.

Spring 1941

Lidia leaned her head back a degree, basking in the warm sunshine as she pushed Sophie along in her pram. When she was a girl, she lived on a farm and the fresh air always made her sleepy by the end of the day. So, it had become a habit for them to have a walk every afternoon, weather permitting. The walks seemed to help Sophie sleep through the night.

She decided to go past the Church of St. Anna, to thank Father Cieslik once more for providing Sophie with birth and baptismal certificates. The clergyman hadn't questioned where the baby had come from...Oddly enough, no one had. It was plainer than plain she hadn't recently given birth, having maintained her slender figure. Everyone she knew, herself included, abided by an unwritten rule. *Don't pry into another person's business.* That way if the Germans took you in for questioning, for one reason or another, you could honestly say that you didn't know.

She rolled the pram up to the church steps but was puzzled how she would get it up and into the building without jarring Sophie. Tadeusz had looked high and low for a wicker pram, something pretty for his little girl. The last thing she wanted to do was leave it outside for someone to steal. A piece of furniture of this quality would sell quicker than a wink on the black market.

A Wehrmacht soldier departed from the church at that precise moment and quietly observed her predicament. "Allow me, madam." He lifted the pram, child and all, and carried it up the steps. Lidia followed, at a loss of what to do. The German set it back down on its wheels and briefly glimpsing inside, he smiled, "What a lovely child. May I hold her?"

"Yes, sir." Lidia mustered out. She couldn't deny him. A Pole couldn't disobey a German soldier's request.

The German soldier eased Sophie out and holding her close against his broad chest, he swayed back and forth to rock her.

The baby cooed, as though she were telling him a story. For a Nazi, he appeared as gentle as a lamb, praising Sophie's Nordic looks. *If he knew the truth...* If he were to discover Sophie was Jewish, he would have ended it all by swinging her by the ankles and smashing her into a tree.

Lidia bit down on her lip until she tasted blood. A new fear possessed her, making the hairs on the back of her neck stand up on end. The Nazis liked to select Aryan-looking Polish children to send home to their Fatherland, to be Germanized, and raised as Nazis. *Oh, Jesus, Mary, and Joseph!* If he wanted, he could take Sophie and there was nothing she could do to stop him.

The German glanced at her and perhaps sensing her unease, he had the good graces to look a little sheepish. "I have a daughter a couple of years older than yours. The last time I saw her, she was about this age. Now she asks my wife what I look like and where I am. She no longer remembers me."

Lidia was at a loss as to how to respond. Here was the enemy doing his utmost to show kindness and carry a conversation with her. A fine-looking man, he was tall and aristocratic, like a prince walking out of the pages of a fairytale. His medium blonde hair was combed off to the side and his grayish eyes, though grayish, were not cold. He was a parent, one who had been separated from his child, and he yearned to see her.

She weighed her options and decided the only thing she could do was show him kindness in return. "I'm sorry, I can't imagine how awful that is. There was a time that I didn't think I could have children and now I have Sophie." She licked her lower lip, to sooth the bite mark she inflicted. "God moves in mysterious ways."

"I pray that, God willing, this war may end soon and we may return to our lives." The German soldier put Sophie back in the pram and tucked her in. He touched the brim of his cap and nodded deferentially to her. "God be with you."

"And with you, sir." Lidia dipped her head, to offer him a little respect.

The German took his leave, but didn't once look back. Lidia, on the other hand, kept him in her sights, watching his retreating figure until he turned a corner and disappeared.

Lidia leaned over and checked on the baby. Sophie was squirming, frustrated that her new friend was no longer there. She directed the pram into the Church of St. Anna and crossed herself, thanking the Lord for His protection. Only then did she notice that she was shaking like a leaf, and must have been when she was conversing with the German.

"Mrs. Sobieska? Are you all right?" Father Cieslik hastened over. He urged her into one of the pews and moved Sophie's pram closer.

Lidia nodded. "This German soldier spoke to me and held Sophie." She took a hanky out of her skirt pocket and fanned herself, creating a little current. "I was afraid but he was gentle."

"The one who just left? Yes, he is a good man." Father Cieslik said, sitting in the pew in front of hers. He turned around to face her. "When he can, he attends Mass and has been courteous to others. Not all Germans are evil incarnate. Some are like you and me, but they have no alternative but to fight."

A good German. The notion seemed inconceivable. Since the war began, every German she countered had been a bloodthirsty beast. Some of the German soldiers were young, and weren't even capable of growing tufts of yellow fuzz on their chins. With her own eyes, she witnessed Nazis slaughter innocent men, women, and children.

But this man proved there were a handful of good Germans out there.

The priest's eyes drifted to Sophie. "Miss Sobieska is adorable... it is a lucky thing that she resembles you." He swallowed, hesitating before he asked. "Do you know anything about her Jewish parents?"

Lidia balled the hanky. She ought to have been terrified that someone had deduced their secret. Instead, she felt relief, that she and Tadeusz didn't have to shoulder this on their own. If they needed help, they could go to him and Father Cieslik wouldn't tell a soul. In the past, prior to the war, in sermons, he spoke about the Old Testament and he would read Scriptures about Jesus' Jewish heritage. He often insisted that the Jewish were the Lord's chosen people and that as Christians, they must love one another, as the Bible commanded. Unfortunately, few took his words to heart.

"We are her parents now." She shrugged. Unable to lie to the priest in a church, she evaded his question. "It is better this way." She waited for him to agree and was dismayed when he didn't.

Father Cieslik frowned. "Be careful, Mrs. Sobieska. The truth has a way of making itself known." He cautioned, and rising to his feet, he bid her a good day.

Lidia didn't know if he meant that someone else might suspect the truth or if hiding Sophie's Jewish heritage would one day come back to haunt her. Neither sounded pleasant.

She leaned back in the pew and found a little peace being within the confines of the sanctuary. Gothic in appearance, the Church of St. Anna had been built in the 15th century. The high vaulted nave was supported by large marble pillars bedecked with images of saints. The apse presented a Mosaic of the Resurrected Christ greeted by a choir of angels. The stained-glass windows consisted of vibrant colors forming pictures of the Lord, the Holy Mother, and other images straight out of the Bible. Statues of Mary and Jesus stood at the front of the sanctuary; Mary looked tender and benevolent while Jesus had His Arms open with His nail-pierced Palms exposed. The whole sanctuary was bathed in natural light and smelled of dust and incense.

This church was her favorite place in the world.

Sophie gurgled and Lidia reached in and stroked the baby's

hand. She hadn't originally wanted to withhold the girl's heritage from her. But it was too late now. Mrs. Altman's note was no more than a pile of ashes in the alley.

Tadeusz was right, he had to be. *Yes, it is better this way.* Lidia shifted in her seat, beginning to feel anxious. The peace she had a moment ago was slipping away and guilt was settling in. In the presence of the cross, she couldn't put the little sliver of doubt out of her mind.

June 1941

"Lidia!" Mother threw her arms around Lidia's neck, her speech garbled by excessive weeping. Parting from her, she gave the three customary air kisses. The first on the left cheek, the second on the right, and the third once more on the left.

"What are you doing here?" Lidia asked, tightly pursing her lips, as though she sucked on a lemon. A small suitcase lay at her mother's feet.

"I came to see you, of course." Mother answered simply.

"Come in." Lidia waved her inside. Chewing on the inside of her cheek, she could feel her temper rising and Mother had yet to utter anything offensive.

The last thing she expected was a visit from her mother. Lately, she and Tadeusz, and everyone else she knew, was the war on the eastern front and Poland's forever shifting borders. Poland's history was a complicated one. For one hundred and twenty-three years, Poland did not exist on the map. One country or another carved it up like a hind quarter of pork and choked it down. Each generation was raised to fight for freedom. It wasn't until after the Great War that their country resurfaced and the Poles declared their independence. Poland had returned to every map, atlas, and globe. They were free for twenty years until the Nazi invasion. For the first two years of the war, Poland was split into two. The eastern half of the country was under Soviet occupation while the western half – where Lidia and her family resided - was under Nazi occupation. In the last few days, the Nazis invaded the east and snaked their way into the Soviet Union. Krakow was not directly impacted and yet Lidia could sense the city was in turmoil. Tadeusz would return home with a newspaper at the end of the day and she would devour every propaganda-filled word. And by word of mouth, they would hear remnants of the truth.

Without sending a letter, Mother chose today of all days to show up on their doorstep an hour before dinner.

Mother picked up her suitcase and carried it into the cottage. "It's been too long, Lidia." Her glistening eyes swept the room. No matter what her mood, her eyes were always watery and her cheeks were always pink, as though she were on the verge of tears. "You haven't been home in ages. I knew if I wanted to see you, I would have to come to Krakow."

"Well, my life is here with Tadeusz." Lidia ground her teeth, counting to ten.

A farm wife in her early fifties, who had borne her share of hardship, Mother possessed a sense of quiet grace. Never a golden lock out of place, never a speck of dirt smudging her cheek, never a trickle of sweat along her neck – she was beautiful. Her figure remained trim despite childbirth and constant consumption of hearty food. Her plain, homespun clothing remained neat and respectful.

Lidia wrinkled her nose and looked down on her mother. The woman was beneath the dirt on her shoes.

Sophie must have woken from her nap and let out a hungry

squall. Thankfully the bedroom door was closed, so her mother couldn't see the baby from where she stood.

"When did you have a child?" Mother rested her hands on her hips. "Why did you never tell me?" she whined.

"I have been busy." She retorted.

Before Mother could reply, Lidia rushed into the bedroom to tend to the baby and locked the door. She cuddled Sophie to her chest and the little girl squeaked, confused by the tension. Despite her numerous attempts to leave her past behind, she could never forget her origins.

Lidia hid in the room until she heard Tadeusz come home. His exchange with Mother was muffled, but she imagined her goodhearted husband would be polite. She reluctantly laid Sophie back in the cradle, preferring to hide until her mother's visit was over. Summoning her courage, she unlocked the door and went straight to Tadeusz's comforting embrace.

He dropped an understanding kiss on her clammy brow. He alone knew the lifetime of pain this woman caused her.

"Well, where is my grandchild?" Mother asked. "May I see her?"

"Sophie is sleeping and I don't want to disturb her. She is getting over a cold." Lidia fibbed. The child might have been found in a basket on the doorstep in the dead of winter, but she was robust.

Lidia set out an extra bowl and divided their meager mess of stew into four small portions, setting Sophie's aside for later. She gave them each a hunk of bread and hoped that would tide them over until morning. They assembled around the table, crossed themselves, and her husband said the blessing.

Tadeusz sent Lidia a nudging look but she gave a tiny shake of her head, refusing to make small talk. He coughed. "How long will you be in Krakow, Mrs. Nowackowna?" he dared to ask.

"A week." Mother swiveled in her chair, her lower lip

quivering. "Lidia, you haven't spoken two words to me since I arrived and you haven't brought the baby out for me to see. Do you still hold a grudge over your father, Roland-"

"That man is not my father!" Lidia threw the spoon into the bowl.

Roland was not her father.

Her real father died when she was a little girl. Two weeks later, when he was barely cold in the grave, Mother married Roland. And Lidia refused to forgive her mother for that. Mother was a mouse. Her expressions, her demeanor, her actions were all mousy. She would hunch her shoulders and burrow into herself. She never wanted more. The woman was content walking two paces behind her husband, treating him as if he were some god.

Tadeusz's hand was on the table ledge and his fingers curled into a fist. "You may stay, Mrs. Nowackowna. However, Lidia will decide when and if you see the baby. But listen, I won't allow you to guilt my wife into returning to the farm. Her place is here, as it has been for well over a decade." He added pointedly, "And keep your mentions of Roland to a bare minimum."

Mother nodded meekly.

Lidia pushed her bowl aside, her appetite ruined. The broth of the stew, which was customarily tasty, weighed heavily on her tongue and stomach.

The remainder of the meal was spent in silence. After Lidia fed and changed Sophie, she brought the little girl out for Mother to hold. But she would not leave the woman alone with the child, not for a second.

Mother petted Sophie's hair, singing her a lullaby. Such affections brought back memories of her own girlhood and how close she and Mother once were. But that was before her father's death...before Roland.

Lidia shot daggers at Mother until she retired to her and Tadeusz's bedroom for the night.

Tadeusz spread a pallet on the floor next to the fireplace while Lidia made do with the divan. Her feet hung off the edge of it, and the cushions lumped into wads, but that was not what kept her awake. It was a string of memories she would love nothing more than to banish from her mind forever.

When her husband began to snore, informing her he was dead to the world, Lidia left the divan and tiptoed into Sophie's room, dodging the creaky floorboards. Standing at the side of the cradle, she was transfixed by the child.

The beautiful baby lay there peacefully. If it were in their power, the little girl would never know an ounce of fear or pain. Only happiness.

"Sophie," Lidia whispered, "I love you and I will protect you no matter what the cost." She glanced up and noticed Tadeusz in the doorway, and sent him a half-hearted smile.

Tadeusz made his way over and claimed her hand, pressing it softly. ""Lidia, are you all right?" Before she had a chance to respond, he continued, "Your mother won't stay long and she will return to the farm. She always does."

Lidia wished she could have spoken all of that was in her heart, but she didn't have the words. Instead, she shook her head. "Promise me that you will never tell Sophie about my past." Her fingers gripped his, frantic not to lose his touch.

"Someday she may have questions." He said.

"I want her to have a normal life, a happy childhood. The best."

"Sophie will have the best we can offer her." Tadeusz placed his other hand on her shoulder. "But that has nothing to do-"

"Please, promise me, Tadeusz." She begged. "Please."

There was a darkness in her past and in her. It sunk its sharp claws into her soul and wouldn't release her despite the number of times she had tried to break free. The last thing in the world she wanted was for the darkness to taint Sophie. Their daughter was all light and goodness. Perfection personified.

"All right, I promise." He acquiesced. "I love you, Lidia."

"I love you too, Tadeusz." Lidia kissed him on the lips.

They stayed at their daughter's bedside, watching her sleep. Mother stayed a week before homesickness got the better of her. But Lidia knew that it would not be the last time she saw her mother.

Chapter Three

November 1941

"It will be fine, Tadek. You're her father, after all." Lidia threw on her coat, disregarded Tadeusz's anxious protests, and swept out the door before he could stop her.

Since they had adopted Sophie, her husband loved spending time with the little girl and playing with her. But he was absolutely terrified of watching her by himself. Having been raised solely by his father and being one of five brothers, he knew nothing of girls and their ways. *Until he met and married me.* After several years of marriage, she trained him well, but a small girl made him skittish as a deer. The man was paranoid that he would harm their daughter, that his paw-like, calloused hands would fumble her, crush her bones, or bruise her pliable skin.

He is going to have to learn. Besides, she needed an hour alone, without a baby hanging off of her apron springs. A walk to the Main Market Square was precisely what she needed.

Krakow was stark and forlorn, having descended into a waiting-state and it would remain so until mid-November, when the first snow fell. The wind was mightier than ever, giving her an intense headache. Even so, she needed this outing because with a new baby and a husband demanding so much of her attention, she rarely had time to herself. This was a treat.

Lidia did a couple of laps around the Square, scanning the stalls. Much of the merchandise she couldn't afford and didn't need. One did pique her interest, a bookseller, and she stopped at it twice. The tantalizing tomes were tempting and it had been ages since she had a new book. Tadeusz had recently brought home a bottle of vodka, likely from the black market. It stood to reason that she deserved a new book. New clothes and fine foods didn't matter as much, but books were nourishment for her soul.

Suddenly, the trumpeter of St. Mary's Basilica stirred and began playing the *hejnal*. The five-note tune reverberated in the streets, ghostly echoing throughout the city. She paused and cast a melancholy glance at the church's impressive tower. Others in the vicinity stopped too and watched. The *hejnal*, Poland's anthem, had been played in Krakow since the 14th century. Legend had it that the tune ended on a quavering note because the original trumpeter was playing during a Mongolian invasion. He was slain at that very moment, by a Tatar's arrow in the throat. The anthem so closely identified with Poland's patriotism that it was a miracle the Nazis allowed it to be played. One missing feature in the Main Market Square – or as they Nazis called it, Adolf Hitler Platz – was the Adam Mickiewicz Monument. A tribute to their great poet, the Nazis dismantled it and shipped it to only God knew where!

When the trumpeter finished, Lidia and everyone who lent an ear waved to the musician above and cheered.

Distracted by the bittersweet moment, she turned and bumped into a tall, dark-headed man. "Pardon me, sir." She apologized, blushing over her clumsiness.

The man brought his arm out to prevent her from stepping away. "A word, madam." He said, in a Yiddish accent.

Lidia was taken aback. *A Jewish man?* He wasn't wearing the mandated band on his arm, nor did he appear to be with a work group. Jews weren't permitted outside of the ghetto, unless they were with a work group or in German custody.

His hands shook, grime corroded beneath his fingernails and lined the creases of his knuckles. Small white dots shifted and leapt from his scalp. *Lice!* She cringed and hoped none would jump on her. Those pests were known carriers of typhus and she didn't want to bring any of that home to Sophie.

Lidia attempted to sidestep him, but he grabbed her forearm and in an unsteady tone, he ordered, "Come with me."

She could have screamed, or should have rather, but she didn't. If she had, the German soldiers patrolling the area would have put a bullet between this man's eyes. They might corner her, suspecting she was connected to him. If they were to investigate, they would discover the truth about Sophie.

He led her to an alleyway, sandwiched between two buildings.

She jerked away from him and rubbed the spot where he held her. "Who are you?" she hissed.

"I- I'll do...do the t-talking." The man stammered, his teeth chattering. "You- you're sh-sheltering a Jewish g-girl, m-masquerading her as y-your own."

"No, Sophie is my daughter." Lidia insisted, the blood draining from her face. She felt for the brick siding behind her and slumped against it, to prevent herself from fainting. "I gave birth to her."

He gave a slight shake of his head. "We b-both know that's not t-true. I-I live in the s-same f-flat as her parents. They're not as qu-quiet as they should be."

Lidia briefly wondered if this man was Sophie's birth father. Perhaps it had been his and Mrs. Altman's plan all along for her and Tadeusz to become attached to the little girl and then be persuaded into having a hiding place provided for them too. But the longer she studied this man's features, she couldn't trace any resemblance in him to Sophie. Not an expression, not his looks, not his coloring. Whoever this man was, he had no connection to her daughter and only found out about their situation by accident.

Fools. She inwardly cursed Sophie's parents for being so careless. *I'll wring their necks if I ever get a hold of them.*

Her eyes surveyed the alley, eager for a stick or metal piping to use as a weapon. Unfortunately, all of the pipes in view were linked together. There was a rubbish can lid that could work, but it was out of her reach.

"Go away, or I'll scream!" She threatened.

"If you were going to, y-you would have s-screamed al-already." His trembling had grown more pronounced. She wondered if he was cold, for he wasn't wearing a coat. But the longer she listened to his voice and studied his demeanor, she realized he was terrified. "I will...I will keep your secret and in return...yes, in return you and your husband will h-hide m-my family and m-myself. There are s-seven of us in all."

"We couldn't possibly." Lidia dismissed him with a wave. "Our home isn't big enough and we couldn't afford it."

Not only that, the last thing she wanted was this man in her home. What if his story about him and his family wasn't true? The Gestapo was known for using people to scout out Jews in hiding. Perhaps the Gestapo was aware that Sophie was Jewish and decided to manipulate them into telling the truth.

"That – that is not my problem." His eyes watered, indicating to her he was full of remorse. Whoever he was, whatever his motive, he didn't want to do this. As if he could read her thoughts, he said, "Despite...despite what you think of m-me, I'm...I'm not a b-bad man. I'm not!" He declared, a lone tear dribbled down into his beard. Drawing in a breath, his stuttering subsided. "But I won't let my children die. I will do whatever I have to do to save their lives. We will come to you next Sunday. If you do not receive us, I will send a note to the authorities telling them the truth about your daughter."

"Please, don't do this." She covered her mouth.

"I have to, I'm a parent. I don't have a choice." He spun around and departed, mingling amongst the crowd of shoppers.

Lidia gulped for a breath, the abrasive brick of the weather-beaten building chafed her back through her coat and blouse. On wobbly legs, she made her way back home.

When she staggered into the cottage, she allowed herself to break down sobbing.

Tadeusz was on the floor with Sophie, but the second he saw Lidia, he shot to his feet. "What is it? What happened?" His fists were primed to pound on whoever dared to make her cry. The man would slay the Wawel Dragon himself if need be.

"I was in the Main Market Square and a man approached. A Jewish man."

"Outside of the ghetto?"

"He claimed to know that Sophie wasn't ours and that she's Jewish."

"How?" The thick vein in his neck protruded. "How could he possibly know that? Neither of us said a word, and Father Cieslik wouldn't."

"He said he overheard Sophie's parents talking." Lidia withdrew a hanky from her pocket and dabbed the corners of her eyes. She twisted it in knots, directing her tension into the material. "He promised to keep our secret if we hid him and his family."

Tadeusz paced the length of the room several times, his fury slowly draining off. "If I weren't so angry that he more or less threatened my daughter's life, I wouldn't be opposed to hiding more Jews. There are rumors of an upcoming liquidation of the ghetto." He lifted and dropped his shoulders. "He is desperate to save his children and himself. I suppose we can't fault him for that."

Lidia couldn't believe her ears. "Well, I'm Sophie's mother and he threatened my family, so I have no pity for him." She was on the verge of saying the man could hang for all she cared, but kept that to herself because it would have been too cruel. "What do we do? Should we report him?"

"We must call his bluff, as they say in poker." Tadeusz cupped her elbow to pacify her. How he could be so calm was mystifying. "We must feign ignorance, ignore him. We must have faith-"

"That is not enough!" Lidia moved away from him and started to do a little pacing of her own. Revenge was not in her nature but to save Sophie from danger, she was willing to try anything. "Turning the other cheek will not protect our daughter from the Germans."

"But we can't report him." Tadeusz placed his hands on her shoulders, preventing her from wearing a pathway into the floor. "If we do, we would be drawing attention to ourselves, to Sophie. The Germans may wonder why a midwife never came or why you didn't go to the hospital when you gave birth to Sophie. They may badger our neighbors; someone may say something and their suspicions will be aroused."

Her spirits sank and once more tears threatened to fall. "So, what, we sit and wait?"

"And pray like we have never prayed before." Tadeusz guided her to the corner of their sitting room.

Mounted on the wall were two portraits, copies of famous originals. The first was of the Divine Mercy Image of the Lord. On receiving visions of Christ, Sister Faustina Kowalska painted it and it became a popular icon in Poland. His right hand was raised, and His left was over the Sacred Heart. Red and white rays beamed downwards, and below was the words *Jesus, I Trust In You*. Sister Faustina died in Krakow before the war, spared of all the suffering it brought. The other was the Black Madonna of Czestochowa. An image of the Virgin draped in fleur-de-lis robes, held up her right hand in blessing, and in her left arm she cradled the Christ child. St. Luke originally painted it, then it was lost, and rediscovered by St. Helena who gifted it to her son Constantine. Later, it came into Poland's possession and was closely associated with them since the 14th century. Two garish scars stood out on the Madonna's cheek. During a Hussite invasion, a soldier had attempted to capture the portrait, but when he failed, he slashed it with his sword. As a result, the soldier was divinely struck down. People made pilgrimages to Czestochowa to pay homage to it.

Jesus, I Trust In You and Black Madonna of Czestochowa seemed to look down through soft, sympathetic eyes. *Surely, our prayers will be answered.* Lidia thought as she crossed herself and knelt beside her husband. They prayed well into the evening. Only Sophie's hungry cry awakened her. By the time she fell into bed at night, prayers were still on her tongue.

Sunday came and went. The Jewish man and his family never showed. She wondered if it was a test from the Gestapo. Tadeusz thought in all likelihood the Jewish man died or had been deported. Night and day the Germans were thinning the ghetto out, using various selection processes. Of course, that was an euphemism. The Jews were being shot or relocated to work camps in the east.

January 1942

"Excellent sermon, Father," Tadeusz complemented, as he and Lidia were on their way out of the church.

Lidia bounced Sophie a little. The baby was quiet through

most of the Mass, but now that they hovered by the door and were greeted by the bitter cold, she made her displeasure known.

"Thank you," The priest said, gratefully. He wore a smile, but it didn't quite reach his eyes. He lowered his voice slightly when he asked, "Would it be possible for me to call this evening?"

Lidia shifted the child in her arms, wondering why he would wish to keep a visit from the other parishioners. There was nothing wrong with a clergyman calling upon his good friends... unless he too had something to hide.

"We can do better than that, Father." Tadeusz replied congenially. "Come to dinner."

The priest nodded his acceptance.

Tadeusz took Sophie from Lidia, to offer her a break. She slipped her arm through his and they continued on home.

She sighed and shook her head.

"What?" Her husband asked cluelessly.

"Never mind." She grumbled.

Lidia was busy for the remainder of the day with preparations. She never minded when the priest visited. Father Cieslik was the first to make her feel welcome in Krakow. The large city had been a new world to the farm girl, but he showed her around, earning her trust. When she was ready, when the dark memories of her childhood surfaced and it became too much for her to bear alone, she felt comfortable confiding in him. Not only as she would a priest, but as she would a good friend. He had become a second father to her, though she never quite worked up the courage to admit that to him.

No, she was more than happy to have him over, but it would have been nice to have been consulted since she was the one doing all of the work. She often had to be creative in planning a dinner for three, in making a meal stretch. *Now a fourth!* The only time Tadeusz was in the kitchen was when he was eating a meal. The one time he tried to boil water for an egg, he burnt the water and caught a dish towel on fire.

Lidia spent the afternoon cleaning and preparing the meal, while Tadeusz and Sophie spent the afternoon strolling playfully about the room. For a couple of weeks now, the little girl had been latching onto furniture and propelling herself up onto her chubby feet. She toddled alongside a chair, or the divan, or a bed, but she was too frightened to cross a room on her own.

Lidia fried up sausage and warmed the sauerkraut she canned and stored in the root cellar in the autumn. The strong aroma of vinegar and cabbage permeated every nook and cranny and would linger for days.

Father Cieslik came bearing a small plate of heart-shaped cookies. Lidia's mouth watered at the sight of the treats and she fought the urge to snatch one straight off the plate as a child might. They had a fine meal and good conversation. To her surprise, the priest and Tadeusz forfeited their cookies that way she and Sophie could have two apiece, which made her feel a little guilty over her resentful mood.

Lidia, Tadeusz, and Father Cieslik relaxed in the sitting room, watching as Sophie played on the rug.

"Miss Sophie has grown so much." The priest commented off-handedly, yet his careworn face betrayed his underlying apprehension.

His blondish hair was thinning, but his features were small and his blue eyes twinkled. He never raised his voice. In fact, his tone was so soft and gentle that when he spoke, it relaxed her. *In his day, Father Cieslik would have been a fine-looking man.* Lidia tore her gaze away, ashamed at finding a priest attractive.

"It is none of my business and I hate to pry," Father Cieslik scooted to the edge of the divan cushion and rested his palms on his knees. "Miss Sophie is Jewish, isn't she?"

A breath caught in her throat and for a second, she felt like she couldn't breathe. For nearly a year, no one questioned their claim that Sophie was their daughter or wondered about her origins. Folks may have suspected, but for one reason or another, they said nothing. First the man in the Main Market Square, and now Father Cieslik. The priest signed Sophie's birth and baptismal certificates without a second thought, but now he was calling them out on it?

"Yes, Father, our Sophie is Jewish." Tadeusz bobbed his head.

"Why are you mentioning this now?" Lidia asked, fidgeting restlessly in her chair.

Their lives had finally settled down and Sophie...Sophie didn't miss her true parents. The truth was, as time passed, the longer the little girl was with them, the less Lidia thought of her as Jewish. Sophie couldn't have been more her daughter if Lidia had carried her for nine months and had given birth to her.

"I don't wish to intrude on your privacy." Crimson spilled out onto the priest's face and trailed down his neck. "Forgive me, I wouldn't mention it at all except there has been gossip amongst the parishioners. And the other day, a Gestapo agent came by to ask me questions, some of which were about you."

Lidia let out a strangled yelp. *That Jewish man.* He was part of the ploy, which was why he never showed. She let her guard down when he confronted her and let some of the truth slip. The Gestapo must have sent him and from her reaction, deduced the truth!

Her first instinct was to pack a rucksack, take Sophie, and flee Poland. *But where could we run to?* They didn't have enough money to bribe someone to sneak all three of them across the border into Hungary. Nor did they have the money to bribe the Gestapo to look the other way.

Tadeusz looked to the religious icons on the wall.

"You're a fine couple and you genuinely love Sophie. No doubt you want what is best for her." Father Cieslik hesitated, observing them carefully. "If you wish, I can take Sophie and place her in another home. One in the country. The Gestapo would likely leave you alone after that and the little girl would be protected."

Lidia touched her brow, feeling the start of a headache.

The priest's offer was generous. The logical thing would be to hand Sophie over to him. She might be safer in the countryside, however, since the Gestapo were watching, they would notice if Sophie disappeared. They would easily track her down. Besides, her new protectors might not be kind to her. Some Poles didn't like Jews and only hid Jews for the money. Sophie deserved to be loved and to be part of a family.

Sophie made a noise, waking Lidia from her from a stupor. The poor little girl had no inkling they were discussing her fate. She picked the child up off the floor and nestled the child to her bosom, forbidding anyone to try and take her. Including the priest. *I'll die before I part from her.* Using her finger, she traced the little heart on the child's neck.

Tadeusz hung his head, beaten down by this revelation. She feared he might be tempted to follow Father Cieslik's advice. "No," He firmly declared, to her relief. "We won't forsake Sophie; she is our daughter. 'A guest in the home is God in the home,' as the proverb goes. God gave us Sophie; we must trust that He will protect her and protect us."

Father Cieslik's look was pained. "If that is what you wish." He conceded, with a respectful nod. "I think it's very dangerous for you to continue on like this, but if I can be of any further service to you, do not hesitate to ask." Pressing his lips into a thin line, he didn't overstay his welcome and left soon afterward.

Lidia carried Sophie to her bedroom. The little girl put up a fuss when she was undressed and a fresh nightgown was put on her. Sophie poked out her lower lip, to get her way and stay up later. But once she was tucked in and had a bedtime story, she dozed off.

If you go, Sophie, I go too. Lidia swore, as she looked down at the sleeping child.

Tadeusz entered the room and his brawny arms encircled Lidia's waist, hugging her to him. Neither said a word; they didn't have to. Despite Father Cieslik's disapproval, they knew their decision wasn't a mistake.

Chapter Four

April 1942

Lidia put the last dinner dish away, hung the towel on the peg, and went into the sitting room. She flopped down next to Tadeusz on the divan, allowed her head to fall back on the cushion and she draped her forearm across her eyes and let out a groan.

"My darling, you shouldn't let what Father Cieslik said upset you." Tadeusz leaned over and patted her knee.

"If I don't worry, who will?" She joked.

The last few months had been difficult...she had been on edge, waiting for the Gestapo to show up on her doorstep. They never did, but that didn't stop her nerves from getting the better of her. She, Tadeusz, and Sophie resumed their normal routines, pretending nothing was wrong. There were mornings her stomach was so knotted that she ended up doubled over the toilet vomiting. A persistent ache developed in the base of her neck and shot down between her shoulder blades, preventing her from moving her head from side to side. Other than the sounds Sophie made, the hours of the day were unnervingly quiet. Not even her daughter or her books could distract her. The return of the storks to Poland didn't lift her spirits. In the past, nothing gladdened her heart more than to spot one of those spindly legged birds nesting on a rooftop, ushering in warmer weather. They could jut their heads back and clatter their upper and bottom bills, rattling their calls *kle, kle, kle* all they wanted- this year, she couldn't have cared less.

She moved her arm and noticed her husband's complexion was a fraction too pale for her tastes. Cupping his cheek, his skin felt moist and a little prickly since it had been hours since he shaved. "Are you well?" she asked.

"Well enough." Tadeusz averted his gaze.

"No, what is it? Tell me." Lidia insisted.

"You had a letter." He exhaled, his thick breath smelling of their evening meal. Digging around in his trouser pocket, he produced a missive and laid it in her lap. "It is from your mother."

Her husband did that from time to time. Whenever Mother or Roland sent something, he would try to intercept it and he'd hide it, until he found the right time to give her their news. Were anyone else in the world to interfere with her private business, she would have been furious. But he knew how much turmoil Mother and Roland caused and did his utmost to shield her from it.

Lidia flung the letter on the table. Later she would burn it, as she did with the others. "Oh, well, that is all right." She shrugged. "Mother always upsets me."

"It is about your step-father." Tadeusz rubbed his neck, feeling the tension too. "Roland has cancer and he doesn't have long."

For years she cursed that wretched man's existence and wished him dead. Her Christian faith led her to view hatred as a sin. But this was a sin she was all too willing to commit and she never had an ounce of remorse for. Cancer was the Lord's judgment on Roland.

"That makes no difference to me." Lidia replied.

"Would you never want to make peace?" Tadeusz didn't dare utter the man's name, knowing it would enrage her. Her husband might have been the head of the house and he was more than twice her size, but when it came to Roland, her temper was uncontrollable. "Death is so final. We never know when we will get another chance."

Lidia shot him a withering glance. For him to suggest making peace or to forgive, deeply wounded her. He didn't understand and he never would. Of course, he could easily encourage forgiveness! Tadeusz had come from a good family. His mother died after giving birth to her fifth strapping boy and his father died young of a heart condition, but his childhood years were happy ones. He had no concept of the evil she was put through. If Roland were not dying, Tadeusz likely wouldn't have mentioned peace or forgiveness. He never had before.

If Sophie were not asleep, she would have shouted at him for having the audacity to say that. "How can you ask that of me?" She demanded. "My father was a good man and he was only gone two weeks before my mother married Roland. What kind of woman marries a man she knows nothing about?" She propelled herself upwards.

"Will you attend the funeral?" Tadeusz asked. "For your mother's sake."

"Oh, that man won't die any time soon. He's not that generous." She stalked to the other side of the room, to put some space between them. "My only consolation is that he will suffer."

Tadeusz gasped, made the Sign of the Cross, horrified that she expressed such hatred. "Lidia, this hatred is poisoning your soul. You must forgive, that is what we pray for every Sunday." He lifted his left hand to the portraits of Christ and the Queen of Heaven, to remind her of Who was watching. "'Forgive us our trespasses as we forgive those who trespass against us.'"

"Jesus didn't have the painful childhood I had." Lidia crossed her arms under her bust. Were they talking about forgiving anyone else, she would have agreed, but in this instance, she didn't care. "If He had, He wouldn't ask me to do such a painful thing." She countered.

She snatched the letter up and through it into the blaze in the fireplace. The flames singed the short blonde hairs on her fingers, but she scarcely felt it. The fire devoured it, but she was left feeling unsatisfied.

Her resolve crumbled and she was soon shaking. Whether the tears were from raw nerves or due to past memories, she couldn't be sure. Perhaps it was a combination of both.

Tadeusz ambled over and wrapped his arms around her. "It's all right, my darling." He placed a kiss on the nape of her neck, murmuring, "Just let it out."

She spent the rest of the night in Tadeusz's embrace in tears. It had been years since she left the farm, married Tadeusz, and moved to Krakow. She banished Mother and Roland from her life, and she had done her utmost to forget about her youth.

But, somehow, the past always had a way of catching up with her.

Friday, 15 May, 1942

Lidia adjusted the straps of her shopping bag on her arm and shuffled forward, eyeing the stalls, considering what she would buy next. It was Sophie's Name Day and she wanted her little girl to have something special.

When she named Sophie, her choice didn't make sense. Oh, "Sophie" was the perfect name for her daughter, she didn't regret that. However, considering that Sophie was born on the 12th of October, Catholic tradition dictated that the child should have been named after a saint that had a Name Day closer to that date. That was how good religious parents generally chose names for their babies. *Silly me, I selected Sophie because it was beautiful.* Now there was a wide gap between Sophie's birthday and her Name Day. Her first Name Day had gone unnoticed. Money was scarce with all of the unexpected expenses that a new baby required.

Money was scarce and there were still unexpected expenses, but she couldn't allow another Name Day to go unnoticed. Not when Sophie was almost old enough to remember. The little girl was too young to realize how poor they were, but she wanted to spoil the child.

She spent the morning scouring the Main Market Square and found a cake, a loaf of bread, and the ingredients to make little dumplings with meat and cheese.

A stall of toys caught her eye and as she approached, the vendor held up a doll. "A treat for your child." He waved it at her. "Spoils straight from the Jewish ghetto! I'll be willing to barter!"

Lidia had been about to buy it, until he mentioned it was from the ghetto. She dropped her hand to her side and surveying his inventory, she wondered how the man came about them. An unbidden thought occurred to her...the children who owned these toys, who played with them and loved them, they were dead. The vendor seemed unfazed that he was making a business out of selling dead children's toys.

She backed away, bumping into someone. Her mind harkened back to the Jewish man who claimed to know the truth about Sophie. She turned around, half-expecting it to be him.

A man in a khaki-trench coat was there instead.

Lidia froze in place, but inwardly she was all aflutter. One glimpse of him and she knew the man was a Gestapo agent. *The one day I let my guard down, I encounter my worst nightmare!* She cursed herself for not staying home.

Flashing her a wide-toothed grin, he withdrew the loaf of bread poking out of the shopping bag.

He brought it to his nose and inhaled, running it beneath his nostrils like he would a cigarette. "There's nothing better than freshly baked bread." The man said, his eye lids rose up a degree, like shades on windows.

"Yes, sir." Lidia squeaked and waited for him to request her identity cards.

The Gestapo agent chortled, lowering the loaf. He wasn't good looking like the German soldier she encountered on the steps of the church the previous year. This one was wiry, with pointed features, and a small toothbrush mustache on his upper lip. A tribute to his beloved Adolf Hitler. The man's balding head didn't appear to be held up by a neck; it perched on his shoulders like a dome.

"Is it a special occasion?" His nasally voice made it sound as though he were speaking through his snout.

"It's my Name Day." Lidia said, hoping he wouldn't be able to detect her deceit. She didn't want him to know of Sophie's existence. Terror mounted within her but she had to stand at attention for however long this German addressed her.

"Ah, well, congratulations!" The Gestapo agent's lips curled disdainfully.

The man held out the loaf, but when she reached for it, he dropped it on the cobblestone street. He raised his foot and stomped it, grinding it under his heel.

She didn't dare object to this treatment; it would have only made this whole trial worse.

Folks gathered around, curious and eager to watch. Her middle-aged neighbor, Mrs. Karlinskowa, was one of the spectators. Her expression was sorrowful, but she didn't dare intervene. To cross a Nazi, one would be crossing the devil. The crowd had to be relieved that they were not on the receiving end of this Nazi's harassment. She knew it from personal experience because she had been a spectator before.

The Nazis delighted in harassing Poles, deeming them sub-human and only useful for slave labor and menial work. From the day of the Nazi invasion – which they claimed the Polish soldiers attempted to defend their country on horseback – the Germans had gone out of their way to remind the Polish population that they were second class citizens. Schools were closed; only small children were permitted a rudimentary education; books had been banned or burned; and the holy days and traditions were suppressed. Children were forced to work at the tender age of twelve. Particular trams were *"For Germans Only"* or the trams had *"German Only"* cars; specific parks were prohibited from Poles and dogs; and pools were closed to Poles and Poles had to make do with cooling off in the rivers. Hundreds of laws were issued, stripping Polish citizens of their national identity.

The German eagle, with a swastika clutched in its claw, had swooped down and punctured the neck of the Polish eagle. The Polish eagle didn't die though. It remained in a purgatory waiting...until life was breathed back into it. Someday, it would be resurrected and it would soar.

The German's cackle brought Lidia back to the present. "Now pick it up and eat it." He seized her by the shoulder and screamed in her ear, "Do it!"

Lidia sank to her knees. *Please, don't let him kill me.* Choking back sobs, she tore off a piece of bread and poked it in her mouth. She mashed her lips together, chewed and swallowed.

"Very good. Now what do you say?" The Gestapo agent asked.

"Thank you." She whimpered.

"Good girl." The man slid his greasy fingers through her hair. He swatted her head playfully and let out a guttural laugh. "Stupid Poles, no better than dogs." He arrogantly sauntered off.

The second the Gestapo agent was out of sight, Lidia began

to gag. Acidic juices in her throat bubbled up and she vomited everything that she had eaten that day. And maybe everything from the day before.

Mrs. Karlinskowa chose that moment to hasten over. She used a hanky to dab the bile from Lidia's chin and drew her upwards. Mrs. Karlinskowa slung the sack over her shoulder and slid her arm around Lidia's waist. They staggered back to the Debniki district, the older woman leading her like a child since Lidia was too muddled to make sense of all that had transpired.

Mrs. Karlinskowa relayed the whole ordeal to Tadeusz, promising to look in on them the following day and she returned to her own home.

Lidia rushed to the kitchen, swished salt water around, and spat out the bitter saliva in the sink. Tadeusz drug the tub over and filled it to the brim with water. He heated another batch of water, risking burning it, and filled the tub. He helped undress her and assisted her in the bath as she might assist Sophie. The next thing Lidia knew, she was coaxed out of the water, patted dry, and sent on to bed.

She lay there, on her back, her eyes fixated on the dusty, wooden slatted ceiling for what seemed like hours. When she grew too restless, she rolled out of bed and crept into the W. C.

Lidia splashed cool water on her face and caught sight of her reflection in the mirror. For years, she couldn't look at herself, due to a combination of shame and self-hatred. But now enough time had passed that she could bear the sight of herself again.

She was less than three months away from her thirty-first Name Day, but her face maintained that youthful artlessness. Her blonde hair waved naturally on its own and it looked its best when freshly brushed and free of its clasp. The dark shadows beneath her blue eyes dimmed their brightness and her full pink lips were drawn into a frown.

He could have killed me. Once more her stomach rolled and she was on the verge of vomiting.

Lidia swallowed and rushed to Sophie's room. Her daughter had become her refuge from all of life's sorrows.

The little girl happened to be awake and on seeing her mother, she pulled herself up. "Mama!" She squealed, bouncing.

Lidia lifted Sophie out of the bed and hugged her. "I love you, Sophie." She nuzzled and kissed the little girl's temple. "You are worth everything."

Holding her daughter made her feel a little better. The celebration of Sophie's Name Day would be postponed to another day. Young as she was, the little girl wouldn't know the difference.

At least the Gestapo agent spared the little cake. Sophie would enjoy it.

Chapter Five

October 1942

"One bite for papa." Lidia nudged the rim of the spoon against the little girl's pinched lips.

Sophie was fussy about eating peas, preferring them raw. She hated them mashed or canned, or worse, in split pea soup. Between rationing and the shortages, fruits and vegetables were only available when fresh. When it was in season, produce was picked straight out of a field and brought in to the green grocer. In the warmer months, Lidia took a fraction of all she bought and preserved it, storing it in their root cellar.

Her daughter wrinkled her nose and kicking her feet, she made the high chair wobble.

"One bite for papa, one for mama; one for Father Cieslik; one for St. Sophia..." And so on, until the last of the mushy peas were consumed.

Sophie filled out beautifully, with dimples in her cheeks, elbows, and knees. *Just the way I wanted her to be.* Lidia beamed proudly. Her daughter was the picture of perfect health and rarely ever sick. She and Tadeusz, on the other hand, had grown thinner on war rations. But it was worth it to ensure that the child had plenty.

A sharp knock interrupted the meal. The knuckles upon the

wood were harsh, each rap making Lidia flinch. Her nerves had improved since the spring, but occasionally little things like uninvited guests flustered her.

"Papa?" Sophie asked.

"No, not papa." Lidia replied, laying the spoon and the bowl on the table. Tadeusz never came home this early. He had no reason to knock either, since he had a key of his own.

As she liberated Sophie from the high chair, the visitor knocked once more. No, it was more than a knock, it was pounding. This was not a social call.

"Coming!" She called out, depositing the little girl into the chair by the fireplace and answered the door.

Lidia was suddenly paralyzed.

The Gestapo agent she encountered last May was on her doorstep and a second agent was a few paces behind. A black sedan was parked alongside the curb.

Smugness slithered across his weaselly face and realization dawned on her that the encounter in the spring was no coincidence. The man had been scouting her out and humiliating her was an added reward. The Gestapo intentionally bided their time, waiting until she and Tadeusz let their guard down before striking like a snake.

This had to be about Sophie. *What else could it be?* Hiding a Jew was a criminal offense and punishable by death. It was the only major crime they committed. They dabbled in the black market occasionally, but everyone in Krakow did that.

Lidia tried to swallow, but couldn't due to the lump forming in her throat. "Yes, sir?" Bracing herself against the door frame, she hoped that her shakiness would be concealed.

It wasn't. If anything, it grew more and more pronounced by every passing second.

"I'm Sgt. Kloster." The sergeant gave a sharp bow and clicked his heels together before resuming his full height. "Mrs. Lidia

Sobieska, your presence is required at Gestapo Headquarters immediately."

Her thoughts raced. "I'm watching my neighbor's daughter and I need to return the girl to her." She glanced back at Sophie, who was bouncing up and down on the chair's cushion. "Please." She meekly requested.

"Make it quick." Sgt. Kloster harrumphed, snapping his fingers. But thanks be to God, he believed her falsehood.

So, they aren't here to collect Sophie. If it wasn't about her and Tadeusz hiding a little Jewish girl, masquerading her as their own, what could the Gestapo want with her?

Lidia snatched her shawl from its peg and wrapped it around Sophie. She hoisted the girl up on her hip and carried her over to the neighbor's, the agents trailing after her. The Karlinski chimney was smoking, a sign that someone was home. Mrs. Karlinskowa came to her aid that day in the Main Market Square. Perhaps she would again.

Lord, please, let her be willing. She knocked briskly on the door. It took only a minute for Mrs. Karlinskowa to answer. Before the woman could offer a proper greeting, Lidia blurted out, "I know I promised to watch your daughter this afternoon, but I have an appointment." She sent her neighbor a frantic, pleading look. *From woman to woman, Christian to Christian, have mercy. Save my daughter.* No other words were required.

A glimpse of the Gestapo agents prowling the property and the woman understood fully. "Of course." She snuggled Sophie to her chest and miraculously the little girl didn't put up a fuss. "Thank you for keeping an eye on her. I'll pay you later."

Lidia battled the urge to give Sophie a parting kiss, but such a display of affection would have betrayed them. She tore herself away and didn't dare look back, otherwise she would have started crying.

Sgt. Kloster seized her by the elbow, spun her around into the direction of the car. He pitched her into the back, causing her to tumble onto the bench seat and practically into the lap of the second agent. The man shoved her into the middle cushion, sandwiching her between him and the sergeant who climbed in after.

The car lurched forward and her stomach rolled into a ball, tightening until sharp pains shot through her abdomen. *They will kill me if I vomit on the floorboard.* Riding in the backseat always made her nauseated. But the thought of being taken into custody, never seeing Sophie or Tadeusz again, terrified her more.

The sedan sped through the winding roads of the city, reaching downtown Krakow. It passed through the gates of Montelupich Prison. The Montelupich family originally erected it as a manor in the fifteenth century and the park across the street was part of its gardens. In the nineteenth century, when the Austrians ruled over Krakow, it was converted into a prison.

Lidia mutely recited several "Hail Mary's" under her breath until the driver slammed on the brakes in front of the prison. The four-story building sprawled out, resembling a beast with its arms open wide, eager to devour. Barbed wire and glass covered the walls. That heinous place…hundreds, thousands of men and women had disappeared into it.

And I will be one of them!

Sgt. Kloster got out first. The second agent barked out the order, "Get out!"

She scrambled out, her skirt tangled in her legs, she ended up on all fours on the sidewalk. Jagged pieces of cobblestone stabbed her palms and kneecaps.

Sgt. Kloster grabbed her wrist and whipped her upwards, snarling inches from her face. "Stop screwing around." His foul breath reeked of stale cigar smoke.

The sergeant was on her left and the second agent was on her right as they escorted her into the building. Before Lidia could take in her surroundings, they ushered her to a flight of stairs. They mounted the steps, leading to the second story. Their three sets of footsteps echoed throughout the empty corridor.

The two brought her into a room, which contained a table and two chairs. A single, twenty-five-watt bulb dangled from the ceiling, illuminating a room. Orange streaks ran down the walls. *Is that blood?* There were no windows. No one would hear her screams if they tortured her.

Her heart slammed into her rib cage, leaving her lightheaded.

The sergeant pushed Lidia into the chair. She put her hands in her lap and winced as she bent her knees, feeling the skin stretch at the openings. Blood oozed from her wounds but it was useless to complain. The Gestapo sergeant didn't care that she was in pain. Unshed tears gathered behind her eyes, causing them to burn.

The sergeant sat across from her while the other agent lurked behind, working a rhythm as he paced.

Sgt. Kloster laced his fingers together. "We noticed a man visiting your house after curfew. To be out after curfew is illegal." He declared softly. The man was acting the part of a gentleman now which was far more unnerving, considering what he was capable of. "Who is he?"

Lidia tilted her head thoughtfully. *Father Cieslik?* A frequent guest in their home, he occasionally visited after curfew. Because of their close connection to the priest, they had fallen under suspicion. The Gestapo didn't know about Sophie...they were interested in Father Cieslik. Though she didn't know the extent of the clergyman's illegal activities, he provided birth and baptismal certificates for Sophie and he once offered to hide the little girl in the country when the Nazis were sniffing around, asking questions about them.

"Just a friend of my husband's. They play cards and talk and sometimes lose track of time." Lidia replied nonchalantly.

"Is that so?" Sgt. Kloster raised one of his brows, obviously not buying it. "What could you have to discuss that can't wait until daylight?"

Since the simple lie did work, Lidia racked her brain for an explanation that would deflect attention from Father Cieslik, but would also be believable. The thought occurred to her; one was too scandalous to be plausible. But what did she have to lose? If a little lie didn't work, why not try a big one?

Lidia chewed on her lower lip. "My husband and I...we have fallen on hard times." She lowered her head, feigning shame. "My husband's friend pays for me to keep him company in the bedroom. It helps make ends meet. We didn't want anyone to know, so that is why he comes at night."

Sgt. Kloster's jaw swung open and for a second, he was dumbstruck. "I see." He said at last.

The agent behind her started to cough.

Here she was a simple house wife confessing to the Gestapo that her devout Catholic husband was prostituting her for profit. And it wasn't Father Cieslik who was calling, but a friend of her husband's.

Lidia let the tears fall freely. "I hate it, it is sinful and immoral sir, I know." She wiped the dampness off of her cheeks. "But we have enough food now."

The sergeant openly gaped at her.

These two worldly men hadn't expected that. The sergeant looked to the second agent. From the silhouette of the man the light made on the wall, she could see the outline of him give a befuddled shrug.

"Well, then," Sgt. Kloster's lecherous gaze swept over her. "Perhaps I can visit tonight and you can entertain me. I pay well."

"I'll have to tag along." The second agent piped up.

Lidia felt her blood turn to ice in her veins. They were having a good laugh at her expense and made a few jokes, but it was obvious they were serious.

A knock sounded, making her jerk.

The second agent answered it and following a short exchange, he addressed the sergeant. "Sir, Lt. Brühl would like to have a word with you."

Sgt. Kloster cursed, stormed to the door and shouted at the one who dared to interrupt the interrogation. The shouts gave way to apologies and profuse groveling, the panic in his tone carried to where she sat.

Lidia cast a sly glance over her shoulder and was bemused that the Gestapo agents were quaking in their extravagant, leather shoes.

The sergeant hastened to his side; his hands clasped together. "Mrs. Sobieska, please pardon me for intruding on your privacy." A splotchy rash broke out over his cheeks. "I thank you for your patience and apologize for whatever discomfort we may have caused you."

Lidia recoiled from him, insulted by his behavior. This man had treated her worse than a dog, abusing her, teasing her about rape. If it weren't risky, she would have spat in his face. But she wanted to be out of the prison as soon as possible.

"May I go home now?" She asked.

"Absolutely," Sgt. Kloster said. "I'm releasing you into Lt. Brühl's custody."

Lidia nodded, but didn't know the Lt. Brühl the Gestapo agent was referring to. Neither she nor Tadeusz associated with Poland's occupiers. They would have rather died than collaborate with the Germans. However, the two Gestapo agents were under the influence that she had connections in high places and she was not about to correct them.

Sgt. Kloster pulled her chair out and assisted her to her feet.

Upon noticing the wounds on her palms and knees, he pressed his handkerchief into her hands. The other did the same, mumbling apologies.

They opened the door for her and she wandered out into the hall. A tall German officer was waiting in the shadows. He offered his arm and she timidly took it, fearful that she was walking straight into a trap. There was no other alternative but to go with him. If she stayed, she'd be in the Gestapo's clutches. Only when they stepped outside and were in the broad daylight did she glimpse at him.

Lidia covered her mouth to conceal a gasp. Her rescuer - Lt. Brühl - was the aristocratic German soldier who helped carry Sophie's pram up the stairs of the church. He hadn't changed much in a year and a half, aside from the hair near his temples had turned silver.

"Sir, how-" She was too bewildered to form a complete sentence.

"I saw the Gestapo agents collect you." Lt. Brühl edged closer and lowered his voice to a faint whisper. "Mrs. Sobieska, we all have our secrets, but in the future, you must be more careful. The Gestapo suspected that because of your friendship with Father Cieslik, that you and your husband have been assisting him in his activities. Or at the very least have shown sympathies towards the Jewish people. If you do have further troubles, please contact me." He slipped her a white card with his personal information on it. "As distasteful as it is, I implied to the sergeant that you are my kept woman. The Gestapo should give you a wide berth. I have also intervened on the priest's behalf. I would walk you home, it is better for your neighbors to not be aware of my intervention. Otherwise, your countrymen might mistake you for a collaborator."

Lidia sighed. While she had quite a walk ahead of her, she appreciated his thoughtfulness. The resistance was known for executing Poles they believed were collaborating with the

Germans. Well, except for those who betrayed Jews. There was no punishment for those who turned the Jews over to the authorities.

"Thank you, sir, and I thank you on behalf of my husband and daughter. God bless you."

"God bless you, Mrs. Sobieska." Lt. Brühl said.

She offered him a small wave and started for home. Her knees throbbed with every step, but she gave thanks to God for His protection. The Gestapo would leave her and Tadeusz alone, they wouldn't bother Father Cieslik anymore, and they continued to be in the dark about Sophie. Lt. Brühl was a godsend.

For the thousands of bad Germans, there was one of him.

November 1942

Lidia took a pause in the story she was reading to Sophie, watching Tadeusz from the corner of her eye. He had remained at the kitchen table following their dinner, to review their household finances.

After a long day's work, Tadeusz customarily joined her and Sophie by the fire. Her husband and daughter would listen with rapt attention as she read various Polish folk tales aloud. Sophie laughed and squealed whenever she created a new voice for one of the characters.

But the last few evenings, Tadeusz spent hours poring over their finances, ticking off figures, tapping the end of his pencil against a thin notebook. He would cast furtive glances at her and Sophie's way. His wistful expression indicated he wanted to join them but for whatever reason he wouldn't permit himself. They hadn't argued recently, nothing out of the ordinary had happened. Yet she could detect a change in him. She knew that man inside out, the good and the bad.

Lidia sensed his attention on them once more. She closed the book and directed her daughter's attention to her father. "Sophie, ask papa why he is staring at us."

"Papa, why?" Sophie wriggled off of her knee and clamored to him.

"Can you blame me?" He swung the child into his lap and kissed her cheek. "With two of the prettiest girls sitting in the living room? How can I not stare?" He chided, then tickled her tummy and said silly words in her ear to make her giggle.

But Lidia wasn't fooled, Tadeusz was holding back. Something was wrong.

She tried to quell the anxiety welling up inside of her. Had one of their neighbors figured out that Sophie was Jewish? Maybe someone was going to try to blackmail them again. Or it possibly had something to do with Father Cieslik?

Sophie restlessly slid to the floor and toddled into her room for her favorite doll.

Lidia hugged the book to her stomach, stood and approached him. "Tadek, what is it?" she asked.

"Things will be hard for a few months, winter and all. We may have to skip one meal a day." Tadeusz looked sheepish, as though he was somehow at fault.

If he mismanaged things, that was understandable. No one was perfect. But for him to suggest that they should deny themselves further was insane. Their meals shrank with each passing month. Supplies were bought off of the black market, if they could afford it. But like every other family in Poland, they struggled to survive from day to day. She supposed she and Tadeusz would have to, if there was no other choice.

"Well, all right, if we must. But Sophie can't skip, she's a child." Lidia stated and that was not something she would budge on. He may make the major decisions in their household, but when it came to her daughter, Sophie was first in her heart. "I could start taking in laundry." She softened her strained expression, and tried to make a joke out of it. "Those German ladies are accustomed to servants. I could wash their clothes."

Tadeusz shook his head, initially disagreeing. But he gradually came to the realization of how wise her suggestion was. "That could work." He admitted. "But we ought to have a little saved up." He leveled his gaze at the book she was holding. "We could benefit from selling your books on the black market. The bookcase too. The dealers will pay well."

"My books!" Lidia exclaimed.

If Tadeusz had suggested that she sell her body on the streets she couldn't have been more surprised. Growing up on a farm, she wasn't a slave to fashion. Her clothing was clean and modest, plain at best. None of that mattered to her. Other than the wedding band and her patron saint necklace, she owned no other jewelry. But the books...her books, they were her only form of entertainment. Whenever the world overwhelmed her, she would lose herself in a book and her troubles would vanish.

"What choice do we have?" Tadeusz slammed the notebook shut and launched himself to his feet. "Either we sell the books or be caught unaware and end up starving. We can't eat books, Lidia. Other than kindling, what good are they to us?"

He provided her with enough reading material over the years, never complaining when books cluttered the sitting room or the nightstands by their bed. All to make her happy. But he never really understood her passion for books. The man read nothing but the Bible, a couple of prayer books, and a newspaper from time to time. Her husband was a simple man. Not stupid, but he was content in his small world and he gave no thought to stories, or characters, or how people lived.

It hurt that he would belittle her interests.

But much as she hated it, he was right. Selling the books might spare them from starving, or they could put a little by. For Sophie to have enough and for them all to be more financially secure, she would sell the books in a heartbeat.

"Of course." Lidia tossed the book of Polish folktales on the kitchen table. It landed with an angry thud. "I'll have them ready tomorrow."

"I know you are upset." Tadeusz rested his hand on her shoulder, in an attempt to calm her. "But this is for the best."

Lidia met his gaze and realized this wasn't about the books or finances at all. No, he was hiding something else. But she couldn't put her finger on it.

Tadeusz turned from her and went outside before she could confront him about it.

He retired early, rolling onto his side and keeping his back to her when she joined him. She tried to sleep, but unable to, she cast the covers aside and padded over to the small bookshelf in the bedroom. Dozens of books were stacked onto the shelves. She withdrew her old copy of "Anne of Green Gables" and stroked it as she would a cat. That book saved her life in more ways than one. If it weren't for Anne Shirley and her story, she wouldn't have survived her childhood. It was one of the few things she brought with her to Krakow.

Plucky Anne Shirley was beloved in Poland. Soldiers were issued copies of the novel when they were sent to defend their country during the invasion and members of the resistance turned to it for inspiration. It was banned in certain places.

Days after the Germans invaded, as she and Tadeusz slept, shots were fired on the street. A resistance worker had been executed. The next morning, she found "Anne of Green Gables" dislodged on the shelf. She examined it and the bookshelf and what she found was shocking. A stray shell penetrated the wall of the house, it went through the bookcase, then it was stopped by the book. If the book hadn't been there, she would have been killed in her sleep.

The other books she could part with, but not, "Anne of Green Gables." *It's damaged anyway.* The rim of the pages was crudely mashed and discolored. *No one will buy it.* She reasoned.

Lidia placed a reverent kiss on the cover of the book While her husband snored, she wedged it under their goose down feather mattress. Tadeusz would never think to look for it there. He wouldn't even know it was missing.

Chapter Six

January 1943

Lidia wiped her tearstained cheek against her shoulder and bent further over the wash tub. Her fingertips were raw from the abrasion of rubbing one of Tadeusz's work shirts on the scrub board. But she couldn't stop now. She needed the distraction.

Her relationship with Tadeusz grew strained after he sold the books. Though she obeyed his wishes, she wasn't happy to forfeit her beloved tomes. After a few weeks, her temper cooled and she made every effort to patch things up. *He rebuffed me time and time again.* She sniffed, tossed the shirt into the filmy water, and sat back on her heels.

To Sophie, he was the doting father morning, noon, and night. *To me he is cordial.* Intimacy between them died, he no longer kissed or touched her. The other night she attempted to show him affection, to relay what she was feeling. He grunted out, *"Lidia, I'm tired. Leave me be."* He rolled onto his side, to avoid looking at her.

There is only one reason for that. Lidia concluded and dried her hands on her apron. *There is another woman.* She never would have thought her good and pious husband was the kind to commit adultery. However, it was nothing new. Many men before him did as much, many continued to, and many would still. Women in her position could only look the other way. After all, the Church and society would side with him, despite the fact he was in the wrong.

In between chores, she spent her time sobbing inconsolably and praying. What could she do? Where could she go? Other than keeping house, she had no skills and never held down a job. While she loved to read, her education was typical of a former country girl's – basic. Returning to her parents' home was not an option, not with Roland still living. She could only hope and pray Tadeusz wouldn't decide to separate and take Sophie from her.

"Sophie..." Lidia's look towards her daughter's room, where the little girl was napping. If she lost Sophie, her life wouldn't be worth living.

Tadeusz could have all of the women on the side he wanted, she would never complain and she would remain in a loveless union for the rest of her days. As long as she could have Sophie.

After Lidia hung the laundry about in the kitchen, she ended up in an hour-long sob in the fetal position. An unexpected knock beckoned her to the door. She answered it, despite her eyes being red-rimmed and her pink nose swollen twice its normal size.

"Mrs. Sobieska?" Father Cieslik appeared taken aback by her mussed appearance.

"Father, come in." Lidia tucked her limp hair behind her ears.

The priest banged his shoes against the doorframe to not track in snow. He shuffled in, closing the door behind him.

"May I fix you some tea?" She winced at how raw her voice sounded.

Tea was a rare luxury now, only available to those who shopped on the black market and were willing to pay exorbitant prices. She and Tadeusz no longer splurged on tea or that vile sludge some considered coffee. However, there were a couple of old stale tea leaves from a few Christmases ago, that she hid far back in the cabinet.

Sharing a cup of tea with the last real friend she had in the world would comfort her in a way crying couldn't.

"I'm afraid this isn't a social call, my child." Father Cieslik inhaled, his chest puffing out. "Mr. Sobieski was at the church, repairing a light fixture, when he collapsed."

"Dear God!" Lidia exclaimed. "Is he-"

"He is in the hospital. It was a heart attack."

She released an agonizing moan. At thirty-five, her husband was too young to have a heart attack. *This has to be a mistake!* Tadeusz was never seriously ill; even when he had a cold, he worked. The man didn't know how not to work. She assumed he was strong enough to pull a plow.

Tadeusz had mentioned the men in his family were prone to heart attacks. He must have inherited the heart condition after all. His size and stamina masked the truth – that he had been sick for a long while.

Lidia fetched Sophie from her room and grabbed the little girl's coat to bundle her up. "We'll be ready to go in a few minutes, if you'll take us to him." She held out one of the girl's arms to slip it into the coat.

"No." Father Cieslik gently took the coat from her and draped it over a chair. "Mr. Sobieski asked me to ask you not to come. The conditions there...are not suitable for either of you to be exposed to." The priest guided the child to the toys spread out on the floor. He gestured for Lidia to have a seat on the divan and sat next to her. "They won't keep him long, not when they have countless German soldiers from the eastern front to tend to. The doctor will release him in a few days and I will bring him directly to you."

69

Lidia propped her elbow up on the arm of the divan and rested her forehead in the heel of her hand. This shocking news and her consistent sobbing left her head swimming.

One moment her husband was an adulterer and the next he was on his deathbed.

Tadeusz would have to recuperate at home. *Can he recover from it?* From what she knew of his family, none of the men survived their heart attacks. He was lucky to be alive.

"I can help make the arrangements for his return home." Father Cieslik offered, his expression a little strained.

She nodded, unable to think of what to say, and where to begin. The priest's level head and calm nature would no doubt be beneficial.

For the next hour, Lidia and Father Cieslik discussed a number of changes she would have to make. One thing was for certain, her and Sophie's life would never be the same.

Father Cieslik arranged for Tadeusz to come home via truck owned by one of St. Anna's parishioners. Lidia brought Sophie into the kitchen to keep the little girl from being underfoot, while the priest pushed her husband in a rickety wheelchair to their bedroom. She didn't want to be in the way either. It may have just been his illness, but Lidia felt that prior to his heart attack, her presence more annoyed her husband than comforted him.

Minutes later, the priest stood in the kitchen doorway and signaled that Tadeusz was ready. The clergyman promised to come by the following day to check on them. She saw Father Cieslik out, thanking him for everything.

There is no prolonging the inevitable. She had to see her husband now. Inhaling and exhaling several times in an attempt to soothe herself, feeling a surge of courage, she led the small girl to the bedroom.

After four days' absence, nothing could have prepared her for Tadeusz's dramatic alteration. The heart attack aged him a decade; his skin was a pasty gray and dark shadows encircled his eyes. Sweat beaded along his hairline and down his broad forehead. Her once robust husband had been transformed into a broken man.

His breath came in rapid, exaggerated gasps. The small move from the hospital to their cottage wore him out.

"Papa?" Sophie whispered.

Tadeusz's lips stretched into a smile. "It's me, baby. Come here." He motioned the child to come closer.

Sophie didn't need to be asked twice. She scrambled into the bed and curled up by his side like a small cat.

Lidia hung back. She longed to forgive and forget, but the breach between her and her husband couldn't be denied and it wouldn't be easily mended. Rather than face this problem together, Tadeusz pushed her aside, making her feel unloved and at fault. Despite their differences, she still loved her husband dearly. No matter how he behaved and how he treated her, she wouldn't abandon him. *In sickness and in health...* That is what she vowed the day they married.

Tadeusz ventured a timid glance her way. "My darling..." he rasped. "I'm so sorry."

"Tadek," Her lower lip quivered. "I am too."

Tears trickled from the corners of his eyes and rolled downward. The man never cried, not in front of her.

"Come here?" He patted the empty space on the bed.

Lidia lay down on the other side of their daughter. She placed her hand on his stomach and he put his hand on top of hers. Their daughter chatted incessantly, scarcely stopping to draw breath.

She studied every inch of her husband's face, as though she were reacquainting herself with him. *My husband, my best friend.* How could she have thought he was seeing another woman? This was the man who confessed every sin to the priest, no matter how small. Tadeusz must have sensed he was ill and maybe he thought was doing the right thing, but instead he hurt her.

Sophie talked herself to sleep, clinging to her papa like he was a large stuffed bear. Her nostrils purred out babyish snores.

Tadeusz angled his head to where his chin was pulled inwards to his neck, sandwiching a small roll of fat. Lidia stared intently into his eyes, speaking without using words. They used to do that all the time when they were courting and for a while when they were first married.

Their introduction had been bittersweet. She met Tadeusz one Sunday Mass when he was visiting his cousins in the village near her family's farm. They both went up to light candles, each in the memory of their deceased fathers. She immediately felt safe in his presence. They didn't say a word, but lingered close, until her mother came to fetch her. Lidia recalled how he bashfully sought her out after the service and asked if he could call. Mother and Roland disapproved of him and did what they could to keep them apart. She and Tadeusz met in secret, exchanged letters, freely professing their love. When he learned of her dark secrets, he never judged her. She didn't think twice about running away with him. Since then, it had been them against the world.

Lidia drew her hand out from under his and laid it on his chest, directly over his heart. The beat was funny, it reminded her of a broken clock whose hands ticked at a manic pace.

"Father Cieslik found a job for me at a munitions factory, as a cleaning lady." She declared. There would be no discussion about this, she wasn't asking permission. One of them had to work and provide a living for them all. He made no answer, so she inched her fingers up to his jaw, tracing the edge of it. He was sticky from dried sweat. Once he was rested, she'd have to sponge bathe him later. "Tadek, talk to me."

"I'm scared." He whimpered, like a small boy. "I've had a father and brothers who died young of heart attacks. I'm going to die and leave you and Sophie alone in this world. It didn't happen this time, but it will next."

Lidia sat up, leaned forward, and kissed him on the mouth. "The only thing you can do now is rest and try to recuperate. Right now, you, Sophie and I are together, so that is enough." She smoothed his short crop back, noting she needed to wash his greasy hair too. "I love you, Tadeusz."

"I love you, too." Tadeusz caught her hand and brought it to his lips. "I'm going to stay around for as long as my heart and body will allow."

Lidia nodded and patted his cheek. The vow he just made to her was as sacred as the vows he made to her on their wedding day before the altar in the church. Perhaps more so.

Sunday, 14 March, 1943

Lidia scrambled out of the church, foregoing a chance to speak with the priest. She owed Father Cieslik so much for securing her a job at the factory. She and another woman managed to keep the factory somewhat tidy. There was something satisfying about receiving her pay, knowing she had earned it honestly, and it was hers to do with as she pleased. Between her demanding job, the errands she had to run, caring for Tadeusz and Sophie, her obligations to the Church, by the end of the day she felt like a tattered wash rag that had been rung out and stretched until the ends frayed.

Unholy screams from the Jewish ghetto bombarded her, making her desperate to get home as soon as possible. The shots and the violence and the wailing started during the church service. The altar boys merely closed the windows to drown out the unpleasant noise. Father Cieslik looked uncomfortable, but continued his sermon, disregarding the terror across the street at the ghetto. A man in his position, who was involved in his own illegal activities, couldn't afford to show sympathy to those doomed to destruction.

Since the ghetto's formation, there had been shootings, round-ups, and deportations. But now the dreaded liquidation had begun. A camp had been constructed at Plaszow for the young, strong Jews the Germans wanted to spare, where they would be ruled by the sadistic Amon Göth.

Lidia picked up her pace, tears blurring her vision and she was soon sobbing hard enough that sharp pains seized her lungs. Others in the street turned a blind eye to what was going on and she prayed no one would notice her distraught reaction. Father Cieslik may have been able to set aside his pity, but she couldn't listen to the Jewish people's suffering and remain unaffected. She was only able to breathe easy when she set foot in their little cottage.

The carnage was in the distance now, but an unnerving fear possessed her that after the Germans eradicated the Jews, they would start in on the Poles. Or somehow, they would discover that Sophie was Jewish and they would come for her.

After dinner, Lidia put Sophie in her nightgown and brought the girl to sleep in their bed. She could not bear to be far from her daughter, not with what was going on in their city.

Lidia slid beneath the covers and she would have pulled the blankets over their heads. But Tadeusz would have suffocated, so they had to endure the raw screams and gunfire throughout the night.

Sophie put her hands over her ears until she dozed off. A child in German occupied Poland, she was accustomed to air raids, bombings, gunfire, screams, and violence and didn't know life could be any different.

"Where is God, Tadeusz?" Lidia asked. No matter how many miracles she had witnessed since the war began, the murder of innocent people made no sense. "How could He allow this?"

"He is with us all." Tadeusz groaned. "The Lord is there with the Jews, He will not abandon them." He reached over and rubbed her shoulder.

"Where is the comfort in that, when He doesn't rescue them? All of those children!" Lidia batted his hand away. The last thing she wanted to hear was cliché platitudes. How those poor people dying were God's Will. How He had a plan for this. That everything would be all right in the end. "You wouldn't be so understanding if Sophie's life was threatened."

"Perhaps not." Tadeusz's eyes were heavy-lidded. The meal and the conversation drained him of his strength. "I imagine whoever her parents were, they're dead now."

Lidia looked at their daughter, relieved the little girl could rest easy.

Months elapsed since she last thought of Sophie's parents. Early on, Tadeusz encouraged her to forget about them and eventually she did. She never could picture them living in the ghetto, or in the new camp, or dying. They merely ceased to exist and Sophie came into the world as a four-month-old baby.

"I heard the other cleaning lady talking at work. Some of the Jews were to be shipped to Oswiecim." Lidia shivered, when she uttered the word aloud.

Oswiecim. What was once a historic city in the midst of swamplands, harmless and forgotten, was now one of the darkest places on earth. Rarely did anyone speak of it, no one asked about it, no one openly acknowledged its existence, and no one could be wholly certain what was in Oswiecim. Yet it was general knowledge that Jews and other undesirables were sent there and no one returned.

"Nothing lives there, no one can survive that place." Tadeusz said. He started to drift off. His snores and Sophie's fell in sync like the chugging of a train.

As if on cue, an actual train faintly squealed from within Krakow.

Lidia couldn't sleep. She lay there with her eyes peeled, hearing every little sound until there was dead silence.

The Jews were gone, one way or another, and Krakow was deemed "Jew Free."

Lidia was on her way to confession and stopped, standing opposite of the old Jewish ghetto. A chill came over her, unable to pass the area without unnatural quiet screams ringing in her ears.

It was haunted. Lost souls inhabited it.

Chapter Seven

Summer 1943

Lidia estimated it was six o'clock in the evening when she strode through the front door. "Sorry, I'm late..." she called out and turned to hang her purse on the peg. The other cleaning lady was ill which meant she had more to do at the factory. Her husband and child were likely starving by now, but since she was the sole provider, she couldn't help being later than usual. "Mrs. Karlinskowa?"

Instead of being greeted by her neighbor, she stumbled upon Tadeusz sprawled across the floor on his back, and Sophie sitting by him. His once muscular arms had shrunken into flabs of limp fat. The man, who used to pick her up and carry her to and fro without breaking a sweat, was unable to lift his own head off the floor. Let alone push himself upwards.

"Tadek!" She dropped to her knees beside him. "What happened? Where's Mrs. Karlinskowa?"

"Her husband got into a brawl at the tavern, she had to go get him." He replied. "I promised to stay put, but Sophie was hungry and you were late." He attempted to shrug, but couldn't do so lying there.

Tadeusz could occasionally move from the bedroom to the W.C. unaccompanied, if he felt strong enough. The man would often get it into his silly head that he could do smaller chores, like light cleaning in the kitchen or picking up after Sophie. But the stamina required to put one foot in front of the other, left him gasping for air by the time he found a dish cloth or bent over to collect one of the little girl's toys. His complexion no longer had any pink pigmentation, he had the skin of a corpse.

After he was struck down with his illness, Mrs. Karlinskowa volunteered to look in on him and Sophie while Lidia was at work. However, whenever the inept and often intoxicated Mr. Karlinski ended up in trouble, he became Mrs. Karlinskowa's first priority.

"Mama, I hep papa!" Sophie wrapped her arms around Lidia's neck. "I bring him what he needs."

"Good girl." Lidia planted a kiss on top of her daughter's head. "Can you go get papa's bed ready?"

Sophie eagerly darted to their bedroom.

Lidia summoned all of her strength and rolled Tadeusz onto his stomach and helped him raise himself to his knees. She retrieved a chair from the kitchen and between bracing himself against it, and a little coaxing from her, he was able to hoist himself onto the divan. He would rest there for several hours, until she thought he could reach the bedroom without taking another fall.

"Tadek, what were you thinking?" She scolded. "You could have broken bones."

The tendons in his neck were taut as he gritted his teeth. "I can't just laze there while Sophie's stomach is growling." He snarled.

Lidia paused, disturbed by his tone. She once thought of Tadeusz as a bear of a man, cuddly to those he loved and frightening to those who challenged him. More and more he was revealing his frightening side, his dark moods caused by the knowledge that life was slowly draining out of him and death was around the corner.

"You don't have a lazy bone in your body, though it'd be easier for us all if you did." She said.

"Don't coddle me, woman." He scowled.

Early on in their marriage, Tadeusz learned never to call her "woman." The manner in which the word was used was degrading. But what consideration he once had for her was waning.

I'm not coddling you!" Lidia snapped, putting her hands on her hops. "I'm trying to keep you from dying."

There was a small cry.

She spun around. Sophie was in the doorway, listening. Upset by her parent's exchange, she burst into tears.

"Oh, Sophie!" Lidia gathered her daughter up, balancing the girl on her hip. "Papa is all right; he isn't going anywhere."

A pang of guilt settled within. What she said was a lie. Tadeusz was dying and he would leave them someday soon. But there was no reason to break her daughter's heart now. Let the child enjoy what time her father had left.

She brought Sophie over to her husband, to prove nothing was wrong. His breathing was labored and was exhausted, but he wouldn't dare refuse his daughter. The little girl rested her head on his chest, poking at his deflated belly.

Lidia dropped into the empty chair she had drug in. She could spend all week in bed and not feel rested. Father Cieslik and Mrs. Karlinskowa helped as much as they could but they had other responsibilities. Before Tadeusz's heart attack, she had been tired then too. But he had been there for her to lean on and confide in. Though he was still living, she couldn't depend on him, not like before.

"Lidia, I'm sorry." He rasped. Since his health declined, his voice was different. It was high pitched, squeaking like that of a prepubescent boy. "Please forgive me. You deserve better than me."

"No," She waved him off. "Don't say that. You're all I've ever wanted."

Tadeusz was about to continue, but rather than listen to further depressed complaints, she fled to the kitchen on the pretense of making dinner. There were three large potatoes left. She sliced them up, peel and all, since it contained the best vitamins, and fried them in colza oil. The oil was black and it reeked, but it was the least expensive and easier to find. Their salt ration ran out the week before, so they would have to eat them plain.

Sophie inhaled her portion. Once she was finished, convinced that papa was no longer on the brink of death, she sat on the floor and played with her dolls.

"You and Sophie should split it." Tadeusz said. He managed a few bites before pushing the plate away.

Lidia didn't wish to force him and laid it on the coffee table, hoping he would change his mind later. If not, Sophie could have it for breakfast. Nothing went to waste in their household. From the defiant look in his eye, she knew what that man was thinking. He believed since he was dying, he could forgo food, that way she and Sophie could have more.

She sank into the empty cushion beside him and leaned her head against his shoulder.

"We must have a talk." He announced seconds later. She was about to get up again and leave the room, when he curled his arm around her waist and pinned her into place. "We can't avoid the truth any longer. I'm dying. My father died young, my brothers died young, and I will die young too. You must prepare yourself for a life without me."

She longed to cover her ears and run away screaming. "You

can't predict the exact moment. You may even have weeks or months." She argued.

"True, but I know my body and it's giving out." Tadeusz insisted. "You shouldn't stay in Krakow. Go to your mother and live in the country."

"I will never bring Sophie there." Lidia glared at him as if he lost his mind.

"Roland won't outlive me for long and you will be safer there than in the city." Tadeusz drew in a lung full of air and exhaled. "And one day, when you're ready, you must remarry."

"No," She silenced him with a kiss. "You're it for me. I could never love or be with another man."

"Just think about it." He sighed.

Lidia held her tongue, but there was nothing to think about. Tadeusz was the only one for her. No one could ever measure up, and she would never be able to be comfortable with anyone else.

Tuesday, 22 February, 1944

Lidia rose the morning of the third anniversary of discovering Sophie on their doorstep, expecting it to be a normal day. But when she found Tadeusz clawing at his pajama top's opening, clutching his chest, there was no denying he was on his deathbed. She sent Sophie over to Mrs. Karlinskowa and sent word to Father Cieslik via the inebriated Mr. Karlinski. The priest arrived not ten minutes later, having sprinted all the way from the church to their cottage.

Father Cieslik waited in the sitting room, while she and Tadeusz said their farewells in private.

Lidia slid into bed and rubbed his chest, to ease the pain.

In less than a year's time, he lost a third of his weight and resembled an old man, rather one in the prime of his life.

"Promise me that once it is safe, you will go to your mother's farm." A tear rolled out of the corner of his eye and dribbled onto the pillow. He rested his stiff fingers on her hip, feeling her body tense up. "I can't bear the thought of you and Sophie being in danger. The countryside will be better for you both."

Lidia shook her head. Even if Roland were to die tomorrow, she didn't think she could bring Sophie there to live. That place was full of too many bad memories for it to ever be a home for them. It weighed heavily on her conscience to deny a dying man his last request. But she couldn't lie to a dying man either.

"I can only promise to do what is best for Sophie." She raised herself up and leaning over, she brushed her lips against his. "Please, don't leave me here, I'm not ready. Sophie needs you. I love you."

"I love you too, but God is calling me and I must go." Tadeusz grappled for the bedding, howling like a woman fighting labor pains. "Where is Father Cieslik? I need Last Rites." He mustered out.

Lidia called for the priest and he sailed into the room, carrying a chair. He seemed unaffected at the sight of them lying in bed together. Perhaps during his time in the confessional, he had heard worse. He simply carried on, administering Last Rites to her husband.

Father Cieslik sat at Tadeusz's bedside, gripping the man's hand, praying and whispering words of comfort.

Tadeusz's lids grew heavy and closed one last time. He bent his arms, drawing his fists up to his chest and became still. His gray mouth pursed, quirking into a faint smile. Haggard as he was, with crow's feet splintering the corners of his eyes, he reminded her of a small child.

Lidia let out an agonizing wail, loud enough to rattle the

windows of the cottage. *My Tadeusz is dead!* She brought her fist to her mouth and bit into her knuckles.

Father Cieslik coaxed her out of the bedroom and into the kitchen. She fell into his embrace, burying her face into the material of his rough, black cassock.

"I know, my child, I know." He whispered. "In the coming days, people will tell you to be strong and I'm sure you will be. But I say you must grieve, because Mr. Sobieski was your husband and your friend."

"Thank you, Father." Her words were garbled by emotion.

Lidia's thoughts went to her father, who she adored. He died when she was eight years old. As an adult, she wondered if she idolized him too much. Roland was the furthest thing from a father. Now Father Cieslik...if ever there were a fatherly figure in her life, he was it. He more than earned his title.

None of this seemed fair. Tadeusz lived his life in such a way to please God and it pleased God to take him before his time. History seemed to be repeating itself. Sophie was only three; she was so young and eventually she would forget about him. She would never know what a good man he was, she would never know a father's love.

The war affected every aspect of their lives, including their mourning practices. Traditional Catholic funerals were long affairs, but because of the war, Tadeusz had a short ceremony. The church bell rang for each year of his life and he was buried in the cemetery by the parish church.

Lidia wore the customary black frock, including a thin, dark lace veil to cover her face. Sophie did as well. Since it was in the middle of winter, they had to forgo putting flowers on his grave until the spring. Once the ground was settled and thawed, they would plant tropaeolum – bright yellow ones because that was Tadeusz's favorite.

After a few weeks, she and Sophie returned to wearing their normal everyday clothes. But Lidia fashioned a black armband for her to wear in remembrance of her husband. Every Sunday, they would light a candle in his memory in the sanctuary and following the Mass, they would visit his grave.

Sophie struggled to understand that her father's soul was in heaven and she wanted to go visit him. They had to have many, many talks about it.

During one of their chats, Sophie was sitting on Lidia's lap near the fireplace, when they had a visitor. The knock was familiar, she recalled having heard it before.

Lidia scooted Sophie off and hurried to answer the door. Mother and Roland were standing on the other side, eager to be welcomed in. A scream swelled in her breast and she fumbled for the door knob, frantic to hold onto something. The demon who made her childhood a living hell was here to cause further turmoil. She was torn between killing him and diving under her bed to hide, as she used to.

"What are you doing here?" She asked, after finally finding her voice.

"We heard about Tadeusz and we wanted to comfort you." Roland responded.

Her stepfather was different from when she last saw him, fourteen years prior. The man who married her mother, the one who adopted her and brought them to live on his farm, had been tall, dark haired with a ruddy complexion, he had a persistent twinkle in his eye. A new man stood before her, one not nearly as tall; his shoulders were stooped and he was gray. It was no surprise to see him thin; they were all thin due to the war rations. Wrinkles matted his skin, making it shriveled and pockmarked. Cancer had been a savage beast to him. *It couldn't have happened to a more deserving person.*

He still wore a beard. The sight of those wiry hairs, which felt like steel wool against skin, churned her stomach.

"No, you're not welcome here." Lidia ventured outside, closing the door behind her. The last thing she wanted was for Sophie to overhear. Or for Roland to catch a glimpse of her daughter. "Just leave us alone."

"Lidia, stop." Roland dared to clasp her wrist.

She smacked his hand away. Tadeusz had always protected her from this man, he gallantly fought every battle. But now she had to stand on her own two feet and take care of herself. Grief and her temper emboldened her.

"The feud between us has to end." Roland tried again. He never did take 'no' for an answer. "It has caused your mother endless agony. I know I'm not your father, but I did the best I could in raising you." He rested his palm on his chest. "If you forgive me, I will forgive you."

Lidia's skin felt as though it was on fire. "Shut up, shut up, shut up!" She screamed and spit in his face. "Leave or I'll send for the police!"

He wiped her saliva off using his coat sleeve. "I'm praying for you." He said before she ducked back inside and slammed the door.

That was not the end of it. Oh, Roland knew better than to try again. Not her mother, though. She never knew when to stop.

A softer, meeker knock sounded.

Lidia jerked the door open once more, not about to give an inch. Not on this. Roland would never be welcome in her home. She would die before she let him in the same room as Sophie.

Mother shook her head. "How could you be so cruel to Roland?" She groped through her purse for a hanky, and on locating one, she dabbed her eyes and nose. "He loves you-"

"I hate him." Lidia ground out those words in a manic hiss. She didn't care if Sophie was ten feet off. Her daughter had to learn this man was evil to the core and there were others out there in the world just like him. "How dare you bring him here! When I'm at my lowest, having lost my husband and my best friend, you bring him. You know how I feel."

"Lidia, you cannot continue to live here alone. The farm would be better for you and Sophie." Mother persisted.

Lidia had lost count of the number of times she tried to talk to Mother about Roland. Nothing she said made a difference. Mother sided with him every time. Again, and again, Mother chose him; disgustingly grateful he was willing to provide for her. Never mind the price Lidia had to pay.

"I will never take Sophie there." Lidia vowed.

"One day you will need us and like the Prodigal Son, we will welcome you with open arms." Tears flowed from her weak, widened eyes, but they had no effect on Lidia.

"Go away." Lidia felt a wave of satisfaction when her mother turned an ashen gray and shut the door.

She rested her back against it and hugging herself, she bent over and let out an ear-piercing wail. One that reverberated throughout the cottage.

Sophie ran to her. "Mama!" She hurled herself against Lidia and pressed a kiss to her tummy, thinking that was where the pain was. "I make it better."

Lidia smiled through her tears and brushed her lips against the little girl's brow.

Somehow, her daughter did make it better.

April 1944

Lidia quickened her pace as she turned the corner and onto her block. She wanted nothing more than to collect Sophie from Mrs. Karlinskowa, make a quick meal, and coax the child into going to bed early. While her daughter slept, she would have a nice long soak in the tub and have a good cry. Her grief was still raw and it took all her strength not to break down crying at work. Sophie needed her to be strong and for the most part she was. *But who will be strong for me?* It was selfish, but she needed someone to lean on. Father Cieslik lent an ear when he had a spare moment, but he had the burdens of his congregation to carry and then his own work with the resistance.

White flakes fell and were accumulating on the ground. However, the ones that landed on her upturned cheek strangely didn't melt and disintegrated when she thumbed them away. *Odd. And a little late in the season for snow.* As she neared the cottage, the sweet, delicate scent of lilacs tickled her nose. A Polish favorite, and a sign of good luck, it was one of her favorite flowers. She stopped in her tracks when she noticed a German soldier on her doorstep. Her thoughts first went to the SS. But when she saw he was wearing a Wehrmacht uniform and he faced her, she realized it was Lt. Brühl.

"Lieutenant, it's been a while." Lidia greeted him with a pleasant smile.

"Mrs. Sobieska," The German politely dipped his head. A basket of breads, cheeses, and fruit dangled from his arm, and in his hand was a fresh bouquet of lilacs. "I wish to speak to you on a matter of great importance."

Lidia nodded, unlocked the door, and motioned him into the cottage. After all the man protected her and Father Cieslik from the Gestapo, she would do what she could to help him.

"Please, have a seat." She encouraged, as he made his way into the sitting room. She shut the door, shed her coat and draped it over the chair. "What do you wish to speak to me about?"

"First of all, please allow me to offer my condolences on Mr. Sobieski's death." Lt. Brühl laid the bouquet down on the coffee table, and placed the basket of food next to it. The German settled on the divan, fidgeting like a schoolboy. He was a fraction paler and he was even greyer than the last time she had seen him. A person gained two years for every year the war lasted. "My wife passed recently...my daughter did too. In a bombing."

Lidia willed herself not to cry. "I'm sorry, sir." Losing a spouse was horrible, but to lose a child, that would be soul-crushing. "There can be no greater pain."

"I have been thinking and praying, and I believe I have a solution. For us both." Lt. Brühl clasped his hands together. "Mrs. Sobieska, will you marry me?"

"What?" Lidia sank into Tadeusz's old chair, stunned by his unexpected proposal. "What did you say?"

"It's sudden, I know." Lt. Brühl admitted, looking a little sheepish. "But if you give it some consideration, it makes sense. We're both newly widowed and we have had our share of loss. We are devout Catholics..."

Lidia's hearing faded as the lieutenant prattled on, listing all of the reasons they should wed. She touched her brow, rubbing it. Never in all her years could she have predicted this. Lt. Brühl was a good man, and a good German at that. Her heart went out to him for his loss, but for him to seek her out, a woman he only met twice was...odd. Not only that, it couldn't be. No church in Poland would permit a union between the enemy and a Pole, and the German General Government wouldn't sanction it either. They considered Poles to be sub-human.

"But it would be illegal." Lidia reminded him. "We couldn't-"

"We could." Lt. Brühl persisted. "The Gestapo already believes we are...together. And I could produce paperwork ensuring you and your daughter have Germanic heritage. You could pass as Aryans." His soft eyes met hers and reaching across, he grasped her hand in his clammy one. "We could marry, I will adopt your daughter as my own, and I could bring you to the Fatherland. We could be a family. You and your daughter would be safe, you would want for nothing."

Lidia casually recoiled from him and went to the religious icons on the wall where she began to pray. Not for guidance, for she already knew her answer. *Lord, give me strength!* She understood Lt. Brühl's pain and loneliness, her longing for Tadeusz was intense and cruel. Her mother may have married right away after her father died, but she was not her mother. Though she respected the lieutenant and considered him a friend, she didn't love him and she doubted she ever could. He didn't love her either; he was only trying to replace the wife and daughter he lost. Sadness drove him, but it was callous that he believed she and Sophie could easily take the place of his loved ones.

I could never bring Sophie to Germany. Being the adopted daughter of a Wehrmacht soldier would be the ingenious way to hide a Jewish child, but she would be compromising all she believed in and what Poland stood for. If he happened to learn of Sophie's true identity, he could very well turn on them. Lt. Brühl spoke well and showed compassion to others, but a moment ago he slipped. He used the term Aryan. Nazism was steeped in him, whether he admitted it or not.

Or, Lt. Brühl could be depraved like Roland had been. There was always that chance. The wicked walked around in the skins of good men.

We may starve or be persecuted in Poland, but in Poland we shall stay. Lidia resolved and searched for the right words to reject the lieutenant. Lt. Brühl was a kind man, but a German officer. Men of power never accepted rejection well.

Lidia took a couple deep breaths and returned to Tadeusz's chair, drawing strength from the fact that though had died, he continued to live in her heart.

"Lt. Brühl..." She began softly, but the words faltered when he held up a finger.

"It is all right, Mrs. Sobieska, you don't have to say it." His shoulders dropped in defeat. The tone of her voice made her sentiments known. He got to his feet and nodded once more to her. "I shall take my leave. Seek me out if you change your mind. I wish you well. God bless you."

Lidia sat stock still, refusing to watch him as he departed from the cottage. She had no regrets about her decision, but she couldn't deny that she lost a friend. But now was not the time to wallow in self-pity. *I have to get Sophie.* Throwing on her coat, she headed outside and wished she waited a few minutes longer, as Lt. Brühl was just stepping off of her walk. He didn't hear her or look back and marched off, but she felt uncomfortable having him so nearby. *The neighbors might think I am a collaborator.*

She crossed onto the Karlinski's property and when her head snapped up, she saw Sophie in the window, waving. Mrs. Karlinskowa stood behind the girl, eyeing the retreating German. The woman turned her perceptive gaze on Lidia.

Lidia blushed, and hoped the woman didn't suspect anything out of the ordinary.

Chapter Eight

August 1944

The nights in bed alone are the worst. Lidia decided, rolling onto her side. The image of Lt. Brühl proposing flickered through her mind and she shook her head, to rid herself of him. She missed the companionship a husband offered, and no doubt the officer would have been decent to her, but she couldn't regret rejecting him. Despite being convinced that she made the right choice, that particular uncomfortable memory cropped up at the most inopportune moments.

She smacked her pillow and moved onto her back, wriggling down further into the mattress. *The silence doesn't help.* Her grief weighed heavily on her chest, threatening to smother her. Sophie had become quite the chatterbox, filling the house with her musings and endless questions. Her childlike innocence dispelled some of the pain. But at night, when the little girl was asleep in her own bed, Lidia couldn't help but be keenly aware of her own loneliness.

It was the little things.

She missed how for sometimes no reason at all, Tadeusz used to hug her from behind. Or how on their anniversary he would give her a bouquet of red poppies. His protectiveness of her and Sophie; he fought all of her battles. His religious faith inspired her own. And it wasn't just his positive qualities, she missed his annoying habits too. From his obnoxious snoring, how he left his socks on the floor until there was a pile, the way he would blame her for moving his tools when he simply forgot where he put them.

Since his death, her days were slow and agonizing. Sophie, work, church, household responsibilities, and errands claimed all of her attention. But there was an emptiness that demanded to be filled.

Tadeusz, from a distant memory, murmured in her ear. *We could adopt more. Many children need a good home. Especially now with the war going on.* He said that the day Sophie came to live with them. She originally wanted several children and though they discussed it, adopting another Jewish child, they never did anything about it.

I could take in another child. The idea struck her like a bolt of lightning. She raised the covers over her head, to shield her from her own thoughts.

There had been an uprising in the city of Warsaw. Upon learning of the closeness of the Soviet Army, the Warsawians revolted against the Germans to free themselves. The rest of Poland watched, waiting for the Soviets to assist. But the Russians didn't. Because of their reluctance to interfere, the Nazis crushed the uprising. Warsawian refugees flooded Krakow – some of them were Jews in need of a hiding place.

In the course of the war, she helped one Jewish child – her own. *Maybe I could have done more...no not maybe.* She should have done more and now was her chance! This decision to help another wouldn't free her from grief, but there was no doubt in her mind that it was the right thing to do.

The next Wednesday, Lidia and Sophie went to St. Anna's to pay Father Cieslik a call. He was the only one in her life involved in the resistance and the rescue of Jews. They attended Mass faithfully every Sunday and did the weekly confessions on Friday, but the church was often crowded then. She didn't wish for other parishioners to overhear her dangerous request.

Lidia entered the sanctuary, with Sophie by her side. She knelt midway down the aisle and crossed herself. Her daughter did the same, mimicking her motions.

Father Cieslik was in solemn prayer and she intended to wait until he was finished, but he must have heard their entrance and rose and met them. "Ah, the Sobieska ladies! Miss Sophie, you're almost as tall as your mother." He winked, sending the little girl into a fit of giggles. "How may I help you?"

"I was thinking..." Lidia looked over her shoulder, a habit she couldn't shake off. No one else was there. Even so, she kept her voice low. The large, airy sanctuary's high ceilings amplified sounds. One wrong word, one wrong look, one wrong move – could lead to death. "With the destruction of Krakow's ghetto and the Warsawians taking refuge here, there must be Jewish in need of a hiding place. Maybe an older one." She licked her lips, savoring the flavor of that night's meager dinner, and disregarded the burning emptiness in her stomach. "Our home is open."

Father's Cieslik's cheerfulness waned. "Mrs. Sobieska, you and Miss Sophie have been through so much." The priest motioned towards a pew, urging her to have a seat. Sophie climbed in beside her and he sat on the other side of the little girl. "Involving oneself in the resistance, it's not a hobby or something to do when one is feeling broken by grief. There are human lives at stake. Is now such a good time to be considering this? If your grief were to subside, would you still be interested?"

Lidia frowned, but couldn't fault him for doubting her motives. If she hadn't lost Tadeusz, she likely wouldn't be considering rescuing another Jewish child. Nor could she fault the priest for his skepticism that she could do it. When Sophie came to them, she was so young and could be easily passed off as her baby. With Tadeusz gone, an older child – or even a young one – couldn't be passed off as hers. But whatever doubts the priest entertained – or that she had about herself and whatever her motives might be - couldn't stand in the way of saving another human life. The Lord would provide a way.

"Please, Father." Lidia said.

"Mrs. Sobieska, I think it would be better if you and Sophie continue as you are." Father Cieslik rested his hand on hers, pressing it softly. "Rescuing another may draw attention to Sophie. We've already had our brushes with the Gestapo, we may not be so lucky if they were to come around again."

He was right. Bringing another person in her home might attract attention and the Gestapo may come around again. Lt. Brühl intervened on their behalf once, but since she rejected his marriage proposal, she doubted he would again if she were to get into trouble.

"The tide is turning against the Germans." Father Cieslik said. "In a matter of months, the war will be over. You must consider the future."

The days of the Nazi occupation were numbered. The summer of 1944 had been an eventful one. Father Cieslik visited one evening in June and gave them a radio. Lidia had initially been petrified at the sight of it; the penalty for a Pole owning a radio was death. Were one of the neighbors to overhear the broadcasts and report it to the Gestapo...But on listening to a BBC broadcast, hearing the propaganda-free news, she hung on every word. A little later, the Allied invasion began and day by day they worked their way eastward, liberating the French. Meanwhile, the Russians entered Poland and came west. In July, Hitler's own generals attempted to assassinate him. The plot failed, but it renewed her hope that freedom was around the corner.

"Whatever plans I made with Mr. Sobieski," Lidia blinked several times to keep the tears at bay. "He is gone now and I must make plans on my own." She didn't try to hide the twinge of resentment in her tone.

"Mr. Sobieski was a good man, but your life didn't end when his did."

"Precisely. I'm still alive and I can help another." She insisted.

Father Cieslik paused, hesitating before he continued, "It may be too early for me to say this, but you will love again. Your heart is too big not to love."

"Father, I want to help another, not be married off. And you're right, my heart is big enough to love another – a child." Lidia refused to consider remarriage and unwanted proposals. Leaning in towards him, she whispered, "Every child is someone's Sophie."

The priest looked at the little girl and sighed. "Very well." He ran his fingers through his hair, scraping his scalp. He could no longer deny her. She often wondered if she was like a daughter to him, and that was why he looked after her. If so, she was a spoiled daughter who he couldn't say 'no' to for long. "There is a young lady – God love her, she has a good soul, but she is reckless. She's from Krakow." The frustration coloring his words couldn't be ignored. "No matter how hard she tries, she can't keep a hiding place."

"Then this young lady is meant to stay with us." Lidia said.

"Perhaps so." Father Cieslik conceded.

"I hep mama care for her." Sophie piped up, bringing her finger to her lips to shush them.

"I see that I'm outnumbered." The priest chuckled.

Lidia leaned back in the pew. Her soul felt lighter with the knowledge she was doing the right thing.

The following night, after curfew, Father Cieslik called at their cottage. He was flushed and mumbling under his breath. A young lady lagged several paces behind, oblivious to his irritation.

Lidia was a little bemused by how flustered the clergyman was. The priest was known for showing kindness to everyone and seemed to have endless amounts of patience. What on earth could this girl have done to annoy him?

"This is Ewa Diamant." The priest ushered the spindly girl forward. "Miss Diamant, this is Mrs. Sobieska and that little girl is Miss Sophie Sobieska."

From Ewa Diamant's face, Lidia judged the girl to be around thirteen years old. Her dark hair was plaited into two tails, one behind each ear. The thick braids caused her ears to comically stick out. The girl's brown depths sparkled. Her two front teeth settled on her lower lip, making her resemble a chipmunk.

"Hello, Mrs. Sobieska!" The girl put her hand out. "I promise, I'll be quiet and stay out of your way." She said in all earnestness.

"Hello, Ewa." Lidia ignored her hand and gave the girl a big hug. "Make yourself at home."

Sophie threw her arms around the girl too.

Ewa's grin widened as they parted. She swung around to speak to the priest, knocking her rucksack into a vase. It shattered on the floor, soaking and staining the faded rug with flower water.

Father Cieslik pressed his fingertips to his temples and scolded the girl for her clumsiness.

"I'm so sorry!" The girl exclaimed.

Perhaps detecting the tension, Sophie hugged the girl again.

"Don't worry about it." Lidia shrugged it off.

After all, it was just an accident.

October 1944

Unfortunately, Ewa had a lot of accidents.

Three days into the girl's stay, Lidia understood why Ewa went from hiding place to hiding place. Her incessant chatter was bound to drive any sane person mad. The number of things she broke, the food she ruined when trying to make a meal even though she had been specifically told not to, playing the radio when Lidia and Sophie weren't home. Ewa's worst offense was moving the curtains back from the windows and peering out in broad daylight. A little peek here and there was understandable, but to show her face in full view was dangerous!

Ewa was a risk to her and Sophie's safety, that much was certain. But Lidia didn't have the heart to make her leave, not when she had been turned out of so many homes. The Soviets were edging closer and closer to Krakow. The war would be ending soon, perhaps in time for Christmas. They just had to hold out a little while longer.

On the 12th of October, Lidia finished her shift at the factory early, scrounged a bit on the black market, and splurged on a small vanilla cake. Sugar was scarce, so the treat was likely sweetened by molasses or saccharine. She and Tadeusz raised Sophie to acknowledge her Name Day rather than her actual birthday. But considering the two of them had a difficult year, a celebration was in order. Ewa would certainly enjoy cake too.

A chilly rain began to fall, the droplets were tinted milky white. She gulped and decided to take this as a sign she should go home. It wasn't snowing, it was too early in the season for that.

Earlier that spring, a peculiar white fluff fell from the sky coating every surface imaginable. She swept off the stoop several times before Mrs. Karlinskowa yelled out from her window, informing her of what it was. At the nearby concentration camp, Plaszow, the Germans lit a pyre of thousands of Jewish bodies on fire, the smoke and ashes rose to the sky. The white fluff, the white in the rain drops, were human ashes. It had been months since the fires, but the milky white ashes continued to fall whenever it rained.

A cold tingle shot down her spine as she prayed these ashes weren't Sophie and Ewa's families.

With bags in tow, she first went to collect Sophie from Mrs. Karlinskowa.

After Tadeusz's death, her neighbor volunteered to watch her daughter while she worked. A middle-aged woman, her graying upswept graying hair made her appear older. She was tall as a man but had a slender frame. Mr. Karlinski was often at the tavern, drinking away most of his earnings and they had no children of their own. She was so kind to Sophie, giving her little presents and treats. Lidia often thought in another time and place, they could have been true friends. The woman had come to her rescue when she had her brushes with the Gestapo and Mrs. Karlinskowa never once mentioned seeing Lt. Brühl enter Lidia's cottage. But for Sophie's and now Ewa's sake, she had to be careful with who she let into her life and home.

She had to knock several times before Mrs. Karlinskowa answered.

"Oh Sophie," The woman said wistfully, when she finally opened the door. "If I could steal you and keep you forever, I would!" She deposited the child into Lidia's arms. "Tell mama how good you were."

Sophie was gumming a peppermint. "I was good, mama!" She pressed her sticky lips to Lidia's cheek.

Mrs. Karlinskowa squinted, the muscles in her jaw tightening. "Mrs. Sobieska, let me be frank. Your Jewish girl has been much too loud lately." The woman could have been discussing the weather, she was that cavalier about what she was saying. "The other neighbors have mentioned it to me, but I convinced them that Sophie was having a few friends over. But really, you should be careful."

"Oh." Lidia managed to squeak out, her grip on her daughter tightening. So, the neighbors did know about Ewa. But because of this dear woman's intervention, they would be spared. Her thoughts turned to Sophie. Did Mrs. Karlinskowa have any inkling that the little girl she loved so dearly was Jewish? *Probably not.* As if on cue, the ashy rain fell a little harder, soaking into their coats, clothes, and skin. "Thank you."

"I think you're a fine Christian woman, foolish to get involved, but nice enough. Just be careful." Mrs. Karlinskowa laid a hand on Lidia's elbow. "Have a lovely evening. See you tomorrow."

Her neighbor closed the door before she could form a response. They were lucky. If it weren't for Mrs. Karlinskowa smoothing things over, she and the girls would have been hung or shot. She praised the Lord, His Blessed Mother, and all the saints above for saving them once more.

Lidia glanced upwards and her eyes bulged at the cottage's chimney smoking black. No one was home – save Ewa. To the outside world, it should have appeared as though the cottage was empty. A smoking chimney betrayed them!

She hurried inside and let out a groan the second the front door shut behind them.

Ewa was crouching on the floor, picking up shards of what was once a serving dish. "Welcome, Mrs. Sobieska!" She waved sheepishly.

"No, not my wedding platter! Tadeusz gave me that." Lidia wailed, setting Sophie and the bags down on the floor. The platter wasn't expensive, but to her it was priceless. It was one of the first things he bought for her to decorate their home. It had a permanent place on a shelf in the kitchen and was rarely used. "Ewa, I told you not to touch it."

"I'm sorry, ma'am." Ewa said, dipping her head. "I wanted to clean the cottage as a surprise for you and it was so beautiful, I couldn't help touching it."

"Yes, you could help it." Lidia counted to ten, drumming her fingertips on her brow. "But you chose not to. Why is there a fire in the fireplace?"

The blaze was high, having been fed one too many logs. Lidia dashed to the kitchen for a cup of water and tossed it on the flames, quickly taming them. Ewa was forbidden to use matches. On the second night of her stay, she had been stirring the embers and a spark flipped onto her skirt. Lidia dove in and patted it out with her hands before it burned the young lady.

"I wanted to make it toasty for you and Sophie." Ewa explained.

"You can't do that when I'm not here." Lidia had given Ewa a variation of this speech many times before. However, none of those talks had been effective and she was ready to tear her hair out. "When we're out, the cottage must look empty. This is your hiding place, remember? No one is supposed to know you're here."

Ewa's lower lip trembled and tears soon followed. "I'm sorry, I forgot." She clasped her hands together. "Please, don't make me leave. This is the best hiding place I ever had. I will convert to Christianity, if you want me to."

Lidia closed her eyes and silently asked for strength.

Poor Ewa. Not long after she had moved in with them, the girl admitted that she had hidden in over a dozen different places. Most of her protectors didn't treat her kindly. Some forced their faith on her. In the end, they always sent her back to Father Cieslik. She would hide at the church until he could place her somewhere else. Her parents had been sent to Oswiecim and likely wouldn't come back. Her sisters were in hiding but she hadn't had any contact with them for two years. She was alone in the world.

Lidia hugged Ewa, rubbing her back. "No one is going to make you leave and you don't have to convert, not to please me. This is your home for as long as you need it." She brushed the moisture from the girl's full cheeks. "But you must be more careful, all right? Now, let's get ready for dinner."

The girl beamed.

Ewa was a welcome distraction. The girl didn't possess an ounce of tact and asked question after question about Tadeusz, as well as a variety of other subjects. In many ways, she reminded Lidia of Anne Shirley from "Anne of Green Gables." Perhaps Ewa was also a glimpse of what Sophie might be like in ten years.

Awkward, messy, clumsy...Beautiful.

After dinner and they each had a small slice of vanilla cake, they turned in for bed. Not twenty minutes later, her bedroom door creaked. While the room was dark, Lidia knew who it was. It had become a sweet little habit.

Eva tiptoed in and climbed into bed and barely a minute elapsed before Sophie joined them. They rested their heads on her shoulders and cramped as it was, it was the perfect balm for the ache in her soul. Her bed was no longer empty and she was no longer alone.

The older girl craned her neck to look at Lidia. "Mrs. Sobieska, do you think much of what the world will be like after the war? What will you do once this is all over?" she asked.

During the war, the youth saw things, had experiences that the previous generations didn't, and they had to grow up so much faster. Naïve as she was, Ewa posed the most profound questions. The girl was wise beyond her years. On the fifth day of her stay, Ewa asked how Sophie had become her daughter. All on her own, without a hint, she figured out that Sophie was Jewish.

So, Lidia confessed everything and Ewa thought it was miraculous.

"I don't know." She attempted to shrug, but their little heads weighed down her shoulders. The war had been going on for so long, she didn't know what the world would be like afterwards. She hoped for peace, a sense of normalcy, but she had no specific plans. "What about you?"

Ewa hummed contentedly. "I have been thinking of Palestine. My sisters and I want to go. I want to be a nurse or work on a kibbutz and I want a boyfriend."

Lidia felt like crying, battling a pang of envy. *This is ridiculous!* She was jealous of a child. Ewa had the world at her feet and Lidia felt as though her life was already half over.

She tried to think back to when she was Ewa's age. The only dream she had was escaping her family and leaving the countryside for the city. That much she had accomplished. But she couldn't recall yearning to be anything except a wife and a mother, and to have a home of her own. Women from her village never had careers.

Sophie was the last dream of hers to come true. Now that she had her daughter, what else could she want?

"Will you remarry, Mrs. Sobieska?" Ewa asked.

"No." Lidia gave a slight shake of her head. "I loved my husband dearly; he was the only one for me."

"True love. There is nothing like it. That is what I want." Ewa mused, her pitch raising a full octave. "You don't want to try and find it again?"

Lidia chewed on the inside of her cheek. First Father Cieslik and now Ewa. Tadeusz hadn't been gone a whole year and they were already trying to marry her off. Father Cieslik confided that a couple of single men had asked after her. Yes, she was a young widow, younger than most, but that didn't mean that she was desperate to have a man in her life. For goodness' sake, she still wore a black band around her arm. Truthfully, she wasn't sure she could find the kind of love she had before. Her childhood left its scars on her. Besides, she liked having her own way and she couldn't bear children. And unlike her mother, she wasn't about to enter into a marriage to benefit herself or her child.

"I have it with Sophie." Lidia brushed her lips against the little girl's fair brow. Her daughter never looked more angelic than when she was sleeping. "True love comes in many forms and she is mine."

As long as she had Sophie, she would be happy.

Chapter Nine

January 1945

Lidia was running errands, picking up supplies when the Germans blew up the Vistula Bridge. The impact hurled her to her hands and knees onto the slick, icy cobblestones. She winced at her bloodied palms and legs, then gathered the sacks and got back up. Disregarding the shooting pains in her wobbly limbs, she broke out into a run and reached the cottage within a few minutes.

The Nazis were desperate to escape Krakow before the Soviets made their descent upon it. They stole everything of value and wanted to destroy whatever remained. The Germans razed Warsaw before they left it, burning it from top to bottom, and she and most of her acquaintances feared Krakow would end up with the same fate. But they must have run out of time because most of the city's landmarks were spared. Blowing up the Vistula Bridge though, was the Germans final attempt to prevent the Russians from entering Krakow.

The grocer didn't have much left on the shelves, having been scavenged by the Nazis earlier that morning. But the proprietor pitied her and sold her two loaves of bread, a hunk of moldy cheese, a can of peas, and a sack of dried beans he had stored beneath a floorboard. Split three ways, it wouldn't last long, but it was something to fill their bellies for a couple of days. *We have to be grateful.* The Karlinski's resulted to roasting pigeons. Others caught stray dogs and cats to turn into a stew.

There was a second boom as Lidia crossed the threshold. The whole cottage shook on its foundation. "Dear Jesus." She plucked their religious icons from the wall and called for the girls. "Sophie, Ewa, I'm home! You can come out now."

Ewa and Sophie joined her from the bedroom, where they hid under the bed. The older girl had a butcher's knife in her raised hand, which she laid down on the table.

Lidia moved into the kitchen and kicking the rug aside, she jerked open the trap door to the root cellar. She rarely went down there, except to put food away. When the Germans invaded Poland, she and Tadeusz took cover down there. It wouldn't have protected them if an actual bomb had dropped, but they did feel safer away from the fighting.

She tossed the sacks down and collected some candles and matches. She shimmied down the ladder to show the girls they had nothing to fear. The cellar was swathed in darkness, the only light trickling in from above. Mice lurked in the dark corners, but she didn't dare mention them otherwise they might refuse to join her.

"Come on, girls." Lidia laid the candles and matches on top of the sacks and waved them down. "There's nothing to be scared of."

Ewa handed Sophie down and Lidia placed the smaller girl on the moist floor. The older girl inched her way down, her knees knocking. The chatty girl was uncharacteristically quiet and when she reached the bottom, she clung to Sophie, as if the younger girl could protect her in some way.

Lidia climbed back up midway and grabbing the cellar door,

she pulled it closed. Fine bits of dust clogged her nostrils and coated her tongue. She swished the saliva around in her mouth and though it was unladylike, she spit it out off to the side.

"Mama, I scared!" Sophie cried out. While she couldn't see her daughter, she was willing to bet the younger girl's red face was puckered and tears were sprouting.

"I know, baby, but we have to. It's for our own safety." Lidia replied.

She groped through the darkness until she located the matchbook. The match hissed as she scraped the tip along the rough patch. One lit candle expelled some of the darkness. The little girl's whimpers subsided when she realized there were no monsters – other than mice – in the shadows.

The cellar itself was a small, enclosed space with clay flooring. The ceiling and the walls were wooden, but there were slatted gaps between each board large enough to rain down dirt on their heads. Mice skittered back and forth, eliciting shrieks whenever they ventured too close.

"It's all right, Sophie." Ewa beckoned the little girl into her lap. "The dark scares me too, but we have to be brave. Soon we will be free."

The girl had become an older sister to Sophie. The younger girl copied everything the older girl did, from how she spoke to how she wore her hair. Lidia may have been Sophie's mother and the head of the house, but it was Ewa's word that was golden.

The girls fell silent. Lidia strained her ears to hear every little noise that happened outside of the house. The world above was muffled but she could make out the faint clacking of steel toed boots on the street. From time to time there were shouts, followed by long stretches of quiet.

She chose to blow out the light, despite Ewa and Sophie's protests, to conserve their candles.

"Mrs. Sobieska," Ewa had begun, then hesitated before she continued. "If the Russians are coming to liberate us, isn't that a good thing? Why must we hide?"

"The Germans are retreating, but there's a chance there could be stray gunfire or more explosions." Lidia gulped and prayed she could come up with a good explanation to satisfy the girl's curiosity. "Also, the Soviets may be good or they may be bad. We don't know what they might do to Jews. I want to be certain it's safe before any of us go up."

The rampant antisemitism in Russia was as prevalent as it was in Poland. Reports on the BBC claimed that once Russians liberated a city, Jews that had remained were no longer in danger of death or persecution. The BBC was a trustworthy source, but after five years of occupation, she wanted to see it with her own eyes before she believed it to be true. There was also something else.

By word of mouth, rumors spread that as the Russians advanced westward, the soldiers were raping women and girls. In Warsaw, some ladies were molested multiple times and little girls were not spared.

Please Lord, protect my girls. Lidia begged. Considering what happened during her childhood and that she had been a married woman for nearly fourteen years, she figured if she were raped, in time she would recover. But Sophie and Ewa were young and should never know such horrors.

"You don't think they will hurt us, do you?" Ewa jabbed Lidia's leg with her sharp fingernail. "That they will...you know?"

Lidia shook her head at herself; she should have known better than to underestimate Ewa.

"Do you think it's true?" Ewa asked, scarcely above a whisper.

For most of her childhood, the girl faced trial after trial and survived. To lie to her wouldn't be fair. Lidia vowed she would do whatever possible to protect the girls, but she had to prepare them for the worst. Still, with Sophie present, she didn't wish the innocent little girl to hear such vile things.

"That is why we're down here. But I promise, Ewa, I won't let any harm come to you." Lidia reached out and patted the older girl's cheek. "But let's talk of something else. What is the first thing you want to eat when we're free?"

"Chocolate." Ewa said.

Sophie clapped and chanted, "Chocolate, chocolate, chocolate!" Her childlike words echoed throughout the cellar. Unfortunately, the poor child had no idea what chocolate was. No one could afford such delicacies since the war began.

But Ewa was right.

Chocolate is the first thing I want too. Lidia mused wistfully.

~

They spent three days in the cellar while the battle for Krakow raged. The actual fighting, the shots, and the explosions were far removed from the cottage, but the noise made it frightening enough for them to stay in their hiding place. They only ventured upstairs to use the toilet, to have a drink of water, and a bowl of bean soup. To pass the time and to entertain Sophie, Lidia and Ewa told stories and sang.

By the fourth day, the fighting came to a complete halt and it sounded as though Krakow itself had died. Or perhaps, had been reborn.

Lidia drew in a deep breath of polluted air. They couldn't stay in the cellar forever. They were running out of food and if they were in danger, she would have to find a way for them to escape.

"Girls," She licked her chapped lips and only then realized how thirsty she was. "I'm going to go up and look around, but you two must stay down here, until I give you permission to come up." She left kisses on the tops of Sophie and Ewa's heads before mounting the ladder.

Lidia shoved the door back and stepped into the kitchen. The cottage was untouched from the last time they went up for the toilet or a glass of water. She wiped her hands on her skirt and cringed over her tender palms. They were brushed and a little bloodied from her recent tumble. Her wool stockings had dried to the scabs on her knees. She tussled her hair loose from its clasp but a musty stench lingered and her scalp was itchy. Rushing to the window, she peeled back the curtain. Aside from a smattering of debris, dislodged cobblestones, and smoke billowing into the sky, Krakow as she had come to know it during the war looked the same.

The rowdy chortles of a thick foreign tongue reached her. *The Russians.* From her position at the window, she witnessed a number of soldiers tearing into houses, shouting, and carrying off pieces of property. Feminine cries resounded...one of which belonged to Mrs. Karlinskowa.

Lidia started back for the cellar, her mind racing at where they could go. *The church maybe.* Father Cieslik would protect them. But she and the girls would have to hurry and sneak out the back. Even then they might not elude the Soviets.

She froze in place when the front door was kicked in. It was too late.

Two young Russians charged in and stopped short when they noticed her. The two exchanged bewildered looks and lowered their rifles.

Lidia looked down; she was a grown woman but as filthy as a street urchin. Unsure of what to do, she waited for them to make the first move.

The soldiers conversed in their language. The tall, dark haired one flicked his finger in her direction and the shorter blonde haired one shrugged. Neither looked a day over twenty. In fact, they looked like they should have been participating in a football match rather than engaging in a war. Other than greetings and a few simple phrases, Lidia knew nothing of the Russian language.

There was a creak from the kitchen. Ewa ran to her, balancing Sophie on her hip.

Ewa passed Sophie to her. The little girl tightened her arms and legs around Lidia, to the point she couldn't breathe. Whatever the older girl had told her, the little girl took to heart. The girls buried their faces into the cloth of her stale, sweat-dampened dress.

"Girls, go back downstairs!" Lidia scolded.

Ewa told the Russian soldiers, "Please, don't hurt us. My name is Ewa Diamant and this is Sophie. We're Jews and Mrs. Sobieska protected us from the Nazis." The girl disregarded Lidia's scathing glare and continued, "Please, don't rape us."

The dark-haired soldier gaped and addressed them in Polish, "You're Jews? I'm Jewish. We would never hurt you." He opened a pouch attached to his hip, withdrew a small stack of rectangular objects, and handed them to Ewa. "Here. We're friends, see?"

Ewa's brow furrowed, but peeling the paper on one back, she gasped. *Chocolate!* Her wish had come true. She broke off a piece and poked it between Sophie's lips. The little girl chewed and let out a squeal.

Lidia put her daughter down and took a piece of her own and relished a small taste of heaven that dissolved on her tongue. "Thank you, young men." She said, with a timid smile. These two boy soldiers might not hurt anyone, but she couldn't expect mercy from all Soviet soldiers. "Sophie never had chocolate before."

Another scream rippled through the neighborhood and gooseflesh prickled her skin.

"Ladies," The Jewish soldier sighed. "There are soldiers who do rape. Is there some place I can take you, where you will be safer? Some place to hide? I will escort you."

"We both will." The other soldier chimed in.

"Our priest will protect us." Lidia was too desperate to spare the girls of cruelty that she had to accept. "The church isn't far."

"Pack a few things and we can go." The blonde soldier instructed.

Ewa packed what meager belongings she had brought with her into hiding. Lidia gathered clothing for her and Sophie, a few toys, the religious icons, and the copy of "Anne of Green Gables." She tucked what little money they had into her brassier. They donned on their coats and caps and on the way out of the cottage, she removed the crucifix from the wall and stuck it in her pocket.

Lidia picked Sophie back up and carried her through the streets to the church. Ewa hung onto her elbow, burying her face into her shoulder whenever something frightened her. The two boy soldiers flanked the little group, their weapons primed to take on whoever might cross their path.

The five passed a group of captured German soldiers, who were in the custody of the Russians. One of the Germans glanced in Lidia's direction. *Lt. Brühl!* The once tall and stately man was now disheveled and battered. His eyes locked with hers and there was a flicker of remorse. But she couldn't tarry. Though it was hypocritical of her not to speak up for him, she couldn't risk Sophie and Eva's safety. *God be with him.* After all the good things he did during the war, she hoped that the Soviets would pardon him.

Tanks ambled through the streets. The Vistula was frozen enough that it could withstand the weight of the tanks and the drivers dodged the bodies that littered the river.

Lidia and the girls made it to the church unscathed.

Father Cieslik was there to receive them with open arms, as though he sensed they were coming. Before they departed, she and the girls bombarded the two boy soldiers with hugs and thanks.

As the priest was closing the door of the church, Lidia caught a quick glimpse of Wawel Castle. The Polish flag was raised on the roof of the castle; the red and white banner snapping in the Arctic breeze. Red for courage, white for purity. The old, familiar tune of the *hejnal* keened throughout the city.

Krakow was free, proving that Poland had not yet perished. After two thousand and seventy-eight days, the war was finally over.

Adam's Story

Chapter Ten

Saturday, 22 February 1941
Kazimierz District, Krakow, Poland

Adam was running behind, but he couldn't resist looking in on his daughter one last time before he left for work detail. "Por Una Cabeza" belted out on the gramophone by the window and he ought to shut it off. But his daughter seemed to enjoy the jaunty tango whenever he played it.

He leaned over the lace swathed cradle, marveling at how perfect his little girl was. Suzanne was a combination of him and his wife. She had Mina's blue eyes and smile, and her hair was the color his had been when he was young before it turned darker. Her skin though was pale and delicate, like his mother's was. There was a tiny heart-shaped birthmark on the side of her neck.

She has my heart.

"Papa has to go now, but he will be back this evening." He promised, smoothing back her curls. And he would do everything in his power to keep his word. But he couldn't predict what might happen once he stirred outdoors. Not when Krakow was swarming with Nazis. One couldn't dwell on the negative; he had to believe that all would be well. "We can read a story and listen to music together before bed. How does that sound?"

Suzanne latched on to this finger and gurgled.

Life was ironic. He never planned to have children. After an unhappy childhood because of a difficult father, he didn't think he was suited for parenthood. Marrying his wife, Mina, and having a successful tailoring business was enough. Mina didn't originally want children either, but when she became pregnant ten years into their union, she was overjoyed. He tried to be supportive, but deep down he was terrified that he'd turn out like his father and in the long run end up hurting the child.

When the nurse put Suzanne in his arms for the first time, his life suddenly made sense. The fear vanished and he was in love for the second time in his life. Crying, he kissed her scrunched face, pledging his devotion to her. Having a baby, a year into Germany's occupation of Poland probably wasn't their wisest decision. But he and Mina held out hope that things wouldn't get as bad in Poland as they did in Germany. They attempted to live their lives with a sense of normalcy. They had Suzanne now, they were a family, and the only thing they could do was work and make themselves useful. Lately, it didn't seem to be enough.

They were Jewish.

For me it's only by technicality. Adam thought bitterly.

He was fully assimilated; he hadn't even set foot in a synagogue before he and Mina wed. He wasn't circumcised and he never had a bar mitzvah. He didn't speak Hebrew or Yiddish, never observed the holidays, never prayed, nor could he decide if he even believed in God. They lived in the Jewish sector, the Kazimierz District because Mina was happiest there. The only thing that made him Jewish was his ancestry and for the Germans that was enough.

The Nazis had taken over his business and the art enthusiasts no longer bought Mina's *degenerate* artwork. No matter how assimilated he was, no matter his beliefs or his actions, he was Jewish enough to wear the blue Star of David on a strip of white material around his bicep, to have the "J" stamped on his passport, and to be selected for back-breaking work detail day after day.

Suzanne deserves better. He frowned.

"Papa loves you." Adam left a parting kiss on Suzanne's brow and he headed out to avoid being too late. The Germans relished beating anyone who lagged behind.

He and dozens of other unemployed Jewish men were to shovel snow out of the streets. The day stretched out before him and he thought it would never end. A little after noon, a cocky young soldier confiscated his gloves. His hands soon cracked and bleeding from gripping the handle of the shovel. That evening, on his way home, he tore his handkerchief in half and wound the material around his blood-caked palms.

Adam let out a sigh on his return to their apartment, relieved that he had survived another day. The sitting room was dark until he turned on one of the lamps. Mina and Suzanne didn't appear to be home, which was odd because his wife rarely ventured out with the baby on her own.

Hours passed and Mina and Suzanne still hadn't come home. He began to pace, played "Por Una Cabeza" again and he smoked what he had left of his cigarette ration. Then he smoked more than he paced, as he often did when he was anxious. It was long past the curfew the Germans had issued. A Jew out past curfew was risking a shot to the head. If anything were to happen to his wife and daughter…there would be no point in living.

Mina staggered through the door after midnight, sucking in ragged breaths. Suzanne wasn't with her.

Adam rushed to her, shutting the door. "Mina, where were

you? Did you receive a summons?" He asked, but he was too flustered to wait for her explanation. "Where is Suzanne?"

"Suzanne is safe now." She answered, sobbing as she sank to her knees.

His wife was an artist with an artistic temperament. She tapped into her moods to create wonderful works of art. Abstracts; she called them. All of her creativity came with a price though. She was prone to severe melancholia, to the point where it debilitated her. There were also times she would make rash decisions and live in a state of euphoria. *Manic depression.* A doctor once called it. But by the way she was crying now, this was something else entirely.

Suzanne is dead. Was his first thought. The room tilted. Adam's legs turned to jelly and he braced his hand against the wall to maintain his balance. Since the occupation began, he heard stories of Jewish parents taking extreme measures to spare their children from future suffering. One couple poisoned their three children and then themselves, believing death preferable to falling into the Germans' clutches.

His heart slammed into his ribcage, hard enough to puncture the muscle. "What happened?" He knelt down and pressed her shoulder softly. "Please, tell me!" He implored.

"No, we're going to die! The Germans will kill us all!" Mina batted him away and she needed a moment of soothing breaths before she was calm enough to continue. "Don't ask me to watch my daughter die, Adam. For her to starve or get sick, or be tossed in the air and shot. As long as she is happy and safe, that's what is important." She said, in an attempt to convince him, and maybe herself too.

Adam sat back on his heels. "Mina, where is Suzanne?" He balled his fists, his nails cut into his wounded palms, but he barely felt the pain. "What did you do to her?"

"I left Suzanne on a Christian couple's doorstep and I watched to make sure they took her in. The wife was kind to me once, she will be kind to Suzanne. Everything will be all right now." Mina wrapped her arms around her waist. "I left a note under the lining of the basket, explaining who she is and who we are."

Adam was on the verge of losing his composure. To endanger their baby, to expose her to the frigid temperatures and abandon her on a doorstep, to allow some strange couple to lay claim to Suzanne...At this late hour, he could do nothing. He could hardly storm over to the Christian couple's home and reclaim his daughter. For now, it may not be such a bad thing if their daughter was with this Christian couple. She would be safer with them and it would only be for a few months at most. Once the war ended and the world was set to rights, Suzanne would be returned to them.

This war had been going on for over a year, certainly it wouldn't last much longer. He ignored the voice in his ear reminding him that the Great War lasted four years. No, Poland couldn't go through another war of that magnitude. It wouldn't come out the same way it went in.

"Well, when this is over, we will find Suzanne." Adam concluded, slowly. "Or at the very least, she will find us."

"Oh, Adam-" Mina groaned, shaking her head.

"No, listen to me." He cupped her cheek, stroking it with his thumb. "We must survive this, for her sake as well as ours. Suzanne is our purpose. When this is over, we will all be together again. Trust me."

Mina blinked and nodded. By her expression, he could tell she remained unconvinced and was just humoring him. She slumped into his arms, burying her face into the crook of his neck. Her tears soaked his shirt collar and his own soon mingled with hers.

Adam lingered outside his apartment, his fingers skimming the door knob, dreading going inside. The last few weeks had been painful, to say the least. But he couldn't stay out in the hall forever. His body throbbed from hours of manual labor at work detail and he needed rest. He entered, quickly closed the door, and was greeted with dead silence. Mina was likely in bed, where she spent most of her days. His eyes settled on the space where a small coffin had resided days after Suzanne had been given to that Christian couple.

Since the Germans had a roster of the Jewish population in Krakow, which included Suzanne, he and Mina were left with only one alternative. No one could know that their daughter was living with the Christian couple. If she simply *disappeared*, someone would figure out Suzanne was in hiding and word might get back to the Germans. To conceal the truth, they told everyone that their daughter died. They claimed Mina got up in the middle of the night and found their little girl dead in her cradle. Such tragedies weren't uncommon in times of war, when food and medicines were scarce.

Mina's rabbi went above and beyond. Rabbi Rosenwieg called on them regularly, he helped them plan a small service, and gave the most touching eulogy for Suzanne. The local synagogues and cemeteries were closed to Jews, therefore the service had to be held in their apartment.

Throughout the ceremony, as he listened to the rabbi's kind words, Adam eyed the little coffin. *This is for the best.* He told himself, disregarding the ball of guilt burning in the pit of his stomach. The coffin was empty, but it was a stark reminder of what could have been if they hadn't sent Suzanne away. He and

Mina were able to give a convincing portrayal of devastated parents. No one doubted their sincerity.

He hoped the Christian couple caring for Suzanne were decent people. Mina believed that they were, but she was more inclined to think well of people than he was. The couple might be the salt of the earth, but that meant nothing if they didn't love Suzanne or offer the finest care. She wasn't fully weaned when she was left on their doorstep – were they able to feed her properly on war rations? Did she have nice clothing? Was she warm enough? Would they buy her toys? She loved when he read and told her stories; did the Christian couple even have books other than the Bible in their home?

They'll baptize her. He closed his eyes in remorse. He never used to entertain such negative views of Christians. Poland was a Catholic country; he might not have been religious, but the world around him was. There was no escaping it. For all he knew, the Christian couple were training Suzanne up to despise her own people. *Training her up to hate me.* He cringed at the thought.

Adam heard sobs and followed the sound to the bedroom. The lights were off and it took a couple of minutes for his eyes to adjust. Mina was beneath a cocoon of bedclothes. She often alternated between weeping and staring vacantly at the bedroom wall. He had the opposite problem: sleep evaded him and he was wound up with an endless supply of energy. In the back of his mind, he knew the second he stopped, he'd break down. And that couldn't be; he had to be strong.

Suddenly, he was too wary to continue on with this charade. Despite agreeing to maintain his distance from Suzanne, watching his wife be in such pain, and feeling his own agony, his resolve was wavering.

"Darling," Adam sat on the edge of the bed and rubbed his wife's lower back. "Please, tell me where Suzanne is. I will go get her and bring her home. We can have her back here in a few hours." He couldn't bear to listen to his wife's turmoil because it reminded him too much of his own. "Mina, please, I'm her father. I can't bear to be without her."

"You'll have to learn to bear it." Mina rolled onto her side. She pushed the covers down, her bloodshot eyes peered out. Her eyes always lost their sparkle when her mood plummeted. "Suzanne is dead to us."

Adam recoiled, sickened by her declaration. "No, don't say-" He protested, but the words died on his tongue.

"You have to. Suzanne is dead to us." Mina sat up and finger combed her tangled hair. "Say it."

"No, I won't." He held up his hand. To deny his daughter's life and their connection to her, would be like her rabbi denying his God. There would have been no greater sin. "Suzanne is alive and she's waiting for us. When this is over, we will find her and we'll be a family again. We could have other children too."

"Adam, how can you consider bringing other children into a world like this?" Mina asked, "You of all people."

He managed a wry smile. There was a time, not so very long ago, when he was terrified of having a child. But Suzanne changed everything, she made him brave, and she made him realize that unconditional love was miraculous. To have more children, for them to be a happy family, would be a dream come true.

"Not now, but someday when this is over." He said. "Living our lives is the best way we can resist the Nazis." He took her hand. "Mina, we can't lose hope. That is what they want."

In the unlit room, Adam was able to make out his wife's expression, which was beginning to soften. For the life of him, he couldn't figure out why she chose to be with him. She was beautiful, striking, really. Light eyes were set in an oval face, her raven curls fell like a curtain past her shoulder blades. She was his height and she could stare him straight in the eye, and when she wore heels, she surpassed him. While most ladies preferred modern styles, she liked flowing skirts, bohemian blouses, jingling necklaces and bracelets.

Vivacious and artistic – there was no reason for her to look at him twice. But for whatever reason, she did.

Adam brought her hand to his lips and kissed her knuckles. "You're the one who always encourages me to have faith. If there is a God, He cannot...He will not forget us." He turned on the lamp and the light pierced his retinas. He opened the nightstand drawer, withdrew the pad and pencil she stored inside, and laid it on her lap. "Now, will you sketch something for me?"

"What? Why?" Mina's brow knitted in confusion. "There's nothing beautiful here. Not anymore, not without Suzanne."

"You're a witness to a dark history. As an artist, you're duty bound to record what you see." He tapped the pad of paper, meaning it wholeheartedly. He had an ulterior motive for urging her to draw. A doctor had prescribed lithium salts to moderate her moods. Even when diluted by mixing in tea, she insisted it interfered with her thoughts and memory. Her moods were best managed when she created something. To survive this and her grief, she had to fight as hard as he was. He couldn't do it on his own. "We can hide your drawings somewhere safe and you can display them in a gallery after the war ends. Think of how proud Suzanne will be of her mother, the famous artist."

A ghost of a smile flickered across Mina's face. "Adam, why do you continue to stand by me?" Her fingers interlocked with his. "My moods, my behavior, my actions. Why?"

"I love you." Adam pressed a kiss into her palm. They may have had their struggles over the years, but he never regretted marrying Mina and he never would. "I came alive when I met you."

They shared a quick peck on the lips and he stretched out on his side of the bed. She was swept away, capturing a scene that was common in their neighborhood, of the Nazis abusing a Jewish man. The Nazis bore expressions of manic glee in contrast to the victim who wore an expression of stark terror. Her art would keep her occupied and hopefully the dark cloud hanging over her would lift.

Adam rolled onto his side and he was finally able to get the first good night's sleep since Suzanne was given away.

Chapter Eleven

Monday, 3 March 1941

Adam slid another small stack of zlotys under the lining of Suzanne's old baby pram. By his calculations, he stashed away several thousands' worth. *Hopefully, no one will go through our things.* Two thousand zlotys was the limit the Nazis allotted them to bring into the Jewish ghetto. But he wasn't about to obey their orders.

Many of their friends and acquaintances had their accounts frozen when the Nazis took power. He and Mina were lucky. Prior to the German invasion, when others were in denial about the possibility of war, he withdrew a good portion of money from their bank account and stored it under a loose floorboard in their apartment. He figured if the Nazis could goosestep their way into Austria and Czechoslovakia without firing a single shot, then they could easily do it in Poland and then he and Mina would have no way to access their savings.

He tucked the lining back into place and filled the pram with various odds and ends that he and Mina decided to take with them. *Only weeks before, I showed Suzanne off in this pram and now it carries our worldly goods.* His daughter's absence was felt wherever he went. If losing his child wasn't enough, they now had to contend with this new edict.

For months, rumors circulated in regards to what the Nazis might have in store. "Relocation" was one possibility. After all they had seen since the beginning of the war, it was ludicrous to take the Nazis at their word, that "relocation" was simply shipping Jews to labor camps in the east, to "work" and be "protected." No one "relocated" was ever heard from again. When the Germans announced that Krakow's Jews would be relocated to a newly constructed ghetto within the city, it was a small relief not to be sent off to the great unknown. But it was also a slap in the face. Generations before Jews gained emancipation in Europe, local governments sequestered Jews from the Christian population in ghettos. A town within a town, it was divided from the rest of the world. This newly constructed ghetto was a reminder that no matter how far he – or anyone else – had gone in life, no matter how assimilated, history continued to repeat itself.

Mina originally hoped that their beloved Kazimierz district would be chosen for the ghetto's location. The majority of the district was Jewish; the area's cultural history would be a comfort and she and Adam wouldn't be forced to move. But to his and Mina's dismay, the Podgorze district was selected. A dank, ratty district, where Krakow's lower classes resided, he loathed that part of the city. The Christian residents of Podgorze were relocated and the day had come when he and the rest of Krakow's Jews had to move in.

Adam stepped back and made one final tour of their apartment, committing it all to memory. Fury raged within him to the point he was feverish. According to the edict, they were only allowed to take what they could carry or push in the cart. All of their hard work, all of their achievements was gone.

They lived comfortably, in a six-room apartment, complete with electricity, a w.c., two bedrooms – one of which had been Suzanne's, and an attic that Mina used as her art studio. The powerful stench of oil paints reeked and permeated their curtains and linens. Their furniture had been imported from Warsaw, they had Persian rugs in every room.

Once they vacated, some German and his entitled family would lay claim to it.

His mouth twisted into a bitter scowl as he surveyed the first place he called home. *We're intelligent, ambitious, and creative... we can and will make this happen again.* He vowed to himself. He wasn't young per se, but as long as he had Mina and Suzanne, he would move heaven and earth to provide for them.

Mina was crying before her favorite piece of artwork, one she created using an array of colors and shapes, representing what she felt when she learned she was to be a mother.

Adam hugged her from behind and pressed a kiss to the side of her neck. "When this is over, all will be well, I promise."

"How can you be so optimistic?" Mina turned to face him, her lower lip quivering. "You're the skeptic."

"I have faith." Adam replied, without a trace of irony. Unable to account for this sudden conviction, it was born around the same time Suzanne was given to the Christian couple. There were no ifs, ands, or buts about it – he and Mina had to survive this, so they would. He grabbed the handle of the pram and nodded for her to open the door. "Let's go."

He and Mina joined a small group walking in the direction of Podgorze. Their destination was several miles off and they had to travel there on foot, for any other mode of transportation was forbidden to Jews. With every step, more and more joined the procession, until Adam estimated that there were hundreds at his side. People from all social classes and religious backgrounds, some intermingling for the first time. The several layers of clothing he put on – to take more clothing with him – and the heavy winter coat, did little to fend off the frigid morning.

The Christians started to congregate on the sidewalks to watch the mass exodus. The majority appeared smug and it didn't take long for some to start raining down curses.

One boy stood out, screaming taunts and pelting rocks. Before Adam could react, the boy intentionally aimed and hurled a rock at Mina, grazing her temple. She let out a wounded cry and went down.

Adam helped Mina back to her feet and maneuvered her to the other side of him, to shield her from further assaults. He was tempted to storm over and whip the boy.

"I'm all right, we must keep going." Mina grabbed his wrist, to prevent him from acting on his impulse. "He's just a child, Adam, he doesn't know any better." She insisted, using the handkerchief he gave her to press to her wound, to sop up the streaming blood that collected in her hairline.

Adam shot a menacing glare at the boy, but stopped short when he noticed some Christians holding babies. Others had babies in prams, like the one he was pushing. *Suzanne!* Could it be possible that his daughter might be ten paces away? Were it not dangerous, were the Germans not scrutinizing their every movement, he would have approached.

"Who are you looking for?" Mina tugged on his elbow.

"Suzanne." Adam whispered.

"Adam, you must forget about her." She cautioned. "For her sake as much as ours."

Adam reluctantly directed his gaze straight ahead and trudged on. He hated it, but she was right. If the Nazis suspected that one of those babies in the crowd was Jewish, they'd murder it. The last thing he wanted was to compromise Suzanne's safety, or cause the death of another child.

They crossed the Vistula Bridge and continued until they reached Podgorze. Cement walls had been erected to surround the ghetto. The tops of each walled section arched like the tombstones in the Jewish cemeteries, which was intentional. The ghetto was their grave and the walls were their tombstones, and it was only a matter of time before the Nazis buried them alive.

When it was their turn to be processed, he and Mina provided their names, ages, occupations, and showed their personal effects to the officials on duty. On receiving approval, the man in charge rattled off an address and a few directions.

The ghetto consisted of thirty streets, which linked and intersected. The space the Germans allotted for fifty-some thousand people made it grotesquely overcrowded. It took a half an hour for them to locate the apartment they had been assigned, in the midst of dozens of dilapidated buildings.

When Adam and Mina entered the complex, they lifted the pram off its wheels and mounted two flights of stairs until they reached their new dwellings. His spirits plunged further. Their new flat, the handful of rooms to call their own, stank of mildew and the ceiling was crumbling from water damage. Filthy wallpaper peeled, the ends curling as it hung from the walls. Insects and rodents scurried along the baseboards.

Adam went to the kitchen and turning on the faucet, he groaned at the sight of brown water that poured out. *This is a nightmare.* This flat wasn't a far cry from the one he grew up in. He and his mother had been poor. They never knew when their next meal would be. He remembered when he was small, his belly would ache until he was doubled over from the hunger pangs. When he turned fifteen, he swore he would be successful and comfortable before he died. He accomplished everything he set out to do, and acquired happiness along the way. Now, here he was, right back to where he started.

"This is barbaric." He said, shutting off the water. "If they don't shoot us, they'll murder us with disease."

"Adam." Mina cleared his throat. Intoning his name had more of an effect on him than scolding him.

He turned around. Seven others lingered in the doorway, four of which were children. Their eyes widened, fearful of what might come out of his mouth next. The Nazis must have assigned them to this flat too.

"Sorry." Adam cringed. Had he known children were present, he would have kept his opinions to himself. His fingers twitched, he needed to smoke. "Excuse me." He darted to the window and wrenched it open.

A draught nipped at his skin, but he desperately needed to purge the rooms of the putrid air before he breathed too much of it in. Who knew what germs festered in this building?

He lit a cigarette and sucked a drag from it. Mina had made him promise to quit. It was also too costly and he hadn't wanted for Suzanne to breathe in his bad habit. Besides, they could trade cigarettes for other necessities. But today, of all days, he needed to smoke in the worst way.

Adam was puffing away when he felt two pairs of masculine eyes boring into him. He motioned the gentlemen over and offered the cigarette to them. They took turns sharing it. He listened as they introduced themselves and shared their history. They were brothers, Simcha and Shmuel Weiss. Simcha was married and had the children, while Shmuel declared he was a bachelor in search of a bride.

Good luck finding her here. Adam thought, but kept his sarcasm to himself.

Spring 1941

Adam decided to make a small detour from the errand the overseer sent him on, stealing through alleyways to go unnoticed. He wanted to look in on Mina, to be spontaneous and show her he was thinking of her. It was the small, good moments that made life bearable in the ghetto. And if good couldn't be found, it had to be created. Time spent with Mina, and the knowledge that Suzanne was safe on the Aryan side, offered him hope.

Those on the Aryan side often stopped and gaped at the ghetto, as though it were a zoo full of exotic creatures. The sun never seemed to shine on the Jewish side, yet when it was hot, it was baking and when it was cold, it was freezing. He, Mina, and the Weiss family did what they could to clean and repair their decrepit flat, but they were no match for the Biblical proportions of vermin nested in the paper-thin walls. Or the leaky roof. They had a w. c., but the toilet overflowed, regurgitating waste. Often, they had to use a bucket to relieve themselves. Privacy was non-existent, with the Weiss children barreling through the rooms at all hours of the day. Adam moved their bed into a small alcove and hung a sheet to give him and Mina a little peace. At night, when they really needed and wanted to be alone, the pesky oldest boy would spy on them beneath the curtain.

One condition of living in the ghetto was that everyone had to work, or they would be "relocated." Mina found a job in a restaurant kitchen, cooking and washing dishes. She surprised Adam the first night by bringing home a few extra bread rations – which she confessed she had stolen. He praised her for her resourcefulness, and unlike her, he didn't feel an ounce of guilt. The spasms in his stomach – which felt as though the muscle was turning itself inside out – overrode whatever scruples he had. He found a job, working twelve-hour days at a sewing machine, under the watchful eye of a vicious overseer, earning thirty zlotys a day. It was a mere pittance when potatoes cost three zlotys, beans were fourteen, and sugar was sixteen. His fingers developed calluses and often bled, but better bloodied fingers than manual labor. Manual labor could kill quicker than typhus.

He stumbled upon Mina behind the restaurant where she worked, not far from the rubbish cans. Despite their unfortunate circumstances, her moods had balanced out and she was having more good days than bad. But that was only temporary, it would change, especially now that she was running low on the lithium salts she brought with her.

Mina moved closer to a small wooden section of the fence, a framed structure with only crisscrossing wood and barbed wires. He didn't know why this small area was wooden whereas the remainder was cement, but it was no use to question. They had to enjoy it; it was the only glimpse they had of the outside world.

"Mina?" Adam said, approaching.

But she didn't hear him. She was fixated on something else.

"Mina?" Adam took his place beside her and touched her shoulder. "What is it, darling?"

He followed her gaze. Across the street from the ghetto was a church. A Polish woman was at the top of the steps, quaking in her shoes, as a German soldier plucked her baby from its pram. He was being gentle, but Nazis were an unpredictable breed of humanity. They could go from being tranquil to raging in a matter of seconds.

Mina's face contorted and she let out a garbled sob.

"No, don't look if it upsets you." Adam urged her to turn away. The horrors they witnessed in the ghetto could never deaden their souls completely. Mina's sensitive nature caused her to suffer especially, and were this situation to turn violent, it could send her spiraling. "Don't cry..."

Her lips moved, forming words, but nothing audible came out.

A familiar coo tickled his ears and then he understood. *Suzanne!* He rushed to the fence, his fingers clenching around the fencing. The sharped points of the barbed wires punctured and ripped his skin, but he was too numb to register the pain.

"Is that our Suzanne? Please, no!" He cried out.

Mina pried him off and pushed him back against the wall of the building. "Stop, don't draw attention to yourself, or he will figure it out!"

Adam bit down on his tongue and watched as the whole exchange played out.

The German soldier was still being tender, speaking in soothing tones. The woman's terror subsided and she began to converse with the soldier like she might an old friend. To Adam's relief, the German placed Suzanne back in the pram and after a polite farewell, he departed. The Polish woman proceeded to push the pram inside of the church, out of his sight.

Adam's thoughts raced rapidly. Suzane was just across the street, in a quiet church. So close, yet so far. *If I could escape from the ghetto and sneak into the church...*If he were lucky, only the Polish woman and a priest would be inside, and with his fierceness, he could reclaim Suzanne as their daughter.

His eyes darted, searching the vicinity for a solution. The fence was too tall for him to scale. Child smugglers wriggled out through small holes in the wall, but there were no holes close. And he'd likely be too big to squeeze himself through. He noticed a manhole leading into the sewer not twenty paces away. The sewer was the only alternative. Many used it to get to the Aryan side.

Adam knelt down by the manhole, mumbling curses as he attempted to lift the cover with his bare hands. It was too heavy, of course. He needed something to pry it off. Sanning the alleyway, he searched for anything that could be useful.

"What are you doing?" Mina stalked over and yanked on his shirtsleeve.

"What do you think?" Adam jerked away. "I'm going to get our daughter."

"You can't go and steal her."

He ignored her and noticing a broken pipe poking from behind the rubbish cans, he snatched it up. He figured if he could wedge the crook of it beneath the cover, he could raise it up.

"Please!" Mina hissed, pressing her hand to her cheek. "This is insane!"

"No, do you want to know what's insane? Allowing this charade to go on." Adam snapped. "We're Suzanne's parents, she belongs with us!"

"She will die here!" Mina grabbed his chin and forced him to look at her. "Do you want Suzanne to die?"

He stopped, only then realizing how foolish he was behaving. Suzanne was safe and living with a nice couple and the Germans were clearly none-the-wiser. He couldn't say precisely what set him off just now. Perhaps it was sleep deprivation, or starvation, the violence, the deaths...or maybe it was something as simple as missing his daughter and not being allowed the opportunity to say goodbye, or not being consulted about giving her away. But the second he saw Suzanne, something inside of him drove him to bring her back home. Whatever the reason, he couldn't permit his own pain to cloud his judgment and ruin his daughter's chance at survival.

He rose and tossed the pipe aside, flinching at the noise it made when it hit the cement.

"Mr. and Mrs. Altman, can I help?"

Adam shuddered, but raised his head. Mina's rabbi, Rabbi Rosenwieg, was at the mouth of the alley. *How long has he been there?* He hoped the man hadn't overheard their conversation.

Rabbi Rosenwieg was older, on the wrong side of sixty. A round man by nature, he lost a fair amount of weight on ghetto rations, accentuating the winkles and lines that indented his skin. A tiny, circular knitted cap cupped the back of his head. For the duration of the acquaintance, the rabbi wore a graying beard which shrouded the lower half of his face. But not long after moving into the ghetto, a cocky soldier cornered the rabbi and crudely clipped the hairs away. To torment the clergyman further, the German ripped patches off to make the man cry. The rabbi's beard had only begun to grow back.

"Mind your own business, rabbi." Adam retorted.

Rabbi Rosenwieg remained undeterred.

"Adam, don't be rude! Rabbi Rosenwieg is our friend. You need to return to work before you get into trouble." Mina pressed a kiss to his cheek and propelled him out of the alley.

"Allow me to walk you back." Rabbi Rosenwieg suggested and Adam found himself too weary to dissuade the man.

He and Rabbi Rosenwieg walked a good bit before the clergyman shot him a sympathetic look. "I'm a good listener, you know. You can talk to me; you can say whatever you like and I will keep your counsel."

Adam covered his mouth, fighting the urge to yell, to curse, to shake, to retaliate. He longed to do something to that German who spoke to the Polish woman…to every German for destroying his family and his life.

"We lied to you, rabbi." Adam despised himself for being weak and allowing the truth to spill out. But he couldn't carry such burdens to himself any longer. "Our daughter, Suzanne, isn't dead. My wife arranged for our daughter to stay with a Christian couple until this hell is over. I saw Suzanne a little while ago, from a distance, with a Christian woman." He swung his foot back and kicked a loose rock across the road. "She let that German soldier hold Suzanne!"

"Mr. Altman, this is only temporary; living in the ghetto, your daughter being separated from you. You will be reunited one day.

Until then you must remind yourself that Suzanne is safe, healthy, well-fed and free with that Christian couple. It's for the best."

Adam held up a hand to silence him, tormented by this inconvenient truth. The rabbi was right, but it was a bitter pill for him to swallow that he had to rely on strangers to care for his daughter because he couldn't. To him there was no greater sin in the world than a parent who had a child but didn't take care of it. He knew that from personal experience.

"I know you're trying to help, but every bit of my conscience screams to go over and reclaim Suzanne." He said.

"You're a good father, of course you feel that way. There must be a reason-" Rabbi Rosenwieg had begun to say.

"Spare me, I'm not religious." Adam said, picking up his pace. If the rabbi planned to sermonize - on how God had a great plan, that they were His Chosen people, and that He would never forget or forsake them – the clergyman had better save his breath.

He had already wasted enough time on what originally began as an errand. A beating awaited him on his return to work, for his tardiness, and he had to brace himself for it. Beatings could be a daily occurrence and he was growing accustomed to them, but they still weren't pleasant and they should be avoided if at all possible.

Rabbi Rosenwieg lagged behind, huffing and puffing to keep up. "What if I could learn the name of the couple who has Suzanne?" He croaked out.

Adam stopped short and turned back to face the rabbi, who now held his undivided attention.

June 1941

Rabbi Rosenwieg was true to his word, though it did take him a few weeks. He provided him the names of the couple, where their home was located, as well as information on who they were. The Sobieski's were a young, religious couple who lived simply. They weren't wealthy or comfortable by any means, relying solely on Mr. Sobieski's earnings as a laborer. Mrs. Sobieska didn't work, she was a housewife who spent all of her time at home with Suzanne. According to the rabbi's connection – who he refused to identify – the Sobieski's adored the child and their world revolved around her.

On the one hand, Adam was relieved to hear the Sobieski's were decent people. On the other hand, he was envious that Suzanne had become their daughter.

The anger stewing inside of him drove him to behave irrationally, especially in regards to his daughter. On the night after the German Army invaded the eastern half of Poland and entered the Soviet Union, his temper got the better of him.

He waited until Weiss family retired, and Mina was dozing, before sneaking out of bed. He dressed carefully, the pitch blackness of the flat was disorienting, but he managed to put his clothes back on. His worn, faded suit hung on his thin body and he resembled a child playing dress up in his father's clothing. But it was all he had.

Adam shifted and bumped his knee into the post at the foot of the bed, jostling his wife awake.

"What are you doing?" Mina stirred, sitting up. "Adam?"

He rubbed his knee and made a face. "I want to make sure Suzanne is all right." There was no use in lying to her. She would get the truth out of him one way or another. "Someone gave me the names of the couple caring for her."

"No, you have to stop this obsession." Mina groaned, rubbing her forehead. "You have to let Suzanne go."

"Let my only child go? My little girl." Adam gripped the bed post, sinking his nails into it. Little crescent moons encircled it. "How could you forget about her so easily? You're her mother."

"How dare you!" She sharply jabbed her finger into his chest. "I carried Suzanne for nine months; I felt her move within me. I nursed her and rocked her to sleep. Can't you see? I'm dying without her! But this is her best chance for survival." Her arm dropped back to her side. "Don't ever speak to me like that again."

Adam sank down onto the mattress, defeated. "I'm sorry. But I can't- I can't abandon her." He rasped. "Suzanne won't understand."

"Is that what you think you're doing?" Mina scooted over and patted his hurt knee. "You didn't abandon Suzanne; you're doing what is best for her by giving her a better life. You're not your father."

The pressure of unshed tears gathered behind his eyes. He swallowed, to not succumb to his emotions. "My father left and I never got over it." He considered pointing out that part of his so-called 'obsession' stemmed from the fact that Mina never consulted with him before giving their daughter away. She made the choice and he was forced to accept it. But now was not the time to say such bitter things. "My father left me and I never got over it. What if Suzanne never forgives us?" He couldn't bear the thought of his daughter growing up to believe that her true father didn't love her. Death was preferable than to let her go through what he did. "She could blame us...she could blame me."

Mina framed his face and pressed her lips to his, to pacify him. "Someday, Suzanne will understand that we loved her so much that we spared her of this. We did what we had to do." She laid back down and turned down the covers to welcome him back in. "Now, come to bed."

Adam mutely obeyed, undressing once more. He slid in next to her, biding his time.

An hour later, Mina was dead to the world.

He dressed again, this time with more care, and tiptoed out of the flat without bumping into anything else. The Weiss family, too, were unaware.

He disappeared down a manhole on Krakusa Street. It was a well-known, well-used route in the sewer which led into the Aryan side of Krakow. On resurfacing, the city was asleep and the streets were empty. The Germans had a curfew in place for the Christian population too. Anyone caught on the streets after 8pm would be arrested. He chose to travel via alleys until he reached the Sobieski's neighborhood, in the Debniki District, on Tyniecka Street.

He treaded the walk softly, memorizing everything. The Sobieski's little cottage was modest, but idyllic; a cream one-story building trimmed in burgundy. Flowers in the front fringed the walkway up to the door. A little fence enclosed the property; bordering what looked to be a small vegetable garden in the back. They had a commanding view of the Wawel Castle. Theirs was the kind of home any good parent would want their child to grow up in.

Adam didn't stay long, or else he'd risk being caught by a neighbor or the police. "I love you, Suzanne, and I will see you again." He vowed, under his breath, in the direction of a window he imagined was hers. "We'll be together, we'll be a family. I promise."

He tore himself away, swearing to look in on her whenever he was able.

Chapter Twelve

November 1941

Adam crept into the flat he and Mina shared with the Weiss family and was both surprised and relieved when he found it empty. He rarely had a quiet moment to himself. Wherever he turned, he was bumping into someone. *It could be worse, I suppose.* There were others in the ghetto who received worse accommodations, or lived with dozens of strangers. He and Mina only had to contend with one, large family.

He tightened the belt on his coat, noting the room felt colder than it did outside. This tenement was determined to be a thorn in his side. With the exception of the wood stove in the corner, the flat didn't have any heat. For fuel, they had to scrounge up sticks and rotted limbs...if any could be found. Everyone else in the ghetto was scrounging too, gleaning whatever could be burned. He and the Weiss brothers postponed prying off the door frames, window panes, and cellar stairs to incinerate, until there was no other alternative. God only knew how long they'd be in the ghetto. They needed to think of the future, and what resources they might need then. To stay warm at night, he and Mina snuggled beneath flea infest blankets. Bathing was a luxury. It was too cold to undress and wash properly. If he chanced washing his greasy hair, he might catch pneumonia and there would be no recovery from that. The water tended to freeze in the pipes anyway. What did eek out from the faucet was not something he wanted on his skin and scalp.

Adam decided to take advantage of his privacy and look over the money they had. He went to their bed, lifted up the mattress, and removed the glass jar of money. Dumping it on the bed, he counted it quickly. He and Mina spent quite a bit but managed to avoid selling some old pieces of jewelry that belonged to his mother. His mother had given them to Mina on their wedding day. Mina suggested they should try and wait until after the war to sell the jewelry, that way they would have something to begin anew on.

His ears picked up at the familiar clomping of Shmuel Weiss' footfalls on the flight of stairs. He returned the money to the jar and stuffed it back in its hiding place. Though he had no reason to distrust the Weiss family, he didn't wish for them to know about their savings. Death and starvation twisted the best of men into thieves. They had children too; that was reason enough to steal. If Suzanne had come with them to the ghetto, he wouldn't think twice about stealing to provide for her.

Adam grabbed up a tattered, old propaganda-filled newspaper, sat on the bed, and pretended to read as Shmuel entered.

"Mr. Altman," The man flushed through his heavy, lice-filled beard. "We need to talk. This isn't easy for me to say, but I want to do the right thing. I hope you can forgive-"

Adam tossed the newspaper aside and narrowed his eyes. "What is it?" He asked, losing his patience. "Well?"

"My brother Simcha overheard you and your wife one night." Shmuel removed his cap, ran his fingers through his limp hair, and then jammed the cap back down on his head. "He knows about your daughter and he's blackmailing the Christian couple your child is with, into providing him and the rest of us with a hiding place."

"What?" Adam seethed with unchecked rage. "I'll kill him!" He shot to his feet.

"Please-" Shmuel beseeched, attempting to block Adam's exit from the flat.

Adam shoved Shmuel aside, stormed out into the hall, and he closed his eyes for a second. He followed the sound of Simcha's throaty voice, locating the man in the corner.

"You!" He pointed and charged at him.

Simcha sprinted down the flight of stairs. A good ten years younger and far more athletic, the man should have been able to outrun him. Fury coursed through Adam's veins, charging him with unparalleled energy. This man had threatened his little girl's safety; he wouldn't allow Simcha to escape.

Adam caught up with him outside, in front of the building. "Get back here!" He tackled Simcha to the sidewalk. Rolling Simcha on his back, he made fists and threw one punch after another into the man's face. Blood spurted like a miniature crimson fountain as he pummeled his flat mate into a pulp.

"Stop, stop!" Simcha begged, bringing his arms up to shield himself from the blows.

"You threatened my daughter's life to save your own skin!"

"Please, I have children too!" He cried.

Adam latched on to the man's ears and raised his head to slam it into the concrete, when a thick pair of arms encircled his waist.

Rabbi Rosenwieg hauled him off of Simcha and pinned his arms down. He nearly slipped the clergyman's iron hold twice, until his wife stepped in front of him and shouted his name. Glancing around, he noticed a crowd of people had gathered to watch the beating.

The rabbi released him when he ceased struggling. "Oh, Mr. Altman." He murmured, smoothing out his red-sprinkled clothing.

Adam wiped his blood-stained knuckles on his trousers, comprehending he had another man's blood on him. *I was going to kill Simcha.* And he would have too, if Rabbi Rosenwieg and Mina hadn't intervened. He wouldn't have regretted it either. Nothing was too much to ensure Suzanne's life and if Simcha had to die, then so be it. That was the effect the war and the ghetto had on his soul. It could transform a pacifist into a murderer.

"Go on, go on now!" Rabbi Rosenwieg clapped his hands, shooing the people off. "There's nothing to see here." To Adam's relief, the crowd dispersed.

They were lucky none of the German guards overheard the commotion and swooped in. No more than two Jews were allowed to walk together on the street.

Shmuel assisted his brother to his feet.

Simcha was moaning, flinching at every little noise from car horns to birds in the tree above. Blood gushed from his nostrils and into his mouth, outlining his white teeth. His eyes were swelling, but he was still able to peer out from the lid of his right one. A long-jagged cut began at his cheek bone and led down to his chin. He resembled a rotted piece of fruit, bloated and decayed by the sun.

"You contact those Christians again, I'll kill you. And no one, not the rabbi or God Himself will stop me." Adam flexed his fingers to rid them of the throbbing. His knuckles were busted open and oozing. "Swear to me, on your children's lives, that you'll keep your mouth shut." He advanced towards the trembling man, stopping only a foot away.

"I swear!" Simcha bobbed his head.

Shmuel led his brother off.

Adam had to hand it to Shmuel; he forfeited a hiding place for his family and himself to do what was honorable. In all likelihood, he never expected Simcha to almost die as a result and probably wouldn't have said anything if he had known what the outcome would have been.

"What was that?" Mina roughly seized his arm, causing Adam to flinch. He had forgotten she was there. She had witnessed him about to kill a man, yet she displayed no fear of him. "Answer me!"

"Simcha knows where Suzanne is." Adam explained, under his breath. Under her unwavering gaze, shame began to fill him.

"You almost killed a man; you do understand how wrong that was, don't you?" Mina said.

"Yes. I went too far, I lost control." Adam reluctantly nodded. "But we have to be more careful than we have been. Suzanne almost paid the price for our carelessness."

"Promise me you won't do something like that again."

"All right, I promise." He gritted his teeth.

Before his wife could get another word in edgewise, Adam withdrew from her and returned to the flat. He collapsed on the bed and threw the blanket over himself. Though he knew he was wrong and felt some shame over nearly taking a life, he didn't regret his actions. Not if it protected Suzanne. *I deceived Mina.* He promised no more violence, but that was a lie. If someone threatened his wife or daughter's safety, he would do whatever possible to protect them. *It's as simple as that.*

January 1942

Adam trudged into the tenement building and up several flights of stairs to the floor of his apartment. It had not been a good day...not that they had good days in the ghetto. He and Mina argued earlier that morning and she slapped him. *She never hit me before.* Between the tension and being without lithium salts, her moods were wild as the wind off of the Tatra Mountains. There was nothing he could do but wait for her moods to change. Mina couldn't help herself...if she could, she wouldn't treat him harshly.

He rubbed his sore cheek and remembered the first anniversary of when Mina gave Suzanne away was right around the corner. While he had seen his little girl a couple of times from a distance and noted her growth, in his mind she was only four months old. From all appearances, Suzanne seemed happy and he was grateful to the Sobieski's for saving his daughter's life. However, the jealousy he felt couldn't be denied.

The Sobieski's witnessed all of Suzanne's firsts. Her first laugh, her first steps, her first words, her first "I love you," and she called them papa and mama.

Adam raised his head and he sighed. Rabbi Rosenwieg was lingering outside the door of their apartment. He was in no mood for company, but since the rabbi was a close friend of Mina's, he couldn't send the man away. The clergyman didn't seem to have any family of his own.

Or any other friends. But he kept such thoughts to himself.

The rabbi visited often. Adam assumed that the rabbi intended to reform him. However, Rabbi Rosenwieg rarely spoke on religious matters and never lectured him about anything.

He motioned the clergyman in and sat down at the table. The Weiss family was out and Mina was late coming home from work. "Apologies, rabbi. We have nothing to offer you." He yawned, patting his mouth.

The room was quiet, except for droplets falling from the mouth of the faucet and plunking into the sink. The silence made Adam drowsy. The muscles in his shoulders were taut from being hunched into one position for hours on end, sewing until he got a stiff neck. For the past several weeks, a fleece blanket of snow covered the contours of Krakow. Forbidden to use the tram or a car, he went to and fro to work on foot. The cold, the work, and daily life in the ghetto – he wanted nothing more than to drop into bed and sleep forever. But for his wife's sake, he feigned politeness to the rabbi.

"If we had tea or coffee, but...well, you know how it is." He shrugged helplessly.

They had no eggs, no meat, no milk, no tea, no coffee...not even that abomination *ersatz* coffee. Nothing that would have given him energy.

Gone were the days when he could invite company over for a glass of hot, milky tea and a slice of honey cake. Or a simple cup of coffee. He could no longer put the radio on and listen to a program, or crank up the gramophone and hear an old record of Chopin or Bach or Puccini. Never mind how he used to lounge around on their old apartment's balcony on lazy Sunday afternoons and read classics. Or take a relaxing stroll in the park. Now their bleak lives consisted of turning the ghetto inside out for a spare potato peel, dodging bullets, and bypassing naked corpses lying in the middle of the street.

Rabbi Rosenwieg nodded knowingly, then he tilted his head.

Adam wondered if he had a bruise on his cheek, but without a mirror, he couldn't see how bad it was. *Hopefully the rabbi will disregard it.* Everyone walked around with bruises, gifts from the German soldiers.

"I was married once." The rabbi said abruptly. "To a wonderful woman named Esther. She died giving birth to our daughter, Tosia. Tosia was my whole world. She married and moved to Warsaw; she had three children. The whole family died in a bombing during the German invasion. When I learned of her and the children's deaths, I wanted to die too."

Adam swallowed and wanted to kick himself for being such an ass. The rabbi sought him and Mina out because he had something in common with them. Their daughters were lost. Suzanne was alive, but lost all the same.

"I'm sorry, rabbi." He wished he could offer the clergyman some comforting words, but he knew nothing of matters of the heart.

The rabbi studied his fingers. Hands that were once soft and accustomed to cradling the Torah and serving others, were raw and chapped from laboring outside. Not at all befitting a rabbi. Adam had tried to find the rabbi a job using a sewing machine but all of the positions were occupied.

"I know how you feel, Mr. Altman." The sparkle long since vanished from Rabbi Rosenwieg's eyes, but he plastered a half-hearted smile on his face. "I think you and Mrs. Altman are a lovely couple and this may sound trite, but I believe it is God's Will that you will someday be reunited with your daughter."

"God's Will." Adam repeated warily, crossing his arms.

If the rabbi was proven right, that God would reunite Suzanne with them…he would willingly lay down his pride and attend Shabbat services, recite prayers, and read the Torah for the rest of his days.

Mina came in and greeted the rabbi by planting a kiss on his hairy cheek. The man's beard was growing back. She bemoaned the weather, how it was giving her a migraine, and putting her in a dark mood.

Rabbi Rosenwieg patiently listened to her woes.

Adam blinked. His wife barely gave him a second glance. He didn't know if she was ignoring him now or had forgotten about their argument…and that she hit him. Perhaps it was best if he forgot about it too. Her dark mood seemed to be waning now that the rabbi was here.

He sent the rabbi a grateful look. He would try and make a more conscious effort to be kinder to the clergyman.

Chapter Thirteen

June 1942

Adam massaged the back of his left hand, rubbing small circles, to loosen the muscles. He wondered if arthritis was setting in because his fingers often felt stiff. *I'm so old.* He let his gaze wander, noting the oppressive silence in the flat. Rabbi Rosenwieg reading aloud at Mina's bedside was the old exception. The rabbi's melodious tone was soothing enough to even make him drowsy.

The Weiss family had been taken in a round-up the other morning and were shipped off to God knows where in one of those notorious cattle cars. Though he wasn't close to the Weiss family, especially after what Simcha Weiss attempted to do and their altercation, he hated that they were sent off to their deaths. Yet he couldn't muster any human emotion, not even for their children. The ghetto had stolen his ability to feel empathy. No sooner had the Weiss's been deported, did the Nazis order for an assortment of new people to move into the flat. First came Rabbi Rosenwieg and then a variety of others that they had no connection to.

Around the same time, manual labor sapped the rabbi of his strength and he could no longer work. Then Mina suffered a nervous breakdown and was fired from the restaurant. It occurred to him how dangerous it was that they kept Mina and

Rabbi Rosenwieg's unemployment from the authorities. The Nazis required everyone in the ghetto to work. The Germans did regular sweeps, gathering up hundreds of Jews, claiming that they were being relocated for work. By word of mouth, news reached the ghetto that the Jews were being sent to Oswiecim. And once they were sent there, they never returned to Krakow and they were never heard from again.

The Nazis have no further use for us. Adam frowned. He, Mina, and the rabbi had to do something, but what. *It's on my shoulders.* Mina and the rabbi were reliant on him for survival. He was the only one with a job. The hours were still grueling and the overseer was a tyrant. But every Sunday morning he was able to catch a glimpse of Suzanne on her way to church and it emboldened him enough to face the coming week.

Mina spent most of her time in bed, her moods bouncing back and forth. She alternated between loathing the very sight of him to being overly affectionate. Adam didn't try to understand; by the end of the day, he was simply too tired and accepted however she behaved. While he worked, Rabbi Rosenwieg looked after Mina. His original theory on why the rabbi was dedicated to them was partially wrong. Rabbi Rosenwieg sympathized with their loss of Suzanne, since he lost his Tosia. But the rabbi viewed Mina as a daughter; he seemed to need someone to be a father to.

A family formed in the midst of hell and he couldn't deny that it was miraculous.

Adam wiped his eyes free from grit, his lids began to thicken. He was on the verge of dozing when the rabbi coaxed Mina out of bed and encouraged her to sit at the table with them.

"I'm sure you'll feel better once you move around." Rabbi Rosenwieg patted Mina's shoulder.

"My skin hurts." She mumbled, but did as bidden. "I hate my skin."

Adam nodded gratefully to the clergyman. "Just sit up for a few minutes." He suggested.

Mina kept her head lowered, refusing to acknowledge him.

"I spoke to a friend of mine; he could help us find a hiding place." Rabbi Rosenwieg proposed, as if he read Adam's thoughts. The man seemed to have a penchant for detecting his low points...and doing what was necessary to help. "He has numerous contacts."

"I don't think we could afford it." Adam rose and shuffled to the counter. He turned and rested his back end against it.

After living in the ghetto for nineteen months, his and Mina's savings had dwindled. His mother's jewelry ought to be reserved for after the war or for Suzanne. He doubted the rabbi had any resources. A hiding place was costly. Poles willing to hide Jews did so for a price. A Jew had to pay as much as two hundred *zlotys* a day for protection and then there was no guarantee the Pole wouldn't change his mind and betray him to the Gestapo. The Germans paid five hundred *zlotys* a head...A man looking to provide for his family wouldn't think twice about handing Jews over to the authorities.

"There's a man, Oskar Schindler, he has Jews work for him." The rabbi stroked his jaw, tugging on the ends of his beard. "He protects his workers. Perhaps we should try to be employed by him."

Everyone had heard about Oskar Schindler. He had a reputation for drinking, gambling, and chasing after any woman in a skirt. But he was generous to his Jewish workers; he took on people destined for death.

"We have to do something." Mina put up. "If we stay, we'll die here or be deported." No sooner had the words left her lips, she slapped her hand over her mouth and rushed to the sink to vomit.

Adam finger-combed her hair off to the side, rubbed her

lower back, and offered words of comfort over the retching sounds she made.

Mina straightened and used the handkerchief he gave her to wipe the remnants of bile from her chin. She refused to sit down, fled back to bed, where she drew the threadbare covers across her legs and began to cry.

"Rabbi, would you..." Adam didn't need to finish.

Rabbi Rosenwieg understood and excused himself, claiming he needed a little fresh air.

"Don't cry, we'll figure something out. I promise." Adam went to his wife's bedside and sat on the corner of the limp mattress. He rested his hand on Mina's slim hip and was disturbed by how pointed her bones felt. "If you want, we can try the rabbi's friend. Or perhaps Oskar Schindler may be willing to help."

"It's not that." Mina chewed on her lower lip. "I'm pregnant."

He was dumbstruck. *Pregnant?* He never wished to pry in her personal business, but when one was malnourished and when there was tension, *things* became irregular.

"A baby? Are you certain?" Adam blinked, still unable to wrap his mind around this.

"I saw a doctor a couple days ago." Mina shot him a scathing look for questioning her. Pregnancy certainly would explain the upheaval in her moods. "He said I was about six weeks along."

Six weeks. Sex had become, well, non-existent. He was always too exhausted and she never felt well. Not to mention they were filthy, flea-infested, depressed wretches. But about six weeks ago, Mina was feeling affectionate and it had been a while...

In the midst of this darkness, in this hell, there was to be a child. *We're having a baby.* He wanted to laugh and cry at the same time. This child wouldn't be a replacement for Suzanne, but maybe this new baby could give them hope. Then when the war ended, he and Mina would find Suzanne and they would be a family.

Tears of joy slid down his cheeks. *I'm going to be a papa again!* For the first time in a long time, he felt happy.

"All right, not to worry." Adam dried his face with the frayed cuff of his sleeve. "We will smuggle you out of here." He smiled and laid his hand on top of hers. Whatever it took, however much it cost, she and the baby would be provided for. "There has to be someone out there who would hide you and eventually a child."

"We must be realistic. No one will take in a pregnant woman." Mina turned her wrist, until his hand was in hers. She gave it a squeeze and said, "I can get rid of it."

His joy quickly dissipated and he was left horrified. Pregnant Jewish women who couldn't afford to have an abortion or find someone to do the procedure, would try to trigger a miscarriage. One woman in their building ran twenty laps up and down the flight of stairs and took a steaming, hot bath. Her husband found her later that night, in the tub, dead, in cold crimson waters.

"What?" Adam got up. "You can't do that. You can't give Suzanne away and abort our second child."

He didn't know if he could survive losing another child. *My heart couldn't take it.* Others may have had no choice, but they could find another way. Or he would make one.

"Mina, I'm begging you." He knelt down at her bedside and bringing her hand to his mouth, he kissed it fervently. "Don't do it. I will find a solution, I promise. Give me a chance and trust me."

Mina looked skeptical, but nodded.

He hugged her and placing a kiss on her damp brow, he believed all would be well.

―――

Adam was panting as he ducked into his apartment building. He took his handkerchief out of his pocket and dried his clammy face. The overseer waited until a couple minutes before curfew until he dismissed them. He enjoyed watching from the window as they scattered like a flock of birds to their residences, to avoid being picked up.

He had a lead on a hiding place for Mina and the new baby. Around noon it came to him. *The Sobieski couple!* They took in Suzanne and treated her as their own. If he were to offer them the jewelry and money hidden in the jar, and a promise of remuneration after the war, he thought they would be willing to take in Suzanne's mother and unborn sibling. Yes, he would have to swallow his pride and do a little begging, but Mina and the baby were worth it.

He'd approach the Sobieski's this weekend.

He drug himself up the flights of stairs and entered their apartment, greeted by an unholy quiet. Mina was in bed, her forearm flung over her eyes. The bottom half of her face was white and her lips had no definition and blended into the rest of her skin. The rabbi had drawn a chair up to her bedside, the Torah was open in his lap, and he was reciting the prayer for the dead that Adam had grown accustomed to hearing others say.

"What happened? Mina?" He crossed the space dividing them. Terror squeezed his heart painfully. "Are you ill? Is the baby all right?"

Her reply was too garbled to be coherent.

Rabbi Rosenwieg put his hand on Adam's shoulder and ushered him back out into the hall. "Mrs. Altman went to the chemist." He averted his gaze, too guilt-ridden to look him in the eye. "She had the baby taken care of."

No! Adam stormed down the length of the corridor, made a fist and punched a hole in the wall.

He tried to swallow, but due to a massive lump in his throat, he felt like he was choking. By God, he wanted that child; he wanted it more than anything. He had only known about it for two days, but from the second he learned of its existence, it breathed life and hope into him. Hope that the war would end someday and they would have a future together. But now, the poor little life had been snuffed out, along with his too. *My poor baby!* It never had a chance, not really.

"Mr. Altman," Rabbi Rosenwieg wasn't daunted by his actions. He never was. "Right now, your wife needs comfort-"

Adam's eyes were burning, but the tears wouldn't fall. "What about me? What about what I need? What about how I feel? That was my child!" He shouted, laying a hand on his chest. "Suzanne was my child too and I didn't have a say about that either."

The rabbi shook his head helplessly. He had no answer. Mina could spend her days in bed, wallowing in her tears and soiled bed linen, mourning for her children. He, on the other hand, had to have a stiff upper lip and carry on. Whatever agony he felt was disregarded. The child was his, but because he was the father, his pain was secondary. With Mina, his pain was always secondary.

The rabbi explained how Mina went to Mr. Pankiewicz. A Catholic pharmacist, the Germans allowed him to run his business in the ghetto. The only Christian in the midst of thousands of Jews, he provided medicines and assistance to Jews free of charge. That included abortions for those who desired one.

Adam breathed in and out, in and out, in and out – until he felt calm enough. He returned to her bedside, perching on the edge of the mattress.

Mina pulled the covers over her head.

Adam tugged the sheet out of her grasp, drawing it downwards.

"Why, Mina?" His temper cooled on observing how small and ill his wife was. "I was going to the Sobieski's. They would have taken you and the baby in."

"And you always said I was the dreamer." A lone tear trickled down Mina's cheek. "The Sobieski's might not have welcomed me. The only reason they were interested in Suzanne was because

I gave her to them to become their daughter. If we had the baby here, it would have starved to death or contracted a disease. That was if either of us survived the birth. It is better that the baby never knew the darkness of the world."

Adam couldn't believe his ears. Mina really preferred death for their child than to give him to do what a father should: protect his own.

"The baby will never know our love either." He pointed out.

"We still have each other." Mina placed her hand on his thigh. He shivered beneath her touch and his reaction didn't go unnoticed by her. "You hate me now." Her chin quivered. "You said you would always love me."

"I hate what you have done. You made this choice without me." He detested how whiney he sounded. Vulnerability was a great weakness in him, but for once he needed someone to lean on. Someone to hear his concerns, his worries, and his troubles. He never wanted to burden Mina, but he couldn't conceal his pain any longer. "You gave Suzanne away without my consent. You ended this pregnancy and I had no say in the matter. Suzanne and the baby, you took them from me."

"You think I don't love Suzanne or this second baby as much as you do!" Mina looked at him in disbelief, as if he betrayed her. "Admit it, you don't think anyone could love our children as much as you do. You don't understand, you never will, no matter how many times I try to explain to you. I did what I had to do." She burrowed back under the covers.

Adam got up and paced the room, then dropped into a chair by the stove. Mina missed his point entirely and accused him of something completely untrue. He didn't doubt Mina's love for Suzanne or for this second baby. He was tired of her making decisions separate from him and having to be the one to live with the consequences. Someday, he would move past the choices Mina made, but for now, there was a wall between them. One that he didn't know how to tear down.

Chapter Fourteen

August 1942

Adam slowed his pace and since Mina was on his arm, she did as well. While they still were at odds, he continued to escort his wife on the rare occasion she left their flat. He couldn't move past what happened to their second child, but the last thing he wanted was for her to come to harm.

Their poor baby...they'd never name it, hold in their arms, tell it stories, or watch it grow. The loss made him relive the turmoil of giving up Suzanne and it caused his resentment to manifest. Had Mina committed adultery, or wanted a divorce, he could have overcome that. But to end their second child's life, against his wishes – it was more than he could bear.

He was lost in his own thoughts...until a soldier let out a harsh chortle.

A couple of officers were in the middle of the street, amusing themselves by taunting Jewish passersby. Slapping, forcing them into degrading positions, shooting them if it pleased them. To one man, they flicked open a lighter and set fire to his clothing, then refused to allow him to roll on the ground to put it out. His screams...He slowly burned alive, the flames gnawing through his flesh until all that was left were fragments of bones. *Every day we go out into the street, we take our lives in our hands.*

There was no guarantee of coming home at the end of the day. There was no guarantee of anything.

Adam drew Mina close, urging in her ear, "Turn around, quick!" If they were lucky, they could avoid whatever abuse the Germans intended to dole out.

But they didn't move fast enough.

"Halt!" One of the young officers shouted.

He and Mina froze and she began to cry like a child. He wrapped his arm around her waist in a paltry attempt to console her.

A sleek-looking officer strutted up, a playful grin slithering across his charming face. His dark eyes beheld depraved enthusiasm. He loved the sins he committed.

"And just where do you think you're going?" He rubbed his chin as he looked Adam up and down. "Humph! You almost look Polish. Almost. Except for the snout." He reached over and flicked the tip of Adam's nose. "Do you speak? Speak!"

"I speak." Adam said. "I can speak."

"Down on all fours."

"What?" He gulped.

"You heard me." The German jerked his luger out of its holster and aimed it squarely at Mina's head. "On all fours, or I shoot her."

"Please, stop!" Mina wailed. "Don't hurt us!"

"Now!" The officer ordered.

Adam raised his hands in surrender. "I'll do it!" He dropped to his knees and peered upwards. *Is this it for me?* Not young by any means, he felt it was too soon for him to die. He hadn't been reunited with Suzanne, or atoned for missing over a year of her life. There was a breach between him and Mina, one he needed to mend. And the rabbi…he never thanked the clergyman for his kindness.

The soldier jabbed the cold barrel into Adam's brow. "Close your eyes!" He demanded. "Close them!"

Adam shut his eyes, but he refused to cry or tremble. If this was his final moment, he wouldn't forfeit his dignity. There would be no begging. Begging never worked anyway.

Click.

He jerked but he felt nothing. *Am I dead?* He dared to crack open an eyelid, and realized the weapon jammed.

The officer threw his head back and howled with laughter.

Adam exhaled. He was still in the ghetto, but at least he was still alive.

The next thing he knew, he was lying face down in the street. Pushing himself up, he spit out red-tinged saliva. The metallic taste of blood coated his tongue. The soldier had hit him in the jaw with the luger. His skin was swelling, an ache pulsated from him facing downwards.

The Nazi, wearing his steel-toed boots, kicked him a couple of times in the ribs for good measure.

Mina's hysterical shrieks felt abrasive on Adam's eardrums and his ears began to ring.

The officer ceased his beatings, asked the other what time it was, and the two casually marched off.

Adam was panting, unable to catch his breath. *I'm not dead!* His lungs and sides constricted. *I'm still alive!* Blood trickled from his mouth, down his chin, like a bright red tear. There was red everywhere! Sobs overtook him; sobs for Suzanne, sobs for their second baby, and sobs for his marriage.

Mina flung her arms around him and struggled to draw him upright. Leaning upon her, they hobbled back to the flat.

She deposited him on the bed and mutely, she dampened a cloth and gingerly dabbed the blood off of him. Too numb to move, he lay there as she unbuttoned his shirt and prodded her sharp fingertips into his chest, tapping on his rips. Unable to ascertain if any were broken, she tore the bedsheet into strips and coaxing him into a sitting position, she wound them around his torso.

Adam felt himself growing more sluggish with each passing minute and sank limply into the mattress when she was finished. "Thank you." He slurred.

"Adam, I'm sorry." Mina reclined on the bed next to him. "I know you don't understand and I'm sorry. I do love you."

"I love you too." He mumbled, incapable of opening his mouth too wide. Every little movement, every little twitch of a muscle, was misery. "But I'm still angry." He slid his around her, drawing her close.

"I know."

Mina slept. In spite of his exhaustion, Adam didn't nod off immediately. His eyes bore into the crumbling ceiling above, his mind too foggy to fathom his recent brush with death.

He tucked in his chin and gazed down on Mina, whose cheek was resting on his shoulder. Part of him would always be brokenhearted over the choices she made, but he had to find a way to let it go. If they wanted to survive this war and if they wanted their marriage to survive, they had to work together.

Sunday, 11 October 1942

Adam lingered in the alleyway across the street from the church, watching as a large group of Christians filed into the stately building. It was the day before Suzanne's second birthday, and a Sunday, which meant his daughter and the Sobieski's would be attending the Mass. *They should be here any moment.* He thought, as the priest welcomed his congregants, ushering them indoors.

Suzanne was walking now. The last time he saw her, her balance was off kilter and she held her hands up while she toddled from place to place. She preferred to climb that small flight of stairs on her own, sassing the Sobieski's whenever they attempted to help her. And she could speak! She chattered merrily, carrying a cloth doll wedged under her stubby arm. Nothing gladdened his heart more than to watch her. While Suzanne and the Sobieski's worshipped, he'd wait in the alleyway for hours, until the service ended and the congregation dispersed.

Mina refused to come; despite the fact he invited her each week. For her, it was too agonizing.

Time passed, the priest shut the doors, but the Sobieski's hadn't shown yet. They were devout Catholics; they never missed a service.

"Something must be wrong." He said. "This isn't like them." Not that he knew them well, but after all of the times he observed them, he felt that he did.

Panic bubbled up inside of him, curdling like sour milk. The Sobieski's were an ordinary couple. There was no reason for the Germans to trifle with them, but images of the Sobieski's being arrested flashed through his mind. If they were taken into custody, then Suzanne would be too. God only knew what would become of her.

He had to find them! He wouldn't be able to rest until he knew Suzanne and the Sobieski's were safe.

As he did numerous times before, Adam navigated the sewers and surfaced on the Aryan side. He removed the armband and stuck it into his trouser pocket, calmly walking to the Sobieski's house. A few folks cast suspicious glances his way, but he disregarded them. His "sad" eyes betrayed him. From the horrors of the ghetto, a Jew could be picked out of a crowd of a hundred due to a pair of "sad" eyes. Coupled with his thinner than average frame and begrimed clothing, the Gestapo could swoop in and snatch him off the street in a second. No questions asked.

But Suzanne was more than worth the risk.

As he turned onto their block, Mrs. Sobieska and Suzanne

disembarked from their cottage. She was balancing Suzanne on her hip and carried the little girl off.

Once they passed by him, Adam straggled behind at a safe distance. *Suzanne...* He stroked his rough chin, shamed by his unkempt, grotesque appearance. Mrs. Sobieska was small and as fierce as he was, it would be easy for him to wrestle his daughter away from her and bring Suzanne back home before the woman knew what happened.

But he didn't. No good father would bring a child into the ghetto if he could spare her. That would have been selfish. He hated to admit that Mina was right. Their little girl was better off in the Sobieski's care.

Suzanne wriggled in the woman's arms. She peeked over Mrs. Sobieska's slim shoulder. The little girl grinned, her two front teeth poking out, and she waved at him.

While he was stunned that she acknowledged him, Adam waved back. He'd give almost anything to hold her again.

A large hand suddenly clamped down on his shoulder and he found himself pitched into the nearest alley. Adam caught himself before he tumbled to the ground.

A man cornered him. "Who are you and why are you leering at my wife and child?" He shouted, his voice echoing into the street. *Mr. Sobieski, of course!* He smacked his palm into the side of a building and was unfazed by the pain it should have caused. A towering figure, Adam estimated Mr. Sobieski weighed two or three times what he did. "Answer me!"

Adam pressed his cracked lips into a thin line. "Get away from me!" He spat out.

Mr. Sobieski took a swing, but Adam ducked. Catching him off guard, Adam tackled the man to the ground. Mr. Sobieski was younger, larger, and stronger...he should have been able to win this fight.

But the large man was soon doubled-over, gasping for breath.

Adam moved away from the man. "Are – are you all right?" He asked. A second ago, he was prepared to fight the man, and now he was concerned about his welfare. "Should I go for a doctor?"

Mr. Sobieski rolled onto his backside, shook his head, and gradually the cough subsided. He was paler than he ought to have been, but his skin started to resume a more natural pigmentation. The man was obviously sick. *Who knows what ails him?* On Krakow's Aryan side, the Poles had it easier than the Jews did. But they, too, lacked food and medicines.

Mr. Sobieski sighed and sat up. A white ball of material was on the ground. He leaned forward and picking it up, he unfolded it and revealed the blue star. The armband!

Adam stuck his hand into his trouser pocket. It was empty. *Oh no!* Mr. Sobieski likely didn't hate Jews. After all, he was raising a little Jewish girl as his own. But there was no predicting what the man would do now.

"You're the father, aren't you?" Mr. Sobieski whispered.

Adam snatched the armband out of the man's hand and returned it to his pocket. "Is Suzanne well?" he asked.

"Suzanne?" Confusion clouded his features, but then he nodded. "Yes. Are you going to make trouble?"

"Of course not." Adam narrowed his eyes, insulted that Mr. Sobieski would insinuate such a thing. "I just...seeing Suzanne safe and healthy gives me hope."

"Do you need a hiding place?" Mr. Sobieski's expression softened. "We have room."

Adam nearly agreed, but bit down on his tongue to silence himself. It was a great temptation. To be able to see Suzanne every day, to hold her, and to be her father again.

But it couldn't be. Were he and Mina – and the rabbi too, they couldn't abandon Rabbi Rosenwieg behind – be able to hide in the Sobieski's home, the chances of them drawing attention would increase. No one suspected Suzanne was anything other than the

Sobieski's daughter. With three more people under their roof, the whole household would fall under scrutiny. Suzanne included.

"No." Adam shook his head, frustrated at how close he came to being reunited with his daughter. And he had been right – the Sobieski's would have been willing to take in Mina and their unborn child. "It's unwise for a whole Jewish family to hide in one place. We could all be betrayed."

"I'm sorry." Mr. Sobieski sounded genuinely regretful that he couldn't help. He attempted to stand but was a little wobbly.

"As am I." Adam sighed and helped the man to his feet. "But don't misunderstand me: I will reclaim Suzanne one day." He brushed past the man. Then recalling a particular incident that occurred not long after the Sobieski's took Suzanne in, he turned and added, "Oh, and tell your wife not to let anymore Nazis hold my daughter."

The time Mrs. Sobieska permitted a German soldier to hold Suzanne never sat well with him. Oh, he could see she had no real choice in the matter. She seemed frightened at first, but it wasn't long before she was speaking to the soldier as though he were an old friend. If she were that chummy with the enemy, perhaps she could avoid putting his daughter in harm's way.

"He was a good German." Mr. Sobieski protested.

"You and I both know there is no such thing." Adam replied.

He departed, eager to get back to the ghetto before anyone else saw him and turned him over to the Gestapo.

November 1942

There was a moment, in the midst of his insurmountable workload at work detail, that Adam realized their days in the ghetto were numbered. According to the rumors, the ghetto was to be split into two sections and then the day would come when the SS would line them up along a wall and shoot them. Or ship them off to the great unknown.

The only thing of value he had left was his mother's old jewelry and Mina's sketches of ghetto life. The jewelry could be sold to benefit the three of them, but what was the point if they were to die in a few weeks? Suzanne, on the other hand, could benefit from the jewelry far better than they could.

That evening, he folded up his wife's sketches and put them in the jar containing the remainder of their savings. He added the jewelry to it and twisted the jar lid on as tightly as he could. He shrugged into his coat and grabbed the shovel by the door.

None of the other flatmates paid any mind to him. Except for Mina.

She woke when he was about to step out and insisted that she accompany him. He hesitated, fearing she would slow him down, but he didn't have time to argue and he didn't want to wake the others. When she was ready, he led her through his usual route via the sewer and into the empty Aryan streets of Krakow. A handful of streetlights and yellow moon glow, guiding them along, lighting their path.

They made it to the center of the city, to Planty Park, which encircled the Old Town. The chain of smaller gardens and clusters of trees provided a shady oasis in the warmer months. In Poland's sixth season though, it was dismal. For a season, Mother Nature turned its back on the country. Like many countries, they had the four official seasons. However, within Poland's springs and winters, there was an early spring and an early winter. They were currently in that dank period between Poland's Golden Autumn and early winter.

Adam scouted out a large linden tree. Its thick trunk would silhouette the hiding place he had in mind. He scolded himself for not doing this earlier, in July or so. In the warmer months, Linden trees bore citrus-like flowers which were beneficial for colds and could relieve heart troubles. The honey from the blossoms could be used as a sweetener. It would have made a world of difference in the ghetto – how many could have been helped! It was too late now.

He stuck the shovel into the earth and dug. The ground was hardened from the cold, and it seemed to take forever to make a decent hole, but he was determined.

"Why couldn't we bury this inside the ghetto?" Mina stood by, hugging the jar to her abdomen.

Rabbi Rosenwieg tried to work with her, but she spent most of her days in a ratty nightgown, in bed. She looked wretched... she was wretched. Adam felt a twinge of guilt and wished he could do more for her, but he was too busy working and scrounging for food.

"As soon as the Nazis deport us, they will ransack the ghetto for valuables. This will be safer on the Aryan side. No one will think to look for it here. We can come back for it later, after the war." He explained.

"We may not survive."

Adam squinted, the hole appeared deep enough now. "At the very least, we can leave it as a legacy to Suzanne." He took the jar from her and squatted down. "She will have something that belonged to her grandmother and she will have your artwork."

He laid it in the hole and packed the dirt around and on top of it. By the overturned soil, it was obvious something was buried there. It wouldn't take long for someone to stumble upon it. He searched and collected whatever loose rocks he could find and made a bed around the tree. After much diligence, it appeared decorative.

"But how will Suzanne even know to look here?" Mina pointed out. "Adam, you're not thinking logically."

Adam stood and bit down on the inside of his cheek. He hated that she was right. They couldn't tell anyone about this little buried treasure, meaning Suzanne would never find it.

"We're not going to survive. For all we know, Suzanne is dead too." Mina said.

"Don't say that!" Adam cringed. He hadn't meant to shout, but he had been too distraught to remember that they were out after curfew and if someone caught them, they would be imprisoned and killed. "I have seen Suzanne; she is still alive." He ran his hand over his face, but couldn't avoid asking the next question. "Mina, do you even want to live?"

"What is the point of living if this is what the world is like?" She shrugged indifferently. "We're barely living now, so maybe we would be better off dead."

He sniffed, shaking his head. He couldn't accept that. They walked hand in hand with death every day; they had no hope of a future, not even the promise of tomorrow. But knowing his little girl was out there in the world, it was enough of an incentive for him to fight.

"I won't let them kill me." Adam replied.

She didn't respond, her vacant eyes bore into him. He didn't want to admit it, not out loud, but...she was dying. She was giving up.

Adam claimed her hand and hoped it wasn't too late, that he could reach her. Despite the mood swings, despite the pain, despite the confusion – Mina was still there. Her soul was there, it was bright, and she needed to believe in something again.

"Listen to me," He began, "Suzanne is alive and she is waiting for you. I see her every Sunday; she is strong and beautiful. You can't give up, Mina."

Mina blinked owlishly, but to his relief, she slowly nodded. "I'll try. For yours and Suzanne's sake."

Adam took her arm and gently led his wife back to the ghetto, where their fate awaited them.

Chapter Fifteen

March 1943

When Adam, Mina, and Rabbi Rosenwieg heard the gunfire and their neighbors' screams, they knew the final liquidation of the ghetto had begun. They took refuge in the attic, behind a false wall he and the rabbi constructed weeks before...just in case. Once they were safe inside the little room, he secured the paneling of thin slabs of unfinished wood nailed together. The gaps between the rows of planks reminded him of a mouth of crooked, rotten teeth. But it was the best they could do since they already burned most of the wood for warmth.

Adam sat close to his wife and the rabbi. He tried to swallow, but the dusty, upper room sapped his saliva and left him hoarse. Quenching his thirst was unthinkable. They needed to conserve what meager supplies they stored in their rucksacks. Including the water. There was no telling how long they'd be in the attic.

He listened as Rabbi Rosenwieg and Mina joined hands and prayed. Envying their faith, he closed his eyes and spoke silently to the God they believed in. Not to ask for deliverance for them. It was too late for that. But rather for Suzanne's protection. As long as his daughter survived, he and Mina would live on through her. The Sobieski's lived far enough away from the ghetto to be safe and no one knew Suzanne was Jewish. But fear had sowed seeds in his soul to where it was second nature for him to be frightened.

The three had been in their hiding place for no more than twenty minutes when the clash of boots on the staircase alerted him that the enemy was closing in. Mina whimpered, sounding like a child.

Adam slid his rough hand over her mouth and drew her to him.

The sun shifted and its beams poured in between the planks of wood, casting a golden spotlight on the three of them.

A heavy-footed man strode into the attic, hitting all of the creaky floorboards. "Out! Come out." He commanded sternly. "I can hear you breathing."

It's done, it's all over now.

Adam loosened his hold on Mina and he removed the paneling, revealing a single German soldier. The man seemed familiar. Hair greased down, slickened to his scalp led to his pallid, thin face appeared pointier. The curve of his lower lip was like a girl's, soft and delicate. He wasn't SS; he was Wehrmacht and he didn't have jurisdiction in the ghetto. But in the course of the last few years, Adam encountered him before.

The German quirked his finger, motioning them out.

Adam climbed out first, followed meekly by the rabbi, and finally Mina, who was quaking from head to toe. Jews caught evading the Nazi's orders were killed instantly. However, this German's weapon remained secure in the holster at his hip.

The soldier's expression softened and Adam remembered who the man was. He was the same German soldier who held Suzanne and talked with Mrs. Sobieska. The one Mr. Sobieski called a "good German."

In the years since the war began, Adam had become convinced that the Germans were evil incarnate. He hoped he was wrong and sent the soldier a beseeching look.

"I can't save you." The German said, as if he could read Adam's desperate thoughts. "The best I can do is arrange for you to be sent on the transport. That will prevent anyone from killing you immediately."

Rabbi Rosenwieg was the first to speak. "We accept, thank you." He drew his arm around Mina, who was still sobbing.

"Then come with me." He instructed, swiveling on his heel.

He descended down the stairs and went throughout the building, checking for others. They trailed close behind, nary a word was spoken. Only Mina's muffled cries filled the building. By the time they reached the foyer, the soldier had accumulated at least twenty others.

"Come along." The German ordered and they followed him outside.

He started to march, and no one thought twice about obeying. With each stride, his boots thudded on the cobblestone, like a rhythmic pulse.

Adam and the rest hustled after the Wehrmacht soldier. A few hands reached out and latched onto his coat, as if they believed touching him would protect them from bloodshed. And it did.

Men, women, children were gunned down, their bodies falling lifelessly. *The screams...*Adam swore he would never forget one woman who was pitched off a balcony. Her shrill shriek rattled in his ears long after she hit the ground. Corpses lay strewn, contorted in every unflattering position imaginable. Some dressed, some not. Each wore a similar mask of terror. Their unblinking eyes seemed to be fixated on the group as they passed by. Narrow streams of blood created a river and drained off into the sewer. The soil was soaked, turning to red clay. Bundles, luggage, and rucksacks were abandoned in the road.

"Listen," The German said, over his shoulder. "When you reach Oswiecim, you must be willing to work. You must use whatever resources, whatever talents, and whatever strengths you possess. Understand?"

Adam stored his advice away in his memory. There was no guarantee of survival, but it was better than nothing. They had a chance, albeit a small one, but a chance all the same.

The soldier brought them to Zgody Square and ushered them to the group selected for the transport. The German departed without so much as a polite farewell, leaving Adam to suspect he was on the search for other desperate souls.

Hours passed and more Jews arrived. Over a thousand had been chosen. The group divided like the Red Sea as a SS soldier stormed past, shouting for them to move.

Adam linked his arms through Mina's and Rabbi Rosenwieg's, to avoid losing track of them in the chaos. The thousand were led to the Ostbahn train station.

He gulped at the sight of the cattle cars, and couldn't believe he was surprised. The Nazis didn't view Jews as human beings; therefore, they didn't deserve to be transported as such. He estimated the wooden cars were not more than fifty feet long and twenty feet wide. A couple had barred windows; others were fully enclosed. The doors slid to the side to open; when closed, a bar came down to lock it in place.

He spun around when he heard a child-like giggle. A small girl, near Suzanne's age was laughing and pointing at the train. From her behavior, he suspected it was the first time she had ever seen one. He often resented the decisions Mina made, but at least Suzanne was spared of this.

"In! Get in!" The Germans shouted.

Adam put his arm around Mina's waist and grabbed Rabbi Rosenwieg's elbow, refusing to be parted. The crowd surged forward, like an ocean wave. If one didn't move with the flow, one would be battered against the side of the boxcar and crushed. Their turn came and they scrambled inside and they were shoved into the far corner of the car.

Seventy-some others were crammed into the tiny space,

wedged like sardines. The door slammed shut and an outcry arose as the dark flooded the car. There was no place to sit, no room to move, no window to look out, and only fetid air to breathe in. A bucket in the opposite end served as a toilet. If one did not make it in time, one soiled themself. There was no food except for what they had in their rucksacks.

The train heaved; the wheels squealed as they turned.

Adam's limp frame swayed to one side and then to the other. The second the good German had discovered them in the attic, he numbed himself to everything that followed. But standing there, without space to draw in a lungful of breath, he felt as though he were on the verge of dropping dead. The walls and the seventy others closed in. A scream lodged in his throat, one that he could not swallow or exhale.

If I could press myself into a corner, I'd be all right. He began to wheeze.

He plastered himself against Mina, burying his face in her oily hair, wishing she could dispel his fears. But their relationship didn't work that way. She looked to him for comfort and protection. *Now is not the time to break down.* The good German advised them to be strong and be willing to work. Weakness would only get him killed.

Mina's cries brought him back to the present. She had been screaming since the door closed, but in his own panic, he tuned her out.

Someone flicked open a lighter and for a few minutes, Adam could see.

"We're going to die, they're going to kill us all!" Mina's downcast eyes protruded from her narrow face. Tiny rivers of tears rolled down her cheeks, leaving dual clean paths amidst dirt pocked skin.

Her fingernails dug into his coat, straight through the material, and cut into his shoulders. She was upsetting the whole carload. They all felt as she did. Hell, seconds earlier he nearly lost it. But panic was contagious and it would soon spread to others.

Adam cradled her face in his hand. "Shh, we have to be strong. We have to get back to Suzanne. She is waiting for us, think of her." At his mention of their daughter, he detected a glint of hope in her eyes and expression. She mumbled incoherently, leading him to fear she might erupt once more. Nudging their friend, he hoped the rabbi might be able to reason with her. "Rabbi, please!"

"We have to have faith, Mrs. Altman." Rabbi Rosenwieg whispered, "Cling to the hope He offers us. He promised to never leave us, nor forsake us."

Adam was relieved when Mina nodded and her sobbing subsided. Her body slackened against his, and the name Suzanne rolled off her tongue like a sacred prayer.

Adam felt his right side go numb as Mina clung desperately to him. As he cooed in her ear, a stray breeze of air whispered across his face. When he felt the cool trail again, he looked around and noticed a slit in the wall, between two boards that may offer him a glimpse of the outside. He deposited Mina into the rabbi's arms, and squeezed his way through.

Peering through the small gap, a quaint countryside flashed past. Snow fell steadily and the sun was masked behind a gauzy layer of clouds. The world was in hibernation. A peaceful enough image, it would have made a picturesque scene on a postcard. He remembered it all. Years before the war, he traveled from Krakow to Oswiecim on business. It was a beautiful city, tucked away in marshy lands. There was a Jewish presence in the community, one that lingered into the 1930s. But like every other Polish city rich with Jewish history, it was eradicated after the Nazi invasion. Along with the Jewish population.

Oswiecim won't be like it was last time.

The rabbi summoned him and Adam reluctantly parted from his little window. He reclaimed his wife and murmured assurances that they would be all right, as long as they stayed together.

He soon lost track of time they spent on the train. Perhaps it was hours, perhaps it was days. It was long enough for his stomach to twist and cramp and growl. Long enough to forfeit his pride and relieve himself in that infernal bucket. Long enough for people to drop dead of dehydration and exhaustion, for babies to choke on their own phlegm or freeze to death.

Then the train convulsed and came to an abrupt halt, pitching some to the floor.

"Ah, we have arrived." The rabbi announced.

Doors of the other cattle cars were wrenched open and Adam heard a chorus of cries.

"Adam!" Mina grappled with his coat, frantic for him to intervene. "I don't want to die!"

Adam grimaced; he would have solved it if he could. But this was beyond his control. He touched her cheek, saying, "Listen to me: remain calm. We will follow orders and all will be well in the end. After this, we will be together again. We will be happy; you will be an artist and I will be a tailor. Best of all, Suzanne will be waiting for us. Think of Suzanne."

"Suzanne," She repeated and closing her eyes, she whispered, "I love you, Adam."

"I love you, too." Adam said, and kissed her softly. Whatever lay ahead, he and Mina had hope for the future.

The door on their cattle car was thrown open. Night had fallen but white fluorescent lights spilled in. A sickly-sweet smell followed, tickling his nostrils and his tonsils.

"Out! Everyone out!" A German soldier roared. "Out! Hurry! Leave everything behind! Out!"

Those on their feet – Adam, Mina and the rabbi included – departed from the cattle car and wandered down a sloped ramp. Dozens of soldiers bounded over.

"Men on one side, women on the other." Another German tore through the group separating the ladies from the men. He wielded a truncheon, slamming it down on random people. "Children, elderly, and the ill to another side. There are trucks waiting for you."

The soldier advanced towards them and Adam released Mina, to avoid a beating. She staggered to the women's side, while he and the rabbi hastened to the expanding group of men.

Adam cast a final glance at his wife. He saw her, all of her, but her widened, frightened eyes were the only feature he committed to memory.

A heavyset, balding man wearing a thick pair of spectacles and a starched white coat, wove through the sea of men. He jutted his thumb back and forth when addressing each prisoner. *Left, left, left, right, right, left, right...*

The man signaled Adam and Rabbi Rosenwieg to the right. Adam dragged the rabbi over before the doctor changed his mind. The ones selected for the left joined the ever-growing group of children, elderly, and sick. Some were placed in trucks and carted off to God knows where.

"March!" The soldiers ordered.

Adam picked up his feet and he and the others chosen to go right, were herded through the gate, then under an iron rod archway that displayed the words, "*Arbeit Macht Frei.*" The group was swept into a building, where he came face to face with men in prison garb who looked more dead than alive.

"Clothes off!"

Sensing the crowd's hesitation, a soldier started to wail on a man near the front.

Adam flung his coat and hat aside and peeled off his filthy clothes. His face was burning with embarrassment, but the room was full of men all in the same predicament. One of the men in prison garb seized his hand and nearly ripped his finger out of its socket until his wedding band came off.

Once naked as the day he was born, he was ushered to one of the benches. Sitting down, he sucked in a ragged breath and held it. A tall, ghoulish man lurked behind him. In the man's hand was a large pair of shears.

The man slid his greasy fingers through Adam's hair and lopped and cropped until his scalp was bare. The snipping sounded like crickets rubbing their legs together. A couple of nicks and pokes to his head elicited no complaints. The blades could easily be used to slit his throat.

"Next!" The barber grunted.

Adam followed the other bald men and he waited in a line leading up to a man seated behind a table. When it was his turn, he dropped in a chair. The man grasped his wrist and twisted it until the underside of his forearm was shown.

In the man's hand was a needle with a long end. Jabbing it into Adam's skin, the point bobbed into the material of his flesh like a sewing machine, leaving behind a blue trail of numbers.

Adam cursed through his clenched teeth.

"You think this is terrible?" The tattooist rubbed a filthy, bloodstained cloth over the punctured skin, smearing a crimson hue. He surveyed his work. "You haven't begun to suffer yet. You should have gone left, avoided this hell."

The man released him, and Adam let his sore arm dangle at his side. When he summoned enough courage, he ventured a glimpse at it. *108224. I no longer exist.* He was dead. The number was all that remained.

He followed the others into a room and stood beneath a shower head. He nearly collapsed when icy cold water spewed down. Pain shot through his chest. Suddenly, the water was shut off and he shakily staggered out, his teeth rattling.

Someone hurled clothing at him – a gray and white striped button up shirt and pair of pants – and then tossed him a pair of wooden clogs. No underwear, no socks, no coat. The material of the garb was thin in places, fraying in others, and it clung to his soaked skin.

Adam was barely dressed before receiving orders to go outside. He and the newly processed men lined up in rows of five and stood for what he estimated to be hours. His wet skin and damp clothing eventually dried. No one had a watch, no one could be sure of the time. There was space between each prisoner to prevent one from leaning on the other. The Germans counted them three times, to be certain their calculations were accurate. He had plenty of time to observe his new world.

Hundreds of army barracks buildings lined the vicinity. Sections of the camp were divided by tall, barbed fences. The wires connected to each fence pole and sizzled. Watch towers containing men with rifles, dotted the area.

Adam inhaled, the air piercing his lungs. That sickly-sweet smell wafted through, carried by an arctic wind. His throat thickened and he gagged. The stench made him queasy, but he didn't dare vomit.

He craned his neck and looked upon the great expanse of the night sky. It was muddled by a filmy red smoke, dimming the moon and the stars. Out in the countryside, the heavens were usually at their brightest. But the glowing lights and the red smolder spoiled the view. His bleary eyes followed the reddish pathway to the chimneys, which belched out plume after plume of smoke. Ashes floated down, like gritty snow.

Where is Mina? Adam pondered. Had she been stripped, shaved, tattooed and been dressed in rags? Was she outside now? What had become of her?

~

When roll call ended, the German soldiers chased Adam and the other men into a barrack, suited for horses or pigs. But, no, the building was filled to the brim with the ghosts of men. Bald, filthy, thirsty, emaciated creatures in rags.

Adam recoiled from them, but then it occurred to him he was seeing a mirror image of himself.

Other than the narrow walkways, the building was crowded with three tiered bunks. Plywood slats with a sprinkle of straw served as beds. A stove near the center of the room generated some heat, but not enough to warm them.

Where are we? Adam surveyed the barrack. He didn't recall dying, but the tattooist was right. This was hell.

Men...he supposed they were once men...they no longer looked human. They looked more like boney deer. Hairless creatures, walking upon stick legs, creeping back and forth, wearing white and black striped prison garb.

An older man seized Adam's shoulder, making him jump. "Mr. Altman!" He licked his colorless lips. "It's me, Rabbi Rosenwieg."

Though the man was closer to Mina, Adam was relieved to see a friendly face. They had been separated at some point and with all that happened, Adam forgot about him. The rabbi's cheeks and head were smooth, except for a smattering of cuts. His shirt was strained across his barrel chest, the seams stretching.

Adam hugged him. He was not the kind to dole out hugs, but this place changed everything. They clung to one another for a few minutes, then backed away to listen in on another's conversation.

"Where are we?"

"Hell. But the Germans call it Auschwitz. The women's side is Birkenau."

"Where are the others?"

"Did they go left?" A veteran of Auschwitz replied. "Whoever went left went to the gas chambers. They are dead. Death is left, life is right. The corpses were burned. They escaped through the chimneys. That is the only way to escape Auschwitz, through the chimneys."

"My God, my God, why have you forsaken me?"

Adam shook his head, unable to fathom what the veteran of Auschwitz said.

"Some of the men and women and all of the children on the train have been gassed to death by now." The veteran said, "They were locked naked inside of a chamber and Zyklon B pellets were dropped in. There was a roar of screams and then nothing. Their corpses were sent to the crematoriums. That red smoke, that stench – that is your families. Or maybe the fat from them is being used for soap and the skin for lampshades." He shrugged nonchalantly.

Oh God! Adam wanted to cry but his tears were gone. It was incomprehensible. Images of red and orange flames swallowing people, roaring, consuming them entirely, flashed through his mind.

He and Rabbi Rosenwieg collapsed on a bottom bunk, alongside another man. Neither of them uttered a word. His mind was too full of all that transpired to make conversation.

Adam dozed with his bare head pillowed on his folded arms, only to awaken to Rabbi Rosenwieg reciting the 23rd Psalm aloud. Bits and pieces sounded familiar. Unlike before when the Scriptures had no effect on him, the passage soothed his troubled soul.

Adam moved onto his side. "Rabbi?" His throat was sore, his tongue sticking to the inside of his cheek. In the morning, if the Nazis didn't provide any water, he'd eat handfuls of snow.

"Sorry, too loud?" The rabbi asked.

"No. I don't know any prayers. Please, help me pray for Mina." Adam pleaded.

Mina was somewhere in Birkenau with the women, at least that's what he hoped. If she went right, she was on her own, without anyone to lean on, in charge of managing her own mood swings and depression.

"Of course." The rabbi said.

He repeated after the rabbi, memorizing Scriptures and prayers. If there was a God, he hoped He would intervene. After all, He could not permit such darkness. Perfection could not abide such evil.

Adam closed his eyes and murmured the prayers, feeling grateful that Suzanne was with the Sobieski couple. As long as she was safe and Mina was faring better than he was, he could endure anything.

Chapter Sixteen

Summer 1943

During his first few weeks in Auschwitz, Adam used a small, pointed rock to carve notches into his bunk's frame to keep track of days. But it wasn't long before he ran out of space and he soon no longer cared to record the length of his internment.

For time didn't exist in Auschwitz. There were no watches, holidays, or calendars. The house of the day could only be estimated by the position of the sun. Mornings, afternoons, and evenings blended together, only divided by the excruciatingly long roll calls and distribution of food rations. There was one roll call at the beginning of the day and one at the end; through snow, rain, and the heat. There were no trees to shade them, nothing grew, not even a blade of grass. Rations were a couple crusts of bread – which were made with flour and sawdust – and a bowl of soup containing bits of meat, worms, or buttons floating in it. Buttons were saved to be used or traded, and the worms...well, the veteran informed Adam early on that worms and other insects were edible by camp's standards.

In spite of all of his attempts to hold onto his sanity, Adam's mind began to work differently. In the beginning, everything affected him. Whether it was a kapo beating on a prisoner, children merrily skipping off to be experimented on by the camp doctors, or a cart piled high with naked corpses rolling past – he couldn't banish those things from his thoughts. Soon enough, such travesties no longer fazed him. The belief that his stay in Auschwitz would be short, died a quick, merciless death.

The average lifespan in Auschwitz was six weeks and then a prisoner would turn into a walking corpse, decaying from the inside out. Under hooded lids, their eye sockets would sink in and their cheeks would hollow. Teeth fell out; sores erupted all over their bodies from lice and mites festering into their skin. Muscles shrank and their skeletal frames would just out unnaturally, their only bit of roundness was their swollen bellies. When they would stand, they would rock back and forth on the balls of their feet from feebleness.

Adam began to suspect that he and the rabbi were in danger of becoming a walking corpse. His tailoring skills came in handy once again and after showing the rabbi how to sew well enough to pass inspection, they were permitted to work inside a building. They mended SS uniforms, clothing, and shoes. Thimbles couldn't be found and their fingers were raw and bleeding by the end of the day. However, it was better than having the life drained out of them through manual labor.

In his early days at Auschwitz, Adam promised himself once he was free and had his family back, he wouldn't give the camp a second thought. But that was impossible.

Auschwitz couldn't be left behind. It wasn't only about the memories. He breathed in its dust – the human ash that floated down from the four chimneys. He never quite got the stench of burning flesh out of his nose. He walked through puddles of the white ash, tracking it everywhere. It landed on his food and he ate it. It settled on his clothes and he wore it as a second skin. When it rained, it seeped into his pores.

He would take Auschwitz with him wherever he went.

Humidity hung in the thick breezes of the marshy lands of Oswiecim. Tucked into the foothills of the Tatra Mountains, the Sola River, an off-shoot of the Vistula, flowed nearby. The swamp tainted the air. Combined with the wind, Adam's head was continually pounding. It reminded him of years prior, when he had a severe migraine and left his shop to go home and lie down. Mina fetched him a couple of aspirin and they napped together. He rested in her arms until the pain faded away.

Mina...

He occasionally wondered if the happy life he lived before the war had been a fantasy – if any of it had been real. *This is it; this is all there is...*

But no, it was real! It existed, Mina and Suzanne existed!

Guilt settled in the pit of his stomach, for forgetting his own wife. She was over in Birkenau, alone, with no one to take care of her, likely facing the same hell he was. He yearned to let Mina know he was thinking of her and that no matter what the circumstances, she should not give up. Suzanne was waiting for her, he was waiting for her, there was hope.

Adam did a little organizing and was able to scrounge up a pack of cigarettes, which was a valuable commodity that could be traded for food, clothing, or medicine. He tracked down a fellow prisoner who had access to Birkenau and gave him the cigarettes. In return, the man promised to pass Mina a message. Just a note of encouragement that once the war was over and they had Suzanne, all would be well.

Rabbi Rosenwieg was scowling as he eavesdropped on the conversation, his arms folded on what was left of his barrel chest.

Adam sensed the rabbi's displeasure, but waited until they returned to the barracks after the day's final roll call before broaching the subject. "What?" He grabbed the rabbi's arm. "You don't agree with what I did?"

The rabbi seemed to be on the verge of speaking, but he sighed and waved Adam off. "My opinion is of no consequence." He settled on.

Rabbi Rosenwieg was wise and intelligent and though Adam hated to admit it, he had come to rely heavily on the rabbi's judgment. Like Mina, the rabbi's faith encouraged him to press on.

"I would really like to hear it." Adam countered.

"What if your messenger can't deliver the note? Or what if he only pretends to?" Rabbi Rosenwieg scratched his head, his filthy nails scraping his scalp. No one could avoid the mites and lice. He and the rabbi were worse than dogs flicking off fleas. "Desperate men do desperate things when they are starving. You should know that by now."

"I have to know if Mina is all right. I need-" Adam paused and studied the man. The rabbi wasn't angry about him trading the cigarettes. No, that wasn't it at all. He sank into their bunk. "You think Mina might already be dead."

"I don't know what to think and neither do you. That is the point. It's better to believe that Mrs. Altman is doing well and coping. That will give you hope."

Adam gasped for air, but he couldn't catch his breath and the room began to spin. *What have I done?* Mina was fragile and vulnerable, more so than the others. How could he have parted from her so easily? He should have fought for her! She depended on him.

He dropped his head in his hands.

"Mr. Altman, please." Rabbi Rosenwieg knelt down by him. "Would a prayer help?"

Since their arrival at Auschwitz, Adam prayed as devoutly as any man would. Hoping that if there was a God, He might be listening and He might intervene.

Might.

I'm an idiot! If there was a God, He wasn't in Auschwitz. He couldn't have been. Auschwitz was hell, they were in hell. All of the prayers and the verses he memorized- it had been a waste of time!

"A prayer?" Adam ground the heel of his hand into his forehead, wishing he could knock some sense into himself. "If God has taken my wife from me, He will never hear from me again."

"Mr. Altman-" Rabbi Rosenwieg cringed.

"No more, please." Adam laid back in the bunk and stared at the slatted plats above him, his vision swimming with of the marks he made with that rock. "If there is a God, He will have to ask my forgiveness for sinning against me."

The veteran of Auschwitz once told a story, that in the early days of the camp, a group of men put God on trial. There were lawyers and witnesses, a judge to mediate, and a final verdict.

God was guilty.

***

A few days later, the prisoner Adam dealt with sought him out, grinning, his toothless gums showing. The man had a yellowed slip of paper in his grimy hand.

Adam snatched it up eagerly, his heart skipping a beat when he opened it and recognized Mina's penmanship. This was no forgery.

"Is it real?" Rabbi Rosenwieg edged closer.

"Yes!" Adam closed his eyes briefly and didn't know why, but he laughed.

Rabbi Rosenwieg covered his mouth, his eyes were shiny.

Adam opened the paper wider and motioned at the rabbi, giving him permission to read it as well. A few other prisoners leaned in and he was fine with that. They didn't know Mina; they didn't really know him either. But there was something about passing secret notes under the guards' noses that inspired them all.

Dear Adam,
I'm as well as can be expected. I found a friend who I went to school with years ago and we help one another. She has been good to me, especially during my low moments. We're sketching all that we have witnessed, just as I did in the Krakow Ghetto. We won't let what we have seen be forgotten. I will fight to be reunited with you and Suzanne. You two are my world. I feel I must apologize for some of my past choices. I did what I thought best but I'm sorry I hurt you, Adam. I love you. Please, send Rabbi Rosenwieg my love.
Until we meet again.
Mina

Adam realized he was crying when the words on the page began to blur. He didn't know he was still capable of tears. *Mina!* He brought the note to his lips and kissed it.

"You must find a way to see her, Mr. Altman." Rabbi Rosenwieg was sniffing and wiping his eyes.

"How?" Adam wanted to more than anything and there were lovers in the camp who found ways of meeting. But he had few resources. It was by sheer luck he came across those cigarettes and traded them to smuggle the note to her.

"Well," The one who brought and retrieved the note piped up, "If you have money, gold, jewelry, I could bring her to you."

"I don't have anything." Adam replied, stuffing the note in his trouser pocket. His wedding ring had been his only piece of jewelry and it was taken from him when he entered Auschwitz. Other prisoners might have smuggled things in, but he hadn't thought to.

"Too bad." The man tutted.

"I have something." Rabbi Rosenwieg announced. He quirked his index finger and peeling back his upper lip, revealing a gold tooth. It was far back enough in his mouth, that the Nazis missed it. "If I give it to you, will you arrange a meeting for him with his wife?"

"Rabbi-" Adam jaw dropped, shocked by the rabbi's offer.

"If Mrs. Altman is to survive, she needs encouragement. She needs to see you, to be reminded she has hope." Rabbi Rosenwieg insisted.

Adam was too selfish to refuse, but vowed he would buy a replacement for the rabbi after the war. It would be the least he could do for such an extreme sacrifice. But the truth was, he could never repay the rabbi for his help.

"Will you arrange the meeting if I give this to you?" The rabbi asked the courier once more.

The man nodded.

Adam gulped and shook the rabbi's hand, thanking him repeatedly. He held his breath as one of the other prisoners used a pair of pliers to rip Rabbi Rosenwieg's gold tooth out of his mouth.

Adam was shivering as he crouched down in the mire, pressing himself against the wall of the latrine. It was partly from fear and partly from Rabbi Rosenwieg's howls when the tooth was removed. *So much blood.* He was hesitant to leave the clergyman, since the blood was still oozing after several hours, but the rabbi assured him he would be fine. Not only had the rabbi made a huge sacrifice, he was risking his health. Blood loss could lead to weakness, infection could set in...

A train whistle informed Adam that another shipment of Jews had arrived and were being led to their deaths. The foul odor of overflowing toilets wafted to him, but the stench of feces and death and human ash no longer bothered him. It was night and except for the moon, stars, and an oscillating searchlight from the closest guard tower, it was pitch black. The bluish searchlight swiveled and shone on him in flashing intervals, but he remained unnoticed by the guards. Every prisoner was confined to the barracks at night...at least officially. Only the insane dared to break camp regulations. *I'm insane then.* Were he caught; he would be killed. But his wife was worth the risk. This meeting was not only for her sake, but for his own. They had not seen each other in...he wasn't sure how long exactly. They needed this crumb of hope life was tossing at them.

The courier instructed him to wait near the latrines until he brought Mina. How the man was able to smuggle another prisoner from Birkenau to Auschwitz was unfathomable.

"Adam?"

Adam first believed it was the whisper of the wind, or his own pathetic imagination.

"Adam?"

He emerged from his hiding place and rushed into his wife's arms, clinging to her as tightly as she had clung to him when they were in the cattle car. "Mina!" He stepped back and drew her closer to the latrine wall where he believed they would be safer. They squatted down.

"We only have a few minutes." Her voice was weak, but he imagined he sounded different too after all this time in Auschwitz.

Adam squinted, but he was convinced he could make out her

face. Like him and everyone else, Mina was emaciated, dirty, and wearing oversized striped prison garb. *My beautiful bride.* She would always be his beautiful bride.

He withdrew his bread ration from his pocket and pressed it into her hand.

"Adam, you need that as much as I do."

"Take it. I'll be fine, I promise." Adam nudged his wife, urging her to put the crust in her pocket and was glad when she did. "I love you, Mina. I will do everything in my power to correspond with you. This will end soon, and when it does, we will get Suzanne and start over."

"Yes," Mina threw her arms around his neck. "Absolutely! I love you too."

Adam's mind went blank, either from exhaustion, terror, or hunger, but was content enough to hold Mina close until the courier retrieved her and took his wife away.

～

For a few weeks, he and Mina corresponded regularly. While the whole thing was originally done for Mina's benefit, Adam found his own spirits improving. He saved every note of Mina's, cherishing them like priceless treasures.

Then on a night when the courier was scheduled to bring another missive, he sought Adam out, shaking his head solemnly.

"Oh-" Adam grabbed his stomach, as though he had been punched.

"I couldn't locate her this time. They may have put Mrs. Altman in a different barrack. Or sent her to another camp. Or..." His words trailed off. He didn't have to say it; he left the other possibility unspoken.

Rabbi Rosenwieg shuffled up beside him.

"Or my wife is dead." Adam said, clenching his fingers.

"I'm sorry." The courier bowed his head, unwilling to meet his gaze.

"All right, thank you." The rabbi gestured for the man to depart. The man apologized once more and left.

Adam wanted to scream, but knew better than to draw attention to himself. Instead, he brought his fist to his mouth and sank his teeth into his knuckles. *No, please!* His thoughts raced. *She can't be dead!*

A dark thought occurred to him; one he could not put out of his mind. Some prisoners in deep despair *gone on the wire.* Rather than continue to suffer this hell, they took their lives by throwing themselves against the electric fence. From their meeting and from her passionate notes, Mina didn't seem to be suicidal. But there was no predicting her moods.

The truth couldn't be denied. During their final months in the ghetto, Mina's moods were on a downward spiral. After the abortion, there was no hope of her moods lifting. The signs were all there, he witnessed them before.

Early in their marriage, after the euphoric ecstasy of being newly married, her moods bottomed out and she attempted to jump from their balcony. He caught her before she made the leap and he talked her down. He took his wife to a specialist. The doctor had seen it before: Mina had what was called manic depression and advised that the best Adam could do for her was have her committed to a sanitarium. But he couldn't lock her up and throw away the key. Doctors and nurses weren't always kind in such places. The treatment of lithium salts was introduced. After some months, she improved and she was never that low again.

Until the ghetto.

In his own turmoil, he missed the truth. Or maybe he didn't want to see it.

Mina could be dead and if she is, it's my fault. Adam hugged himself.

Rabbi Rosenwieg sat down next to him on their bunk, gripping his shoulder, but he didn't say a word.

A few days later, Adam was on his way to evening roll call, when his sadness bombarded him all at once. The woman he pledged his life to, his best friend, the only one he ever loved - he may never see her again. His heart compressed and he sank his knees, his strength draining out of him followed by tears and an agonizing moan.

Rabbi Rosenwieg's arms encircled Adam's waist as he attempted to hoist him up.

The other prisoners cast pitying glances in his direction, but they continued to line up for roll call. The guards would soon come and punish him. Failure to show up at roll call meant a number of things. Gas chambers, shooting, a beating, the dogs released to maul him - all which ended in death.

"Stop it!" Rabbi Rosenwieg whipped Adam around and slapped his face. "Shut up!"

Adam stumbled but regained his balance. He rubbed his throbbing cheek and mutely lined up in formation. Rabbi Rosenwieg's smack had done the trick. Once more, he was calm and doing what he needed to.

The rabbi stood a few feet off and stared straight ahead, acting like nothing out of the ordinary happened.

Adam stole a sideways glance at the man and couldn't deny being a little impressed. He never thought the rabbi had it in him to fight.

The duration of the roll call passed like any other. Later, when they returned to the barrack, Rabbi Rosenwieg stopped Adam before he climbed into the bunk. "Mr. Altman, will you forgive me for hitting you?" he asked.

Adam's skin felt hot, both for losing his composure, for endangering himself. "Why are you still with me, rabbi? Why do we eat together and work side by side? Why did you rip your own tooth out for me?" He ought to have more consideration for the man who continually helped him, but Auschwitz made him beastly and hateful. "You will never persuade me to be religious. Not after all of this."

"We're friends." Rabbi Rosenwieg answered simply.

"Friends." Adam scoffed. "Don't be ridiculous."

During their first few weeks in the camp, he didn't question it. It was a relief to not be alone in Auschwitz. But the more he thought about it, none of it made sense. Before and after the ghetto, Rabbi Rosenwieg had obviously viewed Mina as an adoptive daughter and he accepted Adam since he was her husband. But now that Mina was in Birkenau, or was possibly dead, there was no reason for him and the rabbi to remain close. But the rabbi persisted.

Rabbi Rosenwieg looked pained and his complexion was two shades lighter than normal. The clergyman must have been frightened to be alone. He had nothing outside of the camp. For whatever reason, the rabbi viewed Adam as a friend and it was beneficial to his survival.

"I'm sorry, rabbi." Adam slammed his palm against the bunk frame. All the man wanted to do was help and he stuck back at the clergyman to hurt him. "What is wrong with me?"

"You're suffering, we all are. Whatever you're feeling is natural."

Adam shook his head. "None of this is fair." The tumult of emotions coursing through his veins caused him to tremble.

One moment he wanted to cower in the corner and cry, the next he was feverish from rage. "It's useless to complain, but I fear Mina has killed herself or was gassed. And I will never see Suzanne again."

"You don't know anything terrible happened to Mina." The rabbi said. "In all likelihood, she was moved to another part of Birkenau. You must not think of her as dead."

"I can't lie to myself."

"Why not? If it gives you hope, then by all means, lie to yourself, Mr. Altman."

Before Adam could respond, another prisoner approached. A bit older than the rabbi, he was short in stature, thick around the middle and he had a toothy grin. "Is your name Altman?" He put out his dusty hand to shake Adam's. "So is mine. Maks-"

"Maksymilian Altman." Adam mumbled a string of curses under his breath.

"Ah, so my reputation precedes me." Maksymilian drew back and cocked his head to the right as he studied Adam. "Have we met?"

It had been years since Adam had seen him, but he would have recognized Maksymilian anywhere. Their last meeting was when he had his shop. Maksymilian showed up, in hopes of reconciling. It was all an act. Adam knew his father was only interested because he was successful. When he threatened to call the police, Maksymilian took off and never came around again.

"Yes. Several times actually. We lived together for a few years. You also fathered and abandoned me. You abandoned my mother too." Adam smirked, enjoying the man's sudden discomfort. "I see not even you could worm your way out of this." How ironic that they ended up in the same place, in the bowels of the earth.

Maksymilian had the good graces to lower his head. "I'm sorry-" He muttered.

"Spare me your pathetic apologies and stay out of my way." Adam warned and slid into his bunk.

He rolled onto his side, turning his back on his father. Despite his best efforts to ignore the man, he overheard Maksymilian speaking to Rabbi Rosenwieg, pleading his case. Whatever his father had to say, whatever his story was now, Adam didn't care to hear it.

Chapter Seventeen

August 1944

Adam shuffled through the line, waiting for his daily bread ration. The second it was his turn, he snatched up a coarse, black heel that was hard enough to make a noise when he tapped it on the table. He moved off to the side, stuck it in his pocket, planning to soak it in the bowl of soup he would receive later to soften it

He scanned the area and didn't see the rabbi or his father. Since their impromptu reunion, his father avoided him. Maksymilian sought out Rabbi Rosenwieg though, to gain his trust. Adam tried to warn the rabbi that Maksymilian was shifty, but the good rabbi believed everyone should have a chance at atonement. So, he and the rabbi parted ways. If Rabbi Rosenwieg preferred Maksymilian's company, then so be it.

I can survive on my own. He decided. Suzanne and Mina were all he required in life to be happy. Despite all of his inquiries, his wife was unfortunately still missing. He often feared the worst, but tried to do as the rabbi previously suggested: to believe Mina was alive even if it wasn't the truth.

"Give it to me!" A bawdy shout piqued his interest.

Adam turned around just in time to see one prisoner tackle another. He winced at the sound of a fist pounding into pulpy skin. From what he could make of it, it was over a bread ration. A few bites of food could make a difference between life and death. Out of morbid curiosity, he wandered over, to find out who was fighting.

Maksymilian had Rabbi Rosenwieg pinned to the ground, his hands spanning the clergyman's neck. The rabbi's eyes rolled back into his skull; he was growing paler by the second.

Adam charged over to Maksymilian and shoved him off of the rabbi. He took a swing and punched his father squarely in the eye. The force sent the older man flat on his back.

The bread ration the rabbi and Maksymilian had grappled over, somersaulted into the dirt. A few men dove and wrestled for it until one grabbed it and jammed it into his mouth, choking it down.

Adam knelt beside Rabbi Rosenwieg and patted his cheeks until his color was revived. The rabbi's lip was split open, a crimson droplet dribbled down his chin. Another bright red string of blood beaded from his temple. One side of his face was beginning to swell and his neck bore pink stripes where Maksymilian's fingers left their impressions.

The rabbi sat up and took a couple cleansing breaths. Adam helped him up and let the rabbi lean on him until he got his bearings.

Maksymilian was crying, his bruised eye clenched shut. "Please, I'm sorry! I can't help it, I'm starving." He crawled on hands and knees, stopping when he reached Adam. For a second, he feared his father might kiss his clogs.

"We're all starving." Adam answered. "This is a man of God. Show some respect."

"Please, son, give me your ration." Maksymilian whimpered, disregarding what Adam had said. His father didn't respect anyone, let alone a rabbi. He only cared about himself; he had always been that way. Nothing, not the war and certainly not

Auschwitz, cured him of his selfishness. It made him worse. "I will die if you don't!"

"I don't care." Adam leaned down and seizing his father's shoulder, he brought his face close to his father's. "Stay away from Rabbi Rosenwieg and stay away from me." He released his father and returning to the rabbi, he guided the clergyman away.

Rabbi Rosenwieg sighed. "Thank you." Using the cuff of his shirt sleeve, he dabbed his lip and his temple.

He and the rabbi hadn't spoken recently and Adam blamed himself for that. The rabbi may have been naïve in trusting Maksymilian, but it was out of pettiness and resentment that Adam left Rabbi Rosenwieg to the wolves. It nearly cost the man his life.

"Adam pulled the bread ration out of his pocket and handed it to the rabbi. "Take it." He said. "I'll find something else."

"Careful, Mr. Altman," Rabbi Rosenwieg sent him a knowing look. "I could perceive this as an act of friendship."

"I'll take my chances." Adam shrugged, a smirk tugging at the corner of his mouth.

Perhaps having a friend wouldn't be such a terrible thing. Rabbi Rosenwieg had been there for him and Mina from the start, through all of their trials never once forsaking them. He never judged and Adam's lack of faith didn't deter him either.

The rabbi tugged and tugged and broke the bread into two pieces. He handed Adam one. "You know, one of my duties as a rabbi is to listen to my congregants' troubles. And offer counsel, if it's wanted." He gnawed on the piece of bread, his teeth carved indentions into it and he swallowed the shavings. "You're welcome to confide in me."

"Mina was the only one I ever confided in." Adam said, slipping his portion back into his pocket. "Somehow, she could make things seem not so terrible." Due to her vivacious personality, she possessed the gift of drawing the truth out of him before he knew it. He blinked away the tears blurring his eyes. "My father only married my mother because she was expecting me. When I was small, he was silly and fun. Always joking, always teaching me card games, laughing. He couldn't hold down a job and broke my mother's heart more times than I can count, but I adored him." He set his jaw, refusing to lose his composure. His history with his father shouldn't affect him, it had been decades. But even after all of this time, after all of the betrayals, he couldn't get past it. "He started to take off for periods of time, rack up debts, and run around with other women. My father would return after a little while and we would welcome him home. Then, one time, he never came back."

He and his mother struggled to survive. She had little education and her only experience was as a housewife. But rather than return to her parents' home, she took in laundry and sewing to make ends meet. She refused to sell her jewelry because her mother had given it to her. His mother persevered, but Maksymilian stole the sparkle from her eyes and her carefree smile. Cancer took her not long after he married Mina. He occasionally regretted she hadn't lived long enough to hold Suzanne, but she avoided the war, the ghetto, and Auschwitz.

Adam shook his head. "Really, my mother might as well have left too. She never got over his abandonment, she was too wrapped up in her own pain to notice mine. I had to raise myself." From the second Maksymilian took off, his mother lived as if he were coming back. She continued to wash his clothing, fixed his favorite meals, and spoke as if he were in the next room. "His reputation followed me everywhere and it embarrassed me. My love for him quickly turned to hate. Until I met Mina, my heart was closed off to love."

He first met Mina when she came into his shop to pick up an order for her father. She returned a few times after that, claiming she was in the neighborhood and wanted to say, "hello." It wasn't until her fifth visit when it finally dawned on him that she was interested. Her passion was intoxicating, he never stood a chance. He loved every bit of excitement Mina brought to his otherwise dull life. With it came more than their share of challenges, but he never once regretted falling in love and marrying her.

"Mina and Suzanne are all I have…if Mina is still alive." Adam concluded. "I don't want my daughter to grow up thinking we never wanted her." He would rather die than for her to have a childhood like his. At least from all accounts, the Sobieski's genuinely loved her.

"Or that something is wrong with her and that you didn't love her enough to stay." Rabbi Rosenwieg said. He gave up eating his piece of bread and put it in his pocket. "There was nothing wrong with you, Mr. Altman. The trouble obviously lies with your father."

Adam nodded. What the rabbi said was nothing new, he told himself that many, many times. But when the rabbi said it, it made it truer than ever before. "The thing is, if my father ever returned, asked my forgiveness, and said he loved me – it would have been enough. Even now, part of me still wants that. For him to love me."

"That is what I spoke to him about." The rabbi declared.

"What?" Adam raised his head, daring to hope. "He mentioned me?"

"No," Rabbi Rosenwieg said gently, shaking his head. "He rarely talked about you. Maksymilian is not a good man. But I wanted you two to reconcile, so you could have your father back. I thought it would make you happy. As happy as you could be in a place like this. You would have family again."

Adam's throat tightened and he coughed. The truth had been right in front of him all along. Rabbi Rosenwieg viewed Mina as a daughter, and Adam assumed the rabbi merely tolerated him for her sake. The first part was true enough, but the reason the rabbi had gone above and beyond was not only because of Mina.

Rabbi Rosenwieg viewed him as a son. He was constantly understanding, offered comfort, imparted wisdom, and loved unconditionally. The man had his tooth ripped out to enable Adam to visit Mina. He was as devoted as any father could be. And somewhere along the way, unbeknownst to him, Adam began to look upon the rabbi as a father.

"Thank you for listening, rabbi." He wanted to hug the man, but he held back. "You would make a very good priest." he quipped.

"Of course. Anytime." Rabbi Rosenwieg winced as he smiled, the muscles stretching the crack on his lip, showing the gap where the gold tooth was missing. In a softer tone, he assured him, "Mr. Altman, you will be an excellent father to Suzanne. Never doubt that. And as for Mrs. Altman, I don't know where she is. But you have to continue to hope and believe she is fighting with all of her might to survive. We all are."

Adam nodded and hoped the rabbi was right. *Mina is alive, Suzanne is waiting for me, and someday we will be together again.* Talking to God was impossible, after all he had witnessed. But if he could speak to Him, that would be his prayer now.

Maksymilian died three days later. He had been prowling through the barracks during the night. After fighting over a pair of stockings with another man, he simply dropped dead. Other prisoners stripped him, leaving him bare on the dirt floor.

Adan didn't shed a tear as another prisoner drug Maksymilian's naked corpse out of the barrack and heaved it onto the cart used to collect the dead. Even if the crust of his bread could have bought Maksymilian a day or two more, Rabbi Rosenwieg was far more deserving of the ration.

In the autumn of 1944, after a long day of sewing, mending, and cutting material, Adam and the rabbi collapsed on their bunk, exhausted. He hoped it wouldn't take too long to fall asleep, for every second of rest was beneficial. He must have slept a little, because later, when an explosion struck and the camp and barracks trembled, he was drowsy.

"Earthquake!" Adam scrambled off the bunk.

"Here?" Rabbi Rosenwieg groaned as he climbed out.

The prisoners in an upper bunk had the advantage of looking out the window. The veteran of Auschwitz said, "It's the crematorium, it's on fire!"

Rumor had it that the Russians were sixty miles off and working their way through Poland. New inmates claimed that the Allied armies invaded in June and were coming from the west. Earlier that summer, I.G. Farben had been bombed and occasionally foreign planes flew over Auschwitz. It wasn't uncommon for prisoners to beg God to bomb the camp, that way they might die and to prevent further suffering.

Is it the Allies? Adam wondered, feeling conflicted. On the one hand, it would bring an end to Auschwitz. But if the Allies destroyed Auschwitz, he would die too. And he had no intention of dying, no matter how intent the Nazis were on killing him.

He and the rabbi ventured to the opening of the barracks and watched the Nazis scurry about. Red and orange flames licked the crematoria building, devouring it in one great gulp. Smoke billowed, higher than what the chimneys regurgitated.

We could break free. Adam wrapped his arms around himself. He would hopefully find Mina in Birkenau somewhere, then they could go to a nearby farm and ask the owner for a lift into

Krakow. He would pay the farm with the money hidden in the jar in Planty Park. Then he and Mina would go straight to Suzanne and reclaim her.

A couple more days, I can be that patient. Adam reasoned.

It didn't take long for the truth to spread by word of mouth. The Allies had not bombed Auschwitz after all. The Sonderkommando – the men tasked with incinerating the corpses of those gassed – revolted and blew the crematorium up. A hierarchy existed in Auschwitz. Everyone looked down on the Sonderkommando. They assisted with the gassings of thousands of innocent men, women, and children; they collected the bodies and burned them in the ovens. Then they pilfered through the dead's belongings for food or valuables that could be traded. All to live for a few months longer.

The SS rounded up the Sonderkommando, along with a couple hundred others, and executed them. One after the other.

Adam went about his day as if nothing extraordinary occurred. Though he despised the Sonderkommando for working directly for the Nazis, they had his respect for resisting. He never resisted the Germans; he never considered it. Those who resisted died. The way he figured it, if he were to see Mina and Suzanne again, he had to obey and bide his time until the war was over.

That night, as he tried to sleep, Adam suddenly couldn't breathe and sat up, gasping for air. Rubbing his bare scalp, he swore. His skin was damp, sticky, and reeking...and not from sweat. A prisoner in the upper bunk must have had an accident and his urine leaked down. It wasn't the first time he had been urinated on and it wouldn't be the last. He used the cuff of his sleeve to dry his head. It was the only thing he could do. Washing was impossible. Whatever clean water he found; he drank.

"Mr. Altman?" Rabbi Rosenwieg rolled onto his back. The once plump man had deflated like a balloon. He was a shell of his former self. "Are you ill?"

Adam massaged his closed eyelids. "Rabbi, is it possible that after you lose your humanity, to become human again?" he asked.

"Yes, but you're not the one who lost his humanity." Rabbi Rosenwieg replied.

He and the rabbi had many philosophical discussions. What else could they do to maintain their sanity? If they focused too much on food, they would remember that they were starving. Sometimes he and the rabbi reminisced about the past or about holidays, or they argued about politics. Adam lost count the number of times he and the rabbi tried to figure out how and why Hitler, the Nazis, the ghettos, the gas chambers- all of it- happened. How civilized people became monsters.

"I eat scraps tossed to me, I come when I'm called..." Adam snorted. He pushed his wet sleeve up, flashing the death number on his forearm, which had had an *A* added to it. "I'm branded like a cow, I sleep on straw, and I have to relieve myself on the ground. What the hell am I?"

"No, no, no. Don't you see? The Nazis, they're the ones who lost their humanity. We're the ones maintaining ours. No one can take your humanity away; not the war, not the Nazis, not your father. No one." The rabbi couldn't bear for a conversation to end on a sour note. He continued to believe and hope for the best. "This can't last much longer; this will be over soon."

"We have been saying that for five years. And then what? After all this, after all we have seen, life returns to normal?"

"What is normal? After this, your life can be whatever you want it to be. You will have Suzanne and Mina and you can begin anew."

"Right, Suzanne and Mina." Adam rubbed the back of his neck, using his scabbed fingertips to work a spot that tensed into a knot.

"Think of how happy they will be to see you." Rabbi Rosenwieg sounded wistful.

The poor rabbi had no one waiting for him outside of Auschwitz, other than God. Perhaps that was enough for him. But it occurred to Adam that after he and Mina were reunited with Suzanne, it would be just the three of them. After all he and the rabbi had been through together, their friendship wouldn't end after Auschwitz.

Chapter Eighteen

January 1945

"Cold, eh?" A guard edged close, his grin widening.

Adam lowered his head and tried to maintain his pride, despite standing in line, naked, alongside hundreds of others for selection. He ought to be used to this, the degradation, the beatings, the starvation, the taunts. But there was a small part of him, buried down deep, that refused to be denied his humanity.

Especially after the advice Rabbi Rosenwieg gave him. *It's mine, it can't be stolen from me.*

The Nazis were losing the war. The Soviets were devouring Poland, expelling the Germans from the country. In the fall, they began to ship Jews westward, into the heart of Germany. In an attempt to cover their tracks, the Nazis destroyed what evidence they could of the crimes they committed. From burning camp records, to dismantling the gas chambers and crematoriums. Then came the death marches. Prisoners would set out on foot, with no more than the clothes on their backs and clogs on their feet, and be marched off to a different camp in the west.

The Germans had their selection process first. The prisoners were forced to strip and run past the camp doctors, allowing them to judge their emaciated bodies. Those fit enough would be chosen for the march. Despite the ominous name, Adam hoped he would be selected. Those who remained behind would certainly be killed.

Adam's trembling became more pronounced. He didn't dare look the guard in the eye. The Nazi could view that as a challenge and shoot him. The German had recently eaten, for he could smell the man's savory breath, and it was making his stomach growl. In a few minutes, it would be his turn to run past while the Nazis played God with his fate.

"You're freezing, eh?" The guard adjusted the collar of his fur coat. The man's immaculate appearance, every hair in place, his nails cut perfectly – reminded Adam of how precise he used to be about his own appearance. But that was before life in the ghetto and Auschwitz. "Even if you do survive this, no one will believe you, you know."

Adam didn't answer, but decided he didn't care if he was believed or not. He couldn't imagine ever speaking of his time in the ghetto or Auschwitz. Only survival and reunion with his family mattered.

"But you won't survive." The guard licked his fleshy lips. "You're already dead and this is hell."

Adam's shaking ceased when the German moved on to taunt another prisoner. One of the doctors barked at Adam, informing him it was his turn. He exhaled, pooched out his stomach, and stood tall in an attempt to appear stronger and healthier. Compared to the other prisoners, he was smaller, thinner, and older. On his next birthday, he would be forty-four. Imprisoned in Auschwitz for close to two years, he was an old man. *A veteran of Auschwitz.* But the Nazi doctors only saw numbers and naked bodies.

As he ran past, he heard the doctor send him right, for the death march. He was tossed another set of prison garb and clogs, and motioned to get out of the way. He threw on the clothes and headed out straight for the infirmary.

Rabbi Rosenwieg wasn't part of the selection process. He collapsed earlier that month and was carted off to the infirmary. Ill prisoners avoided it at all costs, as there were no medicines or any means of comfort. Prisoners went there to die.

Adam found his old friend curled in a ball on one of the cots. He sat next to him and swore that he could feel the fever radiating off of Rabbi Rosenwieg's body. The muscles of the rabbi's mouth stretched into a morbid grin; strings of saliva hung from his two front teeth to his lower lip. Sweat beaded from his former hairline and down his brow, falling like tears. He was one stage away from being an Hourglass. Whenever a prisoner became thin and pale in the face, he would swell up like an hourglass and after a few days in bed, his time would run out.

Rabbi Rosenwieg's eyes were clouded but grew more animated when he saw Adam. "Mr. Altman, I heard about the march." Uncoiling his legs, he sat up and gestured to an empty cot behind Adam...where the previous occupant recently expired. The stench of death still hung in the air. "Hide here and you will be safe."

"I can't. They will know; they always know." Adam leaned forward in his seat and grabbing the rabbi's hand, he whispered in the man's ear, "My friend, you will soon be free."

The rabbi was dying. There was no denying it.

Adam drew back and swallowed. *None of this is fair.* The rabbi lasted in Auschwitz for nearly two years, only to die a few days before liberation. He would be free though. Adam didn't know if there was a God or not, but if anyone was rewarded in the world to come, it would be Rabbi Rosenwieg.

"May I say a blessing over you?" The rabbi asked.

Adam couldn't deny his friend a last request. "If you want." He bowed his head and closed his eyes. "Don't know it will do any good though."

"You will be pleasantly surprised then." Rabbi Rosenwieg

placed his grimy hands on top of Adam's scabbed head. "'The Lord bless thee, and keep thee: The Lord make his face shine upon thee, and be gracious unto thee: The Lord lift up his countenance upon thee, and give thee peace.'"

Adam blinked back tears, refusing to admit he didn't feel something. But it wasn't so much the blessing as it was the man who said it.

When he was finished, the rabbi sank back into the cot. A moment later, he rolled onto his side, and leaned on his elbow. He lifted up his pillow and withdrew a shirt. "I have something for your journey." He handed off the piece of clothing.

Adam peeled back the material, finding several days' worth of bread rations hoarded in there. No wonder the rabbi was failing. He starved himself, saving his rations for this. A crust of bread could combat a fever as well as any medicine could.

"I can't take this from you." His voice cracked under the weight of emotion.

"Yes, you can." Rabbi Rosenwieg harrumphed and waved him off. "You will need your strength. "It is God's Will that you're reunited with your wife and daughter."

"God's Will." Adam whispered wearily, and couldn't refuse for his family's sake.

He folded the shirt back up, realizing the rabbi's gift would serve two purposes. The bread would sustain him and a second shirt would offer him a little more protection from the wind.

Rabbi Rosenwieg seemed to be at peace, satisfied he possibly played a part in fulfilling God's Will. Unlike Maksymilian, who would have stolen his last piece of bread, the rabbi was willing to die, so that he might live.

"Thank you, rabbi." Adam said, as the rabbi shut his eyes.

Later, he managed to get a hold of a pencil and a scrap of paper. He wrote a letter to Suzanne, explaining everything. He intended to survive, the rabbi claimed it to be God's Will...but on the off chance he didn't, whoever discovered his body would find the letter and send it to Suzanne. Then she would know what happened to her father and why he never came back for her.

~

Adam turned his barrack upside down, trading and organizing for extra food rations and clothing. He managed to exchange his clogs for a sturdy pair of work boots. By the time he and thousands of others passed beneath the gate reading "*Arbeit Macht Frei*," and followed the tracks out of the camp, he was better equipped. It wasn't nearly enough to protect him from the elements. He overheard the guards complaining that this was the worst winter in thirty years. His skin absorbed the unmerciful winds and it settled in his bones. The feeling in his feet came and went, and he found he preferred the numbness to the stabbing pain of needles.

Snow piled high, drifting to his thighs. None of that fazed the Germans, who wore proper coats. They drove the prisoners on, making them pound down the icy white fluff with their own feet. Adam figured out it was better to be at the center and did his best to stay there. Since others stomped the snow down, it made it slightly easier to shuffle through. Prisoners who lagged behind were shot or beaten to death. Like the birds who fell from the trees frozen, others dropped dead in the middle of the trek. The freezing temperatures caused hypothermia or triggered heart attacks. One prisoner's finger snapped like a crisp carrot.

Adam looked up and squinted. The sky was drained of color, and he couldn't tell if it was day or not, let alone how many days it had been since his journey began. Part of him held out hope that Mina was on this march and they would find each other. The wish wasn't logical. They were all bald and thin, identical to one another, but he thought should be able to recognize his own wife. Yet he didn't see her.

His stomach gurgled and remembering the crust of bread tucked into his sleeve, he fumbled for it. Not paying attention, he slammed into an SS officer, knocking the German face down on the road. *Run!* But out of habit, he became paralyzed by fear.

The officer rose, dusting himself off, cursing. He brandished his truncheon.

Adam bit down on his tongue, his teeth nearly piercing through the muscle. It was ludicrous! He survived all of this time, only to meet his death due to clumsiness. *Because of my stupidity, I will never see Suzanne or Mina again.*

He braced himself for the blows he was about to receive.

The German raised the truncheon high before bringing down on the juncture of Adam's neck and shoulder. Before the officer could hit him again, Adam lost his balance, slid down an embankment. He continued his lengthy plunge into the woods, until he slammed into a large birch tree.

He lay there limply amongst the tree roots, waiting for the officer to withdraw his weapon and shoot. But the Nazi never did. The SS office pressed on, perhaps believing he was dead, and no one else gave him a second thought. He lazily watched as the prisoners and the Germans vanished into the abyss of white.

Adam tried to push himself up, but crumpled when he couldn't summon enough strength. *This is it. I'm going to die here.* He felt more dead than alive. *I may as well give into it.* The letter was somewhere on his person and someday Mina and Suzanne would know what became of him.

He didn't know how long he had been laying there...Perhaps hours, perhaps days...when two older faces – a man and a woman – materialized before him. Their mouths moved as they conversed, but he couldn't hear them. His hearing had long since faded.

"*It is all right.*" The woman mouthed to him in German. She petted his head as she might a small child's.

The man pulled him up and wrapped his arms around Adam's torso, while the woman grabbed his feet. They hoisted him up and carried him off.

He recalled a Scripture that Rabbi Rosenwieg shared with him, not long after they entered Auschwitz. One that he memorized and initially found hope in. Though his friend was still back at Auschwitz or dead even, he somehow heard the rabbi's voice.

"*And the LORD said, I have surely seen the affliction of my people which are in Egypt, and have heard their cry by reason of their taskmasters; for I know their sorrows; and I am come down to deliver them out of the hand of the Egyptians, and to bring them up out of that land unto a good land and a large, unto a land flowing with milk and honey...*"

At long last, he was free!

~

Adam opened his eyes and rays of white flooded him, the cleanliness of the room burning into his retinas. The scent of antiseptic was pungent. He looked around and he seemed to be lying in a hospital bed. *How did I get here?*

"Where am I?" He croaked out, his tongue cleaving to the roof of his mouth. "Hello? Is anyone there?"

He massaged his thick eyelids and a barrage of memories assailed him, blinking past like an old moving picture, looping with voices and thoughts. *Suzanne. The ghetto. Auschwitz. Mina and Rabbi Rosenwieg. The death march. The old couple and the Scriptures.* None of which explained how he ended up in this hospital.

He shifted to his side and peered out the window. A cheerful sun in clear blue sky hovered above a snow-capped mountain range, at the backdrop of a large, metropolitan city. *That isn't the Tatra Mountains and this isn't Krakow! This isn't Poland!* His breathing became labored. *Why am I not in Poland? I should be in Poland!*

"Where am I?" Adam fisted the bed sheets, anxiety surging through his veins. "Hello!" He shouted.

A shadow caught his eye. The nurses hung back, too skittish of him. He wondered if he thrashed in his sleep. The rabbi once said that he muttered things while he rested.

"Sir, settle down." A blond doctor sailed into the room, marching up to his bedside. "Don't upset yourself."

"Don't patronize me! Where am I?" Adam snapped, resisting the urge of grabbing him by his white coat and shaking him. "What day is it?"

"It's the 22nd of February, 1945. You're in Basil, Switzerland, in a sanitarium recuperating."

The 22nd of February? No, it couldn't be! It was the anniversary of when Mina sent Suzanne to live with the Sobieski's.

"How?" Adam clutched his head, which was beginning to throb. "The last thing I remember, I was in the countryside with an old couple."

"We believe you were on a death march, heading towards Mauthausen concentration camp. An Austrian couple found you in the woods, rescued you, and arranged for you to be sent here. That was weeks ago though."

Adam racked his brain but couldn't recall anything besides the couple's discovery of him and how they carried him. Not their names or where they lived exactly. They simply showed him an act of kindness and saved his life.

"Is the war over?" He asked.

"Soon." The doctor shook his head sadly. "Perhaps in a couple months. It's over in the east, which is why you are here. Poland is in chaos now."

"So? I'm Polish. Poland is my country, I belong in Poland, whether it is in chaos or not." Adam reasoned since he had been in hell, a little chaos wouldn't frighten him. His thoughts began to race, like shooting stars across the dark expanse of his mind. "Why bring me here? Switzerland is too far from home; I might never get back."

The doctor frowned but didn't offer any answers. He checked his wrist watch and impatiently tapped his foot on the tiled floor.

Adam held the blanket up, stole a glance beneath, and felt heat rush to his cheeks. Someone had undressed him and put him in a hospital gown. His blue tattoo seemed to glare menacingly at him. It was the only souvenir he had from his days in Auschwitz.

"Where are my clothes? Did you steal them? What have you done with my letter?" He demanded, frantically groping through the bed linen, wondering if it had slipped down to the bed frame. "Where is my letter?"

The doctor looked bewildered.

Adam had enough of the doctor's uselessness, shoved the covers back, and sat up.

"No, you can't leave." The doctor grasped his shoulder to pacify him.

Adam knocked the physician's arm aside. "Try and stop me." His left leg felt heavy. Only then did he realize a cumbersome cast was molded to his ankle. "Why can't I move my leg? What did you do to me?"

The doctor rolled his eyes... as if he had answered all of these questions before. "Sir, it's a miracle you are still alive. You have typhus, severe anemia, you weigh little above fifty-seven kilos, you are malnourished and dehydrated, mentally and emotionally exhausted. And you crushed your ankle somehow, which since it was neglected, has begun to heal improperly. We tried to repair the damage, but it will never be what it was. Let me be frank, if you leave this bed, you will die. It is that simple. Do you understand me?"

"But my family needs me." Adam didn't know why but he started to cry and covered his mouth. "My poor little girl Suzanne is alone, Mina is missing. I miss them."

"Suzanne is your daughter? Mina is your wife?" The doctor said, "What Suzanne and Mina need is for you to fully recover. Then you can be together. But you need to take care of yourself first."

"How long? How long will I be here?"

"A while." He shrugged. "Six months or more. Likely more, due to your condition."

Six months or more? No, he already lost four years with Suzanne and two years with Mina. He couldn't afford to lose another minute.

"Unacceptable." The tears continued to flow no matter how many times Adam blinked and wiped them away. He seemed to have no control over his emotions. "A couple weeks, maybe, but no longer than that." He ran his fingers through the sheets, desperate to find the note to his daughter. "Where is my letter? What have you done with it?"

He figured if he had Suzanne's letter, he could send it off and his little girl would know he was coming for her. That nothing, not life or death, God or the devil, would keep him from her.

The doctor asked one of the nurses what he was rambling about and she shook her head in confusion. "Whatever you came with, it was likely destroyed. You had mites and lice on your person and in your clothes. It carried germs-" he said, gently.

"You had no right! That was mine!" Adam slammed his fist down on the mattress. The Nazis stole everything from him and the letter had been his only piece of personal property. And now, that too had been taken. "If I die, there is no record of what happened to me. Suzanne will never know; she will think that I didn't love her. Give it back!"

The doctor signaled for a nurse.

A woman approached; a syringe primed in her nimble fingers.

Adam burrowed down in the bedding, flinching. Mengele, Clauberg, and the other Nazi doctors never experimented on him. Other than his transport's arrival and the occasional selection process, he never encountered him. But suddenly, Mengele and his associates were crowded around him and intended to inject him with poisonous concoctions.

He swung his fists, shouting for help. He couldn't die now, not when he was finally free.

The doctor wrestled Adam down while the nurse jabbed the needle into his arm. Warmth soon flooded his limbs, relaxing him.

"Sir, it will be all right. Just rest." The doctor advised.

"Suzanne...Mina..." Adam's tongue thickened and his words slurred. "Oh God, I miss them..." His head dropped back against the pillow and his eyelids fell like window shades as he drifted off.

The Way Back

Chapter Nineteen

Monday, February 25, 1946

On her return from the grocer, Lidia found an envelope wedged between the door and the doorframe of her apartment. Her name was scrawled across the top and she detected Mr. Altman's fury blistering from it. She left it on the fireplace mantle, waiting until Sophie and Ewa were in bed before perusing its contents.

It was an official summons to the law office of Mr. Burminski, requesting her presence the following Monday for a meeting with Adam Altman. The last thing she wanted was to see that man again, but he – this problem – was not going to disappear.

She fled to her room and searched through her dresser for a suitable frock. The last time she bought a new article of clothing was before the war. Even with Poland at peace, no one could afford new things. Her clothes were shabby, the cuffs of her blouses were frayed, her skirts faded, and her shoes were lined with cardboard because the soles were worn out.

Lidia laid out her Sunday best, since it was the nicest dress that she had. Hiring legal representation was not possible, not on a cleaning lady's salary. She would represent herself.

After leaving work early on Monday, Lidia went straight home, freshened up and changed. She then hastened to Mr. Burminski's office. Using the tram was an extravagance she could not afford and she arrived at the lawyer's pinked cheeked, sweaty, and out of breath. The secretary showed her in and then the woman went to fetch glasses of tea.

Mr. Altman rose the second she entered and he glowered, clearly irritated that Sophie hadn't accompanied her. The man certainly had a lot of nerve to think he would win this battle so easily.

"Mrs. Sobieska, how are you?" Mr. Burminski offered his hand, which she shook briefly.

Lidia sat in one of the empty chairs. "Let's not pretend this is a social call, gentlemen." There was no need for formalities, they were not friends or acquaintances and she refused to show them the courtesy of politeness.

"Where is Suzanne?" Mr. Altman demanded.

"Sophie is with a friend." Lidia said, intentionally enunciating her daughter's Christian name. She folded her hands in her lap, hoping the pads of her fingertips and palms were hidden. Her calluses and blisters were a hideous sight.

"Her name is-" Mr. Altman started to say but stopped when his attorney held up a finger.

"Mr. Altman, please." The lawyer sighed. "Where is Mr. Sobieski?"

Heat flooded Lidia's face. "He died." She replied, her nails digging into the material of her skirt.

A hush fell over both men. She noticed Mr. Altman sending the attorney a pleading glance. The man was tactless, but she knew he hadn't meant to rub salt in an open wound.

Mr. Burminski cleared his throat. "You have our condolences." He opened the yellow file folder laying on his desk and scanned through the information. "Mrs. Sobieska, Mr. Altman claims that you have his daughter, Suzanne. You found her on your doorstep, in a picnic basket in early 1941. Is that true?"

Lidia didn't look in Mr. Altman's direction. *This can't be happening! It isn't supposed to be like this.* However, she felt him scrutinizing her every move. "How can I know what he claims is true? I don't know him from...Adam." She finished dumbly.

"My wife put a note under the lining of the basket, providing our names." Mr. Altman said and after a lengthy pause, he added, "Suzanne has a birthmark on the left side of her neck, in the shame of a heart."

Lidia turned her head slightly, dipping it, to conceal she was on the verge of tears. She wouldn't give Mr. Altman the satisfaction of losing her composure in front of him.

Her daughter, her precious little girl was being taken away. Ewa was her daughter too, but she had Sophie since the girl was four months old. For years, except for Tadeusz, Sophie was the only one who mattered to her in this wretched world. Terrible as it was, she placed all of her love, hopes, and dreams in that child. Whenever grief consumed her, one glimpse at Sophie, and light flooded in. But if Sophie was taken from her...she would die. It was as simple as that. And if Sophie's father could come back, then Ewa's family could reclaim her too.

The secretary chose that moment to return, bearing a tray of tea.

Lidia selected a glass and downed half of it, trying to maintain self-control. The room was beginning to teeter from side to side and she placed the glass on the desk before it slipped from her trembling fingers.

"Mrs. Sobieska, we understand how difficult this must be for you." Mr. Burminski said. "We don't question your love for Suzanne and that you have done the best that you could. But after everything Mr. Altman has suffered through, shouldn't Suzanne be restored to her father." She remained silent and the lawyer continued with his little speech. "A lawsuit is a last resort. But if that is what it comes down to, then that is what we are prepared to do."

She didn't wish to give up, but certainly Mr. Altman's claim as the father superseded her own as the adopted mother.

"Very well, but I must be the one who tells Sophie about it." Lidia raised her head and met Mr. Altman's hardened gaze. He may be taking Sophie from her, but it would be on her terms. "I may not be her mother by blood, but I'm the only mother she has ever known."

Mr. Altman nodded curtly.

Lidia didn't know how she would break it to Sophie, but she had to find a way. As far as she was concerned, she was Sophie's mother and sacrificing for her child is what a good mother did.

Adam cheered inwardly when Mrs. Sobieska acquiesced to his demands, however he schooled his features into a placid expression. He didn't wish this woman ill, but he wanted his daughter back and he wouldn't let anyone or anything stand in his way. Five years of separation, four of them spent in hell, another spent in the sanitarium – it was all for Suzanne. He'd be damned if he let some doe-eyed little cleaning lady keep him from the daughter that was rightfully his.

"Let's go." Adam said, putting his coat and fedora on. He was unwilling to wait a second longer.

Mrs. Sobieska huffed, begrudgingly rising from her chair. She led him and Mr. Burminski out of the office building and down the street in the direction of her apartment.

Don't go back.
For a Jew to return to Poland would be suicide!
They're still killing Jews there, you know. Now it's the Poles turning on their own people!

Person after person cautioned him not to return to Poland. Every Jew was doing their level best to get out of the country while he was the only one doing his level best to get back in. Things were bad for Jews, but where wasn't it bad for Jews? Word spread about the pogrom that occurred in Krakow in the summer of 1945. Many Jews – some who survived the camps – had been senselessly murdered by the locals and there were no repercussions. One of the darkest stories he heard was of Poles unearthing graves near the death camps, sifting through the remains, in search of gold. Gold fillings in teeth, gold jewelry, and gold coins.

As soon as he had been strong enough to hold a pencil, Adam sent letter after letter to the Sobieski's, informing them he was coming for Suzanne. All of his letters went unanswered and he assumed the couple was ignoring them. Then he began to fear that Suzanne and the Sobieski's were killed during the war.

Through the Red Cross, he got in touch with Mina's friend who had been with her in Birkenau. Through her, he learned she and Mina had been moved to another part of the camp. In the latter half of 1944, his wife was sent to the Scabies block. In October of 1944, Mina and her friend were selected for a transport to Bergen-Belsen and they were there for months. Adam had been initially relieved; Bergen-Belsen wasn't a death camp. However, this friend informed him that typhus ran rampant that winter and into the spring, and Mina died of it a few weeks before the liberation. Mina held out hope to the end that she would be reunited with him and Suzanne. She spoke of nothing else. The news of his wife's death was a catalyst which sent him spiraling emotionally and it took his recovery at the sanitarium longer than he originally expected.

Suzanne was all he had left and if he lost her, life wouldn't be worth living.

When he departed from the Krakow train station, the same station he left in a cattle car on, he went straight to the Sobieski's old cottage. A new family lived there. They didn't know where the Sobieski's were, but explained that after the Russians liberated the city, people were relocated. After a few inquiries, he learned Mrs. Sobieska and her "daughters" were living a few blocks away from the Podgorze district, where the Jewish ghetto once stood.

Adam picked up his pace when the three of them rounded the corner and they made their way up to the Sobieski home. He disregarded the pain shooting through his ankle and pressed on, knowing he would have to elevate his foot later in the evening. The second the tiny house was in sight; he nearly broke away from the group and barged into the apartment. Then he recalled the promise he made to Mrs. Sobieska, to allow her to be the one to tell Suzanne.

Mrs. Sobieska unlocked the door and entered. She was moving excruciatingly slow, as if she wanted to cause him further agony by prolonging this reunion.

Suzanne was sitting by the fireplace, next to an older girl, and the two were playing with dolls. The older girl stood and hurried to Mrs. Sobieska's side, linking her arm through the woman's.

Adam stopped in the center of the room and covered his mouth. *My Suzanne, after all this time!* Tears stung his eyes, but he wouldn't ruin the moment by breaking down.

"Mama, who is that?" Suzanne pointed at him. "Mama?"

Mrs. Sobieska squeezed the older girl's hand and got down on her knees by his daughter. "Sophie, come here." She drew Suzanne into her lap and kissed the crown of the child's head. "I don't know how to say this, but remember when I said it takes a mama and a papa's love to make a baby?" The woman waited for

218

the little girl to nod and continued, her face contorting, "Well, it was this man and another woman's love who made you. He is your true papa and his wife was your mother."

Adam handed off his cane to Mr. Burminski and held his arms open, waiting for Suzane to rush into them. That was always how he imagined their reunion. After all, the last time Suzanne had seen him, she had been in Mrs. Sobieska's arms. She smiled and waved at him, so she missed him.

However, Suzanne stayed in the woman's lap.

Adam let his hands drop to his side, slowly coming to the realization this reunion wouldn't be easy as he planned.

Suzanne shook her head, her expression unreadable. "No, you're my mama." She insisted.

"I found you on our doorstep and I adopted you. I took you in and kept you because I thought your parents had died."

"You lied? You say lying is bad." Suzanne stuck out her lower lip.

"Yes, lying is wrong, but it was for your own good." Mrs. Sobieska paused, perhaps searching for the right words to explain. There was no simple way to explain to an innocent child all that occurred during the war. "You and your parents are Jewish. The Germans didn't like Jews and they would have hurt you if I hadn't lied. Whatever others may tell you, whatever you may think, please know that I do love you."

"Why are you saying this?" Suzanne asked.

"Because this man, Mr. Altman... he is your papa..." Mrs. Sobieska's eyes welled up and the tears fell freely. "It's time for you to live with your papa again." Her voice broke on the last three words.

"No, I don't want to!" Suzanne twisted around and yelled, "I hate you."

Adam staggered backwards a few steps. His chest tightened and he wondered if his heart might explode. *No!* How could he have been so stupid. Over the years, he convinced himself Suzanne was counting the days until he returned for her. That was what he used to do during his father's lengthy absences. But Suzanne hadn't even known she was adopted. As far as she had been concerned, she was Sophie Sobieska, not Suzanne Altman.

The time he followed her and Mrs. Sobieska and he believed Suzanne waved at him...he was mistaken. Mr. Sobieski had been behind him and it now made sense that Suzanne was waving at her adoptive father, a man she knew and loved. *I was so desperate.* Like a dog, he ate up whatever crumbs of hope that had been dropped.

Adam wanted nothing more than to retreat to a corner and crouch down in the fetal position. *There's nothing worse than being reunited with your long-lost daughter only to find out she wants nothing to do with you.* It was like having one foot in heaven and the other foot in hell.

Mr. Burminski shuffled forward, squatted, placing his hands on his thighs. "Come now, Mr. Altman is your papa and he loves you." He cooed.

Suzanne only wrapped her arms around Mrs. Sobieska, burrowing her face into the woman's neck.

"Can't you leave her alone?" The older girl piped up, crossing her arms over her chest. "Sophie is happy here and she's my sister."

Adam bit back a retort. The older girl was a child herself and didn't deserve the brunt of his ugly temper. Even so, he wished she would mind her own business.

"Ewa, please." Mrs. Sobieska shook her head and the older girl fell silent. The woman remained seated, but rocked the child back and forth. "Sophie, this only means that more people love you." She finger-combed the little girl's curls and pressed a kiss to her temple. "You will be happy with your papa, I promise."

Suzanne's cries turned into wails, ones that broke his heart. His child was in pain and he was the one who caused it.

"Little girl-" Mr. Burminski began to say, growing impatient.

Adam ventured towards Suzanne and Mrs. Sobieska, holding out his hand. He couldn't bear to hear his child in agony. "Wait, stop. No one is going anywhere. Suzanne..." He gritted his teeth, hating to use the child's false name. But there was no way around it. "I mean, Sophie, for now you are to stay with Mrs. Sobieska. I would like to come by to visit and you can get to know me. Is that all right?"

Suzanne peaked out from her hiding place and nodded her head.

His daughter still made no attempt to hug or even acknowledge him and she wouldn't. To her, he was the man who came to steal her away from her mother and sister she loved.

Adam looked to the woman. "Mrs. Sobieska, would you walk us out?" he asked in the politest tone he could muster.

Mrs. Sobieska disentangled herself from Suzanne's grasp, promising to return in a few minutes. Ewa waved Suzanne over and the two hugged.

Mr. Burminski passed the cane back to Adam and exited first, bewildered by all that transpired. Nothing had gone according to plan, but the lawyer would receive his fee, and in the end, that was what was important to him.

Adam went next, followed by Mrs. Sobieska.

"Mr. Altman, thank you-" Mrs. Sobieska had begun.

"Nothing has changed, Mrs. Sobieska." He pivoted on his good leg and nearly stumbled, startled by her close proximity.

Adam wasn't blind; Mrs. Sobieska was a beautiful woman. He had been so caught up in retrieving Suzanne that he hadn't initially paid much attention to the lady raising her. She was small, her sapphire eyes dominated most of her round face, and her pink lips curved beautifully. Her golden curls were drawn back in a simple tail. The woman was plainly attired, but her frock couldn't diminish her beauty.

He was flustered as to why he noticed her at all. Mina always had a claim to his heart and he never looked at another woman, even after learning of her death.

Until now.

"I will get my daughter back and we will be a family again." Adam reiterated, unwilling to allow a pretty face to bowl him over. "It may take a while, but I'm a patient man. I have waited five years; a few months won't make much of a difference."

"You're a fool." Mrs. Sobieska frowned, her look hardening once more. "If that is how you view your own daughter, as someone you can manipulate, then I will fight you every step of the way."

"So be it." Adam turned and stalked down the sidewalk, his cane clicking on the cement.

He and Suzanne would be together again, one way or another.

Chapter Twenty

Wednesday, 26 February 1946

Lidia couldn't wait for Friday, the customary day for confession, to speak to Father Cieslik. She needed his ear immediately. The second her shift at the factory ended, she went past the apartment to collect Sophie and Ewa, and then they headed to the church. Between work, errands, and Mass on Sunday, she hadn't had the chance to take in Mr. Altman's appearance in their lives. The other workers at the factory sensed something was wrong, but she managed to put them off. She didn't want anyone to know Sophie was Jewish. She did what she could to protect Ewa from the world's cruelties, but since Ewa came out of hiding and she was observant, word spread about her.

A little girl should be a threat to no one. But considering what happened to their Jewish countrymen and women, Lidia thought Christian Poles ought to go out of their way to accommodate those returning home from war. Instead, Jews were being singled out again and killed. Ewa claimed her rabbi said, that except for the German Occupation, never had it been so dangerous for a Jew in Poland.

I refuse to watch Sophie subjected to such hatred. Lidia held the girls' hands as they crossed the threshold of the church. Sophie had been skipping along but switched to a somber pace. Ewa, who had been chattering non-stop, quieted down out of respect.

She guided the girls into a back pew and they waited for Father Cieslik to finish his prayers, cross himself, and rise. He noticed them, smiled, and swiftly glided down the aisle. The priest bore the responsibility of the parish on his shoulders and he had to be weary. However, he always made time for her, Sophie, and Ewa. When the Soviets tore through Krakow, he had been the only one to stand between them and the soldier's brutality. Once things settled down, he found them a new apartment and some furniture.

"Mrs. Sobieska!" The man of God's congenial expression faded and a concerned one replaced it. He sat in the pew in front of them, crossing his arms on the back of it. "What is it?"

"Sophie's father, her birth father, is alive and he came back from...*the camps.*" Lidia briefly covered the little girl's ears when she mouthed the last two words. So far, her youngest daughter was none-the-wiser about *the camps* and she planned to keep it that way. Ewa, on the other hand, knew of them but didn't speak about it in front of Sophie.

Those who didn't single the Jewish people out for harassment, ignored them. In their minds, life had returned to normal. People went on with their business, behaving as though the Nazis hadn't attempted to exterminate anyone.

Sophie's inquisitive eyes flickered back and forth, starving for every little morsel of information about her father. She had no memories of Tadeusz. Oh, she knew he had existed and asked questions about him now and then. But Lidia suspected her poor husband would be all but forgotten now that Mr. Altman was in Sophie's life.

"Mr. Altman wants Sophie back. He can't have her, can he?" Lidia asked.

"I see." Father Cieslik rummaged through his cassock's pocket and handed peppermints to the girls. He chuckled as they tore off the paper wrappings and jammed the candy into their mouths. "I'm a priest, hardly an expert of legal matters. As the father, I'm certain he does have rights. I believe, though, you already know that." He gave her a knowing look.

Lidia frowned, understanding his meaning. Early on he encouraged her to one day tell Sophie, as the truth had a way of coming out. But she didn't listen.

"But Sophie is my daughter too." She persisted, hoping there might be a loophole in the law. "I have loved and cared for her for five years. Isn't that worth something?"

"Of course, it is."

Sophie grew fidgety and asked to go outside. Ewa volunteered to take her, but Lidia didn't feel comfortable letting them go off on their own. For all she knew, Mr. Altman could abduct Sophie and he would feel no remorse about doing so. Lidia and the priest accompanied them and sitting on a bench, they watched from a safe distance while the girls pelted snowballs at an old oak tree.

"I suppose Mr. Altman intends to reclaim her soon?" Father Cieslik commented off-handedly.

"Well..." Lidia shook her head. "When he and his lawyer came to reclaim her, Sophie became upset and Mr. Altman didn't press matters. He suggested that she stay with me for the time being and then they can get to know one another." She put her chilled hands in her coat pockets, missing her old gloves. But the yarn from her pair had been used and refashioned into small pairs for the girls. "But I'm convinced that is just a ploy. Mr. Altman will take her from me and I will never see her again."

Father Cieslik's face was thoughtful. She loathed that particular expression of his. It was the sort she wore before encouraging the girls to do something they didn't want to. "Well, from what you said, Mr. Altman doesn't sound like a bad man. He put Sophie's wishes above his own, and that must count for something." He nudged her gently in the side. "Mrs. Sobieska, this man has seen and been through things we can't imagine."

Lidia nearly reminded him that she had been through dark times too. But in comparison...*No, there is no comparison.* She remembered witnessing a few horrifying incidents that occurred in the Jewish ghetto, but she was only an outsider. The camps were worse. There were whispers of torture rooms, gas chambers, chimneys, and experimentations.

"Then I should be kind to him." She concluded, noting how childish she sounded.

"Yes." Father Cieslik nodded. "He is Miss Sophie's father and he deserves respect and compassion."

Lidia exhaled. Father Cieslik was right. "I'll try." She said, resolving to invite Mr. Altman to dinner on Sunday.

The man should know his daughter. Sophie may be his last living relative. Perhaps if he was allowed in her daughter's life, Mr. Altman wouldn't attempt to take her. He would understand how happy and safe Sophie was and relinquish all claims to her.

She felt her stomach twist, coiling with guilt. After she and Tadeusz took Sophie in, she prayed for the Altman's. Over time, she forgot about them, assuming they had died. To show Mr. Altman kindness, compassion, and say a few prayers for him would be the least she could do for the man.

~

Adam lingered outside the synagogue's office, too anxious to go in. There was nothing to fear, yet his body trembled and that put added pressure on his ankle. He pinched the bridge of his nose, counted to ten, and knocked.

"Come in!" A deep voice beckoned.

He entered and a smile softened his strained face. "Well, hello, old friend." He greeted.

Rabbi Rosenwieg's head jerked up and he released a gasp. He emerged from behind the desk. "Mr. Altman!" He exclaimed.

Adam shook the man's hand, but that was not enough and drew the man into hug. In the past, he rarely offered hugs, but the rabbi was different. They had been through so much together and the last time he had seen Rabbi Rosenwieg, the poor rabbi was more of a corpse than a man. When he learned the rabbi survived, he couldn't rest until he saw him again. The rabbi's was the first friendly face he had seen since his return to Krakow.

Rabbi Rosenwieg drew away. He almost resembled the man he was before the war. His coloring was ruddy and he had gained weight. His thick head of hair and plentiful beard grew back.

Adam felt there was nothing more just in the world, than for the rabbi to be spared and to resume his position in the Jewish community, spreading *Tikkun Olam* wherever he went. A concept the rabbi first shared with him in Auschwitz, it meant to "repair the world." After all that had happened during the war, the world needed healing.

"I wasn't sure if I'd ever see you again." Rabbi Rosenwieg confessed.

"I wasn't sure about you either." Adam said and though he didn't wish to say it aloud, he couldn't postpone it. "Rabbi... Mina is not coming back."

Rabbi Rosenwieg's soft eyes watered and he didn't speak for a minute. "But Suzanne?" He groped for the desk. "Did you not find your daughter?"

"I did." Adam closed his grasp on cane's handle, his fingers tightening and loosening again and again. It was a nervous tick of his. Whenever he gripped the handle of his cane, it somehow helped him relax. "Suzanne hates me, she didn't want anything to do with me."

"What? That can't be all of it. Sit down, Mr. Altman." The rabbi motioned for him to the empty chair in front of the desk. He sat into the one next to it, scooting it closer. "Begin at the beginning."

Adam sighed and hooked the cane on the back of his chair. The last thing he wanted was to recount how his little girl rejected him. The memory was painful enough. "I found the woman who hid her, Mrs. Sobieska, and I went to her home. She wouldn't let me see Suzanne so I hired an attorney. When I was able to reclaim my daughter, Suzanne refused to go with me." He slumped down in the seat. "Mrs. Sobieska poisoned my daughter against me; she renamed her to Sophie and I know she had her baptized."

Adam didn't have any particular plans in regards to Suzanne's religious instruction, aside from ensuring she understood she was Jewish. The rest would be up to her. But for that woman to decide what religion his daughter would be and for her to be baptized, churned his stomach. It was a smack in the face. Throughout history, Jews were forced to convert and be baptized, or they faced death.

"I'm sorry. None of this is fair to you, or to your daughter." The rabbi's sympathetic expression waned and Adam sensed he wouldn't like what his friend would say next. "You must keep in mind though, if Mrs. Sobieska hadn't renamed her or had her convert, Suzanne would have been killed."

The muscle in Adam's neck throbbed. He wasn't an idiot. Jews survived outside of the ghetto and the camps had to masquerade as Christians. He always figured Suzanne would have to take on a new identity.

"Yes, but the war is over now. Why all of the secrecy?" Adam asked.

"Only God knows." The rabbi shrugged.

"Then He had better tell me." He jutted his thumb to his chest.

"So, you showed up on Mrs. Sobieska's doorstep, demanding to have your child back. That must have been shocking." Rabbi Rosenwieg tilted his head, tugging on the tufts of hair on his chin. "What did Mr. Sobieski do? You haven't mentioned him. Were there other children?"

Adam didn't like the direction the conversation was taking. "Mr. Sobieski is dead. There is another child living there. A young lady, but I'm willing to bet that she's Jewish too." He said shortly. "Mrs. Sobieska seems to like to collect Jewish orphans."

"I see." The rabbi leaned back and crossed his arms. "While I agree you should have your daughter back, try and put yourself in Mrs. Sobieska's shoes. She is a widow, who has cared for Suzanne since she was a baby. She must be very attached, perhaps she even loves the girl. These girls might be all Mrs. Sobieska has in the world, and then you come out of nowhere, to claim Sophie from her."

"So what? I should feel sorry for her?" Adam didn't bother to conceal the repugnance in his tone.

"Well, I think you should be more understanding. Whether you like it or not, Mrs. Sobieska has done you the greatest favor: she saved Suzanne's life. 'Whoever saves one life, saves the world entire.' That is from the Talmud. Your situation isn't ideal but attacking Mrs. Sobieska will hardly endear you to Suzanne."

Adam regretted hanging his cane off of the chair. He was once more feeling agitated. The rabbi was right, the rabbi was always right. *I don't hate Mrs. Sobieska.* How could he hate the one who rescued his child? The woman did seem to genuinely love Suzanne. She obviously wasn't a bad person.

"Very well." His anger was diminishing with each tick of the wall clock. "I can be patient, but at what point do I say enough is enough? Suzanne is my daughter, not hers. When can I put my foot down and demand to have my child back?"

"Since there is a bond between the two, Mrs. Sobieska may always be involved in Suzanne's life. Perhaps not as a mother, but as an adoptive aunt or family friend. Would that be so terrible? For Suzanne to be friends with the woman who saved her?"

"I suppose not." Adam agreed, albeit reluctantly.

As long as Mrs. Sobieska understood that Suzanne was his daughter and she would eventually come to live with him.

Yes, I can be patient. He sighed.

Sunday, 3 March, 1946

To Adam's surprise, Mrs. Sobieska sent a note inviting him for dinner the following Sunday. He accepted, of course, and showed up on their doorstep early, bearing gifts. According to Polish tradition, one didn't come to a meal without presents for the hosts. For his daughter, he found a doll in the Main Market Square. For the older girl, Ewa, a folk necklace. And for Mrs. Sobieska, he selected a volume of Mickiewicz's poetry. He knew nothing of Mrs. Sobieska's literary tastes, but nearly every patriotic Pole adored Mickiewicz's works. The presents cost him an arm and a leg, however if he could make Suzanne love him, then it was worth it.

He shifted from one foot to the other, to take the stress off of his ankle and used the cane handle to rap on the door. Mrs. Sobieska answered seconds later, wearing the same bland dress she wore the day she met him at the attorney's office. He pushed the thought from his mind, but wondered why he continued to take notice of her appearance.

"Mr. Altman." Mrs. Sobieska nodded.

"Mrs. Sobieska," Adam held out the book to her. "For you, for inviting me."

"Thank you." She accepted the gift and stepped aside for him to enter.

Unlike their previous encounter, his daughter practically galloped over. Her inquisitive eyes were drawn to the doll.

"For you." Adam mustered out, handing it to her.

The little girl clapped and jumped up and down. She examined the doll, running her fingers through the yellow yarn hair and tugging on the skirt.

The other girl, Ewa, hung back. Adam knew even less of girls caught in between childhood and adulthood and how to act around them. "For Ewa." He up the necklace, hoping it would suit.

Ewa drew her upper lip back and her two front teeth poked out. He soon realized that was her version of a smile. She grabbed it and slipped it over her dark head.

"Girls, what do you say?" Mrs. Sobieska prompted.

"Thank you!" They said in unison.

Sophie latched onto his hand and she attempted to drag him inside. Adam ambled after her into the sitting room. As soon as he was seated, she jumped into his lap and hugged him.

Adam blinked several times, to maintain his composure. Otherwise, he would have cried. This was the moment he had been waiting for for five years.

"What do I call you?" Sophie asked, withdrawing.

He was speechless. This was precisely what he wanted, for her to accept him and think of him as *papa*. Yet it took him three attempts to form a coherent response, "Papa would be nice, but perhaps it is too early for that. My name is Adam."

"Mama, can I call him by his Christian name?" Sophie asked, shrilly shouting.

He covered the ear closest to her, cringing at the word "Christian."

"That's fine but be respectful." Mrs. Sobieska's voice wafted in from the kitchen.

Adam turned his head, catching a glimpse of the woman and Ewa, who were tending to the meal. He hadn't noticed they moved in there. He watched as Mrs. Sobieska stir the soup on the stove. He had to hand it to her, she raised Sophie well. Not only that, but the woman smoothed things over with the little girl. His daughter no longer feared him and that had to be Mrs. Sobieska's doing.

Sophie either couldn't or wouldn't sit still. If she wasn't bouncing up and down on him, digging her sharp tail bone into his thigh, her feet were twitching or her fingers were tugging on his tie. "Mama said you're not a Christian." She said.

"I'm not. I'm Jewish, as was your birth mother Mina, and as you are too." Adam answered and wondered how much of that she understood.

"Mina was my mother's name? Can I name my doll Mina?"

"If you would like." He nodded, his throat constricting. He crooked a finger under his collar and wished he could unbutton it and remove his tie. But that would be improper.

"Is Mina dead? My papa is dead. I mean, my other papa. His heart attacked him."

"Yes, Mina died." Adam replied and though his knowledge of children were limited, he had a feeling of what her next question would be.

"How did she die?" Sophie's eyes burned a hole through him. The question was so innocent...

Pressure mounted between his temples, his vision blurred, and his mouth went dry.

"Sophie," Mrs. Sobieska swept into the room, bearing collection of papers. Ewa was practically on her heels. She passed the stack of papers to the little girl. "Let's talk about something else. Tell Mr. Altman about your drawings." The woman and Ewa seated themselves on the divan. Mrs. Sobieska had the volume of poetry in her lap and she began to skim through it.

"I like to draw and I draw everything!" Sophie fanned out her pictures as she might a hand of cards. For a small child, she was talented and clearly inherited her skills from Mina. "Can I draw you?"

"If you wish." Adam smiled.

Mina was gone, but in a small way she returned to him through his daughter.

Minutes later it was time for dinner and they sat at the table. The meal consisted of a vat of tomato soup and newly baked black bread. It was delicious, and considering their country was facing a grain shortage and they were on the brink of famine, that was remarkable. Mrs. Sobieska explained that the previous autumn, the Russian confiscated the harvests, leaving Poland in dire straits.

Hearing his daughter recite Christian prayers was disturbing, but he kept his reservations to himself. After the meal, he assisted the ladies in clearing the table and then stepped outside for a few minutes.

Adam took out a cigarette from its case, lit it, and puffed on it, his fingers trembling. He had gone over two years without smoking, but the second he was able to get his hands on a cigarette in Switzerland, he returned to it. He hated to fall back on a bad habit and only did it when his nerves got the better of him.

During the visit, it occurred to him that throughout the evening he called his daughter "Sophie." He thought of her as Sophie too. Losing that small battle bothered him, but if his daughter was returned to him, he figured he could reconcile himself to the different name.

The front door opened and Mrs. Sobieska stepped out. A shawl was draped around her shoulders, but she couldn't be warm enough. He considered offering her his coat, but didn't know how she would respond to that.

"Are you all right, Mr. Altman?" She hugged herself, her tone full of sympathy. "I'm sorry if Sophie was too nosy about Mrs. Altman."

"No, it's all right. Sophie should know what happened to her mother, but it's not a story for little girls. Someday, I'll find a way to tell her." Adam replied. He wished to spare Sophie from the ugly truth for as long as possible. Her innocence did his heart good.

Then there was the fact he couldn't speak of his experiences, or of Mina's. The words simply wouldn't come. To Rabbi Rosenwieg, he said she wasn't coming back and that was enough. The rabbi understood, he had been at Auschwitz. *So many didn't come back from the camps.* For some horrors, there were no words. How could he explain Mina's fate to someone who never witnessed such things. She was starved, diseased, and treated worse than an animal. According to Mina's friend in the camp, in her feverish state, she spoke of Suzanne and the bright future Adam promised of her. One night she died, her body was stripped, she was tossed on a cart, and she was buried in a mass grave with hundreds of others. All because she was Jewish.

His gaze drifted to Mrs. Sobieska and he couldn't tear it away. Nor did he want to. The way she spoke throughout the evening, he could tell she was intelligent. She more than held up her end of a conversation. Despite their initial introduction, and the arguments they had, he liked her company.

"Sophie said Mr. Sobeski had a heart attack. He was young,

yes?" Adam commented. The one encounter he had with Mr. Sobieski; he remembered the man as young. And that a cough plagued him. But he assumed Mr. Sobieski recovered from it.

"The men in his family die young of heart attacks." Mrs. Sobieska nodded. She glanced at the setting sun and she scrunched her face from its glare. "Well, it's getting late and the girls have an early bedtime."

"I see." Adam sighed. He shouldn't have been surprised; all good things had to come to an end. Though she had been polite, she was ready for him to go.

"Would you like to read Sophie a bedtime story?" Mrs. Sobieska asked.

Adam blinked his surprise, but he nodded, and followed her back inside. From his childhood, and the first four months of Sophie's life, bedtime stories were always told at the child's bedside.

However, Mrs. Sobieska insisted that he read in the sitting room, since the girls' room was far too mess for a guest to see.

He didn't object and with his daughter nestled against his chest, and Mrs. Sobieska and Ewa listening from the divan, the tale of Queen Jadwiga transported them from this odd situation.

Chapter Twenty-One

Saturday, 10 March 1946

If the first dinner with Mr. Altman was any indication, Lidia would have thought this arrangement would work. As long as he remembered that Sophie was her daughter and the little girl preferred to live with her. He could visit the child when it was convenient. Sophie liked the man, relishing in the new attention she and presents she received. To his credit, Mr. Altman had been polite, a decent conversationalist, and he brought gifts to show his gratitude. *So unlike his first impression!* She couldn't deny how much she enjoyed the volume of Mickiewicz. Ewa warmed up to him too, at times fighting Sophie for his attention. The older girl's father died in the war. Knowing Ewa, she figured she could just share Sophie's father.

Father Cieslik was right. Showing Mr. Altman kindness made a world of difference.

When Mr. Altman paid another visit, things went well...until he asked if he could take Sophie to the park Sunday morning. A request she denied.

That delicate balance of harmony was abruptly overturned. The *discussion* became heated and Lidia sent the girls to their room. The second they shut the door, she and Mr. Altman fell into a fierce argument, one loud enough to be heard all the way in the Main Market Square.

"I'm her father!" Mr. Altman insisted.

"I don't care who you are." Lidia shouted, putting her hands on her hips. She stood nose to nose with the man. He obviously had a temper, but if pressed, she could shout as loud. "I have known you for a couple of weeks? That's not long enough for me to trust you. Besides, church is on Sunday."

Yes, it was natural for a father to want to spend time with his daughter. But to send her child off with a man they met a handful of times, a man who could easily run off with Sophie, was a chance she wasn't willing to take. *It could happen.* Lidia shivered. She heard stories of Jewish parents abducting their children from their Christian rescuer's home. Or, he could be one of those depraved individuals who preyed on little girls. For all of his faults, Mr. Altman didn't seem to be the type. But one could never tell, not until it was too late.

She would die before she allowed Sophie to go through such turmoil. The man's animosity was a small price to pay for her daughter's safety.

Mr. Altman paced, his cane falling into a steady beat. "I was kind, I stepped back when my reappearance upset Sophie." He threw up his free hand. "Why must she still pretend to be Catholic? She's Jewish."

"Why should religion matter to you? You're an atheist." Lidia shot back. "I can tell."

During the meals they shared, whenever a prayer was said, Mr. Altman blatantly refused to bow his head. Her knowledge of the Jewish religion came solely from Ewa. The girl explained that the Jewish Sabbath was on Sunday. But when Ewa mentioned knowing the rabbi he knew, and asked if Mr. Altman would be there next Saturday, he informed her he wasn't observant and he never attended services. When Sophie mentioned Jesus, Lidia heard him grumble under his breath. Mr. Altman was free to believe what he liked, but she wouldn't allow her daughter's faith to be destroyed.

"Tadeusz and I-" Lidia began.

"Mr. Sobieski is dead. Don't bring him into this." The second those cruel words left him, regret crossed Mr. Altman's features.

Lidia covered her mouth, to conceal a sob. That Mr. Altman could be so vicious about the man she loved, was reprehensible.

Neither of them mentioned their deceased spouses much. She was more apt to speak of Tadeusz than Mr. Altman was to speak of his wife. Other than the fact that Mrs. Altman died, Lidia knew nothing of the woman's story.

"Mrs. Sobieska, please, forgive me." Mr. Altman sighed. "I shouldn't have-"

Lidia waved him off. "Get out." She fetched his coat from the peg by the door and pitched it at home. "Now, get out!"

"This charade has gone on long enough." Mr. Altman threw on his coat but didn't immediately leave. "Either meet me half-way, or I will sue you for full custody."

So, it's back to that. She shook her head at him. *Makes sense.* Mr. Altman only showed kindness when it suited him. The second things didn't go his way, he reverted to threats and selfishness.

"I have opened my hope to you, a stranger." Lidia lifted her chin defiantly. "I let you spend time with my child, despite your arrogance and condescension." She wasn't blind; he put on a good show, but it was all an act. He looked down on her and how she raised Sophie. "If you think for one second that a lawyer will frighten me off, you're mistaken. I will get my own attorney."

"You can't afford-"

"If I have to use my last *grosz* fighting to keep Sophie, then that's what I will do. I'm not giving up my daughter!" The truth was that she had little saved. Between moving to a new place, the rationing, and clothing for the girls, the money had dwindled. But she would never tell him that.

"Sophie...Suzanne is not your daughter, she's mine! No matter how much you pretend, she's not yours." Mr. Altman retorted. A smile materialized on his hardened face, one she longed to smack off. "Do you really believe a judge would grant you custody to a child you have no claim to?"

Since Mr. Altman had been cruel in regards to Tadeusz and challenged her right to Sophie, Lidia felt justified to ignore her conscience and retaliate. "After what has happened in our country, do you really believe a judge would grant custody to you?" she asked, in a sickly-sweet manner.

Mr. Atlan raised his finger. "This isn't over." He turned on his good heel and stalked out of the house, slamming the door behind him.

Lidia closed her eyes, inhaled and exhaled, pressing her fingertips to her temples. Mr. Altman was a man who would get what he wanted or die trying. After all, he survived hell on earth. "Don't let him take Sophie from me!" She fell to her knees before the portraits of the Black Madonna of Częstochowska and Jesus, I Trust in You. "Please, I have lost too much!"

She shuddered. If her daughter was taken, she would lose the will to go on.

No, I can't give into despair. The Lord never failed her before and He wouldn't fail her now.

Monday, 24 March 1946

Adam uncrossed his right leg, crossed his left, and then checked on his pocket watch. As of this morning, Rabbi Rosenwieg and a priest he never met summoned him, Mrs. Sobieska, Sophie, Ewa to the synagogue. The two men of God were shut up in the rabbi's office, and despite his attempts to concentrate, he couldn't make out their conversation.

He was sitting on a bench on the left side of the door while Mrs. Sobieska and Ewa occupied the one on the right. Sophie stood in the middle, like a small bridge between them, undeterred by their tension.

Two weeks passed since his recent fight with Mrs. Sobieska and the only communication he had was through their attorneys. Their attorneys scheduled a meeting to discuss their situation, but very little progress had been made because he and Mrs. Sobieska ended up shouting at one another. If this woman wasn't so stubborn, their situation wouldn't be so complicated.

His request wasn't extraordinary; he only wanted to take Sophie to Planty Park on Sunday morning. He would have been willing to take Ewa too, if it smoothed things over. Was it really too much to ask, considering he went five years without spending time with his daughter? But no! Mrs. Sobieska was unyielding and to dismay, she enlisted the services of an attorney who attended her church.

Fury rippled beneath the surface of his skin, brewing like a lightning storm, but he refused to give Mrs. Sobieska a sideways glance. He checked the pocket watch once more and mumbled to himself. The rabbi and the priest requested that they be on time, however they had been waiting outside the office for a half an hour.

Adam clicked the watch shut, got up, and was about to knock when the door swung open.

The priest greeted him in a friendly manner. "My apologies for the wait. Come in. Mr. Altman, I'm Father Cieslik. Mrs. Sobieska, this is Rabbi Rosenwieg." After the customary handshakes, the priest's warm eyes settled on the girls. "Miss Sophie, Miss Ewa, would you mind waiting in the hall? The rabbi and I need to talk to your parents for a few minutes."

Ewa nodded and the priest laid a peppermint in the palm of her hand. He then pretended to pull a peppermint out from behind Sophie's ear, eliciting a giggle from her. The girls returned to the bench, ate their candy, and the older girl regaled the younger one with stories from the Bible.

Adam stepped aside so that Mrs. Sobieska could enter first. She murmured her thanks, but didn't look his way. *Good, she should feel guilty; she's the reason we're here.* He thought spitefully.

Rabbi Rosenwieg encouraged them to sit in the chairs in front of the desk while took his place behind it. Father Cieslik scooted a chair next to the rabbi.

"I can't understand what you hope to achieve with this meeting." Adam broke in. He had reservations about coming. The majority of his exchanges with Mrs. Sobieska ended badly. There was no reason to believe this one would end differently. Whatever the clergymen intended, at least they knew better than to host this meeting in a church. "Proselytizing me won't work, it won't influence my decision. You should know that by now, rabbi."

Father Cieslik's fair brow rose to his receding hairline. He leaned in and whispered something to the rabbi. Rabbi Rosenwieg chuckled and shrugged Adam's comments off.

"In case you haven't noticed, Mr. Altman, this isn't about you." Mrs. Sobieska interrupted. Her little pink tongue peaked between her teeth and knowing her, she would have stuck it out at him, if she could have gotten away with it. "This is about Sophie."

Adam opened his mouth to respond, but snapped it shut. He wouldn't allow himself to be baited.

"Good grief," Rabbi Rosenwieg teasingly nudged the priest with his elbow. "Their attorneys were right." A laugh rattled in his throat.

"We didn't summon you to discuss religious matters." Father Cieslik said. "Rabbi Rosenwieg and I have been contacted by the gentlemen who legally represent you. They have concerns about this custody battle."

Adam snapped to attention *Concerns?* Why hadn't Mr. Burminski spoken to him about it? If there were issues, why go to Rabbi Rosenwieg and Father Cieslik to solve them? *Why are we even here?* His claim to Sophie superseded Mrs. Sobieska's. In his opinion, she had no rights, but he only humored her to pacify Sophie.

"While the war is over, the situation in our country is sensitive." Rabbi Rosenwieg rested his crossed arms on his stomach, which was once more beginning to pooch out. "Every day there is violence against Jews and our new occupiers only add to our burdens. I think we can agree the last thing we want is for the Communists to put their oar in on this matter."

Adam caught a glimpse of Mrs. Sobieska nodding and felt relieved. At least she was aware of their country's troubles. When he heard it wasn't safe for Jews in Poland, he thought it was an exaggeration. After all, what could be worse than Auschwitz? But the pogroms: Poles murdering Jews outright; property withheld from Jewish owners, Jewish children not returned to their parents...

He encountered it first hand when he was in the Main Market Square the previous Saturday. The trumpeter was playing and he stopped to admire how beautiful it was to hear it again. *Poland has not yet perished.* He nearly swallowed his tongue when he overheard a sweet-looking, little old lady tell her friend, *"The Soviets are the worst. At least the Germans were charming people.*

They didn't kill anyone who didn't deserve it." The woman said it in such a casual manner, as if she were discussing the weather.

"A custody battle between a Jewish man and a Christian woman over a Jewish child who has been raised Catholic." Father Cieslik pressed his fingertips together, tenting his hands. "Can you not imagine the turmoil it would cause?"

"What are you saying?" Mrs. Sobieska's healthy complexion turned ashen. "That one of us should forfeit our right to Sophie?"

"I won't give up my daughter." Adam started to raise his voice.

"No," Rabbi Rosenwieg replied. "We believe the solution lies within the four of you."

Adam wondered how the men of God expected to do what the attorneys couldn't. That he, Mrs. Sobieska, Sophie, and Ewa could find an answer seemed too good to be true.

"If you agree, we would like to speak to the girls and hear their thoughts." The priest suggested.

Adam didn't know why, but he looked to Mrs. Sobieska, to gauge her reaction. He wanted this woman out of his daughter's life. However, he couldn't deny she loved Sophie dearly and she would do right by his daughter. What Ewa had to do with any of this, he didn't know. Yes, she was a member of Mrs. Sobieska's family, but she wasn't a member of his.

"If you think it best." Mrs. Sobieska said.

"I suppose." Adam found her approval was good enough for him to comply. "As long as you don't influence Sophie one way or another."

If it were any other rabbi trying to intervene, he would have taken his daughter by the hand and stormed out of the building. But this was Rabbi Rosenwieg, the only real friend he had in the world. The man had been there for him in his darkest hour, and he had been a fatherly figure. If the rabbi thought it best for him to dive head-first into the Vistula River, he would do it.

Out of respect for his friend, he would go along with what the rabbi wanted.

"Excellent. Let's call the children in." Rabbi Rosenwieg smiled and beckoned the girls inside.

Chapter Twenty-Two

Lidia wrung her hanky while Mr. Altman paced the length of the hallway. She was surprised he hadn't worried a permanent path in the floor from the number of laps he took. His slacks rustled like a bird's wings and every click of his cane grated on her nerves. Unlike her, the man was fidgety.

Something he and Sophie have in common.

The girls were still in the office, speaking to the rabbi and the priest. She was dying to know what they were saying. *I'm not a perfect mother, but Sophie is happy and I love her.* Sophie had accepted Mr. Altman as her father, yet Lidia couldn't imagine the girl preferring to live with the man. As for Ewa...only God knew what would come out of her mouth, but she would certainly insist on Sophie staying.

But what if she was wrong and Sophie asked to live with Mr. Altman? *Perhaps if I were stronger, I could let him take her.* She was selfish in that respect; she wanted Sophie for herself and she didn't intend to share the little girl.

Lidia nearly flinched when the door creaked open. Mr. Altman stopped in mid-stride, his knuckles whitening as he squeezed the cane's handle. The priest motioned her and Mr. Altman back into the office.

She and Mr. Altman reclaimed their former seats and the girls stood in between them.

An eerie silence hung over them, until a gentle chuckle from Father Cieslik broke it. "We have had a nice chat with Miss Sophie and Miss Ewa, and with their help, we have discovered a solution."

"Ladies, I believe it best that you should tell your parents." Rabbi Rosenwieg urged, nodding to the girls.

"You tell them, Sophie." Ewa nudged the younger girl.

Sophie shyly peered at Lidia, then at Mr. Altman, and back again. She worked the toe of her shoe into the worn, faded carpet.

"It's all right, baby." Lidia reached over and petted the girl's curls, regretting she put the child in this position. "Nothing you say will be wrong."

"Yes, no one will be upset." Mr. Altman encouraged.

Sophie claimed Lidia's hand and wiggling her fingers at her father, she wasn't satisfied until his hand was in her tiny grasp. "Me and Ewa think you should get married." The girl said.

Ewa's hand flew to her mouth, concealing a squeal

"What?" Lidia and Mr. Altman cried out in unison.

Sophie started to giggle.

This has to be a joke. Lidia narrowed her eyes at Ewa. No doubt the older girl put the thought in Sophie's head. Ewa was at the age where she was crazy about boys and was on the search for a boyfriend, and Sophie was at the age where she loved hearing stories of princes and princesses marrying. That had to be why they made such an outlandish suggestion.

"Go on." Rabbi Rosenwieg gestured for the girls to continue.

Ewa bobbed from one foot to the other. "I think it would be romantic, that after all you have been through, you found love again." She explained.

"That's insane!" Mr. Altman protested, but a tug on him from his daughter quieted him.

"You're my mama and you're my papa." Sophie's fingers tightened their grip on Lidia. "You both want me. You can get married and both have me. We could be a family. You love me, right?"

Mr. Altman's lips twitched, but he didn't answer her.

"We love you more than anything." Lidia shot a contemptuous look in the man's direction.

Mr. Altman awaked from his brief stupor. "Yes, of course, we love you." He chimed in.

"So?"

"We love you, but Mr. Altman and I don't love each other, and we have different religions." Lidia explained, as carefully as she could. She wondered how a ludicrous scheme had gotten this far. "Ewa, you understand."

"No, I don't. You could be friends if you wanted to be." Ewa replied. "You have a lot in common."

"Papa?" Sophie turned to Mr. Altman, flashing her big blue eyes.

Lidia waited for Mr. Altman to refuse. He wasn't considerate of the feelings of others, so it should have been easy for him.

However, Mr. Altman sniffed and his chin trembled. "We'll talk about it. All will be well though, I promise." He patted his daughter's cheek.

Lidia groaned, clutching her forehead. Now it would be far more difficult to convince Sophie that marrying was unthinkable. Never mind about Ewa. The girl was ecstatic, rocking back and forth on her heels, in her own dream world.

"Sophie, Ewa, will you wait in the hall again?" Father Cieslik requested.

Ewa nodded and dared to wink in Lidia's direction.

Sophie kissed Lidia's and Mr. Altman's cheeks, before she and Ewa traipsed out into the hallway.

"Mr. Altman!" Lidia hissed, once the door clicked shut. "Why did you let them think we would consider getting married?"

"She called me, 'papa!'" Mr. Altman explained. "Do you know how long I have waited to hear her say that? Five years!

She caught me off guard." He scooted to the edge of his chair and addressed the men of God. "Mrs. Sobieska is right though. Have you lost your minds? We can't stand one another and Ewa was wrong, we don't have anything in common."

"Father, rabbi, how could you encourage this?" Lidia frowned. She twisted her wedding ring around her finger, Tadeusz's memory coming to mind. To remarry so soon after his death would be a betrayal. She only lately stopped wearing the black mourning band on her arm. "My husband has only been dead for two years."

"My wife has been gone for a year." Mr. Altman said. You're wise and learned men: can't you see how this wouldn't work?"

"You have more in common than you think." A bemused expression settled on the rabbi's broad face. "You love Sophie more than life itself; you have been through dark times, you're widowed and correct me if I'm wrong, but neither of you have romantic prospects, nor do you desire them?"

Lidia nodded and to her surprise, Mr. Altman was nodding too. While she didn't know the man's personal history, from the way the rabbi described them, it did sound like they had more in common than she originally thought.

"Couples have married for worse reasons than convenience's sake." Father Cieslik carried on the argument from there. "Consider this, Mr. Altman: you would have a home with Sophie, a chance to raise her, you would see her every day. Mrs. Sobieska, with a man in the house, the girls might be safer and when Mr. Altman finds employment, he will help you provide for them."

Lidia ceased playing with her ring. Part of the problem was that Mr. Altman was a man. Trusting Tadeusz came easily. After his death and since the end of the war, a few single men showed romantic interest in her – Lt. Brühl included – and pressed their suit. But because of her past, she couldn't reciprocate their feelings. But if it were a marriage in name only, then perhaps it would work. For all of Mr. Altman's faults, she didn't believe he was depraved.

If it weren't for Father Cieslik's gentle persuasion to hear the girls out, she would have stormed out of the synagogue. That he wasn't concerned about Church doctrine was astonishing. But then again, she couldn't be too surprised. Some of Father Cieslik's sermons and his actions during the war, didn't always coincide with the Church.

"But our religious differences." Lidia persisted. This was the only issue the priest and the rabbi hadn't addressed. "I raised Sophie in the Church. Mr. Altman has no faith and objects that she does."

"Can't you see how difficult it is for me?" Mr. Altman counted. "It's insulting to me that my daughter was raised in an anti-Semitic religion."

"I'm not anti-Semitic, Mr. Altman." Lidia shot back. "Could I love Sophie and Ewa and be prejudiced?"

"You kept the truth from Sophie. You destroyed my wife's letter; I know you did!"

"Because if the truth had gotten out, Sophie would have been killed!"

"Really?" The tips of Mr. Altman's ears reddened. He slapped the arm of the chair. "So, it had nothing to do with you destroying all evidence of my claim to her?"

Lidia thought back to the day she found Sophie and discovered Mrs. Altman's letter. She initially wanted to put it away, so that when Sophie was old enough, she would know something about her heritage. But Tadeusz convinced her that if someone were to find the letter, Sophie could be killed. She went along with his wishes. Tadeusz wasn't solely to blame though. In a sense, Mr. Altman was right. There was a small part of her that rejoiced when she destroyed the letter because it meant Sophie was her daughter and no one could ever take her away.

"I thought...I thought you were dead." Lidia said.

"Hope. You hoped I was dead!" Mr. Altman shouted.

"How dare you!" She gasped. Yes, she thought Mr. and Mrs. Altman had died. Not because she wished for it, but because she couldn't imagine how anyone could survive such evil.

"Mrs. Sobieska, Mr. Altman, lower your voices." Father Cieslik scolded, and motioned towards the door. "The girls can hear you, I'm sure. Do you want them to witness you behaving like this?"

Mr. Altman mumbled an apology.

She hadn't realized how loud they were, in a place of worship no less. But there was something about the man that brought out the worst in her.

Rabbi Rosenwieg had been rendered silent, as he had been listening to their arguments. "There is a story in the Bible. Two women claimed to be the mother of a baby, each desperate to keep the child. They approached the king for a judgment. King Solomon's solution was to cut the child into two. The real mother relinquished the child, to save it. It is called the Judgment of Solomon." His hairy cheek twitched, his expression contemplative. "Now, neither of you forfeiting your rights to Sophie will benefit her. However, if you proceed with fighting over her, Sophie will be torn into two. Is that what you want?"

"Amen." Father Cieslik thumped the rabbi on the back, congratulating the fellow clergyman for his insight. "Also, can't you see how fighting over Sophie will make Ewa feel unwanted?"

Lidia felt as though she were on the verge of running out of the room screaming. She despised her own mother for marrying so soon after her father's death. *What kind of woman marries a man she knows nothing about?* She put the question to Tadeusz years ago. It was one of the reasons she refused Lt. Brühl and her other callers.

But now she was faced with a similar dilemma.

Father Cieslik and Rabbi Rosenwieg left the office, offering Adam and Mrs. Sobieska privacy and a little time to think. The second the door closed, he rose and resumed where he left off with pacing. Mrs. Sobieska was fumbling with the necklace was wearing, the one of a patron saint.

Sophie's suggestion was madness and he shouldn't take it seriously. But it was the only thing she ever asked of him. Then, she called him "papa." Hearing her say that word made up for their less than perfect reunion. His little girl wanted him in her life! But to marry Mrs. Sobieska, the woman who fought him on everything?

"This is absurd." Adam testily rapped his cane against the floor. "Why can't you compromise?" he asked. He compromised for all of Sophie's life – it was someone else's turn to do it.

"Me? Why should I?" Mrs. Sobieska scrunched her nose.

Adam rubbed the back of his neck, to loosen the muscles. He was tired. Five years of fighting to be with his daughter, the majority of that time spent in the worst circumstances. Why did it have to be so difficult for him to be a father to his own daughter? *I'm so close, I can't give up now.* If marriage to Mrs. Sobieska was what it took, then so be it.

"I suppose marriage is the only alternative." Adam said, unable to believe his own words.

Mrs. Sobieska shifted in her seat to unabashedly gape at him. "We can't marry, we hate each other!" She exclaimed.

Adam winced, but he deserved it. From the moment they met, he behaved terribly. Contrary to what Mrs. Sobieska thought, he didn't hate her. How could he hate the woman who saved his daughter's life. Unfortunately for Mrs. Sobieska, upon his return, he directed his anger against her. He couldn't make the Nazis pay for their actions – for murdering his wife or separating him from his daughter, nor could he shake off years of abuse that was heaped on him. He was a miserable person; he had a whole hospital in Switzerland to attest to that.

Incorrigible, miserable, hollow, broken, unlovable...

Adam breathed in and out, and counted to ten before speaking. "What we are doing now isn't working." He hoped she would be willing to meet him halfway, but he could understand her skepticism. "I will be a father to Sophie one way or another. If marrying you is the solution, to bring peace between us, then I'm willing to do that."

Mrs. Sobieska's coldness drained away, revealing that she too was tired. Other than being widowed, working in a factory, and being religious, he knew nothing of her. Nothing of her past. He never cared to ask. And now, here he was, proposing marriage.

"I won't share your bed." She whispered, smoothing non-existent wrinkles from her skirt.

He blinked, shocked she spoke so frankly about... that. In a synagogue, no less. "Not to worry, Mrs. Sobieska. That is the last thing on my mind right now." Warmth flooded his cheeks.

He never had never intended to remarry in the first place. Much as he loved Mina, he didn't have in him to fall in love again. Never mind sharing a bed with anyone. After what happened in Auschwitz, being treated worse than an animal and paraded naked in front of strangers, he couldn't be vulnerable like that again.

"Very well." Mrs. Sobieska leaned over and, seizing his wrist, she dragged him closer. Her touch was cold and it sent gooseflesh across his skin. "But I swear, Mr. Altman, if you harm Sophie or Ewa in any way, I will make you live to regret it."

"Of course." Adam mumbled dumbly. Despite what he had seen, this woman was able to strike fear into his very core.

"And I won't take off Tadeusz's ring." Mrs. Sobieska released him, stood, and stalked out into the hall.

Adam closed his eyes and sighed. *What have I gotten myself into?* Mrs. Sobieska wasn't about to make things easy for him, but reminded himself Sophie was worth it and hopefully there would be peace in their family. He stroked his ring finger, missing the band he once wore. But it was long gone, having been stolen from him on his arrival at Auschwitz.

~

Rabbi Rosenwieg and Father Cieslik officiated the ceremony. Ewa and a few other members of the synagogue acted as witnesses. Sophie watched close by; her large eyes sparkling.

At some point during the whole ordeal, Mrs. Sobieska became simply Lidia. Adam didn't know why, but he couldn't take his eyes off of her. She, however, kept her gaze low and looked as though she were facing her execution. Perhaps it was fright. Or guilt. Her eyes were red rimmed and her nose was pink. *The woman cries before the wedding and the man after.* His mother told him when he married Mina. He probably would shed a few tears later, from stress and relief.

Ewa let out a high-pitched giggle. Sophie soon joined in, jumping up and down.

Adam glanced at Rabbi Rosenwieg for an explanation.

"You may kiss the bride." Rabbi Rosenwieg repeated, for what must have been the second time. The man had the audacity to smirk.

Adam hazarded a glance at Lidia, who was glowering...*If looks could kill.* He stepped closer, tentatively cupped her face with his hands, and chastely brushed his lips against hers. Her mouth was soft as rose petals.

A second later, Lidia broke away and hugged herself.

Adam swallowed. One small kiss shouldn't have made much of a difference. Not after weeks of intense fighting. But it did. For the first time in a long time, he felt something. Something akin to human emotion, which he lost in Auschwitz.

His soul was awakened and he liked kissing her.

Rabbi Rosenwieg laid a cloth covered glass near his feet and pointed at it. "Step on it, Mr. Altman."

Adam recalled this tradition from his wedding to Mina. He raised his foot and stomped it. The sound of glass shattering filled the room.

"*Mazel tov!*" Rabbi Rosenwieg and Ewa cheered in unison.

"I'm so happy!" Sophie clapped.

Ewa wrapped one arm around his waist and the other around Lidia's. The young lady seemed determined to make him her father too.

Adam rested his hand on top of his daughter's golden head and the doubts he entertained earlier vanished. Whatever the future may bring, he had done the right thing. He had Sophie now...and a wife and... an Ewa.

Lidia was chewing on her lower lip, hard enough for her teeth to cut into it. Once more she was wearing the same faded dress he had seen her in time and time again. Only now did it dawn on him that it was the only nice dress that she possessed. He had no room to judge since his clothing was cast offs from an American missionary barrel.

He desperately wanted to put his arm around his new wife, and reassure her it would be all right, and to promise that he would be a good husband to her. But he kept such professions to himself.

Chapter Twenty-Three

Saturday, 30 March, 1946

Lidia stirred the steamy porridge on the stove, sniffing as moisture gathered on her upper lip. Her back was to her daughters and Mr. Altman but since none of them were using their inside voices when they praised Sophie's artwork, she overheard everything. She didn't have the heart to scold them for being loud. Sophie was on her father's knee, which was heartwarming. And Ewa's not-so-subtle attempts of grasping for attention made her smile, especially since Mr. Altman didn't know how to handle a girl like Ewa.

A pang of envy burrowed itself down deep. Her husband... Tadeusz should have been there. *Her husband.* She never expected to use those two words for anyone other than Tadeusz. Especially for Mr. Altman. The kiss they shared at the synagogue had rendered her speechless.

When he went to collect his belongings from the boarding house, she and the girls headed straight home. She cleared out their girls' room and moved all of their things into her room. Three to a bed was cramped, but they had done it before. Mr. Altman arrived at the apartment an hour later and the four of them began their new life together.

Lidia divided the porridge into their four bowls and chose

to sit down at the opposite end of the table. The laughter died down. She counted the seconds, reaching ten, before her new husband broke the silence.

"I'm taking Sophie with me to Planty Park today." Mr. Altman stated smugly. "And Ewa is welcome to come along." He added, obviously as an afterthought.

Lidia dropped the spoon on the table. "And I'm taking Sophie with me to church tomorrow. Ewa is welcome, as always, but she makes her own choices." She shot back.

"Can we stop with this religious charade?" Mr. Altman asked. "What use is it, when Sophie will bear my name again?"

Lidia hadn't considered that Sophie would change her name to Altman. But it made sense, especially since her own name was now Altman. She won the battle in keeping the child's name as Sophie, so he was eager for this little victory. Her prime concern was the hatred Sophie might receive for living openly as Jewish. Then there was Ewa. She might feel left out if she didn't have the same last name.

However, Mr. Altman gave no thought to that. He was too determined to have his own way than to think of what was best for the girls.

"What does it matter to you?" She argued. "You aren't religious."

"Can mama come to the park with us?" Sophie's lower lip curled into a pout. "Please?"

"Yes!" Ewa exclaimed. "That would be fun!"

"Is that what you want?" Mr. Altman asked softly. He wasn't kind to her, but whenever he spoke to the girls, he was gentle.

"I want us to be a family." Sophie said.

"Girls, papa and I are sorry." Lidia went to them, and placed her hands on their shoulders. "We didn't mean to put you in the middle of this. We love you and we will try harder."

Cream and sugar were a rarity, not to mention expensive, and ice cream was usually reserved for special occasions. Father Cieslik, however, was the culprit who introduced Sophie to it and treated the girls from time to time.

"Planty Park, yes. But it's too early for ice cream." Mr. Altman nodded.

Sophie sat down and started on her breakfast.

"I can't wait. I used to love going there." Ewa suddenly grew somber, which was uncharacteristic for a girl as cheerful as her. "During the war, before the ghetto, it was forbidden to Jews."

Lidia sensed that Mr. Altman was trying to catch her gaze and looked up. They locked eyes. His expression was apologetic. Despite the wedding and new living arrangements, they were still trying to cut Sophie into two. Meanwhile, Ewa was left out. This must have been what Rabbi Rosenwieg meant when he spoke of The Judgment of Solomon.

Mr. Altman gave her a small nod, which she returned to him.

They had to do better, for Sophie and Ewa's sake.

―

Lidia was glad she thought to bring along hot tea, for the morning was chilly. Planty Park was beginning to thaw, but the earth still felt solid beneath their feet. The second they entered, Ewa dropped the spherical football and kicked it with all of her might. Sophie chased after it. The girls would be fine running and playing, but she would certainly need the tea to warm her insides. It seemed they would have a good time, but for the life of her, she didn't know why Mr. Altman insisted on bringing a shovel along. He offered no explanation; he simply asked if they had one and grabbed it up when they left the apartment.

As they strolled across the uneven ground, he relied heavily on his cane, which led her to wonder how he hurt his leg. She didn't dare ask, uncertain of the kind of response she would receive.

Mr. Altman surveyed the area, focusing on a specific linden tree and ambled over to it, cane in one hand and shovel in the other.

"Dare I ask why you have a shovel, Mr. Altman?" Lidia followed, her curiosity getting the better of her.

"To dig with, of course." His reply was sarcastic, but she detected a teasing lilt to it. He squatted down, knocked aside twigs and old leaves, dislodging rocks until he found what he was searching for. "My wife...Mina, she and I buried something by this tree a few years ago."

Mr. Altman stood and poked the dirt with the shovel, but it was too solid.

"We must soften the ground first." Lidia grabbed his arm and he stopped.

She unscrewed the lid from the jar of tea and dumped the brew, hoping it would do the truth. If it didn't, knowing Mr. Altman, she was willing to bet the man would claw his way through with his bare hands to get what he wanted.

"Thank you." He muttered.

Mr. Altman jabbed the shovel into the ground, attempting to dig using only the muscles in his arms to push it down. He should have known that to get enough momentum, he would have to hop up and shove it in, using his feet. But he couldn't... not with his bad leg. He didn't have the strength or the balance.

The man would die before he asked her for help, but she couldn't bear to watch him struggle.

Lidia released an exaggerated groan. "You're doing it wrong." She took the tool and nudged him aside. "All me, city boy."

She hopped up and using her feet, she forced the blade to cut through the earth. Scoop after scoop, until she heard a clink. She leaned the shovel against the tree.

Mr. Altman dropped to his knees and withdrew a jar from the hole, and held it up to the sunlight.

A quick glimpse told her aged scribblings and *zlotys* were stuffed within.

"Money?" Lidia asked.

"A little, and jewels and drawings. Mina sketched pictures in the ghetto. They are her legacy to Sophie." He tucked the jar into his deep coat pocket and rose, wiping the dirt from his pant legs. "How is it that a lady such as yourself is capable of manual labor?"

"I was raised on a farm." Lidia replied, but decided not to elaborate. He wouldn't understand. If he disliked her now, he would be repulsed if he learned of her past.

Before Mr. Altman could ask any further questions, she rushed off and joined the girls in kicking the football around. She felt a momentary twinge of guilt for excluding him. When she glanced back, she noticed he abandoned the tree and was ducking into one of the shops across the road.

Minutes later, he returned bearing four small cookies. Sophie skipped over and Ewa gushed her thanks. They devoured their treat.

Lidia chose that moment to rest on the park bench and retie her shoe.

Mr. Altman approached, holding a cookie out to her. "Take it." He urged, his thin lips stretching into a smile. "As a thank you for digging up the jar."

She licked her lips. It had been ages since she had a cookie. "All right." She accepted it and nibbled on it, to make it last longer. The honey spiced dessert crumbled onto her tongue. "What did you do for a living? Before the war."

Mrs. Altman painted a picture of their life in the letter she left with Sophie, but it had been so long that Lidia couldn't recall the details.

"I was a tailor and I had my own business." Mr. Altman joined her on the bench. He bit into his cookie and chewed slowly. "What was your profession?"

"I was a housewife." Lidia responded.

She wasn't embarrassed that she had been a housewife, not really. But that she and Tadeusz lived simply left her feeling self-conscious. Mr. Altman had a business, Mrs. Altman was a great artist, they had this fancy apartment in the Kazimierz District...they were educated, cultured, and comfortable in their former lives.

"Was that something you enjoyed?" Mr. Altman didn't sound condescending, but he seemed genuinely interested. "I mean, if I could be hired somewhere, or eventually start a business, would you want to be home again?"

"I would need to think about it." She replied, finishing her cookie.

"Of course." He nodded and resumed eating.

Lidia dreaded bringing it up, she didn't want to start another quarrel. But she couldn't relent on this issue. Mr. Altman may have no use for religion, but she wanted Sophie to have a proper Catholic upbringing.

"I want Sophie to go with me to church on Sunday." She declared.

"I know." Mr. Altman answered, fumbling with his cane. "I just...I want her to know she's Jewish. It's the reason Mina and I gave her to you and your husband. So, she could survive in case we didn't. She lost so much; I don't want her to lose that too."

"She won't." Lidia said. "You will talk with her and you will help her understand, and make certain she will never forget who she is."

Mr. Altman looked uncertain, but nodded in agreement.

The girls resumed their game and she and Mr. Altman sat back and watched them play.

The discussion about religion seemed to be over, but this wasn't it. One day Sophie would want to know what it meant to be Jewish. *I won't be able to answer her.* Sophie would go to Mr. Altman and he would try to help. But really, their daughter would have to discover the truth on her own, to reclaim the identity she had been denied. She had been born Suzanne Altman, but she became Sophie Sobieska. She was one person, yet she had two separate identities.

But that was something they would worry about later. Today, Sophie was young and happy and free.

"You know," Mr. Altman faced her and he looked almost impish. "You have been staring at my leg for most of the day. I mean, I'm flattered to receive such attention."

Lidia hadn't realized it, but she was staring at his misshapen limb again. "I'm sorry, I don't mean to...ogle you. What happened?" A blush spread on her cheeks and she shook her head over her audacity to ask such a personal question.

"Towards the end of the war on the...on a walk, I fell off a road and went down an embankment." Mr. Altman shrugged, nonplussed by her nosiness. "A tree broke my fall though." He quipped and tapped his cane against his leg. "I crushed my ankle."

Lidia mumbled an apology. But if she hadn't known better, she could have sworn her new husband was flirting with her

Wednesday, 3 April, 1946

Lidia wearily glared at the mirror in the w. c. She gripped the sink and bumped her forehead against it. She was frustrated from her recent disagreement with Mr. Altman. Last night he planned to tell Sophie a bedtime story...at her bedside, and though she knew deep down her new husband wasn't a threat to her daughter's safety, some old habits die hard. She didn't allow it, yelling at him, which irritated him and led to a heated argument. They went to bed angry and she woke up feeling upset. *He really did nothing to deserve my wrath.* She should apologize, but if she did, she would have to explain everything and she wasn't ready for that.

A knock on the front door coaxed her out of the w. c. and as she passed by Mr. Altman, she did her best to ignore him.

Lidia answered the door, coming face to face with a gentleman of middle age, with grayish complexion. He was wearing a heavy coat, beneath it was a blue NKVD uniform!

"Mrs. Lidia Sobieska?" He grunted in his thick, Russian accent. On receiving a meek nod from her, he continued, "I'm Capt. Nikolai Vavilov. You have come under the notice of the NKVD."

"What? Why?" The blood drained from her face. She couldn't fathom why the new authorities would be interested in her. She married impetuously, but people married all of the time, especially now that the war was over. "I don't understand."

"You are to be questioned at Montelupich Prison." Capt. Vavilov grabbed her wrist.

Movement behind him caught her eye. Mrs. Karlinskowa, her old neighbor, lurked near the sidewalk, pacing anxiously. She hadn't seen the woman since Krakow was liberated. *She betrayed me for some reason.* She concluded, but couldn't think of what she had done to get on Mrs. Karlinskowa's bad side.

Lidia whimpered, attempting to twist away from the Russian, but it was no use. *Where can I run to?* Really, in many ways, the NKVD was no different than the Gestapo. They investigated, threatened, tortured, and sent people to Siberia. Word spread about the gulags there, that they were horrific. She wasn't like Mr. Altman; she wouldn't be able to survive if they shipped her there. *I'll never see Sophie and Ewa again.*

"Excuse me," Mr. Altman barged over, wedging himself between her and the captain. "How can I help you?"

"Who are you?" Capt. Vavilov frowned, looking confused.

"I'm her husband." Mr. Altman didn't blink an eye as he stood toe to toe in opposition to the Communist investigator. "She is Lidia Altman now. As I asked, how can I help you?"

"I'm here to take your wife in for questioning, to learn the basis of her connection to Lt. Brühl." Capt. Vavilov pushed past Lidia and Mr. Altman, casually strolling into their apartment, surveying the surroundings. Sophie and Ewa, who were in the kitchen, froze in place. They had been warned to never cross anyone in a uniform, particularly the new authorities. "Mrs. Sobieska...Mrs. Altman, we have records indicating the Gestapo issued you a pardon due to your relationship with Wehrmacht soldier, Lt. Brühl." He paused, waiting for her to speak.

"I- it isn't what you think." Lidia shook her head. "The Gestapo brought me in for questioning once because-" She cast a glance back at Sophie and Ewa and knew she couldn't tell the truth. Those who hid Jews during the war were now targeted for their acts of resistance. The Soviets viewed their actions as a symptom of rebellion, one they needed to quell. "Lt. Brühl..."

"Mrs. Karlinskowa told me everything." The Russian interrupted. "You and Lt. Brühl had an affair; you whored yourself out to benefit-"

"No!" Lidia cried out, but it was no use. The alleged evidence was damning enough. She would be arrested and she'd never see her daughters again!

"Stop, that's not what happened!" Mr. Altman moved closer to her, offering his protection. "I'm Jewish and that little girl over there is Jewish, and she is my daughter. During the war, when it became obvious the Germans were going to kill us, I sent my daughter to hide with Lidia and pose as her daughter."

"Is that true?" Capt. Vavilov raised a dark brow in Lidia's direction.

"It is." Mr. Altman nodded. "Lidia did everything in her power to protect my daughter. Some German sought her out, what choice did she have but to be cordial to him? Now Lidia and I are married." He lifted his hand, palm up, gesturing to her. "Do you think I would have married a woman who collaborated with the Nazis?"

"I suppose not." Capt. Vavilov admitted, his smugness dissipating. "I will have to confer with my superiors. This may not be over." And he was right. The captain might have lost this small battle, but the small war continued.

"And I'll be here, fighting for my wife as she fought for my daughter." Mr. Altman replied, escorting the NKVD agent out the door.

Lidia could hear Mrs. Karlinskowa wailing outside, shouting "Sophie!" Then she understood and wondered how she didn't notice it before. Mrs. Karlinskowa didn't have children of her own. When she used to watch Sophie, a bond developed between them, and she used to joke from time to time about stealing the child away. *Mrs. Karlinskowa figured if I was out of the picture, then she could have Sophie.* But the woman never counted on Mr. Altman and his stubbornness.

Mr. Altman shut the door and locked it, just in case. He turned back to Lidia, his expression unreadable. "Are you all right?" He whispered.

"Yes." Lidia nodded. The breath was knocked out of her when the girls propelled themselves into her arms. "You could have let him take me. Sophie would have been yours."

"We may have our differences, but I would never betray you or the girls." Adam said, managing a strained smile.

She sensed though he was dying to know more about her association with Lt. Brühl. However, he went to the kitchen without saying another word.

Monday, 8 April 1946

Adam couldn't keep from smiling. He, Sophie, and Ewa were supposed to be shopping for groceries, but they took a small detour to the Main Market Square. Until he could find work, he watched Sophie during the day while his wife worked. Lidia's irrational fear of leaving Sophie with him subsided since the NKVD's visit. Other than a few arguments, the tension between them had lessened.

There were scads of rules though. He had to hold Sophie's hand at all times and never take his eyes off of her. Neither she nor Ewa were permitted to talk to strangers, particularly Russian men. And he had to tell the girls "no" at times…and he had to mean it. Otherwise, they could end up spoiled. In his opinion, that last condition was more of a suggestion. Considering he missed out on the first five years of Sophie's life, he felt he had a right to spoil her. And he couldn't very well spoil Sophie without spoiling Ewa.

Unable to be idle while Lidia worked, he took over the day-to-day tasks of running the household. The cleaning, the laundry, and the errands fell to him. Ewa helped where she could, but he preferred for her to focus on her education. Or enjoy what remained of her childhood. Too much had been stolen from her. Lidia insisted on cooking, since his meals left much to be desired, but he always assisted her.

His little girl tugged on his elbow when they bypassed a shop that sold desserts.

"May we have cookies again?" Sophie turned her big eyes up to him. "Please?"

"Yes!" Ewa dug through her small purse. "I'll pay!"

"All right." Adam sighed. They knew he couldn't tell them "no." He shook his head at the older girl. "Keep your money, Ewa. It's my treat."

Ewa thanked him. She earned a little money from babysitting and doing odd jobs around the neighborhood, but he hated for her to waste it on something as trivial as a cookie. With the rationing, it was a costly treat.

"But you have to eat it before we get home." He held up a finger as they retraced their steps. "Don't tell your mother. The last thing I need is to have her nagging for giving you treats so close to your dinner. Agreed?"

The girls nodded eagerly.

He paid for the cookies and they wandered through the park. After a couple bites, he divided up his cookie between the girls. They could use some fattening up.

Despite the war, Planty Park's hundred-year-old chestnut trees remained. The lighted walking paths wound around the whole park, beginning and ending at the Wawel Castle, overlooking the pewter gray Vistula River. He found it remarkable how much of "little Rome" as Krakow was fondly called - due to its forty-nine churches - was intact. With the exception of a couple of bombings, the city's buildings were largely untouched. Many of the monuments were missing, including the Adam Mickiewicz monument, but at least morning, noon, and night the trumpet was played.

"I'm so happy you and Mrs. Sobieska...I mean, Mrs. Altman are married now." Ewa said. "I told her she would find true love. It's so romantic."

Adam reminded himself Ewa was young and she didn't mean for her innocent observations to make him feel uncomfortable. "Ewa, people marry for all sorts of reasons." He swallowed and hoped he wouldn't say anything to ruin her girlish fantasies about love. "Love has nothing to do with why we married."

"But it could." Ewa persisted. "You're nice when you're not in one of your moods, and Mrs. Altman is sweet. When I learned my family wasn't coming back, she invited me to stay with her and Sophie forever. I would never leave her; I'm committed to her and Sophie."

He gave the girl a sideways glance. He originally believed Lidia swooped in and claimed the girl the same way she did with Sophie. For his new wife's sake, he presented the past differently to the NKVD officer.

"How did you meet...my wife?" Adam asked.

Sophie was stuffing the rest of the cookie in her mouth, oblivious to their discussion.

"Well, during the war, I went from hiding place to hiding place because I wasn't a very good guest. I was loud and I broke things. Father Cieslik brought me to Mrs. Altman and no matter what I did, she insisted that I stay." The giddiness faded from Ewa's face and he recognized the pain she was feeling. He often felt the same. "She and Father Cieslik helped me search for my parents and sisters, but they died in the camps. Mrs. Altman and Sophie are the only family I have now. Well, and you, if you want to be my family."

Adam's eyes were stinging. "I'm sorry for what happened to you and your parents and sisters." He was about to touch her shoulder, but stopped himself, unsure if he should. "I would love to be part of your family."

He was stunned when Ewa took it upon herself to hug him. Then Sophie tackled him from behind, clinging to him. His heart felt as though it was swelling, from emotion and guilt. In the short time he had known Lidia, he accused her of a multitude of sins. From being prejudiced, to wishing him dead, to denying Sophie her heritage. She could have used her past to vindicate herself. Even during the NKVD captain's visit, she stayed silent about the truth. *If I hadn't intervened, Capt. Vavilov would have taken her away.* Lidia's connection to Lt. Brühl didn't sit well with him, but despite the accusation, he didn't believe it was an affair. Reluctant to cause further upset, he had yet to broach the subject with her. That Lidia feared he would let her be arrested, so that he could have Sophie, was eye opening.

Adam closed his eyes in remorse. He ought to have listened to Rabbi Rosenwieg's advice and been more understanding.

Grocery shopping could wait. They needed to go home.

～

Adam and the girls arrived in time to find Lidia preparing dinner. Sophie and Ewa went up to her, greeting her with hugs.

He lingered by the kitchen door frame, a little awestruck by the woman he married. Lidia was genuinely a good person. But since their wedding, more specifically since their first kiss, he began to notice things about her. How the sunlight cast a sheen on her flaxen hair. She resembled one of those angels in the stained-glass windows of her church. The way her eyes lit up when Sophie did something cute or when Ewa misspoke. The way her pink lips curled into an easy smile.

Lidia told him straight out that she would never share his bed, but lately, he wished she would. There was a fine line between aggravation and attraction. In the beginning, she aggravated him when she challenged him. Somewhere along the way, that aggravation transformed into attraction. He couldn't deny it, not anymore.

She abruptly turned around, hands on her hips, and a wooden spoon sticking out from her fingers. "You can't fool me, Mr. Altman. I can tell you gave the girls cookies." Her brow was arched, but she didn't sound too upset. "There are crumbs around Sophie's mouth. If you're going to sneak her treats, at least wipe her mouth off before she gets home."

The girls darted out of the room, thinking they were about to receive a lecture.

Adam roused from his musings and taking small steps, he met her halfway. "You have been keeping secrets from me." He said.

"W-what do you mean?" The color drained from her face, betraying her terror.

"Nothing terrible, but Ewa told me everything." He assured her, wanting nothing more than to banish her distress. He only meant to tease her, but clearly, he needed to work on his sense of humor. "Why didn't you tell me you provided Ewa with a home because she had none? Why won't you seek recognition?"

Lidia exhaled and standing on tiptoe, she peered over his shoulder. Sophie was playing with her doll on the sitting room floor and Ewa was thumbing through "Anne of Green Gables."

"Since the war ended, the Jews and those who helped Jews during the war, have been persecuted." She resumed her position at the stove and stirred whatever it was that was in the pot. "I don't regret what I did, but I don't want Sophie to be mistreated because of it. Ewa has had a difficult time. "That's one of the reasons I continued to keep Sophie's heritage a secret."

When Lidia turned her back to him, his fantasies were revived. He yearned to hug her from behind, melding his front to her back. Nuzzle her, kiss the little patch where her neck sloped into her shoulder. He had gone nearly three years without touching a woman...or being touched. Until now, he hadn't realized he missed the intimacy of being close to another person. In Auschwitz, Rabbi Rosenwieg insisted they had not lost their humanity. Having Sophie, Ewa, and Lidia in his life made him feel human again.

Adam edged closer and rested his hand on her arm. "Mrs. Sobi-...I misjudged you." When she looked his way, offering him her full attention, he continued, "The last several years haven't been easy, but it doesn't excuse how I've treated you. I'm sorry for taking my anger out on you. You didn't deserve it. I hope in some way I can make it up to you."

"Thank you." Lidia patted his hand sympathetically. "I'm sorry to have misjudged you as well."

Adam yearned to seal the apology with a kiss. However, Lidia had been adamant in the synagogue. He wounded her again and again, and it would be cruel to betray the trust that was beginning to form between them.

He backed off and collecting the plates from the cupboard, he set the table.

Chapter Twenty-Four

Tuesday, 16 April 1946

Adam lingered at the entrance of the synagogue, hesitant to enter. He had visited a few times. The first was when he married Mina. The second was on his return to Krakow, to see Rabbi Rosenwieg. And the third was for when the clergymen brought him and Lidia together, and married them. He occasionally considered attending Shabbat services, to try and sort out his beliefs and find direction for his life. His time in Auschwitz should have been a deciding factor, but witnessing his family's belief in *Something*, inspired him to call on his old friend for counsel.

One day, I will bring Sophie here and she can learn about her heritage. He finally went inside the place of worship, marveling at the white limestone walls and the multiple chandeliers dangling from the ceiling. Drawing in a breath, he couldn't deny feeling a sense of peace in this light, airy atmosphere. It was a miracle the synagogue wasn't destroyed during the war. Instead, the Nazis used the building for storage and left it intact.

Adam ambled to the prayer hall, where a large engraving of a menorah crowned the opposite wall. He found the rabbi in the front pew. The man's head was bowed and his hushed Hebrew words echoed throughout the room. Adam walked on noiseless feet, to avoid interrupting the man's prayer.

The rabbi ended his prayer and rose. "Mr. Altman? What are you doing here?" He asked, when he turned to him. "Is everything all right with your family?"

"Yes." Adam nodded, and felt a small pang of guilt for lying in a place of worship. His relationship with Sophie was improving and Ewa had become a friend. However, his marriage to Lidia was tumultuous at best. Just when he thought they made headway, they would have a heated argument over a trivial matter. Like when he went into the girls' room to read Sophie a bedtime story, Lidia pitched a fit. The following day, the NKVD showed up on their doorstep to arrest his wife for her connection to a Lt. Brühl. She believed he would have allowed her to be taken away in order to have Sophie. That she thought so lowly of him, hurt. "Everything is fine. I wanted to look in on you."

"You are a horrible liar, you always were." The rabbi chuckled.

Adam met the man in the center of the room. "I want my new family to be happy. I want to have a...friendship with my wife. And I want to find peace." He explained. Friendship – what he wanted was a true marriage in every sense of the word. But to say that in a synagogue seemed disrespectful. "And I want to believe in...God, but I think after what happened to us, I'll always be skeptical of Him."

"Come." Rabbi Rosenwieg motioned towards the pew where he had been sitting. "Let's talk as we used to."

Adam headed over, not paying close attention when the north door opened and slammed shut.

Rabbi Rosenwieg saw something and gasped.

Adam turned and was stunned to find a group of five youths marching in. From their appearances, the way they moved, how they chortled loudly, he knew they weren't Jewish and they certainly didn't come to heal the breach between Jews and

Christians. The five boys, their ages ranging from ten years to the cusp of adulthood, resembled one another and it led him to believe they were brothers or cousins.

"What may I do for you, young men?" Rabbi Rosenwieg grew pale, but he lifted his chin in defiance.

"We're here to tell you Jews to get out!" The oldest boy said.

"Jews get out, Jews get out, Jews get out!" The other four chanted, their shouts filling the room. They pumped their fists, raising them in solidarity.

One of the boys, the second to the oldest, looked familiar. Then Adam remembered. *I'll never forget that face.* On the day of the move to the Krakow ghetto, he was the one who threw a rock at Mina and hit her in the head. *Nothing has changed.* The Nazis were gone, but the seeds of hatred were planted and were flourishing.

"Out of the synagogue?" Adam flexed his hands around his cane, his fingers trembling.

"Out of Poland!" The oldest boy's lips curled back, his spittle flying. "We want you gone. You brought the Communists here and now things are worse than ever!"

Adam outwardly flinched, as though he had been slapped. It was the old antisemitic stereotype, that Jews were connected to Communism and they were out to control the world. Between the Great War and the recent one, fears of Jewish dominance through Communism cropped up in Poland. The Nazis adopted it to turn Christians and conservatives against Jews. And now it was back again. Or perhaps it never left.

"We're not going anywhere." Rabbi Rosenwieg replied evenly. "We have as much right to be here as you do. We're Polish and we've been here for generations. Neither of us are Communists, but even if we were, we still belong here."

"Lying Christ-killers!" The second oldest boy hissed.

"You need to leave." Adam pointed at the door.

The second oldest boy produced a knife and opening it, he

wielded it triumphantly. Light from the chandeliers glinted off the blade, and the boy's gritted teeth.

Adam raised his cane up, planning to use it as a weapon to defend himself. But one look at the boy and he lowered his cane back down. *I can't hit him, or any of them.* Hateful as they were behaving, they were stupid youths. The five didn't know any better. Like many in Poland, they took in antisemitism like they took in their mother's milk.

"Please, you don't have to do this." Rabbi Rosenwieg lifted his arms up in surrender, daring to approach the youths. "This isn't the way."

"Shut up!" The oldest boy dashed to the rabbi and punched the man in the eye.

Oh God! Adam didn't know if he was praying or not. He felt paralyzed. He couldn't flee, he couldn't defend himself, he couldn't beg for mercy. He could barely form coherent thoughts. *Sophie, Lidia, Ewa...* Would he ever see them again?

The boy with the knife closed in, moving at an excruciatingly slow pace.

A whimper escaped from Adam as the boy grabbed his shirt and ripped it open. When he felt the point pierce his flesh, everything went white.

Friday, 19 April 1946

Lidia's fingers curled around Father Cieslik's arm as they walked briskly through the hospital. They didn't dare run, or they would risk drawing unwanted attention to themselves. They hadn't done anything illegal, but after the NKVD's visit, and now this, she preferred to go unnoticed.

Three days.

That was how long it took for Father Cieslik to locate Mr. Altman and Rabbi Rosenwieg's whereabouts. Three days ago, Mr. Altman stepped out for an errand and never returned. It was three days of Lidia scouring the streets for her new husband. Three days of Sophie and Ewa sobbing themselves to sleep. Three days of living in the dark, uncertain if Mr. Altman was dead or alive. Three days of absolute terror. After what Adam went through to be reunited with Sophie, he wouldn't simply abandon his daughter. But until this morning, his whereabouts were a mystery.

During Mr. Altman's absence, she was overwhelmed with a multitude of feelings. Fear to sadness, to the realization she missed him during the time he was gone. At night, she couldn't sleep and she watched out the window in case he came home. Only now could she freely admit she liked Mr. Altman.

Father Cieslik called this morning, with news. Mr. Altman and Rabbi had been viciously attacked in the synagogue and they were currently recuperating at the hospital.

Lidia and the priest entered one of the overcrowded rooms. She nearly gagged from the pungent stench of filthy bodies, urine, feces, and blood. The war ended a year ago, yet people were still convalescing from illnesses, the camps, and local skirmishes. *Dear Jesus, this is sickening!* She pinched her nostrils together, and continued on with her mission.

"Over there!" Father Cieslik pointed to the bed at the far end. "I see Mr. Altman!"

Lidia rushed to her husband's side. He was pale and mussed up, but except for a little bruising on his left cheek, his outward appearance looked much the same as when she last saw him. Eyes closed and breathing shallow, he jerked when she perched on the side of his bed.

"Shh, it's all right." She murmured. "It's me."

Mr. Altman's eyes opened and he frantically fumbled for her hand. "Lidia!" His voice came out strangled.

"What happened? Father Cieslik said you and Rabbi Rosenwieg had been attacked." Lidia hazarded a glance at the rabbi, who happened to be in the bed next to Mr. Altman's.

The priest dragged over a chair and sat close to his friends. They joined hands and prayed. Despite the commotion of the other patients, she distinctly heard the rabbi say, "Thus saith the LORD; A voice was heard in Ramah, lamentation, and bitter weeping; Rachel weeping for her children refused to be comforted for her children, because they were not."

The two men of God wept together.

Lidia looked back at her husband and repeated her question.

"Just what the priest said." Mr. Altman rested his head against the dirt smudged pillow and shrugged. "These young men came into the synagogue and attacked us. There's nothing more to tell."

Odd. If she had been physically attacked and sent to the hospital, she would be in tears. Not her husband though. Mr. Altman's gaze was empty and he sounded strangely devoid of emotion. She suspected him to be in shock, detaching himself from the assault to cope. Which must have been what he did during the war. Or, he wished to spare her and the girls from fear. But since the war's end, incidents like this had occurred all over Krakow.

Lidia stroked the back of his hand, using her thumb to rub soothing circles. Her eyes dropped to a white bandage sticking out from his open collar. "Did they stab you?" she asked.

"One of them...cut me." Mr. Altman looked uncomfortable and used his free hand to cover the bandage. "He drew something on my chest, with a knife."

"What did he draw?" She swallowed.

"A Star of David."

She schooled her features to conceal her revulsion, to not upset him further. To think, a group of young men could be so cruel, so vicious. For a boy to carve a Star of David on her husband's chest...She could only thank God that Sophie and Ewa would never treat another soul like that. Why did some people turn out well, and others turn out wicked?

"I'm so sorry." Lidia lifted his knuckles to her lips and kissed them. "Is there anything I can do for you?"

Mr. Altman shook his head. "No. I'm glad you came though." He admitted, slowly exhaling. "The doctor said I could go home today. But please, don't tell the girls."

Lidia agreed, against her better judgment. Then she was reminded of her own secrets and could understand his wish to keep this private. At home, her husband would be in a cleaner environment and he would heal faster. His spirits would hopefully improve and he might eventually talk about what happened.

Home would be his refuge.

Thursday, 25 April 1946

Lidia's eyes flew open and she sat up in bed. The heel of Sophie's foot was jabbing into her ribs. Her daughter slept like a pretzel, contorting her body into odd shapes. Arm flung back, leg hitched up, and her rear end pointed to the ceiling. Ewa was also dead to the world, snoring. The girl could sleep through a bombing. According to her, she slept through the invasion of Poland in 1939, despite her father carrying her down to their cellar.

But their odd sleeping habits wasn't the reason Lidia woke.

It was her husband. The girls were blissfully unaware and she was grateful.

Mr. Altman was screaming in his sleep. *Again.* The first occurrence was a couple nights after their wedding. His shouts rang throughout the house, bleeding through the paper-thin walls. She initially thought someone broke into their apartment and was trying to murder him. Emotion slurred his speech, but she made out a few words about beatings and shootings. Whether the nightmare was about the ghetto or the camp he was in, she couldn't tell. But she believed this latest nightmare was connected to the attack at the synagogue. Though he was reluctant to speak of it, from what she understood from Father Cieslik and Rabbi Rosenwieg, the boys hadn't been caught and the attack was one of many that day. It was a pogrom. A tiny pogrom in a series of many pogroms.

Lidia shoved back the covers, slid out of bed, and crept into the sitting room. She stood before the religious icons on the wall and crossed herself, praying that God would take Mr. Altman's pain away. From personal experience, it took time for wounds to heal. Even then, bad memories didn't vanish entirely. Bad memories lurked in the crevices of one's mind, eager to pounce and destroy the joy one felt. Mr. Altman's lack of emotional response over the attack led into his subconscious. Only in his sleep could he express himself.

The door to Mr. Altman's room creaked and he shuffled out. He was disheveled, his sweat-dampened hair and wrinkled pajamas made him look like a different person. The pajama top had been carefully buttoned, to conceal the wound and bandage.

He stopped short when he saw her, and squeezed his cane.

"Mr. Altman, are you ill?" Lidia asked. It was easier to ask that than about the truth.

"No. Bad dream." His replies were stunted, his strength had been drained out during his nightmare. "Sorry if I woke you."

"Don't worry about that. I was thinking of having some tea. Would you like some?" Lidia didn't wait for him to respond and fled to the kitchen. She filled the tea kettle full of water and put it on the burner, before lighting the pilot light of the stove. "What did you dream of?"

"The attack at the synagogue." He trailed her, halting in the doorway. "And then Auschwitz."

She laid out two glasses and a couple of shriveled up tea leaves she had stored in the cabinet. When the kettle whistled, she removed it and poured the boiling liquid over the leaves, filling their glasses to the brim. They carried their glasses into the sitting room and settled on the divan.

"Cheers," Lidia wished him, gently bumping her glass against his.

"Cheers." He repeated.

Bitterness stung the tip of her tongue, but she continued to sip. The tea was stale without sugar, honey, or milk. Sugar, honey, and milk were reserved for other things. But tea was beneficial to unsettled nerves.

Mr. Altman scowled at the hot brew and blew on it.

"What was it like there?" Lidia asked. "In Auschwitz?"

"None of your business." No sooner had he answered, did he close his eyes and mournfully shake his head. "I can't talk about it, I'm sorry."

Lidia wasn't offended. He lashed out at others to prevent himself from being hurt. Years ago, she did the same. It took time for her to let others in.

"I met Mr. Sobieski once." Mr. Altman let his head rest on the back of the divan.

Lidia nearly dropped her glass and plunked it down on the coffee table. "What? When?" In the time they had been married, he gave no indication he had known Tadeusz. "Why didn't you say anything before?" she demanded.

"It wasn't the best first impression."

"Our first impressions of one another weren't good." She reminded him.

"Touché." He cracked a small smile. "That day you found Sophie, my wife Mina wasn't far off and she watched you take her in. I was able to figure out who you were and where you lived. I used to watch you, Mr. Sobieski, and Sophie go on errands or to church. The first time I saw you, you let a German Wehrmacht soldier hold Sophie. I was so angry."

"I was scared, I didn't know what to do." Lidia shivered, reliving some of her fear from that day. While there was little chance of the Nazis rising up again, deep down she worried that they would. "I feared Lt. Brühl wanted to Germanize her as they did with some Polish children." She sensed he was dying to know why the NKVD accused her of having an affair with the man. Mr. Altman was blunt if nothing else, and it was uncharacteristic that he never asked about it. "Father Cieslik rescued Jewish children during the war, and gave us papers for Sophie to hide as a Christian. This drew the attention of the Gestapo. Lt. Brühl was a friend, to me and to Father Cieslik. He provided us with an alibi to explain Tadeusz and my close friendship with the priest. He implied I was his mistress and under his protection."

"And the NKDV believes it to be true." Mr. Altman concluded.

"After Tadeusz died, Lt. Brühl visited and he did propose. But I turned him down."

"Lt. Brühl was a good German. I never used to think there was such a thing, but I was wrong." Mr. Altman admitted. "He helped me once too. He helped Rabbi Rosenwieg, Mina, and I survive the liquidation of the ghetto. Do you know what became of him?"

Lidia shook her head. When the two Russian boy soldiers escorted her and the girls to the church, she saw Lt. Brühl in a group of captured soldiers. Countless German officers and soldiers were sent eastward to the gulags in Siberia. Many Poles were taken too. No one inquired about those who went missing after the Russians invaded. Only God knew who the Communists would imprison next. Trials were rarely held and the prison in Krakow was filled to capacity. One could see the over flux of people in the cells from the street.

"Well," Mr. Altman went on. "Back to Mr. Sobieski. He caught me outside the ghetto, spying on you, and we scuffled. He figured out who I was and then offered to hide Mina and myself."

"You didn't accept?" Lidia couldn't hide her astonishment. Tadeusz never breathed a word of this.

"If Mina and I hid with you, if we had all been betrayed...I felt it wouldn't have been wise for a whole family to hide together. Would you have wanted us there?" He asked, with no trace of malice, indicating he knew what her answer would be.

"No. I would have feared that you would have run off with Sophie."

"And I would have." Mr. Altman took a swig and laid the glass down on the end table close to him. "But Mr. Sobieski, he was a good man."

Lidia reclined against the divan's cushion and observed Mr. Altman. There was so much about her new husband that she didn't know. He was trying to do better, but he had closed himself off as a means of defense and no longer knew how to act in this new world. She wished there was something she could do to help, but in a sense, he was like a veteran of war. Those who fought in battles never returned the same as when they left.

She debated on inquiring about his first wife. Mr. Altman had said she was dead, and hauntingly added, it *"was not a story for little girls."* Which was understandable. She kept Sophie sheltered from the realities of war. But she was curious about the first Mrs. Altman.

"May I ask about Mrs. Altman?" Lidia whispered. "Were you happy together?"

A shadow passed over him and he appeared to be on the brink of losing composure. "When times were good, we were happy. Mina made some choices I had trouble accepting. She...she suffered from bouts of severe melancholy. Manic depression, it was called." He blinked and his mouth twisted bitterly. "In Auschwitz, I was able to pass notes and I managed to meet her secretly once. I was afraid she would give up. But Mina fought with all of her strength to survive for Suzanne...for Sophie's sake. In the autumn of 1944, Mina was transported to Bergen-Belsen. She died of typhus, not long before the liberation."

"I'm so sorry." Before Lidia could stop herself, she threw her arms about his shoulders, drawing him into a hug. "I wish I knew what to say to make it better." She mumbled in the crook of his neck.

His arms were slow to encircle her, but then he clung to her like his life depended on it. Soon he was sobbing hard enough that his whole body convulsed, leaving her to wonder if this was the first time he had broken down since his arrival in Krakow.

The next time Lidia stirred, she was lying upon a pliable surface. She nuzzled into it, seeking out further warmth. A spicy scent filled her nostrils as she inhaled. *Cologne?* She eased herself up, squinted, and her cheeks flushed. She had been stretched out on top of Mr. Altman, having spent most of the night sleeping with him.

Lidia placed her hand on his chest, feeling the bandage beneath the pajama shirt. She hoped she hadn't harmed his wound.

He was asleep and looked peaceful, his breathing was evenly paced as his arms were about her waist. There was no sign of his earlier distress.

She considered joining him once more when she heard a girlish giggle a few feet away.

"Mrs. Altman?"

Lidia blushed under Ewa's playful scrutiny, wishing she could dig a hole and drop in.

"Ma'am, did you sleep well?" Ewa asked.

Lidia disentangled herself from Mr. Altman, and brushing past the girl, she ran to the w. c. There was no chance that Ewa would keep this to herself.

Chapter Twenty-Five

Adam stormed up the sidewalk to the flat, his ankle protesting the whole way. Rather than spend the day with his family, or attend services at the synagogue, he wasted the entire Saturday seeking work only to be rejected. He was ashamed that Lidia worked herself to the bone while he was at home. It didn't sit right with his conscience.

"Mr. Altman, you're skilled with the needle, but with things as they are...The Jewish situation, we can't hire you." Was the general response, no matter where he turned. One of the men, who had been one of his business competitors before the war, flippantly remarked, *"So you're still alive?"*

When he was in the hospital in Switzerland, he had been warned that returning to Poland wouldn't be easy. Since he witnessed the worst, he thought he could handle it. The ghettos and camps no longer functioned, but the ghostly presence of what occurred still plagued Krakow. The same old hatred was simmering to the surface. The pogrom at the synagogue shook him up, he did his best to put it behind him. Like Auschwitz, it couldn't be dwelt upon every second of the day.

Adam barely crossed the threshold when Sophie propelled herself at him. She did that whenever he was gone, even for a short period of time. No doubt it stemmed from his five-year absence and his recent three-day disappearance during that pogrom.

She waved a sheet of paper. "Look what I made!" When he didn't instantly praise it, she shrieked, "Papa!"

"Not now, Sophie!" Adam cupped his ear to protect it from her high-pitched squeals. "All right?" He didn't realize how harsh he sounded until she retreated like a whipped dog to the main bedroom.

Ewa glared from the kitchen table, where she was slicing potatoes. The girl was rarely in a black mood, but then again, he was never impatient towards her little sister before.

"Being a parent doesn't depend on one's moods." Lidia took her own knife and stuck it into the cutting board. She approached; arms crossed. "You can't shut Sophie out because you had an awful day."

"I know, I'm sorry." He didn't dare argue, because she was absolutely right.

"No. Apologize to your daughter, not me." She pointed at the closed bedroom door. "Go."

"Right." Adam meekly nodded.

He headed to the room, surprised he was permitted in there. Since he moved in, Lidia forbade him from entering the bedroom. She never explained why. They argued a number of times over it, but he complied with his wife's wishes. For whatever reason, it was important to her.

Adam knocked lightly on the door and went in when he heard his daughter's muffled, "Come in."

Sophie was on the floor, by the foot of the bed. Her face was dry and she wasn't sniffing, which was a relief. He would never have forgiven himself if he made his little girl cry. In spite of all of his love for Sophie, he didn't know how to be a father.

Adam hesitated, unsure of how to begin. He had done his share of apologizing over the years, but never to a child. "Sophie, may I join you?" When she shrugged, he winced from pain as he lowered himself beside her. "I'm sorry for how I treated you. I wasn't upset with you. Papa is sorry."

"Why were you mad?" she asked, raising her head up.

"Well, I went looking for a job today." He tried to think of an easy way to explain how things were in the world for Jews. Unfortunately, there was no easy explanation. The truth would have to suffice. "But no one wanted to hire me because I'm Jewish and that hurt me deeply."

"People want you dead because you're a Jew." She concluded.

"Yes." Adam nodded. He hadn't realized she knew what happened to him. Lidia sheltered her, yet Sophie's small ears took in everything. "Now, what was it that you wanted to show me?" He asked, hoping to distract her.

Sophie pulled a crinkled sheet of paper out from under the bed. "I made this of us at the park." She laid it in his lap.

The four of them were in a line, holding hands, they had "u's" for smiles, and they had no necks. But as far as he was concerned, it was perfect.

"Beautiful. My little artist." He drew her close, resting his chin on top of her head. "Your mother, Mina, was an artist too."

"Am I like Mother Mina?" Sophie wondered.

She was enough like her mother for it to be sweet. But if she resembled Mina more, it would have been painful. He hoped the girl wouldn't inherit her mother's melancholy.

"Some. I think you're like both sets of your parents. You have Mina's talents and my stubbornness. You have your current mother's faith and I think you have Papa Sobieski's goodness. You have the best of all of us inside of you." He planted a kiss on the crown of her head.

"Do you want to watch me draw?" She asked.

"I'd love nothing more." Adam replied, and spent the remainder of the afternoon by her side.

"Mr. Altman?" Lidia murmured, drawing him back to reality. She was in her chair by the fireplace, staring at him expectantly. "What happened today?"

Sophie and Ewa went to bed earlier than they did. Lately, he and Lidia spent their evenings talking about the past, the years before the way. They came from separate worlds, but their differences complemented one another. These conversations gave him the opportunity to get to know her better, and to figure a few things out. She hadn't brought it up, but the night he had his latest nightmare, she comforted him...and they fell asleep together on the divan.

He woke in the early hours of the morning, to find Lidia curled against him, her hair tickling his nose. His chest throbbed, but he didn't care. If he could wake up to that every morning, it would be a dream come true. He nodded off, toying with the ends of her hair.

Adam dragged his chair closer to hers, regretting that they weren't sitting on the divan, that way they could sleep together again. Her soft body pressed into his, their breathing falling in sync. Much as he longed to be intimate with her, he kept to himself. Lidia didn't view him in a romantic way. But to hold her and to be held, that would be enough.

"I couldn't find work today. No one would hire me because I'm Jewish." Adam admitted.

"I'm sorry. I hoped...never mind." She shook her head, sighing. "I can continue on at the factory until the situation improves."

"The situation isn't going to improve, not for a while. Maybe not ever." He said. She had taken his surname and she was sympathetic to his plight, but she didn't understand what it was like to be Jewish. She never would. "I have to find work. It's not fair or proper for you to carry the burden of this family on your own."

She and the girls deserved better. They never complained or asked for more than what he could offer. But after all they had been through, they deserved security.

"Family is never a burden." Lidia said.

"So, we're family now?" Adam felt his throat constrict, which for him, was a prelude to tears.

"Well, we're married, Mr. Altman." Lidia dropped her gaze to her fingers, lacing them together. "We share a child. Two children, really."

"If that's the case, please call me Adam."

"Very well. You may call me Lidia."

Adam scooted forward in his seat. "Lidia, do you think we can call a truce? That we could be allies in raising Sophie and Ewa?" He wanted more, he wanted everything with her. But for now, he would settle for friendship.

"It won't work, but we should try." Lidia said, and was quick to add, "For the girl's sake."

"Why wouldn't it work?" Adam lifted his brow. If there was something she didn't like, about him or their lives, he would change it. He'd do whatever possible to make her happy.

"For the simple reason that we can't make it through a whole day without arguing." Lidia hid a laugh. "We come from different worlds and we have different beliefs, we're bound to clash. But, as I said, we must try."

"So...truce?" Adam held out his hand.

"Truce." Her small hand disappeared inside of his.

Following the old Polish custom of a gentleman's introduction to a lady, Adam gave a slight bow and kissed the back of her hand.

He wished their first meeting had been better, that he hadn't acted harsh and rude. None of the past could be changed, but he could do his utmost to ensure that his family had a bright present and future.

Sunday, 19 May 1946

Lidia shook Father Cieslik's hand as she and Sophie departed from the church, complimenting him on his thought-provoking sermon. The priest thanked her for her kind words, and with a ghost of a smile on his lips, he motioned across the road.

She looked that way and was surprised to see Adam and Ewa sitting on a bench and waving. Her husband was in a gray suit, crisp white dress shirt, blackened shoes, and a trilby hat. His weak leg was crossed over his stronger one, his foot bobbing. Sophie did the same foot bobbing tick whenever she was idle.

Ewa fidgeted, unable to contain her enthusiasm.

What are you two doing here? Lidia wondered.

Adam and Ewa stayed home whenever she and Sophie attended church. When they returned home from Mass, he would have lunch ready and afterwards the four of them would take a stroll in Planty Park. She had to take her hat off to Adam; he wasn't like most men. Tadeusz never cooked for her until he fell ill; he never cleaned the house or ran errands. Infuriating as Adam could be, it didn't bother him to do chores that generally were considered women's chores.

Lidia grabbed Sophie's hand and they hurried across the road. Adam and Ewa stood when they reached the other side.

"Papa, Ewa, why are you here?" Sophie asked.

For once, Lidia was grateful for her daughter's bluntness.

"I was thinking, after lunch, we could go shopping." Adam's mischievous expression betrayed the fact that he had something up his sleeve. "If your mother is agreeable to it, there's a shopkeeper I know who is open today."

The majority of shops were closed on Sunday, for no Catholic would work on the Lord's Day. There were a few exceptions, leading her to wonder if the shop owner was Jewish.

"Of course. Go and I'll see you later." Lidia nodded, ushering Sophie towards her father. She long since overcame her paranoia of leaving the child alone with Adam. He wouldn't harm a hair on their daughter's head.

"No, I meant all four of us." Adam caught her wrist before she could walk off.

Lidia blushed. The last thing she wanted was for Adam to feel like he should buy things for her. She wasn't his responsibility. "I don't need anything." Her teeth sank into her lower lip.

"Yes, you do." Adam loosened his grasp and slid his hand downwards, giving her fingers a tiny squeeze. "I don't wish to be insulting, but you do."

Lidia was close to tears. In his own awkward way, he was being thoughtful. She wasn't offended...she was embarrassed. Sweat prickled her skin and her once white frock – which had faded to a dingy yellow – cleaved to her flesh. She bought it a month or two before the war, and she wore it for every special occasion. Sophie's baptism, every confession and Mass, and the day she married Adam.

Is he ashamed of me? She fretted. Adam wore a suit every day, bathed every night, and always looked presentable. When she first met him, his bones poked out at all of the wrong angles, his complexion was pasty, and he sported a constant grimace. But since he moved in, he had regular meals and he filled out. His eyes were brighter and he smiled and teased more.

"Please, mama! We'll have fun." Sophie latched onto her sleeve and tugged.

Lidia agreed, unable to refuse her daughter's pleas, disregard Adam's beseeching expression, or Ewa's puffed out cheeks from holding her breath.

After they had lunch, he brought them to a shop in Kazimierz, which had been the old Jewish district before the war. The shop owner invited them in to explore his merchandise. There were ready-made pieces, along with bolts of material, shoes, boots, stockings, underclothes...whatever one might need.

Lidia casually toured the shop, impressed by its set up and she worked her way back to the front.

Sophie jammed her feet into a new pair of shoes and tottered around.

"Do they feel all right? Not too tight?" Adam asked, observing her gait.

"I love them!" The little girl exclaimed, skipping through the store.

"Ewa, have you found anything?" Adam faced the older girl.

"This is nice." Ewa was holding a skirt, measuring it to her legs. It barely hit her knees.

"Can't you find something longer?" He stammered. "Boys get ideas."

Ewa rolled her eyes, put it back, and selected a different, longer skirt. She looked to him for approval.

"Yes, that's better." He said.

"Adam," Lidia grabbed her husband's elbow and led him a few feet off. "How can you afford this?" She questioned. There was money in the jar he excavated from Planty Park, but surely it didn't amount enough to fund a shopping trip.

"I have a job here now as a tailor. My employer offered me a nice deal." He explained. "And I sold my mother's jewelry."

Lidia was horrified. Adam didn't have much from his life

before the war. All of his worldly goods could fit inside an average sized rucksack. The last thing she wanted was to benefit from his sacrifice.

"You shouldn't have done that!" She cried out. "That was your mother's legacy to you and Sophie."

Adam rested his hands on her shoulders. "My mother would have wanted for granddaughters and daughter-in-law to be provided for." He leaned forward, his lips inches from her ear. His warm breath tickled as he whispered, "You're my wife, let me do this for you. Please."

Lidia's heart skipped a beat. She wasn't naïve, things were changing between them. Between the NKVD visit and the attack at the synagogue, they had become friends. And in the last few weeks, Adam seemed to be pursuing her romantically.

Lidia stifled a sob. "I'll never be able to repay you." Despite her resolve, her voice was squeaky.

"You saved my daughter's life; you raised her and loved her." Adam's arms encircled her, drawing her close. He rubbed her back as she buried her face into his shoulder and cried. "If anything, I'm in your debt. Please."

She parted and nodded, wiping away her tears.

Lidia walked away with two new dresses, a set of underclothing, a new pair of shoes, a hat, and gloves. She insisted on carrying her own purchases, that way her husband wouldn't be weighed down. Ewa toted her own; it had been the first time in a long time since she had been shopping. He still had to manage his cane, but he was determined to carry Sophie's bags.

The four left the shop and were on their way to the apartment when Sophie stopped in the middle of the sidewalk.

"Look, books!" The little girl pointed towards a shop.

"Yes, Mrs. Altman loves books!" Ewa cheered.

"No, don't even think about it." Lidia shot Adam a look.

His mouth swung open, but reconsidered what he was going to say and pressed his lips into a thin, determined line.

What would it be like to kiss him? The thought came to her as they continued on home.

Lidia didn't know where to store her new purchases. Oh, she had ample space but it had been years since she received such fine presents. She wanted to put them where she could gaze upon them whenever she wished. She didn't dare throw out her older frocks; they could be used for everyday wear.

She opened her dresser drawer and took out one of her new brassieres. Her old ones were tattered bits of material, safety-pinned together where the hooks broke off. How long had she needed new underclothes? One couldn't afford such luxuries, not when there were two growing girls in the house. She had turned three different shades of red when he encouraged her to pick out what she needed.

I wonder if Adam would like to see me in them? She had never been prone to lust after various men. Most men repulsed her. Tadeusz was the only one she ever looked at, the only one she wanted to share a bed with.

Adam was different from Tadeusz in nearly every way imaginable. It only stood to reason that he made love differently too.

Lidia returned the brassiere to the drawer and closed it. She left the bedroom and rushed to the icons on the sitting room wall, making the Sign of the Cross. *Mea Culpa, Queen of Heaven!* Her musings weren't sinful per se, considering she and Adam were man and wife. But it felt like a betrayal to Tadeusz's memory, and the love she once had for him.

The front door opened and Adam came in, a square package tucked under his arm. "Sorry." He looked sheepish. "I didn't mean to interrupt."

"You're not. I'm finished." Lidia smiled and hoped he wouldn't inquire what she was praying about.

Adam stood beside her, gazing upon Jesus, I Trust in You and the Black Madonna of Czestochowa. "May I ask, how is it after everything you have seen and experienced, that you have faith?" He then gave her a sideways glance, seeming genuinely interested in her thoughts.

"I don't think I can explain my faith. But in my darkest moments, the Lord has offered me hope." She sighed, feeling guilt swelling inside of her. God had answered so many prayers over the years, yet she couldn't answer her husband's simple question. "What about you?" She noticed his fingers tightened around the handle of his cane and she covered his hand with hers.

"Well, before the war, I was a skeptic and I still am, really." Adam freely admitted. "If there is a God, He wasn't there with us in Auschwitz. He turned His Back on us there."

She touched his jaw, to let him know she cared, and to bring him a little comfort. He was a lost soul, yearning to be found. His thoughts and feelings had to be respected though. Certainly, she believed God was with them in all circumstances. However, she never experienced the ghetto or Auschwitz. If she had, in all likelihood her faith would be shaken.

Her eyes lowered to the package he had beneath his arm. "What is that?" she pointed.

Adam smiled and held it out to her. On closer inspection, she realized it had to be a book.

Lidia shook her head. "No, take it back!" The clothing she needed, but a book in times like these, was an extravagance. "The money could be used towards groceries or rent."

"Just take it, I want you to have it. Please." He tore back the paper wrapping and showed her the cover. "'The Blue Castle.' It is by the same author of that other book you own, 'Anne of Green Gables.'" He stated, as if that would make a difference.

Lidia brought her hand up to refuse and was about to list her reasons why, when an onslaught of tears overtook her. She didn't know why, but she suddenly remembered when Tadeusz sold most of her books before he fell ill. In a small way, Adam was giving her something back.

Adam laid the book aside and coaxed her in a hug, pressing a kiss in the midst of her hair.

Chapter Twenty-Six

Thursday, 6 June 1946

Adam's fingertips were throbbing as he strolled up to the apartment. He used a sewing machine for the majority of his work. However, some select pieces required the stitching to be done by hand. A thimble helped, but he did occasionally jab himself. On entering the apartment, he froze when he heard sniffing. He followed the sound and found Sophie perched on the kitchen counter, her legs dangling in the sink. Lidia was pouring water over the child's feet, washing blood away.

"I shouldn't have let her do it." Ewa hugged herself, her features scrunched up as she cried. "I'm sorry."

"What happened?" Adam asked.

"Papa, I hurt myself." Two large tear drops rolled down Sophie's cheek.

He removed his jacket and rolled up his sleeves, eager to be helpful. Other than handing Lidia what she required, he didn't do much than stand there dumbly. Tending to his own wounds was easy, but he was useless when it came to dealing with a hurt little girl.

"I didn't mean to take my eyes off of her." Ewa fell into hysterics and flung herself into his arms. "Honest!"

"It's all right." Adam returned her embrace, guiding the young woman back a couple of steps. "No one blames you."

Ewa nodded, but looked unconvinced.

Lidia tisked her tongue at Sophie. "Someone ran through the streets without wearing her shoes." She dabbed the cut with an alcohol-soaked cloth, and then wound a bandage around the small foot.

"You should have been wearing your shoes." Adam scolded. Never before had he sounded so…paternal. When his wife didn't correct him, he came to the conclusion that he was in the right. "I bought those shoes for a reason. Wear them when you go outside from now on."

"Yes, papa."

"Your foot will be sore for a bit, but it will heal." Lidia said, drying her hands on a dish towel.

Sophie wiggled her fingers at Adam. She wrapped her arms around his neck, her legs around his legs, and clung to him. He carried her while leaning on his cane. That was the only way he could physically move her from one place to another.

He dropped into a chair in the sitting room, situating Sophie on his knee.

"Will I have a scar?" Sophie asked.

"We'll have to wait and see." Lidia replied, scrubbing down the kitchen counter.

Ewa collected the bandages and the alcohol and returned them to the w. c.

"Papa, what is that?" Sophie grabbed his arm and twisted it around.

The bluish string of numbers stood out on his skin.

Adam's chest constricted. He felt as though his ribs were stabbing his organs. No one outside of Auschwitz had ever seen his tattoo, except for the doctors and nurses in Switzerland.

But after he left for Poland, he wore long sleeves, no matter the weather. This was far more mortifying than the Star of David on his chest. At least that could be hidden from the rest of the world.

"Sophie," Lidia swept into the room. "Little girls shouldn't ask such questions."

"I've seen other Jews have numbers like that." Ewa said, joining them.

He resisted the impulse to cover himself back up. They were a family, but there was much he kept from them. Often the words wouldn't come. But Sophie's discovery of his death number, it could be his way to share part of his story. A small part, but it was a start.

"No, it's all right." Adam motioned Lidia over and she edged closer. If he were going to share this with his daughters, he needed to share it with his wife too. "This is called a tattoo. For some of the war, I was in a camp called Auschwitz, which is near the town of Oswiecim. The camp was like a prison, and the Nazis...the Nazis killed people there. The Nazis decided that I should live and to keep track of me, and other prisoners, they put numbers on our arms. It's ink in the skin. Here, feel it."

"It won't come off!" Sophie poked at his forearm. "May I have numbers too?"

Ewa gasped loudly.

Adam closed his eyes and counted to ten. He wasn't angry, but the thought of Sophie in Auschwitz haunted continued to haunt him. If Mina hadn't made the choice that she made... Sophie never would have lasted to the quarantine stage. They would have sent her left and she would have suffocated to death in a gas chamber. Ewa might have made it past the quarantine stage, however, sensitive girl that she was, she would have died an early death. Lidia would have lasted longer, but not by much. He was one of the rare few who survived any length of time in Auschwitz.

"Sophie!" Lidia put her finger to her lips.

"Sorry." Sophie lowered his head. "The numbers are bad?"

"Very bad." Adam admitted.

Sophie leaned in and pressed a kiss to his cheek. "Does that make it better?"

"More than you can imagine." Adam nodded, and kissed her cheek in return.

Minutes later, the tattoo was forgotten. Sophie went to play with her doll on the floor. Ewa joined her, but he sensed the older girl watching him. The dinner that followed was nearly as awkward as the first dinner he shared with them. Sophie and Ewa chatted, but Lidia was peculiarly quiet. She spent most of the meal nudging her potatoes back and forth on her plate with her fork.

Does my number disgust her? Adam's stomach rolled, and unable to eat another bite, he laid his utensil down.

While Lidia tucked Sophie and Ewa in for the night, Adam lingered by the window, gazing at the moon, watching as gray wisps of clouds swam in front of it. The moon, the stars, the whole sky was so clear and bright compared to what it had been in Auschwitz. There was no reddish smoke to drown it out. Sometimes when he looked at the stars, it was difficult to believe such evil occurred in the world. The serene night sky banished a multitude of troubles.

"Adam?"

He spun around too quickly and grimaced when he wrenched his ankle.

"I'm sorry about-" Lidia approached cautiously, eyes widened.

"No, it's all right." He dragged his leg, wincing from the pain, and met her in the middle of the room. "She didn't understand. Neither did Ewa, really."

"I'm not sure I do either." Lidia confessed, softly.

"No one does, not even me." He shrugged hopelessly.

"May I touch it?"

Adam was too shocked to form an audible reply. So, Lidia wasn't revolted by it. She pitied him.

"I'm sorry, I can be as thoughtless as Sophie sometimes." She started to back away.

"Wait." Adam rasped, his mouth and throat was dry.

He unbuttoned his cuff, rolled up his sleeve to the elbow, and extended his arm to her. He nearly bit through his tongue as her fingers stroked, like a delicate brush of feathers. Except for when they kissed during the wedding ceremony, they hadn't been intimate. Inches apart, the temptation became too great.

Adam grazed his lips against hers. It was innocent but it left him breathless.

Lidia let out a gasp, but she didn't retreat. To his delight, she settled her hands on his shoulders.

"Forgive me, I want you." He said.

"What?" She whispered, her chest heaving.

"I want you." Adam repeated, licking his lips, savoring the flavor of her. Sweet and perfect. "I can't help it." He ventured to cradle her cheek, thumbing along her jawline.

"I want you too." Lidia answered, rising up on tiptoe until their lips met.

The next thing he knew, they were in his room and he was falling on top of her in bed.

Lidia slipped the buttons through the holes of his white dress shirt and opened it. The shame he had of the Star of David wound was dispelled when she ran her fingers over its puckered ridges. *Reading the braille of my skin.*

Her arms slid around his neck and she drew his head down and kissed him once more. Considering they were in bed together, he expected more than the simple kisses she was giving him. Then he realized Lidia had no concept of any other kind of kissing. Tadeusz must have never...

Adam nudged her lips apart, dipped his tongue within, making her moan and shover. He let his hands wonder, gentle touches at first before he grew bolder. He pulled back for a moment and smiled shyly.

Lidia was panting, her lips swollen and the pupils of her eyes were large. A cherry red flush broke out across her cheeks and flooded downwards, disappearing beneath the collar of her dress.

He kissed her once more and fumbled with the buttons on her bodice. Her body tensed and she was breathing harder.

Lidia let out a yelp and shoved him off, slipping out of the bed. She was clutching her bodice together, quivering from head to toe. He wondered if she was going to faint.

"Lidia?" Adam sat up, bewildered. "What? What is it?" He scooted to the side of the bed.

"I- I have to go." She held up her hand. "I'm sorry, Adam."

"Wait, talk to me." He pleaded. "Please!"

Lidia shook her head, flung the door open and rushed out. He heard her duck into the larger bedroom, where the girls were.

What just happened? Adam raked his fingers through his hair and rebuttoned his shirt.

He wasn't stupid. Something was wrong. Terribly wrong. Prisoners in Auschwitz wore similar traumatized expressions.

Someone had hurt Lidia.

Saturday, 12 July 1946

Lidia reread the letter a second time and then a third, concealing it between the pages of "The Blue Castle." While she looked it over in her chair by the fireplace, Sophie, Ewa, and Adam were sprawled on the floor playing with dolls.

The letter was from her mother. Roland, her step-father, had died. The cancer had eaten away at his organs and he died a long, agonizing death. Never one to wish evil on another, she couldn't help but feel that his illness was justified. The letter arrived a couple days ago and she just now worked up the courage to read it. In the past, Tadeusz handled her mother and Roland, but now that he was gone, she was on her own with this.

Adam wasn't aware of her past and she intended to keep it that way. He wouldn't understand. *Who could? Who could accept me as I am?* Tadeusz had, and that was one of the reasons she thought the world of him. Tadeusz was a good man, kind and fiercely protective, but her love for him had been a youthful love. He rescued her from a bad situation. But with Adam, it was different. The thickest onion didn't have as many layers as he did. A stubborn, argumentative, cynical man, he was also thoughtful and considerate. He voluntarily did "women's work" and bloodied his fingers daily to provide for his family. Adam would live and die for those he loved.

But he would be disgusted by her past.

Her skin blistered with heat, sweat broke out over her body. She longed to fan herself, but didn't wish to draw attention. She never used the word *molested*. Or *raped*. Not in regards to herself. Refusing to think along those lines, she put the memories out of her mind and functioned like that for years. It was the only way she could cope.

Lidia flinched when the front window facing the street shattered and a rock soared through the room. Glass splintered everywhere, raining shards down on Sophie, Ewa, and Adam. She flung the book aside and dove, throwing body over the girls to shield them from whatever else might be thrown into the house.

Adam was the first to come to his senses. He tugged on her arm and drove her and the girls to the w. c. "Go, go on!" He shouted.

The second she and the girls were in the windowless little room, he closed the door, and braved the perpetrators on his own. She regretted not staying with him, but she couldn't leave the girls alone.

"What happened, mama?" Sophie asked. "Who did that?"

"I don't know." Lidia attempted to sound nonchalant. "I'm sure it was an accident."

"But Mrs. Altman-" Ewa shut her mouth when Lidia shushed her.

Of course it wasn't an accident, but she didn't want to frighten the smaller girl. Thoughts went to the Polish gang of boys that attacked Adam and Rabbi Rosenwieg at the synagogue. Could they have discovered where Adam lived and did this to continue their harassment? Or was it someone else? Either way, she and Adam let their guard down.

Tiny glass crystals twinkled in Sophie's and Ewa's hair. Lidia unplaited the smaller girl's braids and had her shake the bits out. Ewa did the same to her own. She had the girls undress and change into their nightgowns; in case any glass was embedding in their clothing. Despite the early hour, she ordered the girls to bed. Ewa took Sophie and grudgingly led her to the main bedroom.

Lidia returned to the sitting room, but Adam wasn't there. She heard his voice through the broken window and went outside. A police officer was scribbling down information, but he seemed nonplussed when informed of the pogrom Adam had been swept up in in April.

"Incidents like this are happening all over Krakow. All over Poland too." The officer commented aloud. "Unless you can identify who did it, I doubt there is anything we can do about it."

This country isn't safe for your kind now." He tipped his cap and bid them a good evening.

Adam was crestfallen after the officer departed. Clutching the rock in his hand, he returned inside and she followed. He wandered into the kitchen and listlessly slumped into his customary chair. Without saying a word, he passed the rock to her.

Pasted to it was a sheet of paper, bearing the words, *"Jews, get out of Poland!"* It wasn't a confirmation that the culprit was the gang of Polish youths, but she believed it was too coincidental for her tastes.

"I'm sorry, Adam." Lidia's hand flew to her mouth.

Her husband was wearing the hardened expression that he wore when she first met him. "I had hoped things would be better now that the war was over." Bitterness laced his words. "I had hoped they would never strike us at home."

Lidia reached over and pressed his hand. She wished she could encourage him, but what could she offer but false hope? Pogroms were cropping up all over Poland. Christians were murdering Jews who returned for their property, property that the Christians claimed as their own. Spring and summer had been rife with killings. Some Jews had been shot, others who were traveling were abducted and tortured before being murdered. Twelve were killed attempting to cross into Czechoslovakia.

These incidents reminded her of the pogrom that struck Krakow in August of 1945. Polish youths had thrown rocks into a synagogue on Miodowa Street, interrupting services. When confronted, a riot broke out. Christians attacked the Jews in the synagogue and violence spread to the streets. The number of innocent men and women murdered had never been determined. Ewa had been visiting a neighbor girl when the news of the pogrom rippled through the neighborhood.

Lidia had Sophie hide under the bed, until she found Ewa and brought her home, thankfully unharmed.

But Lidia never expected hatred to come to her door.

"You, Sophie, and Ewa would be safer without me." Adam concluded, starting to pull away.

"Stop it!" She exclaimed, her hold on him tightening. "You can't abandon Sophie, she needs you. She already lost one father; she can't lose another. Ewa is attached to you; she considers you her adoptive father." She shut her eyes and added in a breathless murmur, "I can't lose you either. I need you."

Lidia considered this a miracle. Not so long ago, she wanted nothing more than for Adam to renounce his claim on Sophie. To leave and never return. And now...now he was the father of her daughters; he was her husband, partner, friend...and perhaps more.

Her lashes fluttered open when he touched her cheek.

Adam was gazing intently at her. "To stay in Poland is suicide. Forty Jews perished in that pogrom in Kielce. It could easily happen here." He stated.

The Kielce pogrom...the radio reported that a Christian boy in Kielce had gone missing for a day and when he returned, he told everyone that Jews had held him captive. According to the boy, the Jews were going to sacrifice him and use his blood to mix in their *matzah*. That story wasn't a new one; it had its origins in the Middle Ages. Despite living in this modern age, people still believed the tale to be true. The village of Kielce turned against the Jews, many of whom were camp survivors, and over forty Jews were murdered. When news spread of what happened there, the Jews of Poland were eager to escape. Many had already begun to flee. Bishops and clergymen refused to condemn the attack in the official pastoral letter. Then, Polish primate Cardinal August Hlond issued a statement declaring the Jews to be at fault for the pogrom. This new wave of anti-Semitism was never going to end.

"*Ha-Shoah* could happen again. That's what Rabbi Rosenwieg calls what happened to us Jews during the war." Adam explained, reclining back in his seat. "We can't stay in Poland."

Lidia nodded. Now that they all used Altman as their surname, it would only be a matter of time before something worse happened. Something worse than a rock through a window. Worse than a beating and a star carved into her husband's chest. They should have left after Adam was attacked. To stay was tempting fate.

"I understand. Do you have relatives abroad?" Lidia asked.

"Yes, in America. I have an American cousin who tried to help Mina and I to immigrate before the war."

Lidia never considered living in another country. She always assumed she would live out her days in Poland and eventually die there, as her first husband, father, grandparents, and great-grandparents had done before her.

"It will take time for me to locate them. The four of us could begin anew." Adam dipped his head, averting his gaze. "Would you be willing to leave your homeland?" He sounded uncertain and she felt sorry for him.

Adam had no idea where she stood and that was her fault. The kisses and caresses they shared a month ago, Lidia enjoyed it and thought she was ready for more. Tadeusz had been so... perfunctory in his love making that when Adam took charge, it frightened her. Beneath all of Adam's reserve was an unchecked passion. Unused to it, she fled and abandoned him. The next morning, she acted as if nothing changed and he never brought it up, taking his cue from her.

"'For whither thou goest, I will go; and where thou lodgest, I will lodge: thy people shall be my people, and thy God my God.'" Lidia glanced at her old wedding band, the one Tadeusz had given her. She gingerly removed it from her finger and laid it on the table, nudging it aside. Asking for strength from Above, she placed her hands in Adam's. "'Where thou diest, will I die, and there will I be buried: the Lord do so to me, and more also, if ought but death part thee and me.'"

Adam's eyes glistened. He lifted her hands to his lips and repeatedly kissed her knuckles.

Lidia retrieved "The Blue Castle," from the floor, took the letter out and handed it to him to read. "Until you do find your relatives, there is a place we can go that is more secluded." She suggested. "My mother's farm."

She had vowed to never return to that hellhole. But Roland was dead, and now that she had Adam and the girls' safety to think of, the farm would suit them temporarily. No one would learn what happened to her there when she was young and Mother wouldn't speak a word about it.

"Why didn't you say anything?" Adam scanned the letter, his jaw dropped. "You have my condolences."

"We can stay and work there until we can escape." Lidia said, avoiding his question.

Adam paused, mulling it over in his mind. "I know nothing of planting or harvesting." He said slowly. "You would have to instruct me in everything."

"A chance to order you about? Sounds like heaven." Lidia teased.

Adam smiled and quickly sobered. "The sooner we leave, the better."

She agreed. Soon enough, this would all be over.

Chapter Twenty-Seven

Tuesday, 22 July 1946

Lidia stood opposite of Tadeusz's grave, her old wedding band lying in the palm of her hand. She couldn't fathom how it had come to this. She and her family were leaving Krakow for...forever. Years ago, she came to the city as an enthusiastic eighteen-year-old, her head full of dreams. Nothing quite worked out the way she planned. None of that mattered, not since she had Sophie, Ewa, and Adam.

"Where will I go, Mrs. Altman?" Ewa asked, after she and Adam announced their plans of eventually leaving Poland.

"With us, of course." Lidia assured the girl. That Ewa thought they would leave her behind, was heart-wrenching. "You're our girl now."

"May I call you mama and papa?" Ewa clasped her hands together. "May I be an Altman too?"

"We would like nothing more." Adam leaned forward and kissed her brow.

Between preparing for the move, packing their belongings, selling things they wouldn't need, the last few weeks were chaotic. She scarcely had a moment to catch her breath, let alone consider the recent changes. In the midst of all of this she realized something.

I love Adam. When she precisely fell in love with him and how, she couldn't be certain. Maybe it was when they first kissed at their wedding, but she was in denial of it. Or during one of their arguments. When he saved her from the NKVD, or bought her clothes and a book. The other afternoon, "Por Una Cabeza" played on the radio and he invited her to dance awkwardly to it.

But yesterday evening they were washing up the dishes, he was sharing a memory of his childhood with her. His father was largely absent when he was growing up, but when he was young, he pretended his father was a revolutionary who played a hand in resurrecting Poland as a country. He was in the middle of his tale and as she observed his playfully boyish expression, it dawned on her that she was in love with this stubborn, strong, complicated man. And she wasn't entirely sure what to do about it.

Sophie's giggles drew her out of her musings. Her daughter showed no interest in visiting her adoptive father's grave, preferring to chat with her father, sister, Father Cieslik, and Rabbi Rosenwieg. Lidia didn't want to push it, believing Tadeusz would understand. For Sophie, he was the past and Adam was the future.

The crop of bright yellow tropaeolum that they planted now flourished and splayed across the ground. Its fresh scent tickled her nose. Plump bees floated from one blossom to the other, purring affectionately.

Lidia felt a lump forming in her throat. "Tadek, so much has changed since I last visited." The last time she paid her respects was the Sunday before Adam showed up on their doorstep. She used to visit faithfully every week after Mass, speaking to Tadeusz as though he were beside her. But Adam's arrival changed all of that. "Sophie is growing up. The war didn't touch her and for that I'm grateful. I can only pray she remains innocent and happy. You never met Ewa, but she is silly and clumsy, messy and perfect. To think, I thought I'd never have another child, but I do. I'm married to Sophie's birth father, Adam Altman, and I hope you understand why. I didn't like him at first, but he is a good man." She would give just about anything to know what Tadeusz thought of her new husband. Perhaps he would approve and give his blessing. "I wish you could advise me. I love Adam, but after everything, love seems impossible. Who could ever want me?"

Tadeusz wanted her, yes. But Adam was the opposite of Tadeusz. There was a chance that if he knew the truth, he would be repulsed by her. She was occasionally repulsed by herself, so she couldn't blame him if he was.

"I do miss you and I will always love you. But my place is with Adam, Sophie, and Ewa now." Lidia laid the ring on top of the tombstone and said, her voice cracking, "Good bye, Tadeusz." She took one last glance at the grave, turned, and walked off.

Adam laughed, finding his daughter's giggles contagious.

Father Cieslik was crouching and pulled coin after coin from behind Sophie's ears. *A priest who does magic tricks, who would have thought?* Unfortunately, he would never get to know the clergyman. He should have tried when he had the chance, but on his return to Krakow, he was too busy with his family to give much thought to friendships.

Father Cieslik faced Ewa and teased her about all of the American boys who would fall in love with her.

"You have a beautiful family, Mr. Altman." Rabbi Rosenwieg nudged his elbow into Adam's side.

Adam's heart clenched. *Another regret.* In Auschwitz, the rabbi had become a father figure. On his return to Krakow, when he learned Rabbi Rosenwieg was alive, he intended to resume the friendship. Yet after the attack at the synagogue, his visits with the rabbi waned. After a little trouble, Sophie, Ewa, and Lidia welcomed into their world and he fit there perfectly. His old friend didn't seem to bear him any ill will. The rabbi was often busy helping other survivors, sharing the concept of *Tikkun Olam*.

"Rabbi, it's been a year since Mina died, I should miss her more than I do." Adam cast a glance at the small cemetery where Lidia was having a private moment at Tadeusz's grave. Not much changed, he was in a perplexing situation and he needed the rabbi's counsel. "Now all I want is Lidia. Is that wrong?"

Poor Mina deserved better. For years she struggled with melancholy, then the war came. Sophie had been her bright spot – their bright spot. When she gave Sophie away, to protect her, he didn't understand and he resented her decision. But Mina's choice saved their daughter's life. He encouraged her to place her hope in reuniting with their little girl. Mina fought hard, but she died and never reaped her reward.

But Lidia...she was his wife now, his best friend, and his equal.

"I believe Mina would understand. There's nothing wrong with you and the present Mrs. Altman loving each other. You will figure it out." Rabbi Rosenwieg clapped him on the shoulder. "This is what I wanted for you: to have a family and to be happy."

"This is what we hoped for all along." Father Cieslik said, approaching with Sophie and Ewa in tow.

"What?" Adam asked.

"I don't know you, Mr. Altman. Not really." The priest began, rubbing his arms which were covered by the cassock's sleeves. The clergyman had to be stifling in that black garb, but he wore it in every season. "But I have known your wife for years. Since Mr. Sobieski died, her life has been empty. She had the girls, but she needed more. You two have so much in common. The rabbi and I thought you would fall in love. None of this is a mistake. God's Hand has been in this from the start. He knew you needed each other."

Adam nodded, the reality not at all lost on him. He found his daughter, adopted another child, and had a chance for love. It was nothing short of a miracle.

Things between him and Lidia weren't ideal. One moment she was embracing him, the next she was pushing him away. She was conflicted, and still troubled by the one who hurt her. He, of all people, understood how traumatizing memories could surface at the most inopportune moments. Whatever she needed, whatever she desired – he would do it. She deserved a measure of happiness.

"For a couple of clergymen, you're shifty." Adam said.

"I helped. It was my idea." Sophie chirped from his side.

"I know." Adam reached over and tweaked her little pug nose. "You're quite a matchmaker."

"I'm ready." Lidia announced, as she joined the group. Her eyes lacked their sparkle and were red rimmed, but she managed a watery smile.

Adam drew his wife close and pressed a kiss to her temple, letting her know he was there for her.

"Take care, Altman's." Rabbi Rosenwieg was beaming, like a proud father.

"One mountain can meet another mountain; one man can meet another man. So maybe we will meet again." Father Cieslik reflected thoughtfully.

The skeptic inside of him doubted that he would see Rabbi Rosenwieg or Father Cieslik again. However, he was reminded that he recently reunited with Sophie after years of separation. Nothing was impossible.

Adam touched his forehead to Lidia's. Their tears mingled together as the sun eclipsed them.

Thursday, 1 August 1946

Adam hired a man to drive him and his family, and their luggage, to the Krakow Glowny Osobowy station. They arrived early, and boarded the train before the other passengers did. They settled in a small, grubby compartment.

Lidia made a face. The little room reeked of cigar smoke and the windows were smudged brown, spoiling their only view of the countryside. A hodgepodge of patches and stains marked the cushions. The German and Soviet soldiers had done their worst to it. With the economy as it was, it was unlikely that the railway company could afford to refurbish it. The station itself was lucky to be standing, since it was the only part of Krakow to be bombed during the war.

No sooner did she and Adam get everything situated, did Ewa beg him to read "Anne of Avonlea." In spite of all of their many expenses lately, the silly man found a copy of it and bought it to take on their journey. She claimed his left side, Sophie cuddled to his right, leaving Lidia unsure of where she should be. Adam detected her hesitancy and gestured her over. She sat on the other side of Sophie and she rested her head on his shoulder. Between the rocking of the train and his soothing tone, Lidia's eyelids thickened and she began to nod off.

"Mama's sleepy." Sophie whispered loudly.

"Shh!" Lidia could imagine Ewa pressing her finger to her lips.

"Let her rest." Adam said. She felt him winding the ends of her hair around his fingers, and she enjoyed it. She burrowed closer, noticing how well their bodies fit together.

She hadn't slept well the night before, saddened by the fact they were leaving Krakow for forever, she would soon be in the place she hated most in the world. Her only consolation was that her family would be safe.

Lidia stirred when she heard boisterous commotion outside of their compartment in the hall. Two voices bellowed. Her stomach grew solid and she looked to Adam for an explanation. He felt ridgid against her.

The door slid open, revealing two men. One was huge and the other was gangly, but he had a gun clenched in his sweaty fist.

Adam got up and though he was no match for the intruders, he stood as tall as he could, despite his dependency on his cane. "May I help you?" he asked.

The large man hocked a mouthful of sticky saliva near her husband's feet. "Are there any Jews in here?" He jabbed his dirty finger in Adam's chest. "You look like a Jew."

Adam knocked the man's hand away.

Sophie drew her legs up, resting her chin on her knees. Ewa gathered the smaller girl close.

Lidia wanted nothing more than to cower in the corner, but she couldn't abandon Adam to face this alone. "Are you the police?" She went to his side and linked her arm through his.

"It's none of your concern." The large one's movement disturbed the air; the stench of his unwashed body stung her nostrils. "Unless you're a Jew too." He sneered.

"Of course not." Lidia scrunched her nose, loathing the disgust she feigned. If she didn't pretend to be insulted, the fool might suspect the truth. "Andrej, Helena, Sophie, and I are good Catholics."

She was relieved when Sophie didn't contradict her. Ewa was old enough to accept that though the war was long over, the hatred persisted and that she had to masquerade as a Christian for now. They had explained to Sophie, they must keep hers, Ewa's, and Adam's heritage a secret. Otherwise, it would lead to danger. The little girl seemed to understand.

A lewd grin slithered across the gangly man's face. "Prove it. Let me see your papers." He grunted.

The evening before their departure, Father Cieslik called. He brought them forged passports, identifying them as Christians, and proceeded to convince her and Adam that they would need them. The priest heard the most alarming reports of Jews being abducted from trains and killed in the countryside. Their bodies littered the fields. Lidia wanted to believe the best of her countrymen, but after numerous pogroms, the attack at the synagogue, and the rock thrown through their window, she could ignore the truth.

Lidia retrieved the papers and presented them. The two men had no authority whatsoever, but since one was carrying a weapon, she didn't dare refuse.

Adam looked calm, but clutching his arm, she could feel him shaking.

"These are good, but I don't buy it." The large man concluded after examining the documents. He took them and pitched them to the floor.

"Persuade us." The thinner man chortled.

Adam stared the two men down before releasing a sigh. "Let's step out." He said finally.

The two men filed out of the compartment.

Lidia refused to release him.

"You stay with the girls." He instructed, and placed a bittersweet kiss on her cheek.

Adam followed the men out into the hallway, sliding the door closed.

Lidia sank into the seat and slapped her hand over her mouth, preventing herself from crying out. Her first thought was that Adam might try to bribe the men into looking the other way. But they stored their small bit of savings in the cloth body of Sophie's doll. The toy was a little worse for wear. Her yarn hair was receding and her poor peach head was dented in several spots. But she still held a special place in Sophie's heart. And she made the perfect vessel.

Father Cieslik was right. For all she knew, those men were taking Adam away to kill him! *Lord, please, no!* She prayed. *I can't lose Adam now, I just found him!*

Sophie scooted over to Lidia and poked her leg. "Will papa come back? Mama?" Her daughter's usual sing-song voice became hysterical.

"I don't know." Lidia stood once more, pulled out one of the suitcases, opened it, and grabbed the religious icons. Propping them up against the cushioned seat, she instructed, "Pray, girls, pray hard." She crossed herself and dropped to her knees. "Please, Lord Jesus, please. Adam doesn't deserve to die. Please, save him."

"Please!" Sophie mimicked her, movement for movement. "I need my papa. Please, don't take him away again!"

Ewa remained standing, and rocked back and forth on her heels. Lidia heard foreign words on the girl's tongue. They were Germanic, leaving her to speculate it was Yiddish.

The door was wrenched open, causing them to flinch.

Adam appeared at the threshold. Other than being a fraction paler, he was the same as when he left. "What is this?" He asked.

"Papa, I didn't think I would see you again!" Sophie hurled herself at him.

"We thought they were going to kill you!" Ewa exclaimed.

Lidia rose and wrapped her arms around her midsection. She wanted to both laugh and cry.

"I will always come back to the three of you." Adam reclaimed his seat. Sophie climbed up on his lap and Ewa took her place beside him. He patted the empty spot on the other side of him. Lidia sat down and he slid his arm around her, drawing her close. "Nothing will keep me away from my family."

Lidia allowed herself to relax against him. *Thank you.* She told the Lord. Losing Tadeusz broke her head, but if she lost Adam, it would destroy her.

She waited until later that night, when the girls were resting, before nudging her husband awake.

He roused, blinking away his sleepiness.

"Adam, what happened?" Lidia laid her hand upon his jaw. A bit of stubble had broken out along his chin, but unlike most facial hair, his didn't bother her.

Adam glimpsed at the girls, to ensure they were asleep. "I had to show them I was never circumcised." He replied carefully.

Heat flooded to her cheeks. Only Jewish men and boys were circumcised. During the war, if the Nazis wanted clear proof of whether a man was Jewish or not, they would make him drop his trousers.

"I'm so sorry." Lidia blinked away her tears. She wanted to kill those two fools who forced her husband to humiliate himself.

"Don't cry." Adam brushed his lips against her hairline. The warmth of his soft breath soothed her. "Listen, I will do everything in my power to protect Sophie, Ewa, and you. We will be all right, as long as we're together."

Lidia nodded, slipping her arm across his abdomen, nuzzling against him.

Adam was right. As long as they were together, they would be fine. But they had to get out of Poland as soon as possible.

Things wouldn't get better. Their Russian liberators had become their new occupiers. On the last day of June there was an election – the People's Referendum – in which the Polish population voted overwhelmingly in favor of the Communists. However, neither she, nor Adam, nor anyone she knew voted for Communism. The election's outcome was rigged. Earlier that spring, Polish students and a large number of others made the mistake of attending church in large groups. The security police attacked them, and when the students returned to their dormitory, the Red Army gunned the building. Whoever survived was arrested and imprisoned. It was another good reason for them to leave, in case the NKVD took an interest in her again.

Then there was the news of Katyn. During the war, the German Army stumbled upon mass graves of thousands of Polish soldiers in the Katyn Forest. The Nazis blamed the Soviets and the Soviets blamed the Nazis for the mass execution. However, everyone had an inkling that the Soviets were the ones at fault.

Poland had traded the Swastika for the Sickle and Hammer, Hitler for Stalin, Nazism for Communism, the Wolf for the Bear. The Nazis had only wanted them for a thousand years, but the Soviets wanted them for forever. A Christ among nations, Poland was to be sacrificed on the altar of freedom for the remainder of the world.

Chapter Twenty-Eight

Adam nearly laughed when Lidia proposed hiring a wagon to relay them to her mother's farm, but then he realized she wasn't joking. She went on to explain that many country folk didn't own cars or Lorries. He nodded, choosing to trust her in this. After all, she was more familiar with the countryside than he was. A kind, old farmer bartered with them and let them ride in the back of his wagon. He toted the four and their luggage for three kilometers.

The jostle of the horse drawn wagon encouraged him to look at the sky and relax. It brought back the memory of when the older Austrian couple discovered him in the woods, and carried him to freedom, the verses from the Torah ringing in his ear. It also offered him plenty of time to review their journey from Krakow.

The train ride only lasted a day and half, but to him it went on forever. He hoped his fear of trains wasn't too obvious. They were the only mode for transportation available, but the persistent rumble through the cars, the shrill whistle, and the speed put him on edge. Blue nakedness seeped through the wispy clouds in the sky. The sun rolled in and out, trees blurred together in an unending wall of brown and green. More than once he felt as though he was back on that transport to Auschwitz. He tried to distract himself, by reading to the girls and cuddling with Lidia. Having the three close did him a world of good.

The two Poles barging into their compartment ruined that. The false papers they had were good, but the man barely looked at the documents, leading him to doubt that the men could read.

They demanded that he prove to him that he wasn't Jewish. There was only one thing he could think of. Adam brought them to the nearest W. C. and showed *himself*. It was enough and the two went on their way to terrorize some other poor soul.

Adam put himself back together and had to sit on the toilet for a few minutes to catch his breath. Not only had he survived yet another brush with death, images flashed through his mind unbidden. The ghetto, Auschwitz and the degrading selections, the death march, the gang of Polish youths, the rock through the window…Splashing cool water on his face calmed him enough for him to be able to head back to his family's compartment. He coped until the train arrived at the station.

"Mama, look!" Ewa pointed.

As the horses sluggishly dragged the wagon on the uneven road, a modest farmhouse on a hillside was above the low sloping land. It was simple, trimmed in green and crowned with green gables, and it reminded him of the house in the book Lidia and the girls were always reading. The one he bought the sequel to.

"It's a castle!" Sophie rolled onto her knees. "Can I have my own horse?"

"There should be a couple of horses." Adam observed that Lidia's smile was forced, but for the little girl's benefit she kept her tone even. "If they are gentle enough, you can ride them."

His wife reprimanded Sophie when she started to bob up and down in the wagon bed.

The driver jerked on the reins, halting the horses in the middle of the road. They had arrived.

Adam scooted out first and helped his ladies down. They collected their luggage, thanked the driver, and the four advanced towards the farm house.

Green shutters covered the windows. Missing gables from the roof made him think of a checkerboard. A blue spring followed the length of the acreage and a roughhewn fence encircled a small portion of the property, dividing it from the fields. Other than a chorus of livestock in the barn and the soft whisper of the wind, Adam was met with silence. He couldn't get past the differences between this farm and Krakow.

His surroundings, however, somewhat resembled the countryside leading to Auschwitz. Similar trees, fields, expanse of the sky. The only difference was that this country was teeming with life. Nothing lived in Auschwitz. Still, this peaceful serenity made him feel oddly claustrophobic.

An older woman emerged from the house, ran over, and threw her arms around Lidia.

Adam noted how his wife stiffened and she didn't reciprocate the hug.

Lidia disengaged from her mother and drew Sophie next to her before the woman could scoop the child into a hug.

"My darling girls." The woman's eyes glistened. "Where is Tadeusz? And who are they?" She gestured to Adam and Ewa.

Adam coughed nervously and Ewa sucked in a sharp breath. Lidia told him she had written to her mother, informing the woman that they were coming. But she obviously didn't say a word about remarrying or adopting a second child. Not that he could judge, considering the relationship he had with his father. But Lidia was a warm and loving person. That she didn't get on well with her mother spoke volumes.

"Tadeusz died a few years ago. This is my new husband, Adam Alman, and our daughter Ewa." Lidia claimed Adam's hand, lacing her fingers through his. She nodded for Ewa to come close and the girl did. "There's something I never told you. Sophie was adopted and Adam is Sophie's true father. Adam, Sophie, Ewa, this is my mother, Aniela Nowackowna."

Mrs. Nowackowna scrutinized him and Ewa, giving them a thorough once over. "You never thought of telling me that you married a Jew. Or that you adopted Jew girls?" She pursed her lips, lines fringing her mouth. "Have you lost your mind?"

Adam gritted his teeth. He longed to lash out at the woman. They left Krakow due to the rampant anti-Semitism and no sooner had they arrived, hatred greeted them at the door. Yet their stay at the farm depended on this woman and he didn't want to risk upsetting her further.

Ewa began to cry.

"Sophie and Ewa couldn't be more mine if I gave birth to them. And Adam is my husband and best friend." Lidia inhaled, her chest puffing out. "If I'm to take over the work here, you will show my husband and daughters the respect they deserve. Do you understand?"

Sophie's little head snapped back and forth, watching the two argue.

Mrs. Nowackowna's expression faltered. "I...I see. Come this way." She lowered her head and gestured for them to follow her inside.

Adam gave Lidia's shoulder a comforting squeeze before grabbing one of the suitcases and carried it into the house.

The rooms, the furniture, and the fixtures were simple and rustic. A far cry from how he and Mina lived in Kazimierz, but considering for two years he lived in a horse barracks, slept in a wooden bunk and rarely bathed, he couldn't complain.

Mrs. Nowackowna led the four through the small foyer and up a flight of steep, narrow stairs to the second floor. She stopped outside the first door on the left. "Your old room will do for the girls and one of the guest rooms will do for you and Mr. Altman." The woman decided.

Lidia opened her mouth, but no words came.

Adam recognized terror better than anyone. Sometimes the

past overwhelmed you to the point where you couldn't think, speak, or move. One thing was clear, Lidia didn't like her old bedroom. *Why?* It was a mystery, but for now, all that mattered was putting her at ease.

"Lidia and I may be married, but we don't share a bed." He ushered his wife and the girls in the direction of a guest room. "I will take the old bedroom and Lidia and the girls will have the other."

"Very well." Mrs. Nowackowna sniffed, turned, and headed back downstairs.

The luggage was set near the foot of the bed in the guest room. Lidia instructed the girls to get ready for a bath, for they needed to rid themselves of the dust from traveling. He soon learned there was no tub in the w. c. and a wooden tub in the kitchen would serve as a bathtub. He settled himself in the old bedroom before going downstairs.

Ewa was assisting Sophie in the bath when Adam found Lidia returning upstairs to fetch more towels. "Lidia, wait." He stopped and reached for her hand, cradling it between his. "Touched as I am by what you said, I can defend myself." He sighed. "So, your mother doesn't like Jews. How is it that you do?" he asked.

"I should be honest." Lidia looked shamefaced. "There was a time in my life when I didn't like Jews. If there's anything good about me, it's because of Father Cieslik's influence."

From what he gathered, she met the priest not long after her marriage to Tadeusz and arrival in Krakow. What prejudices Lidia had probably originated with her mother and step-father. He couldn't blame her for being naïve; everyone was at eighteen. She more than atoned for her past wrongdoings.

"We all make mistakes." Adam shrugged. He of all people couldn't hold a grudge against her. "You're the best person I know. Father Cieslik would agree with me, I'm sure."

"What about Mina?" Lidia blinked several times.

"I loved Mina and part of me always will. Her spirit lives on in Sophie. But she is gone and you're my wife now. I...I admire and respect you." While he meant every word of his little speech, his words were inadequate when he felt so much more.

No, he didn't just admire and respect Lidia. It was love. He was in love with her. A love first born out of aggravation, then attraction, and finally friendship. It would be the kind that would stand the test of time.

"You shouldn't." Lidia responded.

Adam frowned, wishing he could free her from whatever caused her pain. He would take it on himself in a heartbeat, if he could. A man of sorrows, he had more than his share of turmoil. Another one wouldn't make a difference.

"It'll be all right, I promise." He assured her.

Lidia gave a nod and pulling away, she went back upstairs.

Monday, 5 August 1946

Adam choked a little on his coffee when Lidia entered the kitchen wearing a man's work shirt and trousers, and took her place at the table. Aside from movie star Marelene Dietrich, he had never seen a woman wear men's clothes before...and wear it so well. He had to avert his gaze from ogling her backside.

He moved to the stove and spooned porridge into five different bowls. Then he laid them out on the table.

During the war, men's and women's roles were challenged. However, he hated the idea of Lidia doing manual labor while he remained in the house. He rarely gave his weak ankle a second thought since he had worse demons to face. But now it was a thorn in his side, preventing him from doing his share of the work. Ewa volunteered to assist Lidia and though she would do her best, the girl always ended up adding to their work in the long run.

Adam shoveled in a couple of bites. "What should I do around here? Can I help with some outside chores? I learned some things in..." He stopped himself before he mentioned Auschwitz. "I learned some things during the war."

Sophie was oblivious to his little slip up. Ewa let out an exaggerated gasp and then clapped her hand over her mouth. Mrs. Nowackowna's hawkish gaze darted to him. The BBC and the papers reported on Auschwitz and the other camps, but the majority of the population feigned ignorance. Either way, Auschwitz was not a subject for the breakfast table.

"Adam, don't worry about it." Lidia curled her fingers around her tea cup and took a sip before putting it back down. "This is your chance to get to know Sophie. You could teach her to read."

Adam was tempted to propose that Ewa or Mrs. Nowackowna could keep an eye on Sophie while he didn't something productive. But his wife's uneasy demeanor convinced him that she didn't want Sophie to be left alone with Mrs. Nowackowna. Ewa would be able to move about a barn and the fields quicker than he could. The niggling memory of his pathetic attempt to dig up the jar in Planty Park surfaced. If he couldn't dig a hole, never mind manual labor.

He grudgingly nodded his head.

Lidia excused herself to go outside and Ewa was on her heels seconds later.

He and Sophie washed and dried the breakfast dishes before heading to the sitting room. Sophie grabbed the old, damaged copy of "Anne of Green Gables" and "Anne of Avonlea" from her mother's suitcase and climbed into his lap. An old schoolbook or primer would make it easier for Sophie to learn, but until he scrounged around for one, the novels would suit.

"What are kindred spirits?" Sophie wriggled in his lap until she was facing him.

The phrase cropped up numerous times in the story. Having never read about the comical, red-headed orphan before, he truly enjoyed her adventures and misadventures. In many ways, Anne Shirley reminded him of Ewa.

"Friends." Adam said simply. "Very good and close friends."

"Are we kindred spirits?" Sophie looked thoughtful.

"The best."

Sophie put her hands on the sides of his face, mushing his cheeks slightly. "I love you, papa." She declared.

Those words took his breath away. He had so long to hear Sophie say it. The separation, the ghetto, the camps, the hospital... waiting and waiting for years! Then when they were reunited, her rejection nearly broke his heart. But now, at long last, she finally said she loved him. All of the strife had been worth it.

"I love you, too." Adam's voice cracked. He hugged Sophie and never wanted to let her go.

"How sweet." Mrs. Nowackowna commented. He hadn't realized she was in the doorway, observing them. "That reminds me of when Lidia was a little girl and my second husband would read to her before she went to bed." Unlike when they were first introduced, the woman sounded congenial. "You would have liked Roland."

Sophie drew back and pointed at the book, eager to resume the story.

"Would I now? Lidia..." Adam began to reply, but his words tapered off.

Roland. The blood drained from his face and if he hadn't been seated, he would have passed out. Roland...Roland was the one who hurt Lidia. The truth had been before the whole time, but he didn't see it until now. Lidia rarely spoke of her step-father. When she learned of the man's death, she didn't shed a tear.

Adam recalled when he was first reunited with Sophie, Lidia wouldn't allow him to be alone with her or Ewa. Her actions made sense. She feared that he would be like Roland and hurt the girls. And it had to be the reason why Lidia panicked when they began to make love.

He found himself praying that he wouldn't unleash a litany of profanity on his new mother-in-law. Since they married, he made a conscious effort to watch his language. Lidia would pitch a fit if Sophie picked up such a bad habit from him.

"Lidia adored Roland when she was young." Mrs. Nowackowna continued, oblivious to his mounting rage. "Then when she grew up, she was prideful and was embarrassed of her home. She believed she was too good for this place and became wild. Kept trying to run away and she did when she was eighteen. That was when she married Tadeusz."

Adam wished the woman would stop talking. If she didn't, he wouldn't be accountable for his actions. "Something must have made her particularly unhappy." He leveled his gaze at Mrs. Nowackowna, letting her know he wasn't fooled by her. She often put on a meek façade for Lidia, duping his wife into believe she was of a retiring disposition. But he had seen her kind before. The woman was shrewd; she had a way of manipulating Lidia and the rest of the world into doing her bidding. Mrs. Nowackowna had to have known what Roland did to her daughter, but she turned a blind eye to it. "It had better never happen to her again, or to Sophie and Ewa. I won't have it."

Mrs. Nowackowna recoiled and timidly retreated from the room. But he felt no guilt for snapping at her. For once his temper worked in his favor.

Adam strode in the direction of the barn, leaving Sophie with Burek. Burek, the shaggy mixed breed dog flopped down in the grass, rolling on his back, so that the little girl could rub his belly. Ewa was leaving to fetch some water for them, but she got distracted by playing with Burek too.

Adam couldn't help but be wary of the animal. Before the war, he never had any pets. And in Auschwitz, there were dogs. The guards often used them to maul prisoners, ripping them to shreds. Burek wouldn't harm a fly, of course. But still, he couldn't shake off the terror he felt, even when the dog's sappy eyes gravitated towards him. He had to find a way to overcome his fear though. When they settled in America, the girls would want a Burek of their own.

He entered the barn and started to cough, which led to gagging. The foul stench of excrement and soiled straw was overwhelming. Livestock stank, but the odor brought him back to the barracks and latrines in Auschwitz. *For crying out loud, will there ever be a day when I don't think of Auschwitz?* He fumed. If only he could think, feel, reminisce, and live his life without images of Auschwitz flickering through his broken mind. But no matter where he went, what he did, or the people he interacted with, Auschwitz was always waiting to rear its ugly head.

He forced himself to calm down and found Lidia mucking out a stall. Perspiration dotted her forehead and hairline. Her pretty features were twisted into a grimace. *She deserves better than this.* In America, he would find a way to give her everything.

"How is it going?" Adam asked, waving at her.

"Well enough." Lidia leaned the rake on the wall and drew closer. "Where are the girls?" She asked.

"Playing with Burek. You know when we get to America, they will want a Burek too. I should be able to tell them 'no' but you know me, I can't." He managed a sheepish smile, but it quickly faded when he saw how miserable she looked. "Lidia, if you hate it here, we can go back to Krakow and bide our time there."

He faced more than his share of anti-Semitism and he didn't want to be subjected to anymore of it. But he would do it for Lidia. She shouldn't have to be in the same house where the abuse occurred. America would be good for all of them. They all needed a fresh start.

"No, I'm fine." Lidia said shortly.

A tiny piece of straw was poking out of her hair. He raised his hand and plucked it out, tossing it to the ground.

Her lips curved into a wry smile.

"What happened to your father? Your birth father." Adam asked.

It was a painful subject, but he wanted her to know that she didn't have to struggle alone. He was strong enough to carry her burdens too. And nothing would change how he felt. He wanted a true marriage, in every sense of the word. Mostly, he longed for her to trust him, to lean on him the way he leaned on her.

"He died." Lidia squinted at him. "The doctor said it was an aneurysm. I was eight."

"And your mother remarried right away?"

"Two weeks later. Moved us out here."

"Was your-"

"Adam, I really need to finish this." Lidia interrupted, impatiently tilting her head. "Can we talk later?"

"Of course. Sorry." Adam nodded, regretting that he pried. He, of all people, should understand boundaries. "When you're finished, I'll make a cup of tea for you."

"Thank you." She responded and resumed her work.

He shuffled out to where the girls and Burek were playing, hoping his daughters didn't notice his distraught expression.

Chapter Twenty-Nine

Friday, 13 September 1946

Since they arrived at the farm in time for the harvest, Lidia considered hiring a young man from the nearby village to assist her with it. Poland was facing the possibility of another grain shortage, which would lead to another drought, continued rationing, and starvation. But Adam insisted on helping her. She didn't wish to overtax her husband. With the exception of when he explained his tattoo to her and the girls, he never went into great detail on what he experienced during the war. But she could tell even after a year and half of freedom, he was still recuperating. Aside from his limp, he was fine physically. What concerned her was his mental and emotional wellbeing. Her husband needed to heal.

The man wouldn't take 'no' for an answer though. No matter how much he favored his ankle, he accompanied her out to the fields before dawn and only returned at night when she did. Ewa watched after Sophie, but both girls soon joined them, eager to lend a hand.

Close to the middle of September, a letter bearing a foreign scrawl arrived for Adam. The second he found it on the kitchen table after a long day's work, he snatched it up and tore it open.

His dark eyes scanned the contents of the note and a smile broke out across his face.

"Well?" Lidia observed, bemused. "What does it say?"

"It's a letter from my cousin in America, the one Mina and I wrote to before the war." There was a streak of dirt across the side of his nose and cheek. He looked cute. Boyish. "He says he will vouch for us and has sent us information regarding immigration. This is our first step to a new life. Once we have our passports renewed and we receive our visas, we can go."

"Go where?" Sophie stood on tiptoe and peered at the sheet of paper, her brow knitting together in frustration. She was beginning to master reading in Polish. But English was an enigma to her.

"To America. Our new home." Lidia felt flustered saying those words aloud.

America was a beacon of hope for most, but moving to a country she knew nothing about left her uneasy. She only knew a smattering of English words; the American customs were a mystery to her, and she wouldn't know how to behave there. She might never fit in and be an embarrassment to her family. It was only a matter of time, too, before Adam figured out about her past. Once he did, he would be eager to be rid of her.

"America is where all of the movie stars live." Ewa told the smaller girl.

Lidia bit her lip. *Perhaps I should stay here and Adam should take Sophie and Ewa to America.* She didn't think she could bear being separated from her daughters. Sophie was the one who kept her going during the darkest times and Ewa was the one who could always make her laugh despite herself.

"But I like it here." Sophie protested. "We have animals now."

"It's not safe for us here." Lidia used her pinky, which was the cleanest of her fingers, to duck the girl's braid behind her ear.

"Sophie," Ewa tried once more. "In America, you can go

to the movies every week and there's a candy shop on every street corner."

"I see." Mother had been eavesdropping from the other room and proceeded to join them. Her lips were pressed together, tight enough her skin grew white. "So, you live here for months and abandon me to fend for myself?"

For most of her life, Lidia had believed her mother was meek and timid, but since Roland's death, the scales fell away. Her mother had been playing a part all along. To marry and stay under Roland's protection, Mother became obedient and she looked the other way when Roland turned predatory. *Had she ever loved me? Or my father?* Perhaps her mother was an opportunist and nothing more. Though she was at odds with her mother, and may always be at odds with her mother, she couldn't leave the woman alone in Poland. She couldn't be as uncaring as her mother.

Adam whipped around; his expression hardened. Nothing Mother did fazed him. "You let your daughter fend for herself. Not another word out of you. Am I understood?" He only drew back when she gave a submissive nod. "Good."

Dear God, Adam knows! Lidia cringed at what he could be thinking of her. She did her best to conceal the truth, yet she failed miserably.

Lidia parted from her family, rushing to the sink to wash her hands. She used a brush on her skin until it was pink and raw and close to bleeding. Then she excused herself to go upstairs to change. A full bath right now was out of the question, but she would like nothing better than to scrub her filthy away.

The evening went well. They tuned into the radio for a little while to hear about Amon Göth's trial. According to the broadcast, it was the first major trial of its kind in Poland. During the war, his evil knew no bounds. He was the commandant of Plaszow Concentration Camp, he participated in liquidations of two ghettos and a labor camp...it was speculated he killed approximately eight thousand Jews. He was convicted on five different counts, he was hung, cremated, and his ashes were flung into the Vistula River.

Neither Adam or Ewa encountered that beast, though both were grave as they listened to the news. Lidia didn't know about them, but she couldn't help but feel relief that such an evil being no longer walked the earth. Not long after the broadcast, she and her family decided to turn in.

Lidia attempted to rest, but the first few nights at the farm, old nightmares interrupted her sleep. She waited until the girls were snoring before creeping downstairs to the sitting room. Camping out on the narrow sofa was hardly comfortable and the memories of Roland still disturbed her slumber, but at least she wasn't bothering her daughters with tossing and turning. She was an early riser and she would be sure to bring the pillow and blanket back upstairs before the others came down for breakfast.

But after a couple of hours, in her drowsy state, Lidia began to dream. In that dream, Roland wasn't dead and despite all of her attempts, she couldn't stop him from going into Sophie and Ewa's room.

Suddenly, a warm palm rested on her brow. She let out a yelp and pushed herself further down into the cushions.

"Shh." The touch was familiar and comforting and now stroking her head. "It's all right. It's me, it's Adam."

Her eyes flew open, the nightmare receded and reality set in.

"Sorry." Adam drew back and sat on the edge of the coffee table. "Are you all right?"

"Yes. I didn't mean to wake you."

"You didn't, I couldn't sleep. Bad dreams. Why are you down here?" He released a weary sigh when she didn't respond. "Please, don't shut me out."

"I don't sleep very well upstairs." Lidia admitted, struggling to sit up.

She could feel his gaze on her, although in the darkness she couldn't tell if it was one of disgust or sympathy. "Lidia, you don't have to tell me, but did your step-father hurt you?" His tone was hesitant, as though he feared the question would upset her further.

"Yes. Please, don't ever tell the girls." Before Lidia could stop herself, a choked sob escaped her. She couldn't bear it if her daughters learned the truth.

"Whatever you wish. Just know, there is nothing you can't tell me." His fingers settled on her forearm, skimming it lightly. "I'm your friend, your husband, and I love you."

Lidia couldn't believe her ears. He must not have understood the kind of abuse she had endured. Otherwise, he wouldn't be able to stomach the sight of her. After all, since their arrival at the farm, she could scarcely stomach the sight of herself.

"Don't say that. Not until you know everything." She rasped.

"Nothing will change how I feel about you." Adam peeled back the blanket covering her legs and tugged on her wrist. "But let's go upstairs. Will you join me to talk?"

Lidia dreaded going up there. Oh, she knew he would never try anything. But she didn't know if she could bear to see his face as she confessed the truth to him.

A couple more tries and he was able to coax her up to the spare guest room. It was rarely used, preferred more for storage, but sometime in the last few weeks Adam switched rooms. His belongings were in there and the bed was freshly made up. A candle had been lit and cast a dome of light in one corner of the room.

Lidia situated herself near the head of the bed and drew her legs up to her chest, hoping to hide herself. The bedspread beneath her was a pretty, geometric rose design heavily woven in blue, pink, and lavender.

Adam positioned himself at the foot of the bed and was silent. He didn't act as though he were repulsed. On the contrary, he looked remorseful.

Lidia found encouragement in this and began. "My mother remarried two weeks after my father died. She had no skills, no experience outside the home. Roland seemed like a good and honest man. Religious. He brought us out here and though I missed my father, Roland was kind to me. I loved the animals and he taught me all sorts of things. I trusted him. He would read me bedtime stories at night." She accepted the handkerchief Adam offered her and dabbed the corners of her eyes. "Then Roland would come in once the lights were out. He said it was all a game and he gave me presents to keep me quiet. I thought it was normal."

His eyes were blazing and he trembled. She knew his moods well enough to know he was enraged. "When... Did your mother know?" He asked, finally.

Lidia shook her head. "She had to, but she ignored it. By the time I was twelve, I had a few friends and it dawned on me that their fathers weren't like that. Their fathers were normal. I told my mother everything and she scolded me for making up such terrible lies. She said I was a dirty, dirty girl." This happened over twenty years ago yet she could still feel the sting from her mother's rebuke. "I stayed outside as late as I could, but it would get cold or I would get tired. I ran away a few times, but the police always found and returned me."

"And Tadeusz, where did he fit in all of this?" Adam asked.

"Not long after I turned eighteen, Tadeusz was in this part of the country visiting cousins and we met at church. We liked each other right away." Their courtship began innocently enough and her step-father disapproved. Lidia feared that Tadeusz would head for the hills once he found out the truth. "He sensed something wasn't right and I told him. He offered to help me escape, without promise of engagement or marriage. But I wanted to be with him. We married in Krakow and that was that." She fingered the fringe on the hem of her cotton nightgown. Since she had told him the worst, she figured she might as well tell him the rest. "I'm damaged goods, Adam."

"Sweetheart..." Adam scooted closer and settled his back against the headboard. "You're not damaged goods. Tadeusz must have told you the same thing."

Lidia forced a wobbly smile. Tadeusz was a good husband. He had a big heart, and in the end, it gave out. He never judged her and no matter how much the wind chapped his cheeks, he never grew a beard because Roland had a beard and Tadeusz knew it would bother her. He was her first love and she would never forget him.

"In the beginning, is that why you never wanted me alone with Sophie?" Adam nudged her softly. "You feared I was like Roland?"

She gulped. How could she have ever thought Adam would hurt Sophie in that way? He was troubled certainly, but he adored their child. The man would lame his other leg if he thought it would benefit Sophie and eventually, he extended that love to Ewa, and then to her.

"I'm sorry." Lidia grasped his hand and brushed her lips against the ridge of his knuckles. "You're a good man, Adam, and my dearest friend. I'm glad that you found Sophie and if it weren't for you, we would be lost. You saved our lives."

"No. You and Sophie and Ewa saved mine." He cradled her cheek, stroking it. "I love you."

"I love you too, but I can't...I don't know if I can be enough for you. How can you look at me? Maybe it would be best if you left me here and took the girls to America to start over."

"How can I look at you? How can I not? I love looking at you." Adam slowly shook his head at her. "Even before we called our little truce, I would watch you out of the corner of my eye. You're beautiful, inside and out. Nothing of what you told me changes how I feel for you. But if I caused you pain-"

Lidia cut him off by flinging her arms around his neck. "Never. I thought... Some men might not want a woman who is soiled." She sank into him, cursing herself for being foolish. They had wasted all this time first arguing and then misunderstanding one another, when they could have shared their love freely.

"Nonsense. Listen to me, you're not soiled. No more than I am." Adam rolled up his pajama sleeve, revealing that tattoo he had received in Auschwitz. He guided her finger tips to it, encouraging her to explore it as she had before. "The Nazis... where do I begin? I have been hit, beaten, shot at, spat upon, urinated on, and starved. I became no better than an animal; branded, naked and bald. I have eaten bowls of soup with worms in it; I came running when I was called; I slept on straw; I relieved myself on the ground."

Lidia tightened her grip, shocked by his admission. She knew it had been terrible there, but to think Adam spent two years in that hell and lived to tell about it!

"I'm the one who is dirty." He added. "Damaged goods."

"No, you're a survivor. My survivor." Lidia tilted her head back and shyly pecked him on the mouth. "You are the best man that I know. How did you survive any of that?"

"How did you survive the war?" He asked breathlessly.

"Sophie." She said, without giving the question a second thought.

"Me too. And now we have each other." Adam dipped his head and nuzzled his lips to hers, developing into an intense kiss. "If you stay here in Poland, then Sophie, Ewa and I are staying too. 'For whither thou goest, I will go; and where thou lodgest, I will lodge: thy people shall be my people, and...thy God my God: Where thou diest, will I die, and there will I be buried: the Lord do so to me, and more also, if ought but death part thee and me.'"

Her eyes welled up; this time they were tears of joy rather than tears of sorrow.

"I love you too. May I sleep in here with you?" Lidia asked.

"Of course." Adam twisted to blow out the candle and flattened out onto his back. She laid her head on his chest, feeling the wound through the material of his nightshirt, and beneath that his heartbeat. His arms encircled her waist. "Are you comfortable?" His voice rumbled as he spoke.

"Yes. This is perfect." Lidia replied.

From now on when one of them had a nightmare, the other would be there to chase it away.

THE END

ReadMore Press

DISCOVERING THE NEXT BESTSELLER

Would you like a FREE WWII historical fiction audiobook?

This audiobook is valued at 14.99$ on Amazon and is exclusively free for Readmore Press' readers!

To get your free audiobook, and to sign up for our newsletter where we send you more exclusive bonus content every month,

Scan the QR code

Readmore Press is a publisher that focuses on high-end, quality historical fiction. We love giving the world moving stories, emotional accounts, and tear-filled happy endings.

We hope to see you again in our next book!

Never stop reading, Readmore Press

Printed in Dunstable, United Kingdom